Daniel Nick

WAR DOG

THE HOUND OF THE GODS BOOK ONE

War Dog

Hound of the Gods Book One

Daniel Nick

World KDC Publishing

Contents

This book is only possible through the support of my family, but I dedicate this first book to the man and woman who inspired my life's work in "The only Holy War worthy of the name."
I borrowed heavily from the trail you blazed and used the knowledge you shared in this book. I hope I did you proud, Andrew and Alice Vachss.
Mr. Vachss, you can rest now, we'll take it from here.
For those that have never had the life-altering experience of reading his books, know that I reverently stole many terms and concepts from his life's work and dropped them straight into my story.
https://www.vachss.com/index.php

The recipe for monster is really kind of simple: you take a small human being and you surround him or her by the people that, having been designated to be the protectors, now mistreat the child. You have the child's cries being heard by the larger parent, the government, and you have that government pat the abusers on the head, giving a seal of approval, and walk away. You have now created a child that will believe that all that can be relied upon is himself. That all he should care about is himself, because after all who cared about him?

Andrew Vachss

About this Universe

Hi folks.

Astute readers will catch several historical inconsistencies in this book.

Dates that are wrong.

Real events that actually happened a year before or after stated in this novel.

That's because this universe in which this story takes place ain't ours.

It's a lot like ours. A scary amount of a lot, but it isn't ours, okay?

These are not the Druids from my ethnic and cultural heritage.

This is fiction, of course, so it's easy for an author to be facile and dismissive of readers' concerns, and the excuse "IT'S FICTION!" has been used to cover up lazy writing before. I hope that this is not your opinion of my work.

There's a whole lot of truth in these pages. A whole lot of overlap between this world and ours.

And so, I've spent some significant time reaching out and asking, listening, and learning about various cultural mores and beliefs, and I have tried to keep my story general where I've been asked to avoid specifics, and fictional where I've been asked not to appropriate or take. At the same time, pretty much all locations, countries, and myths are about 98% the same as our universe because that's pretty essential to where this series is headed.

I was asked by one person, "Why not just make it all totally different? Why not Fantasy in a modern setting, but a whole other world?" (They also hinted that maybe this was a smart idea since I'm...well...a cis-het-white-male and maybe I need to really think about the challenge of writing about other perspectives and cultures at this current point in history – and they're not wrong).

But the answer is, "Because I can't." For reasons that will become clear later in the series, this HAS to happen in a nearby universe almost the same as ours. It's integral to the whole point of the damn books.

The movies, songs, general histories, wars, and even certain historical leaders – same names and time frames. Maybe you'll catch that a few years don't sync up, or that a few presidents, Premiers, or Kings don't exist, but that America, Canada, and Mexico have roughly the same borders and history as our universe. Europe is really familiar. As is Asia. World War Two happened with the same names in charge, but the battles went a little differently sometimes.

That means that – if you happen to study or belong to a culture or faith that finds itself "represented" in these pages – you are DEFINITELY GOING TO SEE DISCREPANCIES AND "ERRORS".

Those are intentional because –

This is not our universe, and these are not your Gods. This is not your religion. Think of it like the Mandela Effect.

It's a universe filled with cryptids that don't quite match ours, Gods that don't quite measure up to our myths, and cultural histories that might be just 2% off from what our history books tell us (which doesn't even mean accurate at this point, but that's a whole 'nother outrage). Please understand that all discrepancies are mine, all parallels are in service to the story, and I wrote every word with reverence and respect for all the people who shared their concerns and requests.

I'm sure I made mistakes, and I apologize in advance for them. Just please know I tried very hard to minimize them and I'll keep trying to eliminate them from future works.

But the movie quotes – they're all real. That's how close this universe is to ours.

> "If we shadows have offended, think but this, and all is mended: That you have but slumber'd here, while these changes did appear." – Puck (in a play, somewhere, and in some universe much like ours)

Chapter One

The End

For somebody as well acquainted with death as I am, I was doing an exceptionally shitty job of killing myself.

A few months ago, I had started missing time. I'd look at my old watch and be shocked that only a few minutes had passed in what seemed hours of ennui. Then I'd look again to find it was three in the morning and I hadn't moved from my couch for over fifteen hours.

I also had recently started having flashbacks. At least I think they were. They were snippets of faces and places I didn't remember. Living alone, I had no one to talk to about it.

It had just gotten progressively worse from there. A soul-crushing nothingness some people call "Down in the Zero". An impossibly heavy absence of anything worth holding onto.

I had gone through something like this a few times before, and the cure was always to go find a war to fight in. But there was no escaping this time. No war, no Army that would have me. This time I was at the end of it.

Despite this, the household lights were bright and cheerful. I was sitting in my nearly empty living room listening to a fun, lighthearted audiobook.

I had the windows open on a glorious, wet, September afternoon in Maryland, and a freshly brewed cup of a Sumatran coffee blend was steaming on the table.

I had done all of that to feel something - anything - and maybe have a reason to go another day.

It wasn't working.

This morning, I made my decision and scheduled the power and gas to be turned off.

Thanks to some bad life choices in my youth, I'm pretty hard to kill. I'm not making tough-guy talk, I mean I am literally very hard to kill.

That's why I was staring at the coffee table in front of me. Besides the mug, it held the only two things in my life that I considered work essentials; that battered, old, white-faced Omega Speedmaster watch, worn in countless deployments, and my old Glock service pistol.

I was thinking on how pointless that gun was compared to the much better odds of success that the fucking painkillers in my bathroom offered, when the doorbell rang.

I grabbed the gun on instinct and went to pause the mp3 right as the narrator was about to explain how the streetwise and plucky Wizard managed to fire an accurate bolt of fire over his shoulder whilst diving through the air to take cover behind the statue in Central Park, but I missed the button. I didn't have enough mental energy to try again, so the story droned on through the Bluetooth speaker mounted under the TV on my wall.

I was irrationally annoyed at the interruption but also intrigued as to who could be knocking at my door. See, I lost my last friend the day I was brutally and forcibly discharged from the military. I had been working hard for months to recover from the trauma of the experience that led to that. Trying and failing.

That meant I was living the life of a semi-hermit and hadn't talked to nor seen another human being other than the gal who delivered my groceries for almost eight weeks.

The bell rang again as I shuffled to the door and looked through the eyepiece. Outside stood a woman I had seen in pictures, but never in person. Confused, I thought for an instant that this was another flashback.

I automatically tucked my pistol into my waistband and reached out, opening the door to stand awkwardly staring at Sarah Egils, wife of that man I once called a friend from the service.

"Hello, I'm-"

"You're Frank's wife, right?" I interrupted.

I realized how weird that was and tried to come alive long enough to have a conversation. Painting on a pretend face of humanity, I said, "Wonderful to meet you! I'm Drustan Seta. Please, call me Dru."

With the faintest trace of a southern accent, she said, "Thank you, Mr. Dru." She stood still for a moment. "Well, can I come in?" Before I could recover my manners, from behind me the speakers let out a yelp and a mild curse as the bad guy got clipped by a bouncing fireball sent his way by the Wizard. "Am I interrupting something?"

"What? Oh, not at all. Come in and make yourself comfortable. I'll turn off the book."

She smiled a little bit wryly at that comment and I felt the need to explain myself. "Hey, I enjoy reading as much as the next guy, but I love listening to a well told story."

She walked into my house and across my floor timidly, her steps hesitant and her eyes searching my walls and floors for something. "Is everything alright?" I asked as she made her way deeper into my living room.

She deflected, "I like your house. It's simple."

Huh. Unintentional backhanded compliment aside, my house is a simple affair. It's one large living room that could act as my dining room assuming I ever had a guest. At the back of the house is the small kitchen hiding behind a half wall. You can see straight into and out of it.

On the left side of the house and behind a blond-stained wood door are my bedroom and master bath. Off to the right behind one plain white door is a bathroom for those same non-existent guests who get to eat in the dining room. It also connects to the room behind the other plain white door in the wall that is a second bedroom I had turned into a training space complete with heavy bags and fighting dummies. I'm not sure why because I never use it.

The interior of the house can pretty much be summed up as wide open and a shade of white or green, with a minimum of effort spent on decorative stuff.

As Sarah looked around my nearly bare walls, her gaze settled on a huge black-and-white picture of some ancient faded swirls carved in stone. It is the one thing other than a flat-screen TV (and the Bluetooth speaker) on my walls.

"Oh, I know that, I think. That's from Newgrange in Ireland, right?" she asked.

Surprised, I answered, "Yeah. I took that photograph myself. Nobody alive today is certain what the three spirals mean, but it gets lit up every year on the Solstice when the sun strikes it. I figure it must have been important."

"Are you Irish, Mr. Dru?"

"Whole family is," I replied, "but most of us come from Ulster, not County Meath," as I gestured at the photograph.

"Was that where you were born?"

"I'm a naturalized American now. Look, Sarah, is there something I can do for you? You seem...How's Frank? Is everything alright?"

Sarah sat on my old, Amish-built sofa and stared down at her hands. "You knew my Frank well, didn't you?" she said.

I took a seat in the chair near the sofa, mainly to give myself time to think. This was getting into risky territory because Frank and I met in a military unit euphemistically called "irregular" by the government. We did what other special forces couldn't, and we did it with a mix of soldiers who weren't all, technically speaking, human.

Seriously.

And Frank was one of the guys not quite human.

"I knew him about as well as anyone on this earth, Sarah. Frank was my Lieutenant and my friend. What's going on?"

She met my eyes for the first time and said, "So you know my Frank wasn't normal?"

I looked her over as I tried to figure out how much to say. Sarah looked somewhere between the ages of thirty and thirty-five and was a beautiful woman. Standing about 5'8", her blond hair was done up by a professional, and her attire was quality-made. She was wearing a gray business jacket and skirt with a pair of high-end, low-cut heels on. And no, I have no idea who made them. I'm a guy who spent the last seven years wearing combat boots, not a fashionista. They're only shoes to me, but even I could tell they were expensive.

Frank had told me she worked for some big tech conglomerate in Texas, but he never said her exact job, so I felt like I was looking at the C.E.O. of a billion-dollar company rather than the wife of a soldier.

Maybe if I was a detective or a cop or something I would have noticed the he never told me anything about what his wife did for a living, but I'm only a fighter; some would say killer. But it was strange. I mean, if I knew he wasn't human, what else would he have to hide?

Still, it isn't like I told him every little fact about my life either. Everyone has stuff that doesn't come up in conversation. We were friends, not therapists. And I'm worse than most with relationships. I can admit that.

"Sarah, I know he wasn't like you at all. I don't know what he told you about our unit, but it was made up of all sorts of "different" people like Frank. We are not allowed to tell you more than that, but I'm betting LT – Frank – did anyway?"

"Mr. Dru, I know everything about my husband. All that *Extra* stuff..." The special emphasis on Extra was all I needed to hear. Frank probably hadn't held anything back from her. I briefly wondered what she knew about me.

What the world calls Cryptids or fairytales, we soldiers called Extras. As in extra strong, fast, hairy, ugly, whatever. They were Extras.

Fuck it.

"Okay. I'll lay it out. Technically, we were a special forces unit for the United States Air Force, but that's about as far as it went for a normal military structure.

"In fact, if LT told you as much as you say, you know that we are the most classified group of people to ever exist on the planet. We are so far outside the normal chain of command that few people outside of combat zones even know about us. Our orders actually come from civilians in an organization known by its initials, right? Seriously, we're so black ops we pretty much scream 'Big 'ole tired cliché!' But we exist and we kill other real shit you have never heard of." I looked at her face, "But you already know all this, right?"

"Yes. Frank never told me stories, but I know what he did, and who he worked for."

"You have any idea what's out there, really?"

She looked down at those expensive shoes and forced out, "No, not specifically."

"Well, let's be specific then. We called ourselves the Nightmare Squad." I held up my hands. "I know, I know, minus points for lack of creativity, but the name fits. The world is a scary place, and every country has its units made up of similar people. Sometimes we even worked together to kill something extremely bad. There are real monsters out there, Sarah."

"Frank just called you the 'Squad'."

I remembered that not all the guys and girls in the unit were like Frank. Most wouldn't settle down at all, and the few that did have a regular girl or guy had to weigh what they could tell their significant other very carefully. Most never told the whole truth, just little white lies to explain away injuries that healed overnight, sensitivity to the sun, the need to shave five times a day, whatever.

The "regular" humans had it worse in some ways. We couldn't say a word about any of it to our families unless we wanted to disappear forever. Forever ever.

"So, are you getting me, Sarah?"

She looked up at me and her face set into a stern frown. "Yes, Mr. Seta, I get you quite clearly. You handle what most people think is fantasy," she waved her hands, "or horror maybe. And I'm well aware we're not supposed to be talking about this. I honestly don't give a damn."

"Good. Me neither."

"But you're a normal human, right? Why were you there with my husband?"

Reluctantly, I admitted, "A regular, plain old 'normal' will never make it to Nightmare Squad. You have to be a savant at something deadly. I was sent to the unit for one reason only. I could shoot off the back of a fast-moving vehicle and hit whatever I was aiming at. I mean, I'm good in a fight, and I know how to handle myself as well as any soldier out there, but what actually got me sent to the Nightmare Squad was my ability to hit shit from far away with a .50 Cal from the back of a Humvee at fifty miles per hour."

I also had what psychologists call a highly adaptable subjective character of experience. That means I don't freak out and try to deny what my eyes are telling me when I see a monster, and I don't lose sleep over killing it. The shrinks were pretty excited over my "adaptability" of thought. None of the other guys and girls in our unit handled the gray areas of our mission better than me. I simply didn't mind killing anyone I had to. Stupid bastards never thought to ask why.

I wasn't sure how this skill set made me the "go-to" guy for whatever Sarah had to say.

Leaning forward a bit, she asked, "You were a sniper?"

"No, I was a shooter," I replied. "The Barrett rifle was a useful tool, but I'm pretty much the best you've ever seen with a gun of any type. There's a handful of people on this planet that might be better, but I doubt it."

"Mr. Dru, don't let the business clothes fool you, I'm a southern gal and know my way around guns. Are you telling tales? You pick up a gun and bam, you hit the bullseye?"

Forcing a laugh out, I said, "Umm...no. I'm not magic. I have to pick up the gun, shoot it, maybe set the sights, or zero in the scope, work with a spotter, or whatever else the tool and setting requires. But after practice and familiarizing myself, I'll be well above average. With the right tools dialed in properly, I'm the best."

I hate this part. I didn't want to tell her more, but I was beginning to get worried about the reason she came here to find me. "There's more to me than that, though. Did Frank ever tell you about the soldiers with knacks?"

"No, I don't believe he did."

"What can't be explained by training is often called a "knack". Some people have a weird, almost unexplainable ability in something. It's rare, but it's acknowledged by people who matter, and normal folks with these knacks are often scooped up by their governments. I have one. They don't know how or why, but I can do all the things great shooters do while moving."

"How is that a, what did you call it, knack?"

"Well, let's stick with the "Sniper" thing for a minute. A good military sniper can hit targets from extremely far away. They lay or position themselves carefully, calm their heart rate, practice breathing techniques, and, well it's fucking hard to hit something a kilometer or more away from you, right?"

"Right. Sure, but..."

"I once shot a target over a kilometer away from a moving vehicle."

"That's impossible!"

"Yes, it is. Yet I do it - did it. Regularly."

She wagged her finger at me like a school teacher scolding a student as she repeated, "That's not possible."

"That's a knack," I shrugged.

"Wait, you're telling me that you guys..."

"...Not only guys, Sarah. The Squad was a totally integrated unit. Girls, guys, neither, both. Didn't matter as long as you were the best at what you did."

"I didn't mean men. I'm aware that you had women in your Squad. Frank told me about," she hesitated, "some of the women."

I bet he did.

"You mean Jo."

She had genuine concern plastered all over her face.

"Yeah. LT, me, and a woman named Jo. Jo wasn't even close to human. Her long, dark face looked like a statue from some ruins in the Chilean Andes, which made sense seeing as how most of those statues were made to honor and appease her family. Not ancestors, Sarah. Family. And she could drive like a bat out of hell.

"Frank rode shotgun and managed ground support for our unit. I killed anything bad around us, and Jo got us into, and out of, the hot zone."

She didn't seem surprised by this information. Apparently, she knew all of it already.

Dreading the answer, I finally asked, "What is this about then?"

"Frank asked me to come to you if..."

"If what?"

Sarah looked back down at her hands all twisted up in her lap and whispered, "My Frank has disappeared."

"Disappeared from where, exactly?" I asked. As far as I knew he was still with the Nightmare Squad somewhere in the sandbox.

She looked perplexed for a minute, and said, "What do you mean? He's disappeared – totally gone. He left the house nine days ago and never came home."

I was flummoxed. "He was home? What, like on leave?"

She looked confused and shook her head, "No, he retired about a month ago. You know that."

I sat forward on the chair and leaned towards her, "No, he didn't," I whispered.

"I beg your pardon?"

"No. He. Didn't."

"Well, of course he did," she half yelled. She stood up as if to leave so I moved quickly and grabbed her hand. She looked at her hand in mine, then up with a look on her face as if she was torn between crying and slapping the shit out of me. Real heat in her eyes.

"Sarah," I said, still quiet but letting go of her hand, "Frank wasn't due to retire for several years yet. Either you're lying to me, or you have been misled."

"What are you talking about? You boys were talking to each other all the time."

I stared dumbly at her for a short eternity. "What?"

She stared back. "You mean you weren't? Then who..." she trailed off and her eyes went unfocused as she reordered some facts in her head.

I, meanwhile, was totally lost. "Maybe you'd better start at the beginning."

Numbly, she sat back down. I had to hand it to her. On her last reserves both mentally and physically, she was able to pull it together and regroup a few seconds after regaining her seat. I've seen experienced soldiers struggle longer over less.

"Sarah, what is going on? When did Frank come home and why?"

She held up her hand for an extra moment to compose herself, so I sat my butt back down into my recliner and fidgeted and waited. Not my strong suit, let me tell you.

Finally, she began, "He called me about four months ago to tell me that he was retiring early from the military. They were letting him go early for "valorous service above and beyond," he called it.

"Wait a sec. Letting him go early? You know that he wasn't strictly speaking a volunteer, right?"

Her features hardened and she glared at me as she said, "Of course I know that. You don't think I know that our wonderful country blackmailed my husband into service? Do you imagine he didn't tell me that they left him with the choice of service or deportation, or worse?"

"Well, I wouldn't call it blackmail," I began.

"Oh really! What would you call it, Mr. Seta? Coercion? Or maybe you'd call it press-ganged or..."

"Slavery."

That stopped her. "What?"

I repeated, "Slavery. What they do to the Extras is slavery; indentured servitude at best. Frank had to give twenty years of military service in exchange for an official identity and status in this country, Sarah."

"Worse than that," she spit out. "He had to give twenty years for one life, Mr. Seta. Do you understand what that means?"

I did. It meant that a guy who lived for damn near five hundred years like LT had to do it each time he wanted a new identity. Can't just live down the street from your good friends the Smith's for six generations, can you? Every "new life" required him to sacrifice twenty years doing the most dangerous, thankless, and dirtiest tasks for the privilege of being a US citizen for the next sixty.

All the global powers did it, and it was so fundamentally wrong that some Extras refused outright and ran. But when it came to a runner, all the countries cooperated.

Couldn't have Extras thinking it was possible to refuse their slavery and get away with it, right? So they were hunted down and killed without fail. Every single one. There was no deportation, that was a lie. There was service or assassination. I know because that was part of my job; to hunt down and kill the runners. It was part of Frank's job too.

And no Extra ever ever got released early. Especially not a leader like Frank. He was too smart, too level-headed under fire, and way too experienced to let go.

"Are you trying to tell me that he was allowed to come home early from slavery?"

"Yes! I know it sounds crazy when you put it that way, but yes!" she said, "My husband called me and told me he was released and coming home. He said that they had to let him go. That he had earned it. A few weeks later he arrived at Austin Bergstrom and I took him home."

"That's right. You two live in Texas. He said something about a Big Rock."

"Round Rock. We live in Round Rock, north of Austin."

"Right, so what happened after he got home?"

"Well, nothing," she said. "We celebrated for a few days, and after I went back to work, he settled into the house and began looking for a job." She looked at me again before continuing, "He talked about you a bunch that first week, and started taking long phone calls several times a day. I assumed it was with you and his other friends from the service staying in touch. That was the impression he gave to me, anyway."

"If you were at work, how did you know about the phone calls?"

"Well, I didn't at first, but he did take a few calls later in the evenings after I got home. Twice last month I called during the day and got sent straight to his message. When I tried back later, I got sent to the voicemail again. I suppose it could have been two different phone calls, but I assumed based on his evening calls that he was taking long calls during the day."

"So, Frank got to go home to you, his wife, but spent all his time on the phone? That doesn't track with the man I know."

"It wasn't that bad, Mr. Dru, but it was the reason I assumed he was talking to you. I couldn't imagine another person being important enough to take up that amount of time." She leaned over and put her hand over mine, "He genuinely likes you, you know. I think you may be his best friend."

I sighed and sat back, pulling my hand free. Damn it! I did not need this sort of thing in my life. I'm out of the Squad for a nasty reason, and LT knows that reason. I kinda figured Frank didn't care for me all that much anymore. I couldn't imagine why he would send his wife to me, so I decided to ask.

"Why are you here, Mrs. Egils?"

To her credit, she didn't repeat what she said before. She understood what I was actually asking.

"Eleven days ago, Frank took me out to dinner downtown. During the meal, he was distracted and jumpy. A waiter dropped a plate in the kitchen and I thought he was about to go through the roof. It scared me a bit. When I asked what was wrong, all he told me was that he had a job offer to work for a private military contractor called Broadhead Securities."

Shit. "Are you sure? What would his job entail?"

"That's the thing, it was a dream job. He would be a consultant. No overseas deployment, no combat, no risk. I know what you guys in the squad think of Broadhead, he was crystal clear on that, but he seemed to think this job was a good opportunity."

"I find that incredibly hard to believe, but we'll get back to that in a sec. Why was he 'distracted and jumpy', as you called him?"

"I don't know! It doesn't make any sense! He shrugged it off, saying how important getting the job was to him. And later at home, he told me he had to leave in two days to meet the president of the company for lunch in Dallas."

"That's their home office?" I asked.

"Yes, but Mr. Dru…The last thing he told me that night was that, of all the soldiers he knew, you were the man who would understand why he was taking the job."

"Why did he say that?"

"I don't know, but he left for the meeting, and later that day he and I had a video call and he told me he needed to stay in Dallas another few days for meetings and onboarding." And with that, she broke down and began quietly crying with her face buried in her hands. "That was nine days ago," she whispered between small shudders.

I went to the kitchen and grabbed a roll of paper towels since there was no tissue paper in the house. Tough guy, remember?

"Sarah, I have to ask you – is that conversation the real reason why you came to me?"

She was able to look up at me again and answer, "No. That day on the video call, as he was about to hang up, he told me he loved me and looked around at the sky like he was taking in all the clouds and sunshine. Then he said, 'If you need anything while I'm gone, call Dru,' and I swear I heard him mumble under his breath as he hung up, 'He'll know what to do.'" She broke down and started crying again.

Interesting. Cryptic. Weird. Call me? Despite what she thought, I hadn't talked to LT in over ten months and never thought to hear from him again. He and I had been tight, but my last days left us with what could only politely be called a strained relationship. Why would he want his wife to come to me?

"You know what? This doesn't track straight. You've heard of contractor security firms like Blackwater, and the like? They're always in the news for the wrong reasons, aren't they? Well, Broadhead is the worst of the lot."

She looked up at me and got herself under control. "How so?" She asked.

"Broadhead has multiple contracts with countries to supply logistics and manpower to their Extra units and missions. They employ many people from the squad after they get out of their units. Many soldiers turn around and join Broadhead, going right back to doing what they did for their country. Murder for hire."

She wrung her hands in confusion, "Why would they do that?"

I shrugged, "Because a lot of Extras and people like killing things."

"Not my Frank."

"No, definitely not LT. That's why I'm confused. Honestly, most of the squad, we hated Broadhead. They tend to start fires that we have to put out, then blame us for the trouble. They have friends in extremely high places, and they do it for the money. Period. No morals, no international relations, no diplomacy, no politics. Purely mayhem for money."

"So, why would my husband take a job there?"

"I don't think he would. This whole thing makes zero sense."

"Oh Lord."

After the quiet tears subsided, she wiped her red eyes and asked me the question I had been expecting since the story came out, "Mr. Dru, will you help me find my husband?"

I'm nothing but a retired killer with an addiction to pills. I haven't the first clue how to find a missing person in a civilian setting, and I sure as hell don't have the money to go chasing all over America to find him. Hell, the last time LT had seen me I had been covered in Jo's blood up to my armpits and holding a gun to his head.

But here was an option beyond eating the painkillers in my bathroom. I felt my heart start beating a tiny bit faster as I realized I might have found my next war. So I said the only thing I could do in that situation.

"Of course I will. He's my friend."

Chapter Two

Children of the Secret

The black slowly resolved into gray and white as I opened my eyes. I was sitting in a lotus position and had been meditating for a little over four hours. The sun was low in the sky, but there was still enough light to see the bare, white wall in front of me.

After Sarah left and went back to her hotel, I spent the rest of that day packing a kit to take with me to Texas, figuring that was the place to start. Soon, it was obvious I had no idea what to pack. After staring at a week's worth of opioids, socks and underwear for five minutes, I realized that I was completely lost.

What does one bring to a manhunt?

Let's get a few things crystal clear. I am not a detective. I do not have "contacts" I can call on to do "leg work" in investigations. I loathe computers, though I am competent in their use. I am merely a retired soldier. I am not a patient man, either. I tend to pick a direction and start going until I meet a wall, at which point I usually shoot it.

In order to prevent such occurrences from happening in civilian life, I have found that the study of Tai Chi, along with meditation, helps me find pathways that my target fixated bull rush approach might otherwise miss. This time, however, the meditation was primarily to get these Gods-damned flashbacks under control.

After Sarah had left, I had started seeing bright flashes of gunfire out of the corner of my eyes, and once a face that looked a lot like mine, but couldn't have been, because he was dead in my arms.

Anyway. No time for that insanity just now. Now I need to pack.

What does one bring to a manhunt? A hunter of men, and I am that. In spades. The battleground is different this time, as are the rules of engagement, but at the end of the day, I spent a lot of time tracking, chasing, and yeah, killing Extras. I'm actually good at it. All I have to do is acquire a slightly different set of tools for my toolbox this time. Or maybe a better image would be a different set of armaments for the rucksack.

Whatever image you prefer, I needed intel, so the first stop after flying into Austin would be to sit down with Frank's wife again and ask some relevant questions. As for packing, this battleground is a quiet, hidden one. The Barrett .50 caliber sniper rifle would stand out like...well...exactly what it is – a man killer.

But I was going to Texas, so I doubted too many eyebrows would be raised by a big game hunting rifle and a large caliber sidearm or two. Pack some hunting camo, some outdoor clothes, and a decent shirt and pants for appearing human, a big bottle of grey market pain killers, and I was good to go. Let's pretend it's a week-long hunting trip as a long overdue vacation.

I was getting the hang of this whole detective thing already.

Sarah had bought me a ticket on the same flight she was on, so we sat in excruciatingly uncomfortable silence on the airplane all the way to Austin. The less said about the trip, the better. I'm horrible at small talk, and Sarah obviously had a lot on her mind. I had eventually plugged in my headphones and listened to my Plucky Wizard overcome all odds to save the day. I was a chapter from the end when we began our descent. I still couldn't figure out how he shot those accurate over-the-shoulder fireballs whilst running away all the time.

When we landed in Austin, I went to stop at the first coffee shop I saw in the terminal. I looked up and got a gut punch when I read it's name: Jo's. It stopped me in my tracks and gave me a little superstitious twinge.

I mumbled, "Shit," as my joint pain flared up and a headache started in my temples. I shook it off and made myself walk up to the lady behind the counter, finishing my mumble with, "You can get past this, soldier, it's just a cup of coffee."

She met me with a tired, "What can I get you?"

I forced myself to say, "What's a good, strong, cold drink?"

Her eyes lit up a tiny bit and a smile crept into the corners of her mouth, "Our specialty is the Iced Turbo."

My eyebrows rose. "Turbo" sounded right up my alley. "What's that?"

"It's an iced hazelnut and chocolate cold-brew. Delicious."

"Sounds sweet. I'm not a huge fan of super sweet."

The smile slipped, "It is sweet. What you want is the Belgian."

Bemused, I asked, "And the Belgian is...?"

"Half Turbo, half black Cold Brew."

"Sold!"

The Grin was back as she rang me up and the drink was put into my hands in less than a minute. I took my first sip, and the drink was the best thing that had happened to me in seven months. "Oh. Oh yes, thank you."

Sara and I met back up at the baggage claim. As we looked for the luggage to start down the chute, we stood around nervously fidgeting and studiously not saying anything. After about two minutes, my ADHD got the best of me and I had to ask, "Do you realize there are two bands playing in your airport right now? At the same time?"

She smiled a little and replied, "Austin is the live music capital of the world, and we take it seriously."

"Sure, but two bands at once?"

"That's a little unusual, but there must be a special occasion of some sort going on. Hardly a rare occurrence here. You know, Dru, you are not what I expected."

I looked around the airport like I was searching for something, "I'm not?"

She adjusted her carry-on bag strap on her shoulder and said, "Oh, I know better than to assume anything where Frank's...friends...are concerned, but the way he described you, I thought you were going to look like Rambo."

Straight-faced, "I thought I did."

She laughed and seemed surprised at herself for doing it. I immediately realized why he fell in love with her. It's not easy for a guy who can expect to outlive humans by four hundred years to let himself fall for a girl who will be lucky to make it to ninety, but she had a genuine laugh that would make a glacier melt.

"So what you're saying," I continued, "is that Rambo isn't a few inches shy of six feet and one hundred and sixty-five pounds of pure awesomeness?"

This time she didn't hold back with the laugh and answered, "Oh sweetie, I'm pretty sure he doesn't have red stubble on his face or grey eyes either."

I immediately stopped laughing and stared at her hard. Her smile faltered and dropped, and her face registered concern. "I'm sorry. Did I say something wrong?"

I leaned in close and replied, "You callin' me a ginger?" It took her a second, and she and I both broke into a laugh at the same time. "It's a curse, dark brown hair and red beard. The Celts strike again."

She finished her laugh and put her hand on my arm in a simple gesture of friendship. Frank, you lucky bastard, why would you risk this? Where have you gone?

Don't worry, I wasn't thinking impure thoughts about my friend's wife. I'm not normal as far as relationships go. As in I don't want a physical one. At all.

I'm not a loner per se (that's a lie, yes, I am), but I've wanted nothing physical from anyone for as long as I can remember. Those relationships seem to be a non-starter for me. But that didn't mean I couldn't recognize an amazing person standing in front of me.

As we left the airport, a wave of heat slammed into me and damn near took my breath away. "Wow," I said, "I had no idea it would be this hot in Austin. It must be a hundred degrees! In September!"

"Yes sir, it's getting more and more common to have these temps even into early September. Good news is that it's supposed to drop into the low nineties starting tomorrow. This should be the last day over one hundred until next year."

After we located her SUV in the aptly named "Blue Garage", I found myself a passenger in the largest non-military vehicle I had ever seen. Sarah's SUV was a Chevy Suburban in silver grey, and it was approximately a city block long. Inside it was tastefully appointed in enough leather to clothe a large herd of cows, and it had all the bells and whistles available. The damn thing even talked to her and let her know we were headed to her house.

"You don't know where you live?"

"What? Of course I do. What are you going on about?

"Why do you have a navigation set up larger than my television, telling you where your house is?"

"Stop being silly."

"In a way, I'm being serious. There's no way a Lieutenant's salary bought this car, and he was never one to buy technology for the sake of technology. This is your car bought with your money, right?"

She drove on, silent for a few beats, eventually answering, "Yes. I work, make money, and spend it. Women do that these days, Mr. Seta."

"What do you mean? I didn't mean to imply you belonged in the kitchen making me a sandwich. I just wanted to know why you have a monster truck with enough technology to go to the moon."

"My husband and I are different people, Mr. Dru; beyond the obvious. I'm a certified techie. I love tablets, smartphones, computers and all that stuff. I work for a company that designs, builds, and sells the most popular examples of those toys on the market. I make about five times as much as he did in the Squad, and I run an entire division of the company. Research and Development, no less."

"Then why does he need to get a job?"

She eyed me sideways as she drove, "Are you serious, darlin'?"

"As a heart attack."

"He doesn't," she shrugged, "I make a strong six figures and he has been saving money for over two hundred years. We're quite well off. But he wanted to get a job, and if we're being honest, he still has a little of that macho male provider bullshit left over from being born in the early 1700's."

There's a trick southerners have when they speak where they can take a simple sentence and make you know exactly how low their opinion of you is, and Sarah nailed it as she said, "I'm sure you understand Frank's thinking."

That was about as clear a "shut the fuck up, man-pig" as you can get without actually saying it. Fair enough. I probably deserved it. A quick flash of a woman's face, framed in bright red hair, and calling me an idiot ran across my brain. That was a new one. Wonder who she was? Was she real? Did I once know her?

We arrived at the house about forty minutes later and I was invited inside for lunch. As we walked up to the door, I looked up at the big Texas sky as the sun shone down hard on me. I noticed a black bird high up in the air circling the neighborhood and felt a chill.

Sarah saw me, looked up, and said, "Yeah, it's a big Texas sky, isn't it? Bright blue and goes on forever sometimes."

I pasted a fake smile on my face. "It sure is."

"You looked like Frank did that day on the call, standing there staring at the sky."

"I'm taking in all the clouds and sunshine." I kept the smile on my face and looked one more time. The bird was gone, but that didn't stop the shiver that went down my spine. We went inside.

I entered the front door to find myself in a large foyer with a nice limestone tile floor and some artwork on the walls. No idea who the artist was, but it looked like scenes of local locations, so I assumed it was a local artist.

I followed Sarah past the dining room on the right, where she looked over her shoulder with an innocent smile and asked, "Want me to make you a sandwich?"

"Uhh...there's no right answer here, is there?"

Laughing, she replied, "Bless your heart, you're going to have to loosen up a little and get used to it. I've been teasing my husband about his old-fashioned thinking for our entire relationship, and you have to admit, you kind of set yourself up for that one."

"Listen, I'm sorry if I said or did anything to upset you, I do recognize that a lifetime in the military did not do me any favors in the 'toxic masculinity department', but I certainly don't think I have any hang-ups about gender equality. I'll try to watch my attitude."

"Huh. I'm...apology accepted, and I'm sorry too. I'm being a little defensive. Probably a habit from being the boss of a bunch of socially inept men who think their brains are bigger than mine because I have different plumbing than them. But you're still going to make your own sandwich. Come on into the kitchen."

Having come in through the front door, and passing the formal dining room off to the right, there was a weird little sitting room to the left.

Immediately after that, a stairway to the second floor was in front of me to the right creating a "wall" for the dining area and going up to my right-hand side. Walking past this stairway led me past a hallway to the right side of the house and into the living room with the large kitchen with a dining nook to my right. It was an interesting layout with the back door almost directly across the house from the front door, and the bulk of the house extending away to one side.

We walked almost all the way to the back door, then turned right into the kitchen.

I made myself a big, classic, Italian-style sandwich on a surprisingly delicious sub roll after Sarah pulled out all the meats, cheeses, and other sandwich stuff from the gleaming, stainless-steel fridge. Italian Subs might be the greatest gastronomic invention in human history...as long as you have a great sub roll to build it on.

And as long as you don't include coffee in the definition of "gastronomic", of course, because coffee is in a class all by itself.

Sarah made something I'll politely call vegetable-based with some cheese thrown in. She grabbed a bag of potato chips, tossed them onto the counter, and said, "Help yourself, Mr. Dru".

We sat down to eat and Sarah looked at me and said, "You really aren't what I expected."

"So you said at the airport."

"No, not your physical appearance, well, not just your physical appearance. For example, what kind of name is Seta? It doesn't sound Irish."

"I changed my name legally. My Stepfather's last name was a real Irish "Mac". For personal reasons I'll have nothing to do with that family."

She sat back in her chair, "Interesting, but it sounds like maybe you don't want to talk about any of that."

"I don't, thank you. How about you, Sarah. Family?"

"Frank was...is...my family. That's it."

"Well, I know Frank loved...loves...shit I'm sorry, this is hard." I grabbed the edge of the table for support.

"Yes, it is. Let's please assume my husband is alive until proven otherwise. I don't know what I'd do without him."

"I agree. LT is alive, and I'm going to find him." I looked up at her face. "He loves you very much. Said you were his world."

"You know, my husband liked you, but he also thought that maybe you were..." she looked away from me and over at the wall as if the words she needed to say would be printed there.

"What? What did he think?"

"Well, that maybe you weren't only an excellent soldier. He told me many times he thought that the skills – what you called your "knack" – was more than you let on. Mr. Dru, he told me many times the world was far stranger than we modern folks knew, and you were part of that strangeness."

Well shit. I am a little different from most, and honestly, I don't want others knowing. I'm not an Extra, but my "knack" has a few warps and twists to it I've worked hard to hide. I don't want to lie about everything, so I figured it was time to try to change the conversation or deflect. "Sarah, I don't know anything about that. I know what I can do. Not why or how."

"My Frank was born in 1723. He's seen a lot, and he thought maybe you were more than you appeared or pretended to be, but he understood why you kept it quiet."

"Sarah, Frank was born in the seventeen hundreds, yes. But it's only in the last few years that psychology and medical science have understood the behaviors of humans in any meaningful way. I need to be honest with you - I am a messed up person. I have seen lifetimes of trauma for sure, but that's simply my bad luck. I do not function like you, think like you, or behave like you."

I rested my elbows on the table and learned in towards her, "Sarah, I get what he was thinking and why. I am different. Even taking our profession into context. But that's because I'm basically a functioning nightmare. Regular, healthy, normal people - like you - cannot understand."

Sarah's eyes hardened. "Oh, you think so? You think little old me can't understand? Mr. Seta, how many human beings do you think could accept and come to terms with a three-hundred-year-old husband? I'm trying to get to know you, but you sure seem to think you already know all about me."

I sighed inwardly and tried to make her understand. "That's not what I meant. I honestly meant that you have no frame of reference for my experiences and the things that shaped me."

"Like what?" she challenged.

I honestly don't know why I said it. There is not one time in my life up to this point that I can remember ever speaking about my childhood. Hell. I pretty much never even allowed myself to think about it. But before my brain could realize what my mouth was saying, I blurted out, "Like my entire abusive nightmare of a childhood."

She got quiet and looked at me with an understanding that curdled my stomach.

Oh shit no.

A switch was thrown in my brain, my ears started ringing like a bad case of tinnitus and my vision began to tunnel, tinged with red. I began to panic.

"I'm sorry Mr. Dru, but you're wrong. I understand that completely, sweetheart."

She suddenly noticed my labored, heavy breathing and said, "Are you alright?" It sounded like it was coming from miles away or maybe underwater or something. I couldn't tell, and I couldn't answer. I was starting to hyperventilate. My knees, elbows, and shoulders exploded in agonizing pain and I crashed up and out of my chair, stumbling back against the wall behind me, using it to hold me up. Snapshots of dead faces played across my eyes in a rapid fire migraine of death and violence. Bodies, blood, and agony in flashback form causing my head to pound like a sledgehammer had come down on me.

She stood up to cross over to me, and even through my blurred vision I could tell she was concerned, "Dru, are you okay? Breathe, sweetheart. Relax and breathe."

I was waving my arms feebly. This hadn't happened in a long time, but I knew what was coming next and Sarah was in real danger. I gasped, "You need to get away from me. Get back!"

She stopped a few feet away from me, not understanding the danger but trying to put me at ease. "It's okay Dru. Don't speak, just breathe. Just listen. You don't have to talk about it. You don't need to speak. Just breathe, just try to relax. It's okay."

It was as if being given permission to stop opened a floodgate, letting the panic and hurt drain away. I began shuddering with relief and slid down the wall until I was sitting on the floor.

Sarah looked at me for a long time and I could tell from the set of her mouth and eyes she had come to some sort of a decision.

Eventually, my breathing began to return to normal and I was able to hear and see clearly again. I felt exhausted and could barely lift my head.

"Dru, I'm going to tell you my story, because you need to hear it. Can you listen to my story? It will be hard for you, I think."

I nodded my head. "I can listen, so long as I don't have to talk much, I think."

"Alright." She visibly gathered herself together before she continued, "I was an orphan at age four and was placed in five different foster families before I ran away at fifteen. And yeah, it was every bit as bad as you could imagine. I was a very pretty little girl." She sat as still as a statue and pinned me with her eyes, "They started whispering that to me in my bedroom late at night when I was eight."

I sat there stunned. I forced out a whispered, "Then how...how the hell did you wind up..." I waved my arms weakly around the kitchen, "...here?"

"Frank."

"Frank?"

"He showed me how to save myself. Plain and simple." She nodded to herself, "If I tell you this, you'll be the third person alive to know my secret. Don't make me regret it. Please."

I swallowed hard and nodded my head a fraction of an inch, "I won't. I understand."

"I was a fifteen-year-old runaway, smart but undereducated, and I was trying to hustle and con people on the streets to survive, desperately trying to avoid the fate of so many others like me. My eyes were wide open. I knew prostitution, drug addiction, and death were waiting for me, but I thought I was smart enough to play the game and win."

I guiltily thought of the painkillers in my pocket.

"I was sure I could beat the odds. Then I met Lucas and we became partners. I knew shortly after he punched me for the first time I had gambled and lost. By the third beating, I did what he told me to do and tried not to make him angry.

"Then one night I tried to con Frank."

I tried talking, "Where?"

"Atlanta. I came onto him as he left a bar, figuring the middle-aged drunk guy would try to take me home and I could talk him into driving into a quiet parking lot where my partner was waiting.

"Lucas was a big kid full of steroids and all muscle. He would bang on the car yelling and screaming about the mark 'molesting' his little sister and we'd shake our marks down for money, get their driver's license and threaten them with exposure if they were married, or violence if they were single.

"Frank started talking to me. He saw right through the con, offered me *five hundred dollars* so long as I went to a woman's shelter for the night, and somehow kept me talking for almost an hour right there on the corner. I can't explain it. I should have hightailed it out of there and looked for another mark. I knew Lucas was one bad day away from becoming my pimp, and I was terrified of him. Somehow Frank talked me into walking away.

"I explained to him about Lucas, and he shrugged that way of his, smiled a sad little smile, and said he'd handle Lucas. I laughed. You know what Frank looks like. I thought, this middle-aged skinny guy is going to handle Lucas? No way! But he patted my hand and led me to the shelter.

"The next morning, for the first time in my life, somebody made good on their promise to me. He showed up, handed me five, crisp, one hundred dollar bills, took me out to meet Lucas, and beat him into the hospital in 30 seconds. I was stunned, and I was in love. Immediately. I turned to Frank and told him he was going to be my husband and I was going to take care of him forever.

"To this day, I'm not embarrassed about that. This wasn't some childish fantasy in my head. This was me seeing a man treat me like a human being for the first time ever, and I knew - *I knew* - this was the way forward and out of my dead-end future. But there was also something in Frank that told me he needed me too. I can't explain it, but I felt for the first time in my life that I was an equal part of the equation. I trusted him completely and I realized he could trust me too. I was one hundred percent committed.

"I'll never forget his response as long as I live. He said, 'I believe you mean that, but you can't even take care of yourself yet. That five hundred can get you away from here. Take it and grab a bus to Florida or somewhere. Learn how to take care of yourself.'

"I was furious. I yelled, 'Don't tease me, I'm serious! You are going to be my husband and I am going to take care of you!'

"He replied, 'I said I believe you, but do you even have a high school diploma?' I punched him in the shoulder and yelled that I didn't need one to love a man.

"I was fifteen years old, Dru, but he could tell I was no stranger to what I was offering and that I meant it. I had no shame. I would have seduced him right there on the street if I could have."

She had tears in her eyes as she continued, "And he said, 'As soon as you get your Masters degree from a college, I will accept your marriage proposal, if you still desire it. Not a day sooner. And until then, if you're really serious, you will move into my spare bedroom and we will do the proper paperwork to make me your guardian so that you can legally stay in my house. Come on, we're going home'. And he took me to his home, moved me into the guest room, and helped me get a GED so I could enroll in Georgia State by age seventeen."

She looked at me and raised her hand to forestall my comments. "Obviously he didn't mean it when he said he'd marry me, and it was clear he wanted me to learn to think of him like a father, but I knew how flimsy and useless the word father could be, and I wasn't interested in that. I decided to prove to him that he was going to be my husband." She smiled a wry grin. "That first night I tried his bedroom door to find it locked. He locked it every night for over four years.

"I busted my butt at Georgia State and spent three and a half years buried in books. At age twenty I had my bachelor's in Computer Sciences and we moved to Austin – Frank sold his house and moved with me to Austin – so I could get my Masters. He never once tried to sleep with me, and I never once tried to sleep with anybody else.

"By then I knew all about him and his past. He had dropped hints for years, but he told me everything during my senior year at Georgia. He was trying to explain why we could never be husband and wife. Oh Dru, I cried so hard when I realized I couldn't keep my promise to take care of him for the rest of his life, and apologized over and over again.

"A few years ago, he confessed that's when he began to fall in love with me. Until then, he was simply doing a good deed. Who does that? Who just saves lives for no reason?"

I was moved in a deeply unsettling way I couldn't define. "Frank, apparently."

"We got married at the courthouse three hours after my graduation ceremony from UT, and that was seven years ago. You already know that four years ago he had to go back to slavery in the Squad, and now he's gone and it's my turn to either save my husband or avenge him. Because I promise you, if my husband is gone, I'm going to kill every single bastard involved."

"Where were people like you when I needed them?" I mumbled.

"I'm sorry sweetie, but I know what it's like being a Child of the Secret."

"Oh, it was no secret in my family," I replied bitterly. "My step-father passed me around like a party favor."

"My Lord."

"Yeah. I've killed a lot of people; I really wish he was one of them."

"He's still alive then?"

"Oh no, he's long dead, but I didn't get to do it. In fact, the son of a bitch died a hero and accidentally saved my life. How's that for a kick in the teeth?"

"But Dru, people like us understand more than most that family has nothing to do with blood. Frank was my family of choice, and you are part of his family. That makes us family too."

I had an electric jolt of self-loathing shoot through my whole body and I had to step away from her. I stood up and walked away from the wall. "No, it doesn't. Only a fool would choose to call me family, but LT is my friend, and friends are rare." I stared into her face, willing her to understand. "That's why I'm going to help you kill all of these motherfuckers."

I dropped my eyes and began to fidget. Gods I could use a few painkillers all of the sudden. "Sarah, this was a lot for me. Too much, really. I'm not ashamed to admit it. I think I need to be alone now. I'd better get on up to my hotel in Dallas."

"How?"

"Umm...good question. Can you actually get an Uber to go that far?"

"Mr. Dru, why don't I drive you?"

There was no way I was going to be able to sit next to her for that long in a car after what we had shared. No way. "And then you'd have to drive all the way back? Isn't it like, three hours each way?"

"Well, I have a car you can borrow, I guess."

"Actually, I don't want any connection between you and me yet. I'm not sure what's going on, but I do think it'd be better if everyone assumes I'm Frank's lone friend. So. Can you get an Uber from Round Rock to Dallas?"

Turns out you can, but it's not fun. I sat in the back of the car for the whole trip thinking about Sarah's childhood and how I've spent my entire life trying to forget mine. But it's impossible to forget when everything you are was shaped in that crucible of hell.

And the real punch to the gut is that I hadn't told her even a tenth of it. I couldn't. We shared a horrific past, us children of the secret, but there are things in mine that would send her right over the edge, and she'd never trust me to be sane if I shared them with her, because I'm not.

Oddly, there were no flashbacks for the entire ride.

Chapter Three

Broadhead

The next morning, I shook myself awake from the usual nightmares and slowly recalled I was in my hotel room, took a quick shower, and dressed for a job interview. And coffee. Always coffee. I've had nightmares for as long as I can remember. Not from "PTSD" like that last defective shrink tried to insist. That's a myth. I mean, yeah, I've got that too, but the nightmares are mostly from my childhood. Post Traumatic Stress Disorder comes from an inability to regulate the threat response. I live in a high threat state all the time. I have reason to, but it's not supposed to be this way.

I wake up and have coffee. And two painkillers for luck.

I figured the only thing for a guy like me to do is to go to the last place I thought Frank went. I looked up the address of Broadhead Securities and caught another Uber. The car pulled up to a huge modern glass building that looked like it was designed by an architect who loved Tolkien but managed to totally miss the point of the Shire. Glass, steel, and chrome had been tortured into "organic" shapes and circular windows and doors.

Hardly any straight edges or ninety-degree angles anywhere. I honestly hated it on sight.

In surprisingly "Ye Olde Lettering", the huge gleaming silver signage and emblem of Broadhead Securities was writ in giant letters across the building between the second and third story, with a surprisingly well-done image of a broadhead arrow tip in the upper right-hand corner of the top floor of the building. I guessed it was ten, maybe twelve stories tall, and maybe should have counted floors, but honestly, who the hell cares?

I walked towards the main entrance, noting the presence of two security guards stationed by the entrance doors, of which there were three - two doors that opened up next to each other and one near the left-hand side of the building. All three were shaped to look round, I guess, but the end result of the architectural nightmare was doors that looked like two parentheses connected by steel bars top and bottom. Fugly as hell. As I approached, I had a quick glimpse of a sour-faced old man dressed in a green woolen cloak waving a stick at me. He wasn't real.

The security guards did what all doormen do - stand there and let everyone through - but they did give me a once over I thought was professional and included a recognition of one soldier to another when they made eye contact with me. I nodded a tiny head nod to them both and walked to the security desk. All incoming people were funneled neatly from the doors to the security desk, where there was a set of two metal detectors, and - I swear I'm not making this up - a sign saying "All firearms must be declared and run through x-ray machine." So, I did.

"Hi. I'm here for a job interview. I have two pistols and my permit to carry, "I said as I took the backup out of my ankle holster and placed it on the x-ray machine. As I placed my Glock from my waistband holster on the belt, I asked, "What exactly are the metal detectors for?"

"For the safety of the employees here."

"How, exactly?"

He looked up sharply from his screen and stared at me for a few seconds. "You applying for a job today?"

"Yes sir."

"You might want to curb the sarcasm then. Step through and go to the desk to sign in for your interview."

I stepped through and immediately set off the detector because I "forgot" to get rid of my pocket knife.

BEEP!

I looked over to the security desk to see a shit-eating grin and smirk at the same moment he asked me to turn out my pockets.

"Shit. I'm an ass. Forgot my knife."

"I'm sure you're right, sir."

"...I ...deserved that." We got through the process after that, I re-holstered my firearms and was through the security checkpoint with the security desk having forgotten completely to check who I was supposed to be interviewing with. Which, of course, was the whole point. I learned that little trick a long time ago from a soldier I fought with who watched far too many spy movies. That's me, Double O six and a half walking into Spectre like a boss.

I was feeling really good about it until the Security officer called out to me, "All you guys interviewing are to wait in room 118. Down that hallway past the elevators and on your left."

Well, shit. I guess it's better to be lucky than good. What kind of evil henchman doesn't even care about your name?

I walked to room 118 grumbling about the recurring theme of making a fool of myself for no reason and went in to see seven other clearly ex-military sitting around flexing, chewing gum in a manly, macho way, and wearing sunglasses inside a building. Three of them female, four of them male, all of them thinking they were the Alpha apex predator in the room. I felt like I was home again.

Don't get me wrong, I'm so fucking sick and tired of that macho shit, and in truth when you find yourself in a group of soldiers with shared experiences of the boredom of staging, the exhaustion of training, and the terror of combat, that macho shit is gone. It's the tightest comradery I've ever experienced and there are men and women I've served with who I count among the best examples of life on the planet.

But put career military in a room with *strangers* who all did the same thing? Break out the rulers, start measuring metaphorical dicks, and your gender gives you no advantage. Those women in the room would be among the first to feed you your balls in order to show you who's are bigger.

That posturing and ego drive has been around since the dawn of mankind. After all, fighters are defined by their ability to fight and *win*, because losing means you're dead. That means every soldier in the room was an undefeated champion of the world. But Godsdamn it's tiring to be around it your whole life.

I went to the chair as far away from the rest as possible, sat down, and put my sunglasses back on to cover up my eyes to prevent any eye contact dominance triggers. If this was a movie, this is the moment some buzzcut asshole would come over and start screwing with me, but these men and women are real-life professionals, and so we all sat with discipline waiting for our cattle call interview to start. Nobody here was dumb enough to screw up a job opportunity by being a bully in a room full of potential special forces soldiers.

I sat for about twenty minutes in peace while three more soldiers arrived. Once we were all there, two suits walked in with our interviewer who was clearly cut from the same cloth as us soldiers. I immediately wanted to call her Sarge from her bearing.

"Listen up!" she said. "I am Karen O'Connor. You men and women were invited to apply for a job with Broadhead Securities because of your military experience, but that's not the only reason. All of you have at one time or another been in the field at the same time as Broadhead securities and we," she cleared her throat and adjusted her tablet, "noticed you. Something in your performance of your duties made you a clear candidate for employment with Broadhead Securities."

She continued, "The ten of you are here today to ask us questions you may have and fill out paperwork to begin your employment. You are all offered a job at this time, and it is up to you to accept or decline. Questions?"

The soldier to my right called out, "Wait a minute, we don't know anything about the job. What are we signing up for?"

"This position is what we consider entry-level. You will be folded into an existing unit of contractors and after training you will be sent to the Middle East or Eastern Europe for a six-month deployment. No Broadhead Securities assets - that's you all - will ever be deployed on an assignment longer than six months. Most will be much shorter. Six months a year you will be home, reporting for training and maintaining your fitness and skill sets, and six months a year you will be on call for ops worldwide."

"Wait, we're working six months a year and training six? Really!?"

"That's correct..." She raised an eyebrow at the man with a questioning look.

"Master Chief Petty Officer Andrew Fuka, formerly Seal Team 4, mam."

From behind me, I heard one of the women soldiers call out, "What's the pay?"

"Who asked that?" said Karen.

"Former First Lieutenant Elizabeth Washington, mam!"

"Former." Karen repeated with a smile. "Well, Elizabeth, as you are all starting here at the same level, you all will make our base salary of two hundred and twenty-five thousand a year."

Well, as you can imagine, that set us all off. That's absurd money for most soldiers, and indeed even as a base salary for contractors, that's still stupid money. Everybody began talking at once and Karen had to call out to quiet us down. After we did, she continued and I decided it was time to draw some attention to myself. Obligingly, Karen gave me an opening immediately. Holding up her tablet that, I assume, had information on all the soldiers in the room except me, she said, "You ten soldiers..."

"Eleven." I interrupted.

"Excuse me?"

"There are eleven of us here."

"And you are?" She asked after a quick head count and then looking at the tablet.

"Drustan Seta, rank and branch redacted by the National Securities Act."

There was a pregnant pause as ten soldiers swiveled their eyes to me, Karen looked up, and both suits behind her seemed to wake up and take an interest in the room for the first time. Both stared right at me. Karen went back to the Tablet and said, "I do not have your name or file here. You are not supposed to be here."

"I was referred by my friend who I think got a job here a little while ago?"

Karen was looking pissed, "Mr. Seta, we do not take "referrals" nor do we encourage employees to try to get their friends hired. Who was this friend of yours?"

Watching carefully both Karen and the suits I said, "Frank Egils."

Karen did nothing but write the name down, but Suit Number One wasn't a poker player. His eyes got wide and he leaned over to Suit Two and whispered in his ear.

Karen began the process of kicking me out, "Mr. Seta, I'm afraid we're going to have to ask you to leave immediately, security will come and escort you out..."

Suit Two interrupted, "Actually, I think we will take Mr. Seta to a private interview for a position he might be much more suited to than an entry-level operator. Mr. Seta, you say your name and rank are redacted?"

"Yes indeedy!" I said, pasting a stupid grin on my face.

"Your career had *extra* security?"

For fucks sake. How clever of them. Like everyone in that room wasn't smart enough to figure that out if they ever came across a unit like mine. Meh, let's play the game. "You got in one, sir."

"Right this way, Mr. Seta." And as easy as that, I was led away to the elevators to have a private interview. Now let's all be clear-eyed here; I knew we weren't interviewing for a job. These suits didn't know me, but they recognized LT.'s name immediately. I figured it was an interrogation room I was headed for, and it was an even chance I was about to get either waterboarded or subjected to an attorney's threats of non-disclosure.

I did not expect what actually happened.

As we walked down the hallway towards whatever soundproofed room they planned to lock me into, I figured I might get a little information myself if I played it right. "You guys taking me to the same room Frank interviewed in?"

"Please follow us, sir." replied suit one.

"I know it's a big company, but did you guys ever get to meet Frank? You sure seemed to recognize the name."

"Sir, let's get to the interview room and your interviewer will be able to answer your questions. I'm sure you understand the need for discretion about you and Mr. Egils out here in a public hallway." Suit Two seemed to be the brains of the duo.

"Oh, sure. Yeah. It's just..."

"Just what?" Suit One asked.

"Quiet, Jason." snapped Suit Two. Yeah, definitely the brains, but now I knew a name. Might not seem like much, but you'd be amazed at what you can do with a name. For me, it's limited to a few psychological tricks. Like, pissing off a guy by using it in an overly familiar way, especially if said guy spent most of his adult life being referred to by rank and last name. In fact, I'm sure suit two used it as a power play because my old friend Jason clenched his right fist and his teeth are grinding a tad. Excellent.

"Hey Jason - Jase? Can I call you Jase? Jase, you ever hang out with Frank? Know him at all? He's a fun guy to grab a beer with. You wouldn't want to mess with him, cause he'd kick your ass, Jase, but he's a great guy in general."

As we turned into another short hallway with a nice oak door at the end of it, Jase opened his mouth to reply, but Suit Two put himself between me and Jase and said with a smile, "That's a bad idea, Mr. Seta. Please do not antagonize Jason."

Well shit, maybe I'm not all that good at this. I was hoping to get Jase pissed off and talking, but Suit Two might be smarter than all of us in the hallway. I'm used to it, honestly. I'm smart enough, but I'm not a genius. It's cool, I've got other skills.

Not that these other skills prepared me for getting punched in the back of my head as Suit Two passed me to open the door. No sir, that surprised me quite a bit, for the brief instant I was still conscious.

***

I woke slowly to arguing. Suit Two was berating Jase. Based on where they were in the conversation, I guessed I'd only been out a minute or two. Long enough to have my guns and knife removed, I was sure, but not much longer.

"...she'll want to question him! How can she do that while he's unconscious or concussed?"

Good question.

Damn it, Sean, he'll recover good enough to answer the questions. It's not like it matters after that."

Nothing matters after that, huh? Well then. That changes things.

"Let's pick him up and get him into the truck so we can get him to the safehouse. You get the arms, Jason, I'll take the feet."

It was at this point I decided to feign unconsciousness for a little bit more while I tried to figure out exactly what was happening, because Sean was right, a concussion is no fucking joke, and I had one. I'm pretty sure I'd have a hard time fighting my way out of the room and out of the building since I couldn't remember where I was. Letting these guys secret me out of the building to a parking garage actually sounded pretty smart to my addled brains.

In a shockingly short time these guys had my mildly concussed and faking unconscious body down a side corridor, into a stairwell and out into a garage. As they carried me along, grunting, swearing and generally trying to haul a limp sack of flesh and bones, I cracked an eye open to take stock of the environment.

See, there's one incredibly important thing you learn early on when your job involves both retrieval of dangerous creatures and elimination of others. If it's an elimination, you eliminate them immediately. Right there, right then. No hesitation. Giving the opponent time to fight back is never the right choice. That's bad movie stuff, not real life.

However, there are times and situations where you can't eliminate them immediately. Perhaps there are witnesses you can't avoid, or the environment isn't safe to be in, or - most often - there's information you need to get from the victim first. In that case, it's a retrieval and you take the victim to a safe and controlled environment, at which time, they are done. There will be no escape, no miraculous rescue, no chance.

So here I am on the other side of this situation, and Jase has said there's no future for me. That means if I let them take me wherever they're planning, I'm done. Dead. And most likely unpleasantly.

What am I saying? I'm saying if somebody wants you hurt or dead, but they are taking you somewhere else first, you fight like hell, run like a deer, or make them take you out right there, because obviously, they still feel you're a threat, or have a chance, or can't take you out there. Force the issue, because once you're in that truck, your life is over. Or worse, maybe it isn't over for a very long, very painful time.

Never go where the bad guys want you to go. That's what I'm saying. And yes, I am aware that I have officially classified my job as being one of the bad guys. Truth is I'm not a good guy, so it's accurate.

When we got to the truck and Sean dropped my feet to the floor to open the back door, Jase straddled my body and let go of my arms to grab me under the armpits, which left my hands and legs free, and well…you know what? I decided I might want to grab Jase around the throat with my right hand as I brought my feet under me.

Unlike the Tai Chi and meditation I learned over the last year, earlier in my life I discovered a martial art system from Southeast Asia - Myanmar, specifically - where they study fighting from all sorts of different ranges, including up close and personal. The up close is based on a combination of an ancient Python based grappling art and Burmese wrestling known as Naban. You can think of it as joint locks, joint breaks, chokes, and the judicious application of violence while wrestling. I studied it for years.

Jason's eyes bulged and his hands let go of me as I stood up, I shoved my fingers as deep into his throat as possible and made a fist. This had the effect of closing off his trachea while I snaked my left arm up and over his right arm in a swim-like move, pushing it down so I could tuck my head into his neckline, wrap my arms together around his neck in a choke hold, push my hip into his, and pivot as hard and as fast as I can into a hip throw.

Only when I threw him, I didn't let go of his head.

As is the way with physics and bones, his neck snapped with an audible crack as it tried to hold his entire body's weight in a violent, twisting throw.

I let go of the body and turned to a shocked yet thoroughly professional soldier named Sean drawing his pistol from his shoulder holster. One of the drawbacks to shoulder holster draw is that it takes longer to orient on a target than a waist draw. Fractions of a second, but fractions matter as I slammed into his body, using my shoulders and trunk to pin his right arm across his torso momentarily so that I could put my right hand on his pistol, thus making the fight about who controls the gun rather than who gets to shoot me several times until I'm dead.

The bonus factor here is that I can engage my latissimus muscles to push and hold down, but because of how his arm was across his body, he needed to engage a whole host of secondary muscles to start twisting and turning to break free. In a movie, I'd now disarm him and kill him with his own gun. In real life, this advantage lasts a half a second and he had a far better grip on the gun than I did, so I did something I've found to be effective many times in my life; I let my opponent fixate and obsess on the weapon while I used my free hand to cause massive trauma to a different part of his body. In this case, I used my left hand to put out his right eye.

Fight over.

He screamed and I had a full second or two to knee him in the testicles, wrench the pistol up and over our heads, and punch him in his throat as hard as I could.

At that point the gun practically fell into my hand, and since I was in a car park I used it like a hammer to beat him unconscious rather than fire off a massive bang sure to attract attention. Plus it saves ammo. I finished it with a solid stomp to his neck.

Sean joined Jase among the dead.

Speaking of ammo, good news. A brief inspection shows me both Sean and Jase carried the same firearm - the classic Glock 17 with one spare mag each. Unfortunately, they both carried them in a shoulder rig, so I was forced to stuff the Glock into my own empty holster even though it didn't fit quite right. Still better than sticking it in my waistband. I also found my pocket knife in Sean's front pants pocket, but my guns were nowhere to be seen. What the hell? Where did they put my guns?

No time for questions right now, I guess. The Glock 17 isn't a small gun, so I took one but left the other. Now armed with one Glock 17, sixty-eight rounds in four magazines, and one hell of a headache, I jumped into this conveniently waiting truck and slowly drove towards the exit.

In what I can only describe as anticlimactic, the gate was automatic, unmanned, and I drove away. I pulled around the last turn of the parking garage with the Glock resting in my lap with my right hand down next to it, but this garage must have been reserved for the inner group because there was no guard at the exit either. However, at the entrance to the garage on the other end of the building, the security guard there did glance over as I pulled out and drove off. Honestly, I was sure there was going to be a problem, but never look a gift horse and all that.

I got a few turns away from the building and sped up, making a beeline to Rt. 35 South and driving the three hours to Sarah's house.

Or at least I would have if the sons a bitches hadn't caught up to me as I drove through Waco.

Chapter Four

Meet Sam

I saw the Broadhead Securities SUV in my rearview mirror. They weren't trying to hide. Shortly after that I saw the other one further back on the highway gaining on their friend and me.

Beside me for an instant there was a chariot with a driver and a crazed man about to throw a spear at me. That wasn't real.

I started psyching myself up for an altercation on the road, adjusted my seatbelt, put the gun on the seat beside me with a spare mag in the cup holder for easy access, and waited for the inevitable high speed chase and attack.

Sixty seconds later I was feeling like an idiot as I remembered we were not in a warzone, and Broadhead wasn't stupid enough to recreate every bad James Bond chase scene in history on I-35 on a Wednesday afternoon. Having caught up to me, they got in the lane behind me and followed.

Now it was up to me. I could speed up and try to lose them, but I figured they found me with GPS or something, so they probably don't need to be in sight to follow. This gave me a little bit of a pause. If they didn't need to be in visual, why did they let me know they were following me at all? I can't imagine it was anything other than psychological because it was actually a bad piece of fieldcraft to let me know they were there, but Broadhead has a lot of pull and connections, and I'm positive they already had my file pulled and knew who I was and what I used to do.

Why do something so stupid? What the hell was I missing?

Uneasy, I pulled out my phone and dialed Sarah. Well, I started to, but my phone suddenly rang in my hand, surprising me so much I almost dropped it. Normally, I don't answer my phone if it's an unknown number, but this was not a normal day, so after staring at the phone for ten seconds or so, I answered, "Hello?"

"Hello Dru. In a bit of a pickle, eh?"

"Who is this?"

"Not super important right now. Right now, you should be worried about those two SUVs behind you."

I took a deep breath and willed myself to remain calm. "Nah, I think I'll worry about the strange guy on the phone. The SUVs are pretty well behaved so far."

"That's a mistake, Dru. I'm on your side, but not much interested in chit chat right now."

"Yet you called me. You are real, right? This isn't my imagination?"

"Seriously?" he laughed. "You're going to act like this in the middle of a fucked up situation? Man, I might actually enjoy this!"

"You know talking on a cell phone while driving is really dangerous. I'm going to hang up unless we get to the point here."

The strange caller burst into what sounded like a genuine belly laugh and took a few seconds to get himself back under control. "You're wonderful, Dru. So, here you go - the point. You got mixed up with Broadhead by accident when you killed Jo. Frank got mixed up with Broadhead because you killed Jo. And now that you announced yourself to them, it's only a matter of time until they kill you like they did Frank."

I paused for about eternity. "Frank's dead? This is known fact?"

"Mmm...let's say I'm about ninety percent sure. I haven't seen the body, but we were working closely on this until he disappeared."

I exhaled a little breath of relief. LT isn't dead until I see the body. "So, who are you?"

"Oh no, Dru. That's not in my nature. I don't work like that. You'll have to figure out who I am the old-fashioned way. Go think back to your childhood and ask yourself who would you least like to see again? That will lead you to ask the right questions about the right types of people. Have fun!"

Oh hell no. We're not going down that rabbit hole. My childhood? No way. "Wait a damn minute! You don't know shit about my childhood. What the hell is this? Why are you calling?"

"Oh! Right. Almost forgot! Broadhead is obviously afraid there's a group of people you're working with. They're following you and monitoring your phone. Not this call, obviously; I've got skills, but if you call Sarah, she's dead. What the SUV's are doing is hoping you make decisions under pressure.

"Run little rabbit, run. Get it?

"If you decide to stay away from your "group", they will monitor your communications and track them down, and kill you when you get somewhere more isolated than an interstate. If you go for help, they'll see who you have, call in appropriate reinforcements, and kill you all. It's pretty hilarious that you are NOT with a group, actually."

"Well," I said, squeezing the steering wheel as hard as I could, "this sucks."

"Why? You've got a gun and there's only six of them in two vehicles. I'm sure you have some ideas of what to do. I'll even help a tiny bit- take the next exit towards Lorena and turn east under the overpass. It's pretty isolated about a mile out. Look for a warehouse that looks empty. Good hunting, I'll be watching with great interest!"

"Oh! One more thing, Frank and I talked about you many times. I know a lot more about you than you think."

And with that, he hung up. Shit.

Looking at my cell phone's map, I quickly located the exit and road my mystery caller was talking about. The only real question is should I listen to the weird caller and do what he recommended? I mean, honestly, why should I? I don't know what the hell is going on or who the caller is, and taking advice from strange voices over the phone doesn't strike me as smart or even particularly sane, but...Goddamn it, fuck me if I wasn't actually smiling! I mean, I know I'm not the most put-together guy around, but dammit, was I actually starting to have fun?

Yes I was! I'm sitting here driving down a side road into the desolate Texas countryside with a shit-eating grin on my face as six guys follow me with the express purpose of killing me and anyone else they find who might be working with me. Assuming the voice on the phone isn't full of shit, of course.

But I'll let you in on a little secret. I just realized I don't care. Taking out those two thugs back at Broadhead hadn't bothered me at all as it was pure self-defense, but these guys in the car are declaring war. I kinda like war. I'm going to find out what's going on here and I'm going to figure this weird shit out. I don't know how yet, but I know it starts with those two SUV's that took the same exit as me. I fished in my pocket for two painkillers and took them dry, my grin becoming a full-on expression of joy.

As I drive down the two-lane blacktop that winds its way out of the small town, I see some Ravens circling a large series of warehouse-like structures surrounded by a fence, but with a large, open parking lot where I can assume the employees park every morning. That smile slips a tiny bit. I have a flashback of a raven sitting right next to me laughing. What the hell?

Ravens. Not the best sign if you're a little superstitious and you spent a lot of time hanging around creatures out of myth and legend. And I remembered it's the second time I've seen birds circling around since I got to Texas. I had forgotten seeing a few flying around near Sarah's place.

Ravens or Crows have a place in every supernatural pantheon where the birds naturally exist. North America, Europe, everywhere, actually. And they're almost always associated with a God or a person you'd definitely rather avoid if at all possible. And while there are no "Gods" on the Earth, there are plenty of personal reasons I don't like them. Most have to do with fields of battle and the aftermath when the birds feast on the slain. Mostly.

I slow down to get a better look and see that the parking lot wraps like an "L" shape behind the three largest buildings. Slamming my foot on the gas, I turned hard into the parking lot and raced around the back side of the building, leaving the startled drivers in the SUV's to react far too slowly to keep up with my surprise move. Forget the Ravens, I need to focus on surviving the next two minutes.

By the time they slow down, make the turn into the parking lot, and speed up to go around the back, I've already passed a row of concrete traffic walls I always called a Jersey wall (but I think are actually called "K" rails), turned the car around, put it in park with the engine still running, and sprinted out the door and over to the concrete barrier. Whatever you call them, you see them all over America - about eight feet long, three feet high and lining every highway construction zone you've ever drove past.

When the SUVs come tearing around the corner of the parking lot, I'm kneeling down behind concrete with my pistol braced on the top and in two hands. Both drivers seemed to see me at the same time.

Both drivers were very different people. The first SUV saw me and panicked, slamming on the break and swerving out into the open parking lot space to my right. That action saved his life, for the moment.

The second saw me and the gun aimed right at him and decided to keep the pedal to the floor and aimed straight back at me, presumably to smash me into putty with his vehicle. That action killed him.

For most people, facing down an accelerating SUV moving and bouncing on a crappy parking lot pavement would make for a challenging shot with a pistol, even braced on a wall for support. I'm not most people, remember?

Orienting on the SUV, I put two rounds through the windshield into the head of the driver from about twenty yards away. The utter destruction of his head caused the body to jerk and collapse and the car drifted a little bit to my left. I sprinted out to my right and put six more rounds into the SUV as it went by and slammed into the K-rail, which had a disastrous effect on the SUV.

Nothing exotic like an explosion or a flip happened, it smashed into the rail and stopped almost dead as it stood up on its nose and the back wheels left the ground, but it didn't flip over. The K rail disintegrated, but not before inertia sent both characters in the backseat into the front seat, one of which kept going right out the front windshield and onto the pavement.

All three were already dead as I knew my shots had found their targets, and nobody without a seatbelt was surviving that impact.

I had nine rounds left in the mag, which was three per person in the second SUV if my mysterious phone friend was accurate. More than enough. I turned to the SUV which had screeched to a stop and as the doors opened up, I had a moment to realize I was standing alone, uncovered, in a parking lot. Oops.

The K rails weren't going to offer me much protection from this angle, but there was a trashed SUV sitting there that would give me concealment and little cover. It could work long enough to give a little lesson in the difference between the two concepts.

The men in the SUV had swerved around while breaking and wound up with the vehicle pointing back at me, and the operators were smart enough to know that sitting in a vehicle without armor was a death sentence, but they had all seemed to forget that car doors are only concealment, not cover.

Wanna know the difference? Here it is.

I popped up over the hood of the crashed SUV I had run behind and put three fast rounds through the passenger side door. The man behind it fell down bleeding from three bullet holes in his chest. I couldn't see him because the door concealed him from view, but the door wasn't any real protection. It ate up a lot of the bullet's velocity and kinetic impact, but my rounds punched more than enough power to lodge in his chest. No cover from fire.

I, on the other hand, dropped down behind the front quarter panel of the SUV where an entire engine was between me and the return fire. Sure, a smart man might think to drop down and look to shoot my feet or legs, but I was concealing myself behind the front wheel. Not perfect by any means, but a damn sight better than a door.

Employing a simple rule I have of never shooting from the same spot twice if I can help it, I leaned out around the front bumper while still in a squat and, you know what? I *am* a smart man, so I decided to shoot out the legs of the second guy hiding behind the driver's side door. My first round blew out his left ankle and he fell screaming to the ground where my second shot took him neatly in the head.

One bastard left. Four bullets. Nice.

He blasted my SUV with a surprisingly accurate rapid fire of about ten rounds while screaming at me, "You motherfucker!"

When his gun ran out of bullets and he went to switch his magazine out for a fresh one, I popped up to take a look and found that bad guy number three had the brains of the bunch, he was all the way behind the SUV and I couldn't see his legs. Well concealed, and with a lot of SUV to provide cover.

"Hey," I yelled, "all your boys are dead. What's the deal, huh? Why are you all so hell-bent on killing me?"

"Fuck you! Backup is coming, and you're fucking dead, asshole!"

"Now wait a second," I said, "you started this shit. I just wanted to know what happened to Frank, and you guys started trying to kill me."

"Above my paygrade, asshole. I don't know what the hell you did to piss off my boss, but you killed my friends and I'm going to fucking put you down like a dog."

A dog. He had to say it. Dog. Goddamn, that pisses me off. Not his fault. He couldn't know how much I love dogs. Hell, in my early days, I was proud to be called a dog of war. We soldier types love that shit. Dogs are better than people, and that's a fact. A dog even saved my life once.

"Alright, asshole. I got your Dog right here. You want a piece of me? You think you're man enough to put me down? Come fuck around and find out!"

His response was five rapid shots that slammed into the side of the SUV followed by a thunk sound that reminded me of a frying pan hitting a kettle, and a sound suspiciously like a body hitting the ground.

I shuffled towards the back of the SUV in order to change my position and peaked around the rear bumper to see a tall, thin man in faded jeans and a ragged white t-shirt that read "Free Leonard Peltier sooner next time!" in red letters standing over an unconscious Broadhead securities guard with a huge grin on his face and an honest to gods cast iron frying pan in his hand.

He stood a solid six foot plus in his well-worn cowboy boots, and his long, black hair was pulled back into a ponytail showing off the high cheekbones and dark complexion of a man native to the Americas. His eyes were filled with mischief as he turned to me with a smile inviting me to join in on whatever joke he was pulling.

"You looked like you could use some help," he said.

Standing up, I aimed my pistol at the new guy and started walking toward him. "Drop the pan, take two steps back, and put your hands behind your head! Now!"

"Really? Is that any way to greet a friend?"

"I don't know who you are, or how the hell you got here without me seeing you. Drop the pan! Take two steps back! Hands behind your head!"

Frowning, he made it seem as if I somehow let him down. Shaking his head side to side, he dropped the pan onto the head of the downed shooter and took two dancing steps back like he was in a musical.

"That better, Dru?"

"No, dammit! Who are you and how do you know my name? I've never seen you before. And put those fucking hands behind your head or I'm going to shoot them off your wrists. Swear to God."

He grinned wide and barked out a laugh, "Remember you said that. It's going to be funny real soon." And with that, he put his hands behind his head. "Now what little doggy? You gonna bark all day or are you going to bite?"

"What?"

"Reservoir Dogs? Tarantino's masterpiece? You had to have seen it!"

"Who the fuck are you?"

"You can call me Sam. Sam Dodson. But I'd also like it if you'd call me friend, because hear my words Dru, you need a friend bad." And with that, he pointed at the guy on the ground and said, "Don't you think we should take this guy inside one of these empty warehouses and ask him a few questions when he wakes up?"

I slowly lowered my gun and asked him, "Why, exactly, are you my friend, and why should I trust you?"

He lowered his hands to his side, "Because Frank did. And now we both need you to finish what he and I were trying to do before he died."

"Well Sam, this is about the most screwed up thing to happen to me ever."

He shook his head, "No it isn't. Not even close. You can't bullshit a bullshitter, Dru."

"Forget it. Fine." I popped the nearly empty mag out of the gun and swapped it for a fully loaded seventeen rounds and tucked it away in the holster. "Pick that guy up and move him inside, and afterward you and I are gonna talk a little bit before he comes around and I start questioning him."

"You're not going to help?" He looked genuinely upset that I wasn't going to walk over and pitch in.

"No, Sam. I'm not. I don't trust you that much and it's the fact that you seem to know a whole lot about Frank that is keeping me from shoving this gun in your face while I ask you these questions. So lift, my frying pan marauder, lift. I'm going to destroy some cell phones and see if I can find a GPS device on the SUVS."

"No need. I already took care of it. His call for backup didn't go through either."

"How the hell did you do that?" I asked.

"Trade secrets, but trust me, it's taken care of."

"Trust you," I laughed, "For real?"

"Obviously it's your choice, Dru, but what are the chances you'll find anything anyway? Are you some super sleuth? Do you even know what to look for on the vehicle? No, you don't. Stop being silly. I took care of it."

"Christ on a crutch." He wasn't wrong. What was I going to do, call up my imaginary science and tech guy?

Letting it go, I walked over to the warehouse to see if I could break in. It was easy, the door didn't even have a deadbolt.

Sam dragged the body up behind me and stopped at the door. "Well, that was lucky," he said deadpan.

Yeah. Yeah, it was. "This a trap, Sam? Cause I promise you, you'll die before I do."

"Awfully dumb and convoluted trap if it is. I send these guys, call you up to tell you how to beat them, help you beat them, and even allow myself to become your manual labor - typical exploitation of an Indigenous person, by the way. I had hoped for better from you - all so I can get you in an abandoned warehouse in order to...what? Kill you? Nah, Dru. Not my style."

This was getting ridiculous. Everything was spinning out of my control and becoming chaotic. My thoughts were trying to catch up to reality and my temper was disappearing fast. Taking a deep breath, I counted to four in my head and then let the breath go for another count of four. It was my favorite "don't kill everyone in the room because it's bad for morale" breathing exercise and I tried to focus on what was in front of me.

I rubbed my eyes, this lunatic was going to give me a migraine. I turned as I heard a thud and saw that Sam had dropped the thug in the middle of the open floor and was walking over to a small office that had a desk and chairs plainly visible through the windows.

"Want me to grab the chairs, boss? Maybe find some rope, a hot poker, razorblades, a car battery and cables?"

"Sam, and I mean this sincerely, what the hell is wrong with you? This isn't funny. Get the fucking chairs and bring them out here. We need to talk seriously and you need to explain what the hell is going on."

"Well in that case, no." He abruptly plopped right down on the floor cross-legged and stared at me. "Get the chairs yourself, tough guy."

"Christ, I don't have time for this. Fine. You sit there like a child in time out. I'll get the chairs."

"Damnit Dru, you are not nearly as much fun as I thought you were going to be." He seemed genuinely saddened by the concept that I wasn't going to treat this like a party or something. How crazy was this loon?

I went into the office, grabbed two chairs, dragged them out next to the unconscious guy, and sat in one. "You want to sit in this chair here and talk to me like an adult, Sam?"

He grinned and quickly stood up, walking over to the chair and sitting down as he said, "Now we're getting somewhere! You ready for a serious conversation that'll blow your mind?"

Sighing, I said, "Yes."

"So, Dru, this is where we share info."

"No," I replied. "This is where you spill your guts and tell me everything I want to know so I don't shoot you in the face."

"Ha!" He barked. "Okay, maybe this will be a little bit of fun after all. Alright, Dru, ask a question, but I feel it should be noted that I'm only going to tell you what I want to, and I think you'd be well served answering my questions as well. I'd like to work together, but if you're not going to trust me, there's no way I'm telling you everything. Sorry."

I stared at him with my best death stare. He smiled and stared back, grin getting wider and wider.

Sigh.

"Alright Sam, let's start easy. Who the hell are you, how do you know Frank, and what is going on?"

He started laughing hysterically. "Oh my! Ha! Oh my. Start easy he says! Oh my. Dru, you are simply marvelous." Wiping his eyes, he slowly regained control of himself and looked up at me.

"I'm afraid you're going to need a story to make sense of this Dru. But this is a group participation story. I'm going to tell you this tale, but you're going to have to fill in some blanks and give me some detail. In fact, we're going to be telling this story to each other. And you know what? You'll have to go first! Ha!"

"Why me? What are you talking about?"

"I'm actually quite sorry. Sincerely. But this story starts - for you - with the day you butchered Jo."

My heart froze in my chest and I couldn't breathe. Jo? No, he couldn't know about that. "Who the fuck are you?"

"No, Dru. I'm sorry, but we either do this right, or not at all. I wish it was otherwise, I honestly do, but you need to know this, and I can't tell you everything unless you share. Unless you can start at the beginning, you might as well pull out that gun and shoot me now. This all started with you killing your squadmate, and honestly, Frank and I don't know precisely why. You wouldn't tell him."

Wouldn't? More like couldn't, I was so close to losing myself forever into insanity at that point, I actually couldn't talk. It took a week under supervision before I woke up screaming strapped down in a bed in the field hospital. Until then I had been a nonverbal killing machine. A danger to most everyone. Three months after that I was quietly discharged and sent home. No longer a trusted resource for killing the enemy.

"Dru."

I looked up into Sam's dark eyes. In them I saw understanding and even a little empathy. "I'm not sure I can talk about this."

He refused to let me look away. His eyes held mine like a magnet and I felt myself being drawn deeper into his gaze. I was locked in. I couldn't turn away.

"Let it go, Dru. Let it out. Talk and let's see if we can help each other."

Amazingly, astonishingly, I began to do what I would have sworn I was incapable of doing. I began to talk about the last day I spent in the war. Repressed memories popped back to the surface.

"There were two teams out of the nightmare squad working together. Frank, Jo, and I were working alongside Tony, Juan, and Keith. Tony was the squad leader and was about six feet tall and five feet wide. And he had one eye. He hadn't lost one. One eye was all he'd ever had. Right smack dab in the middle of his forehead. Of Greek descent, he was what legends called a cyclops, albeit without the massive height Odysseus had to deal with. Extremely smart, pretty strong, and with a real weakness for drink, Tony was a great guy and a seriously good tactician.

His "shooter" was Juan, a tiny guy legends called an Anchimayen - who looked like a Chilean child, ran faster than an Olympic sprinter, and was perplexingly obsessed with Jo in our crew.

His driver was Keith, a Japanese American soldier who had red hair, a red face, and was the single person on the planet who could drink Tony under the table. He was what they referred to in Japan as a Shojo. His story about his family emigrating to America was one of the funniest stories I've ever heard.

Two crews were overkill for a simple job like this, but what the hell. Beats going in by yourself, I guess.

We were converging on the outskirts of this small Afghanistan village about three klicks from a larger village on the side of Mount Noshaq that had been the main focus of our attack yesterday. It was a total clusterfuck, as usual. Yesterday, we had gone in with exceptionally good intelligence that a group of three Taliban insurrectionists were working with an Extra commonly mistaken in history as a yeti or a bigfoot. A nine-foot-tall beast of a humanoid that ranged across the mountainous areas of the world and had a nasty temper and a real taste for human flesh.

The good news is that they were essentially big and tough but with no real other advantages. In fact, they tended to be rather stupid, as opposed to real Sasquatches of North America, but it was easy for them to thrive in the mountains of Afghanistan. With the war they were becoming more brazen in their behavior, venturing out, joining hunting groups, killing and eating American soldiers, you get the idea.

That's exactly the kind of thing that gets the monsters out there targeted by us. If you start killing people in a way that will get you noticed, we go and kill you before you end up on the news. Extras are one thing, real, honest to goodness monsters are another. The general public can't handle that level of truth and honesty in their worldview.

We went in to eliminate the group and kill the bastard. Should have been a simple elimination job. I would have set up in a good sightline, sniped the Extra, and Jo and Frank would have killed the other three with me on the hill as cover. Only he wasn't there and neither were the insurgents. It took all day, and most of the night, but we were able to figure out through questioning the villagers that the bad guys were up the mountain a few clicks away in this tiny little group of huts. Hiding out, or so we thought.

That morning, we all went to mount up, but bizarrely there were new orders merging our squads together. While not unheard of, the particulars were bonkers. Jo was to stay behind with Juan to secure the village until Broadhead contractors showed up to question the villagers and make sure we got the maximum amount of intel out of the locals as possible, while Keith and Tony took their Humvee and I got to be driver for once and motor Frank and I to deal with the Extra and his Taliban friends. It was ridiculous since Tony could have kept his team with him and we could have gone on to do the work as an unbroken team, but we all figured, "that's the military for you".

Of course, halfway there I broke the damn vehicle. Pulling over, it was quickly decided that I needed to go back and get Jo to help me fix the damn thing, but Frank decided that he, Tony, and Keith were more than enough for four assholes on a mountain, and we didn't want to spend another twenty-four hours out there if we didn't need to. So, back to the village I went. It was about two clicks, so I left my gear inside the vehicle and ran back to the village.

What I saw when I got there...what I saw..."

"Dru. This is extremely important," he said in a whisper. "What did you see?"

"I...all the people were dead. Every adult in the village. Executed."

"What else?"

"What else? What else does there need to be?" I yelled, standing up and knocking my chair over. I was shaking all over. I was staring at Sam, but I couldn't see. My vision was tunneling. From a long way off I heard the cry of the Raven on the battlefield - the chooser of the slain, maybe? Reaching out to me, "Remember" it seemed to cry.

All at once, I remembered. Oh God help me, I remembered.

"Children. The children. I ran into buildings looking for Jo and Juan, sure they had been killed. Instead, I found them with the children. Some kids were dead. Dismembered, staked out, bodies cut open. Some were still alive, crying out in agony, screaming for help. Begging for mercy. Confused, stunned, uncomprehending why this was happening to them."

From a million miles away I heard Sam groan, "Oh shit. Too late. We might be too late already."

"I turned the corner of the doorway screaming for Jo and Juan, hoping they were still alive, and they were right there. Unharmed.

"It was them. Butchering children! Why were they killing the kids? I...I snapped. I can't remember what happened next, but the last thing I do remember, I was pounding something that used to be a body...Jo's body...I was covered from head to toe in blood and someone was grabbing me, trying to pull me off the corpse of my squad mate that...that I had butchered like she had butchered those kids."

I was gasping for breath, fighting to say the words stuck in my throat, "Frank. LT was trying to pull me off and I turned on him, putting a pistol...where did I get the pistol? I put a pistol to my best friend's head and screamed at him. DID YOU KNOW?!?! DID YOU KNOW?!?! Then everything went black."

Then everything went black again and I crashed to the floor in front of Sam, unconscious.

Chapter Five

Meet my Memories

I woke up sobbing uncontrollably on the filthy floor of an almost empty warehouse. Sam was sitting about twenty feet away watching me, while the thug was sitting up against a wall trussed up and tied like a hog for butcher. Awake and terrified.

I honestly have no idea how long it took me to get myself together. My brain was disassociating from reality pretty hard. It was almost like all the trauma I've ever experienced in my life was crashing in on me all at once, and let me tell you, I have a whole lot of trauma.

Eventually, Sam cleared his throat and said, "So, it was children."

"Yeah," I replied softly. "Children."

"I wonder why Frank never told me that?"

I looked over at him dully.

"Do you think maybe Frank didn't know?"

I shrugged listlessly and patted my pockets looking for a pill.

"How the hell wouldn't he know Dru?"

I sat back on my heels, squatting on the floor. I was too weak to stand up, what with about a billion pounds of emotional baggage sitting on my head.

Eventually, I said, "When I came back to myself and was coherent enough to explain the events, I couldn't remember what happened. Total blank. And in the reports of the event, there was no official mention of any children. Not a single report from a single eyewitness. Somebody was hiding the fact that Jo and Juan were torturing and killing kids."

"Well, Dru. It's worse than that. Are you sure Frank wasn't hiding this due to guilt or complicity?"

I looked up at him and between ground teeth replied, "Not Frank. No way. I was crazy at that moment, but I believe that LT wouldn't have anything to do with stuff like this."

"Good. And I agreeThat means somebody way higher up the chain of command was able to remove the evidence while you were in the middle of killing two Extras with your bare hands? Geez Dru, how many problems do we have with that scenario? You wanna start?"

"You're right. There's no way. It makes no sense."

"Ha! Understatement of the century, my friend. And get this, Frank and I were able to get a look at that report of the incident, there's no mention of Broadhead at all, yet they were there."

"What the fuck? What are we talking about here? And again I have to ask, who the hell are you?"

Sam sighed, looked at the floor for a few seconds, and took a deep breath. "Alright, I'm going to tell you some things, and I need you to keep an open mind about it. I mean a really open mind."

"I've spent many years of my life fighting with Extras, killing monsters. How open do you want my mind to be?"

"More than that."

I dug my last pill out of my pocket and popped it into my mouth, dry swallowing it. "No promises. Start talking."

"Okay, Dru. I'm a Shaman of my Tribe in Alaska."

"Alaska? You lost or something?"

He smiled. "No, not lost. Hungry. Austin has the best tacos in the world, the second-best smoked brisket, and breakfast burritos to die for. I love this town. Also, Frank was a friend and he and I were looking into some serious shit."

"Alright, maybe you need to back up and start at the beginning?"

He smiled and his eyes gleamed with mirth. "In the beginning, humanity was stuck in a clamshell. Well, the guys at least. The ladies were..."

"Stop. Stop. Stop. Are you always like this?"

"Pretty much, but you're right. This is actually terrifyingly serious."

"So, stop with the sarcasm, and please get to the point."

"I am getting to the point, Dru. In the beginning, there were more than humans and Extras, there were actual Gods."

I kept my face neutral, "You don't say."

"I'm serious, Dru. Frank knew. His father had met some of the last Gods right here in America. "He met my eyes and held them, "In fact, you *specifically* wouldn't exist if there were no Gods."

It got real quiet in the warehouse, and I itched to have my gun in my hand. "What do you mean?"

"That thing you call a knack? It's commonly called God-Touched. Are you a hundred years old?"

I replied truthfully, "No."

He paused and smiled before going on, "Then sometime back in your family's history, before the Gods disappeared, a relative of yours drew the attention of a God and got gifted some skills."

"Bullshit. No way. This is ridiculous. Because I can shoot real well, you're saying there are Gods? I don't see any around."

Sam was staring at me intently. After a few seconds, he sighed with a wry smirk and said, "If you say so, Dru. As far as the world knows, all the Gods are gone. Have been since the mid-1900's."

I shrugged incredulously, "Come on, Sam, what are you trying to sell me here?"

"I'm not selling you shit, white man. The last Gods to leave Earth were our Gods. Gods of the First Nations peoples, like mine. They were the last to go for some reason. But there are many Extras who were alive long before they went and know for a fact they existed. And many God-touched humans like you wandered the earth being heroes and villains of extraordinary abilities. Less now, of course."

I shrugged him off, "God touched heroes?"

"Heracles, Gilgamesh, Beowulf," here he hesitated and looked at me again, "others."

I had to ask, "Well, where are these Gods now, then? Where'd they go?"

"Nobody knows for sure. All we have are theories and guesses based on the few hints the Gods left us. They unfortunately faded one by one until the last one...Tia was her name...well... its ideas and explanations were less than reliable."

"Less than reliable?" I repeated.

"Yeah. At the end, they were scatterbrained confused beings, half child-like and half...kind of like Alzheimer's, I guess? They were "fading" - their words, not mine. This world had changed at a fundamental level and they didn't...fit...anymore.

"All we know for sure is that the last gods of Europe and Asia to leave were the Gods and Goddesses of War, while the last indigenous Gods of America to leave were Gods of Death. "

I looked at him and waited for more.

"Honest, Dru, I'm forced to guess here, but Quantum theory has offered some fascinating directions to look into. Those of us who are doing so think that Gods didn't actually exist within our universe. I mean, that much is a pretty safe bet as almost all Gods live...lived in a special land or place, right? Heaven, Asgard, Tir na Nog, a mountain you could climb but still not find the Gods in like, Olympus, Jade Mountain, Kunlun, or Fuji?"

I nodded, "Alright. For argument's sake, let's assume my mind is open and I accept this as true. So what?"

"Bear with me here. If Gods used to be able to manifest on Earth, but something changed gradually to lock them out, what was it, and why did the Gods of death and war last the longest?"

"You got me, Sam, why did they?"

"We don't know! But we can certainly guess at one thing. Those European and Asian Gods of War? They all disappeared within three years after World War One ended. Pretty much all the other Gods but about half dozen American Gods were long gone by then."

"Uh, you're saying...what?"

"I'm saying maybe the world changed until it wasn't habitable or hospitable anymore for the Gods, but that our behaviors as a species had a strong effect on how good or bad it was for individual Gods."

"Sam, you've lost me. Why do I care about this?

"Because some Gods thrived and existed in cultures that engaged in human sacrifice. And Dru? Sacrificing innocents has always been believed to be the most effective sacrifice."

"And nothing is more innocent than children," I said.

"Nothing is innocent at all *except* for children. And sacrifices go straight to the Gods."

"As in, maybe they actually disappear from existence and physically go to the Gods? Bullshit!"

"I admit it's far-fetched. If the Gods were *that* close to returning, I think we'd see lots of obvious signs. No, I think those poor murdered children were right there, but people were unable to see them. Or the Broadhead operatives."

"How does that work? You're talking out of your ass now, Sam."

"Oh man, you still don't get it. I know far more about this than anyone alive today."

"Because you're a Shaman? Of some little religion up in Alaska? Give me a Godsdamned break!"

"When Gods intervene or their believers are powerful enough, we get back into that Quantum realm of supposition and educated guesses, but my guesses are good. Trust me."

"Trust you? I don't know who the hell you are!"

"Dru, if the world once changed to become inhospitable to Gods, it can be changed back. I, and a few others you don't need to concern yourself with right now, believe that there is a group trying to make the world hospitable for Gods again.

We believe this group founded Broadhead Securities back in the 1970s to try and bring back the Gods of War, but it simply wasn't working for some reason. Now we're afraid they've switched tactics and are trying to bring back other Gods through focused sacrifices and different actions instead of general "battlefield offerings".

"What other actions are we talking about here?"

"Well, we've been watching and researching Broadhead for years now, and they have - through lots of shell companies and business acquisitions - begun trying to make the world a little more "viable" for the manifestations of Gods, and we believe it's working. We think making actual old-fashioned sacrifices like what you saw are the final steps in actually trying to call back a few specific Gods."

"Why on earth would Broadhead want that? What does bringing back Gods do for them?"

"Well, Dru. You're not going to like this, I don't think, but Broadhead Securities is run by a religious order. And that religious order used to be quite powerful when their Gods were real. And they're true believers. It's the worst-case scenario - true believers that miss being the boss."

A sick feeling spread in my stomach. "I've had some bad run-ins with religions and the religious before, and I'm Irish. There's a little history of religious conflict there."

"You have no idea...well, maybe you do, but this is worse. Dru, Broadhead Securities is essentially the modern Druid religion. They want their Celtic Gods back, and they're willing to bring all the Gods back to make that happen. Do you have any idea how fucking bad that would be? To have a dozen pantheons of gods suddenly return to Earth? It'd be the end of days for humanity, maybe the whole world."

It was at this point the guy we had tied up in the corner tried to kill us both.

A frenzied screaming brought my head whipping around as our bound and gagged prisoner started thrashing madly trying to break free of his restraints. It was crystal clear this lunatic was trying to get to us and it was equally clear he meant to murder us.

But Sam had done his work well. The poor bastard writhed and twisted screaming himself hoarse through the gag and rubbing his wrists and ankles into a raw, bloody mess.

"Is...is he going to stop?" I asked

"You know, I really don't think so."

We watched for several minutes but his frenzied thrashing didn't let up a bit.

"This is amazing," I said. "What's wrong with him, and how is he still going? I'm getting exhausted just watching him."

At that moment, his eyes bulged, rolled up into his head and he sighed out a breath before collapsing.

Sam looked at me and said, "Did he just die?"

"Son of a bitch. I think he did."

We looked blankly at each other for a few long seconds.

"Well shit," he said. "This is bad."

"What the hell just happened?" I asked.

"I think we witnessed the levels Broadhead goes to ensure loyalty and commitment to the program. I think that poor bastard was compelled to kill us both as soon as he woke up and heard us talking about the real Broadhead connection to Druidism."

"Compelled?"

"Conditioned. Mind fucked. Brainwashed. A stupid magic spell. Something."

"A...wait...what? Magic spell?"

"There's more to this world, etcetera etcetera. Go with Brainwashed. It'll be easier on you."

"Seriously, who the hell are you?"

He hesitated, "You should keep calling me Sam."

"Fine. Sam, you seem to know everyfuckingthing going on, so what next? What are we going to do about these bodies, and how are we going to find Frank?"

"Find Frank? Frank's most likely dead Dru, you know this. We need to stop Broadhead."

"Whoa whoa whoa, stop right there Sam. I'm here to find Frank or kill the bastards who killed him. First step is finding out where he or his body is. That's my job, that's what I'm going to do."

"For fucks sake Dru, that's not right. Frank was a good guy. I liked him. But we're trying to stop a literal Armageddon brought about by literal Gods."

"What do you mean we, Kemosabe?"

"Oh fuck you, white boy. This is no joke."

"Well Sam, then you get your ass to work and call me when you find Frank's body. I've suddenly realized that if you're correct, and these guys condition their own soldiers to berserker suicide to prevent people from finding out what they're doing, killing these asshats is going to trigger an escalation and they're going to most likely go scorched earth. That means all loose ends and a lot of collateral damage. That means Sarah is now in the crosshairs. I'm going to go get her right now."

"Crap. You're right. Sarah is a potential threat and loose end now. Alright. I'm going to clean up here and go reach out to friends to see where we might look next, but Dru..."

"Yeah?"

"Don't kid yourself. You're in this now. You know damn well Broadhead is the villain. You know they're the ones who killed Frank."

"We still don't know he's dead."

"Fine. But when we find the body, by your own words, your job is to kill these sonsabitches. And I need you to realize there's a bigger reason to kill them, and it's going to be harder than you think. Don't piss me off and lose me as an ally. You'll need me before all this is done."

"Now you do prophecy too?"

He smirked, "Always have," and walked out of the warehouse. Over his shoulder, he yelled, "Go save the damsel in distress and all that Campbell shit, but don't take too long!"

That's when I realized this guy doesn't know as much as he thinks. Sarah would tear him a new one if he ever said that in front of her. Plus, Joseph Campbell wasn't as smart as he thought...Monomyth my ass.

Smiling, I jogged out to my stolen truck and climbed in. As I pulled out of the parking lot I dialed Sarah and she answered on the fourth ring.

"Mr. Dru?"

"Hey Sarah, you need to grab a go bag and get out of the house ASAP. We were right. Broadhead is the bad guy and they tried to kill me."

"What? Oh my lord, where are you, and what happened?"

"No time right now. Get essentials, get in your car, and drive. Drive. No toll roads, no GPS, and turn off your phone. Turn it on and call me every fifty-five minutes, you got that? Fifty-five minutes. Not forty-five, not one hour."

"Wait..."

"No Time. Get going!"

"Dru..."

"Sarah, are you listening? I said..."

"Shut your mouth for a second! Sweetie, I'm at work! I have to shut down, make an excuse, tell my staff, and drive to the house to pack before I can leave."

"Shitshitshit. No, don't do that. Don't go home. Go from work to the closest ATM, pull out all the cash you can and then drive. Turn off the phone as soon as you hang up and don't turn it back on until you call me..." I checked my watch, it was a little after four pm. "at 4:55pm. You got that? I'll answer all your questions then."

"Okay. I hear you. Call you at 4:55. I'll head out towards the Hill Country. No toll roads."

"Perfect. Goodbye. And Sarah?"

"Yes?"

"Be safe."

"You too."

I hung up the phone and drove south on I-35 while looking up "Hill Country" on my phone. Damn. It's pretty much everything west of Waco, Austin, and San Antonio. But there was a place west of Austin called Fredericksburg that seemed to be central to the traffic of that area, so I decided to head that way. I figured we could coordinate our meet-up during our phone calls.

I drove to Temple, then west. Eventually, my phone rang. It was 4:55 on the dot.

"Sarah?"

"Mr. Dru."

"Listen. The next call will be at 6:22 pm exactly. We're going to keep our phones off and call at random times until we meet. Tech is apparently the enemy's tool, not ours. Fill me in on your situation and tell me where you'd like to meet. I'm outside of Lampasas and planning on heading towards Fredericksburg."

"That's a great idea. I'm heading out Route 1431 towards Marble Falls. I'll get there before you, but not way ahead of you. What on earth is going on?"

"Broadhead went after me and I took out six - no - eight of them." I amended as I remembered Jase and Sean died today too. I heard a sharp intake of breath over the phone.

"You killed them?"

"Hell yes, I did. They tried to kill me first, though. Hey listen, do you know a guy named Sam? Friend of Franks, Perhaps?"

"Sam? No, why?"

"Because he helped me and said he and LT were involved in something with Broadhead. I don't have time to discuss it on the phone, but I will fill you in when we meet up."

"Okay. What's going on right now? Why am I driving around?"

"Well, now that Broadhead is moving overtly, I believe they have decided that there's too much exposure to them and too many people asking questions. I'm pretty sure you and I are on a list of people they intend to make dead. And Sarah, these guys move fast."

"Okay."

I was impressed. "You seem pretty calm about this if you don't mind my saying so."

"Well, I've been thinking, now that I've met you. If my husband told me to get you, he must have been worried about violence of this sort. I've been kind of mentally preparing myself for it."

"Damn, rich and smart. Frank sure can pick 'em."

That got a small chuckle out of her as I had hoped. "Bless your heart, but you know I picked him. Thank you for the thought." She changed the subject, "Why did I need to get cash? Are they so connected that they can trace my credit cards?"

"I have no idea, but this Sam guy told me they were pretty well tied into the networks of law enforcement. We can't take the chance yet. How much did you get?"

"Well, my bank has a withdrawal limit on the bank card, so I went into the bank lobby. It was a short hop from work. I took out five thousand dollars and afterward drove to the nearby sports store and made a purchase - five hundred rounds of 9mm ammo and another two thousand dollars in Visa gift cards, so we're pretty set for a few days."

I could tell she was smiling. "My god you're a genius. But why so much ammo?"

"You mean besides the fact that I'm a Texan? I wasn't sure what gun you had, but I was sure you had one, and my pistols are all 9mm. Last night I packed a small bug-out bag and two pistols into the car but didn't have much extra ammo to go with it. I figured if you didn't have a nine, you could use one of mine if needed."

"You did all that based on a lunch conversation?"

"No, sweetie. I told you; I did that based on some thinking about my husband, you, and our current situation. A southern lady believes in being prepared."

"I take it back, you're not a genius. You're Wile E. Coyote, Super Genius!"

A genuine laugh this time, "And you're old. Who even quotes Road Runner cartoons anymore?"

"Alright, let's get off the line now. Turn off the phone until 6:22, at that time we'll see where we are and plan our meetup."

And that's exactly what we did. When we finally met up, it was dark and Sarah had booked a double hotel room under an assumed name and paid in cash at an old hotel in Fredericksburg run by a sweet old German lady who assumed we were a couple out for an adventure in – I swear I'm not making this up – Texas Wine Country.

We went into our room, and I told her the whole story of my encounter with Broadhead from the time I entered the building until I called her on the road. When I was finished, we were both exhausted and famished, so I took a shower while she ran out to get food from a restaurant across the street. I was clean and dressed by the time she got back and the food smelled incredible as she took out a German food feast.

"Wow! German food and Texas wine. So not what I expected." I said laughing as I stuffed a bite of some heavenly potato-based side dish-looking thing into my mouth.

"Oh, yeah," she said, "There's a strong German immigrant history here. It's pretty much the identity of this town. Take a look out that window, there are six German restaurants and three breweries on this street and all of them are excellent. I grabbed a Wurst sampler for us and a few sides. But if I'm being honest, I'm not sorry I didn't get any Texas wine."

"Is the wine bad?" I asked.

"No, but it's not going to set your world on fire either, and when in a German town, eating German food..." She said as she reached into a bag full of clinking bottles "...one really should drink the German beer."

"Yes!" I pumped my fist into the air as she pulled out a dark, Schwarz bier brewed locally and handed it to me. I popped the top and took a deep pull as the delicious nectar flowed down my throat and into my stomach.

"Ahhh...This hits that mythical and long-sought-after 'spot'." I said, patting my belly.

We ate the rest of the meal in silence as our hunger took precedence over talking.

When we finished the meal, I broached the subject that had been weighing on my mind since I realized Broadhead would be after Sarah. "So, what are we going to do about you?"

To her credit, she didn't ask me what I meant, she simply started talking. "I already told my higher-ups that I was taking a week off to help authorities in their search for my missing husband and to spend time with family. They understood, and I figure I can stretch it out a few days past a week if I have to."

"Well," I replied, "That's good, but we need to figure out exactly what we're going to do. I don't see any way else to put this, but Broadhead is huge and if they want you dead, they're going to kill you if you stick around. They're going to kill me too, unless we figure this out. I mean, they're huge, have multiple offices worldwide, and have a rather terrifying reach. On the other side of this equation is you, me, and a lunatic not named Sam."

"Dru, I understand what you're saying, but they can't be all-powerful, and they still have to operate with deniability here in public. This isn't a war zone. It's Texas. My house is in a suburb of Austin. It's one thing to attack you on a nearly deserted road at an abandoned warehouse. It's another to attack two well-armed people inside their home in a wealthy neighborhood."

"True." I replied. "Are you're saying we should head to your house? I'm not sure about that. I mean, sure, maybe we don't find ourselves in the middle of a Hollywood gunfight, but they've got to be staking out your house."

"I'm sure they are, but if we can sneak in or get in and out fast, there are a few things I'd like to grab that can be beneficial to us."

"Like what?"

"Well, I've got basics I'll need like clothes, but that's not vital. I've got more guns, more ammo, burner phones, laptops and tablets."

"Wait...burner phones?"

"Focus, Mr. Dru. I've got lots of unlocked phones and tablets - I tend to collect models of phones and stuff because of work, and many are sitting at my house - unlocked and available."

"Oh. That makes sense. I was worried you were actually 007 or something."

"Don't be silly, no."

"Ok. Well, honestly I am not sure that's important enough to return for. We don't need a lot of guns. In reality, we only need an AR and a pistol - maybe one big rifle... and a couple of shotguns..." I looked up to see her smirking at me. "Oh alright. The phones and computers will come in handy, but don't waste time with clothes. In and out as fast as we can. We can buy what we need to wear. Now, do you have a way to avoid their people who will most definitely be sitting right outside your house and most likely driving around the neighborhood looking for your car and my stolen truck?"

She grinned. "Well, first of all, that truck stays where it is when we leave. Also, did you notice what was sitting on at the corner next to the Rockbox theatre a few blocks away?"

"No. What?"

"A Ford pickup for sale. $3500. That's a cash sale for sure."

I smiled, "Is it a four-wheeled drive?"

She smiled right back, "It sure is. And unlike most Austin trucks, this one is a work truck. Nondescript."

"Perfect. Will we call the owner up tomorrow morning and buy the truck?"

"I called him three hours ago. Told him I'd meet him at nine in the morning tomorrow."

"Are you sure you don't do this for a living?"

"Pretty sure, sweetie."

"I'm not so sure," I joked. "Where do you want me to sleep? I think I should settle down and get some rest. Tomorrow promises to be a hell of a day."

"It's a double. Pick a bed and go to sleep. I'm taking a shower before bed, but you're right. We need rest. Tomorrow we'll avoid the stakeout by sneaking in from the back - my house butts up against a green space. We can park about a quarter mile away and go in the back door."

"Sounds easy", I replied.

"Like you said before, this isn't a movie, so we can sneak in, load up, and get out. Right?"

"Piece of cake."

About 30 minutes later I was in bed and starting to suffer some serious painkiller withdrawals when Sarah came out of the shower and got into her own bed. I had to ask something that had been on my mind since she went into the bathroom. "Sarah?"

"Yes?"

"What's a green space?"

"Seriously?"

"Seriously."

She mumbled something that sounded suspiciously like "Yankee," and continued louder with, "It's a cross between a park and a temporary pond. It's undeveloped land that acts as a flood plain in big rains, but it is usually dry, open fields and used by the neighborhood as a play-space, soccer field, or makeshift baseball diamond."

"Oh. Thanks.

"Sarah?"

"Yes."

"I'm not sure how to ask this...but..."

She let out an exasperated sigh and rolled over to face me. "Yes?"

"How many guns do you have?" Her answering smile warmed my heart.

Chapter Six

Ole Bessie

We woke up around seven in the morning, both of us because of my nightmares. Not being a morning person, I can't tell you what it was like waking up in a hotel room with my friend's wife in the bed across the room from me. I rolled out of bed and into the shower. When I came out, I was dressed, she was dressed, and there was a large, black coffee on the nightstand for me.

So, I guess it was pretty much heaven, because coffee.

Coffee is literally the greatest human accomplishment since the wheel.

I went downstairs and out the door to take a walk around the block looking for anything out of the ordinary, like a death squad or something. Luckily for everyone, my imagination almost always outstrips the reality in front of me. There was nobody around skulking in shadows, no fedoras pulled low over the eyes, and no sudden shouts of "There he is!"

I went back inside and ate a hotel breakfast that was fine by hotel standards but a far cry from the amazing dinner of last night. However, since all I actually cared about was loading up on energy for the day, it was exactly what the doctor ordered. I've gone without painkillers for several days at a time, so I knew I'd be okay, but right now, it was playing hell with my appetite.

As nine a.m. approached, we walked down a few blocks to the Ford truck for sale. It was about fifteen years old and well worn, but looked like it had been taken care of by a man who relied on his truck for a living. The paint was faded, but the tires were new, the rims clean, windows sound, and all around a tight ship.

Looking in the windows, she was spotless inside if a little threadbare. The upholstery was good though, with no rips or holes, and it sported a stock radio.

A few minutes later old farmer number three ™ from central casting (that's the one with no hair, a big beer gut, a baseball cap, and stained denim overalls) moseyed up to us and asked if we were the couple that called yesterday about – again, I swear I'm not making this up – 'Ole Bessie.

"Yeah, that was me, darlin'," Sarah replied, her faint southern accent transforming into a solid, thick southern drawl. The woman who ran a major department in a billion dollar company had been replaced by a sweet Southern Belle.

He looked us over a bit before he said, "Y'all don't look the type for an old work truck, you don't mind my saying."

I opened my mouth to say something, but Sarah cut me off, "It's for our boy. He recently got his license and we want him driving something reliable, tough, and...well...not new, God love him."

He tipped his ball cap back and scratched his head for a second, and said, "I can't blame you for that. Boys and their first truck don't usually last long before they're up to trouble." Sarah laughed, put her hand on his arm and said, "Bless your heart. Sounds like experience talking."

The old man smiled and nodded, "Three boys of my own."

Sarah stared at the truck for about thirty seconds before turning to him with a big, warm smile, and said, "Would you take three thousand cash for it?"

He scratched behind his left ear and said, "Well, since it's for your boy and it's his first truck, I guess I will."

Sarah handed him a wad of cash and he signed the title over. He finished counting and without looking up he called out to us, "You might want to tell your boy that 'Ole Bessie has more under the hood than it appears. She's no monster, but that's a six-liter V8 under there and she's never had any trouble getting up and rollin' on down the road. Tell him to keep his foot light on the gas."

Sarah jumped behind the wheel and we were off on our way to the town of Round Rock and Sarah's house.

A few minutes later I laughed despite feeling like an addict in withdrawal and said, "I sure hope our boy appreciates this fine machine."

She smiled and said, "I almost feel bad lying to the man, but we're on limited funds and he doesn't need to know we're on the run from evil Druids."

"All Druids are evil. Always were. But fair enough."

Sarah gave me the side-eye, but said nothing as we took off down the road.

It was a completely uneventful ride to Round Rock. It took about two hours to get there and the truck performed flawlessly. And yes, she had plenty of power for an old truck. Sarah had a lot of fun driving the thing at eighty-five miles per hour down the road.

As we neared her neighborhood, she finally slowed down and we drove a few back roads to approach the neighborhood on the other side of the shared green space. We filled the tank about ten minutes away from our target because the V8 was a gas hog and we wanted a full tank just in case.

We drove slowly along the road trying to find a parking space that would allow us fast access to the green space and once we found it, we pulled in and parked 'Ole Bessie.

Pointing almost directly across the wide open field in front of us, Sarah indicated a cedar fence and gate that looked like it led directly to the back door of her house. "We go in through that gate and head upstairs to my room. We'll grab the guns and the ammo from the safe and throw it into a big bag I've got in the closet. Then we'll go back down the stairs to my office and grab any small electronic thing we see. Sound good?"

I replied, "Sounds perfect. Let me lead the way to see what's going on. You stay behind me about ten feet and two steps to my left. You cover my six to nine o'clock. Do you know what I mean?"

"I cover behind us and to your left." We started walking quickly, but not running.

"Bingo. You ready?"

"Yeah. Scared, but yeah." We were approaching her gate.

"Stick close and let me lead," I said again, "We'll be fine. Remember, it isn't Hollywood, right?"

"Right." I could hear the smile in her voice. "No shootouts, no explosions."

"Right. We are but two sneaky bastards stealing your own shit from your house. In and out and away we go."

"Away we go," She repeated.

We reached the gate. Sarah had a key in her hand and she unlocked the gate. I pulled the pistol from my holster and grabbed the latch. She put her key away and pulled out her own gun. She was breathing fast and heavy and I could see the intensity of her feelings.

I reached out with my left hand and rested it on her shoulder. "Look at me Sarah. You've got this. In and out. Easy as pie."

She swallowed and nodded.

I opened the gate and we went through into an empty yard. We walked straight to the back door and as Sarah went to unlock it, three things happened all at once. I saw a raven fly overhead, three men came around the side of the house, and somewhere in Hollywood a director yelled, "Action!"

The guy in front pulled up short, opened his mouth to yell, and the two men behind him piled into his back. Sarah damn near jumped out of her skin and everyone raised their guns except me.

"BLAM BLAM BLAM!" My gun was already raised.

Three men dropped to the ground dead and as Sarah automatically leaned over towards the door lock to fit her key, I simply reared back, kicked the door in, and pulled her inside.

"Upstairs now! Get the guns!" I screamed. I ran through the kitchen into the front in time to see the front door knocked in by two guys in armored swat gear and a breaching ram as a third guy leveled a shotgun in the doorway and yelled "Target!" while looking straight at me.

I braced on the wall framing out the weird little seating nook on my right and fired straight into his face, which was the only unarmored part on him. At the same time, he discharged the shotgun and I felt a sting and a searing pain in my right shoulder. Luckily, the slug in his shotgun didn't hit me, but it hit the edge of the wall and a wood splinter went straight into my shoulder. He fared much worse, dropping to the ground dead with a 9mm bullet lodged in his brain.

However, the two men who had breached the door had dropped the ram and grabbed their AR's slung across their bodies and I realized I was bracketed by two guys I could totally kill, except I couldn't kill them both before getting shot several times myself. Also, walls in a modern house are mostly concealment, not cover. The .223 round coming out of those rifles will go straight through a wall unless they hit the 2x4 framing, and even then, they will probably ricochet off and still go through. I dove to my left to get behind the stairs rising up to the second floor whilst firing off a round at the guy standing to my right. The bullet nailed his helmet and knocked him on his ass, but it didn't kill him.

Ah. So *that's* how the plucky wizard did it in my book I *still* haven't finished listening too yet.

Meanwhile, the guy on the left-hand side of the door opened up with three rounds, slamming the stairway and wall, but unlike a single wall, a stairway has solid hardwood treads, and two walls acting as cover.

I was in a narrow hallway created by the stairs and the wall of the kitchen behind me. I knew from my first visit it ended at an opening into the main dining room, so I pulled myself up to my feet immediately, ran to the corner, and came around in a crouch.

The shooter was running towards the foot for the stairs and I sent a round at his head, where it creased the skin at the back of his neck, missing the vital arteries because that's how my luck runs sometimes. However, with my next shot I had a clear view of the guy who had been shot in the helmet a second ago turning to face me, so I dropped him with a face shot, same as his shotgun wielding friend.

Now we began to play a deadly game of "ring around the rosy" as the wounded but still very much active and pissed shooter with an AR began retracing the route I took around the stairs while I crept in the same circle trying to keep the stairway between us so that I didn't get my ass shot off.

It would have been embarrassing as hell if it hadn't ended almost as soon as it had begun when the guy circled back around to the foot of the stairs and got greeted by both barrels of a shotgun being fired from upstairs by Sarah.

BOOBOOM!

Two rounds of 000 buckshot pounded the shooter to his knees and I turned towards him, pointed my pistol at his grimacing face and pulled the trigger.

Sarah started down the stairs when I realized a bad thing. Out in the field, I had worked with Broadhead several times. Like us in the Squad, they loved using groups of three, and *three* groups of three was their typical attack squad. I looked up at Sarah and started pounding up the stairs.

"Run back up! Run back up!"

No sooner had I shouted than rounds started pouring through the open front door, the window next to the front door, and the back door. Team three had split up and caught us inside.

Having never been upstairs before, I was momentarily at a loss of where to go, but Sarah said, "Back to the bedroom" and I followed her around to the left and into the master bedroom that overlooked the stairway and gave an excellent view down towards the front door and entry foyer.

The firing stopped as she came back out other bedroom with her own AR in her hand and tossed it to me saying, "Here. Use this. It's Frank's and full auto capable." She turned around without waiting for a reply and went back into the bedroom.

Thanking the tendency of ex-U.S. military members to break federal laws regarding automatic firearms, I turned back to the railing and looked down as someone outside of the front door tossed in a flashbang grenade. I turned away and closed my eyes, yelling "Flashbang!" while realizing that probably wouldn't mean much to Sarah.

The grenade wouldn't do that much damage to either of us up on the second floor, but it would provide some cover for the bad guys entry and it could easily set Sarah's house on fire. I waited until the Grenade went off with an insanely loud BAMF! and flash that practically burned my eyes even though they were closed. The percussive WHUMP I felt in my chest was impressive, even from the second floor. However, I'm quite experienced with flashbangs and used them often so they don't intimidate me. Right after the flash I opened my eyes, spun back to the railing and thumbed the selector switch to automatic. I pointed at the doorway, pulled the trigger, and held it until the magazine was empty.

I was rewarded with a yelp and curse, but I could tell it wasn't anything lethal. Wounded, not dead. We still had three to worry about. I had missed the breach and now at least one was safely inside the house. I had to assume the back door shooter was inside too, but I could tell that the window shooter was still on the outside because I could see his shadow.

Sarah came out holding her shotgun, a large bag, and a bit wild-eyed. "I have a rifle, a shotgun, and ammo in the bag. Is that good?"

"It'll have to do." I replied as I reached into the bag and grabbed a fully loaded magazine for the AR. "We need to get out of here ASAP. There's three left, one of which is injured, and there's going to be a shit ton more on the way." I replied.

"Wait!" she said as she spun back into the bedroom and crossed over to a nightstand, "I have two phones right here."

Then, a flashbang arced gracefully up into the air and sailed towards my head as one of the assholes downstairs came up with the great idea to risk losing a hand and throwing the grenade at the last seconds before detonation.

Without thinking I raised the rifle to my shoulder and shot it out of the air. Of course, that was going to make it explode about ten feet in front of my face. A fact my ADHD ass realized as my finger finished pulling the trigger.

BAMF! WHOMP!

I tried spinning away, but the blast knocked me onto my ass, blinded, deaf, and stunned. I rolled violently away from the explosion for all intents and purposes completely out of action, on fire, and in massive pain. Writhing on the floor and up against a wall I struggled to get right, knowing I had lost. In a few seconds I was going to feel the searing pain of bullets entering my body and then die. There was nothing I could do about it. I was completely disoriented and in agony. I had failed Frank, Sarah, and myself.

Somehow, seconds passed and turned into a minute as the ringing in my ears subsided and my vision slowly came back. I saw a shadow on the floor beside me and recognized it as the AR. I scrambled for it still barely in control of my own body, flopping around and trying to make my limbs work.

A million years later I got a hold of the gun and braced myself on the wall, lifting the rifle to my shoulder, my vision slowly resolving from spots and shadows into actual shapes. I was still going to die, but the inexplicably slow approach of the bad guys meant I would take one or two with me when I did.

Then I sat there.

And nothing happened.

My hearing and vision eventually came back to functional levels and I heard Sarah's voice, "Dru! Can you hear me?"

"Dru! Can you hear me!" She was yelling. I could barely hear her.

"Dru! Can..."

"Yes! Where are you?" I shouted

"Downstairs! Can you move? Can you come down?"

"Not sure! Let me try. Are you safe?"

"Yes! But not for long!"

"I'm on my way! Where are the bad guys?"

"Two are dead, and one is on the ground!"

"What?!?!"

Sounding desperate, she yelled, "Just get down here!"

"On the way." I repeated. Feeling and looking much like a drunken fool, I gingerly got to my feet and staggered down the stairway trying to maintain good discipline with my firearm. I'm sure I looked like a drunk rounding the stairway and trying to avoid the two bodies cooling at the foot of the stairs and finding a third sprawled up against the front door jamb staring down a furious Sarah standing in modified Weaver stance pointing a pistol into his face.

"What in the hell happened?"

With me now pointing a second gun at the bad guy, she seemed to relax a little and turned to me. "Well, after the flashbang went off, you screamed like a twelve-year-old," she briefly flipped on a stressed smile, "so I ran out of the bedroom and looked over the railing, and two guys were rushing the stairs. I screamed and they both looked up at me like idiots, so I pulled the triggers on my shotgun and...and...they both died. I only had my pistol left so I ran down the stairs and this...this...jerk was coming in the door. I shot him three times and knocked him on his butt. So I shot two more times. They have exceptionally good body armor. He's only bruised!"

I stared at her. "Yes, they do", I slowly replied. "Exactly how did you kill two at once with buckshot?"

"They looked up...face and neck exposed...like idiots. I had two rounds of 000 shot loaded."

"That'll do it." I agreed. Incredible. She wasn't even shaking anymore. Ice-cold and professional as hell. Some people are like that. When the shit hits the fan all the fear goes out of them and a laser-like focus takes its place. If that's what's happening here, she will probably fall apart into a complete mess about an hour after we survive this. You know...assuming we survive this.

I walked up to her and kept my rifle pointed at the guy on the ground. "So, what are we going to do with you?"

Sarah chimed in, "Whatever it is we do with this guy, we need to do it fast. I can't believe there aren't police all over the place."

The Broadhead guy on the ground relaxed fractionally and said, "Cops are holding a cordon of three streets for us. Another team is on the way. You're both dead."

"Bullshit. There's no way you have the entire police force in your pocket."

"Of course not," he sneered, "we don't need the whole force. The boss is enough. We pull strings you couldn't dream of. This won't even be on the news tonight."

Sarah snorted, "You don't know my neighbors, they'll be screaming about this for years. This is a southern town: gossip is practically a sport here. They'll be all over the news."

"They won't even remember this by tonight."

"What the fuck are you talking about?" I asked

"Forget it," he smiled "You're gonna die in a few seconds anyway."

I looked over at Sarah and she seemed to understand my glance. Turning back to the asshole on the floor she said, "Take off your helmet and strip out of the body armor. Now!"

Smile gone, he reached up and unsnapped the chin strap and pulled the helmet from his head. He reluctantly loosened his vest and pulled it off. I quickly stepped in reversing the rifle and smashed the stock into his head, knocking him out. "Grab the bag. I'll grab this guy. We're leaving now." I threw the guy over my shoulder in a fireman's carry and headed for the back door while Sarah sprinted up the stairs to retrieve the bag and the shotgun. Together we ran out the back door, across the yard and into the greenspace.

Amazingly, there was no second kill team, no police, and no witnesses looking out of windows, doors, or even people on the street. Impossible. Yet it happened. We ran, me loping along with an unconscious man on my shoulder, Sarah carrying a small armory, all the way to 'Ole Bessie without another soul seeing us.

Sitting in the front seat smiling was Sam.

Sarah raised her pistol and Sam raised his hands in the air saying, "Don't shoot Annie, I'm on your side!"

"Who the hell are you?" She yelled.

"That's a guy definitely not named Sam", I answered. "Who is Annie?" I asked him.

"Annie? Annie Oakley there? No? Too soon? Too niche?"

"Too old," I replied

Exasperated, Sarah asked, "Boys, what is going on here?"

From the cab of the truck, Sam waved and said, "Hi. I'm Sam, an old friend of your husband."

Sarah ran around to the driver's side. "Hi Sam. Get out of my truck before I shoot you. Pretty please."

"Ahh. You're a lot like Dru, I see."

"If by that you mean I'm in the middle of a life and death situation and a stranger is sitting in my car wasting time, yes, I'm a lot like Dru. Same thing is happening to him right now. Last chance, sweetheart, move or get shot."

"Ha! Wonderful. I'm moving." He got out of the truck and quickly jumped into the truck bed. "Let's get the hell out of here. Throw me the dummy on your shoulder."

I think it says more about my still addled brains than my trust that I did what he asked and threw the unconscious guy into the back and slid into the passenger seat of the truck and shut the door.

Sarah looked at me incredulous and said, "Really? You're going along with this?"

"It's faster, trust me. And we need to get out of here now."

Sarah hesitated less than a second, shrugged, got in, and took off down the street.

"Turn here!" Sam yelled through the rear window and pointed down the street to our left.

"Where are we going?" I yelled back

"I know a great little warehouse about an hour from here where people can interrogate to their hearts content!", He laughed back.

Great. Okay.

Chapter Seven

Not the Good Guys

About thirty minutes later we were headed north on I-35 back towards the warehouse that Sam and I had first met and killed a few Broadhead employees. Sam was tucked down in the back of the truck out of sight and watching our unconscious prisoner, I was in the passenger seat, and Sarah was driving along at seventy-five miles per hour.

I was deep inside my own head, trying to control the after-action jitters that were being exacerbated by my withdrawal pains from the pills I had run out of. I wasn't doing well. After the truck swerved three times, I came up out of my own thoughts and noticed Sarah was crying.

"Pull over," I said, trying to stop my shaking hands. "I'll drive from here."

She didn't say anything, instead staring straight out the front windshield while driving. I reached over and put my hand on her arm. She flinched, swerved the truck, and caught herself before she could sob.

"Sarah. Please. Pull over. You've done enough. You need a break. I'll drive from here."

She took the next exit ramp and parked it on the shoulder of the road without a word and without taking her eyes from the road. When she stopped the truck, I jumped out the door and ran around to the driver's side. I completely ignored Sam yelling, "What's going on?" and opened the driver's side door to find Sarah sitting there breathing deeply.

Unbuckling her seatbelt, I quietly said, "Sarah. Slide over on the seat. I'm driving the rest of the way."

Nothing happened for a second and I was afraid she was going catatonic, when she abruptly shifted over to the passenger side of the truck cab. I jumped in, shut the door and took off, crossing the road and taking the feeder ramp down to I-35 and merging back into traffic.

A few miles later, I heard her softly crying and glanced over to see her curled up against the door. I left her alone for a few minutes. She was processing the trauma of life and death combat and it packs a real wallop. Especially for those not trained or experienced in violence at that level.

Keeping my voice calm and quiet, I quietly said, "Hey there, it's over for now. You're okay. I'm here when you're ready to talk about it." And then I shut the hell up. I'm not a psychiatrist, but I do know what's helped what feels like hundreds of my fellow soldiers and warriors through their first action, and more often than not, it's quiet words of support and an ear when they're ready to talk it out.

About fifteen miles down the road, I heard her straighten up and looked over to see her wipe her eyes and nose. She asked, "Who the hell is Sam, and what the hell is going on?"

"That's a hell of a question." I replied.

"Which one?" she asked.

"Both. I already told you about what happened to me the last time I met Sam, and the conversation we had."

"Yeah, and you told me he couldn't be trusted. I thought you didn't believe what he said."

"I don't believe *everything* he said. I don't trust him much at all, but he does seem to know Frank and want to stop Broadhead from doing whatever it is that they want to do."

"Bring back actual Gods?"

"That's what he says."

"Dru, what do you believe? Because the more I think about this, the more concerned I am about how they thought they were going to get away with blowing up my house and sending nine men into my neighborhood with guns to kill me in the middle of the day!"

"YEAH DRU. WHAT DO YOU BELIEVE?" yelled Sam from the bed of the truck, his face and body pressed up against the back cab window like a kid looking into a candy store.

After jumping almost high enough to smash my head into the roof of the cab, I turned in my seat and yelled, "DON'T FUCKING DO THAT, SAM!"

Laughing so hard he had tears in his eyes, Sam replied, "SORRY, DRU!"

"Fucking asshole," I said while glancing over at Sarah. "Sorry about that."

"It's okay, Dru. Mr. Sam is an asshole, I get it."

"HEY!"

I smiled. "Very true, Sarah. Very true."

"NOT NICE!"

Holding my middle finger up to the window, Sam got the point and scrunched back down in the truck bed to hide from sight.

"He also obviously doesn't want us thinking too hard about the firefight at your house," I said.

"Why?"

"Probably because then we might ask ourselves why he was there, how he found us, and what was he doing?"

She was silent for a moment, turned to me, and said, "There are two distinctly negative possibilities in the literally dozens of actual reasons for that man to be here."

"Yeah, I know. He may be one of them."

Surprised, Sarah said, "No. Not that. I don't think he's part of the bad guys at all."

"No?"

"No. Like you said when you told me the story, it's too crazy and convoluted. Worse, it's inefficient and stupid. The Sam you described isn't that. No, I think the two possibilities that are worst case are these: One he's a total nut job living in a fantasy world and playing his own crazy game that has nothing to do with us or Broadhead specifically, or he's a total nut job that believes every single thing he's told you so far."

We were both silent for a minute before she said, "Actually, option three in the worst case scenario is he's actually right about everything he's saying."

I snorted. "Gods and Armageddon? No." That wasn't an idea I wanted to even entertain.

I didn't say anything else because we were turning down the road to the warehouses. We'd be there in about five minutes. But I thought about a lot of things. Things from my fighting past.

As we pulled into the parking lot I asked, "Did Frank ever tell you about Jo?"

She was silent for a moment. "Jo is the woman you killed. On your own team."

After a short eternity where my guts flip-flopped around and my brain tried to shut down, I replied, "Yes, she was. But she deserved it and more. That's not what I'm asking. Did he describe her specifically to you?"

"Only that she was an Extra."

I parked the truck and shut it off. "Jo was what legends call a Cherufe, from Chile. She was a creature with a long face and skin that looked like rock. In the legends, it is said that Cherufe lived in lava pools inside volcanos and created earthquakes and eruptions. Way back in history, Jo's family played upon these superstitions and required sacrifices from the Homo Sapien natives of Chile."

Sam climbed out of the parked truck and said, "Tell her the rest, Dru. Tell her the way to satiate the Cherufe's appetite was with human flesh.

Tell her how they demanded that they throw a sacrificial victim into the bowels of its volcanic home. Tell her the Cherufe's preferred delicacy came in the form of virgins. Tell her they ate children."

"My God, is this true?" Sarah looked at me.

"Yeah. It was true. Jo talked about it from time to time to shock us all. Called them the good old days. She was Evil. When I killed her, she had butchered every child in a village. Like sacrifices. Like cattle."

Sam piled on, "What else did she tell you, Dru? She ever talk about, say, Ayar Cachi?"

"Who?" Sarah asked.

Sam continued, "Ayar Cachi, the Incan God of Storms. In mythology, he was an incredibly powerful, mean, and nasty God. He would use his slingshot to shoot stones at the sky, creating rain and thunder." Then he smiled a nasty smile and asked, "You like slingshots, Dru?"

I ignored him and he went on, "He had three weaker and apparently kinder brothers who feared and hated him. Cachi was one of three triplets, and he had an older brother who was a protector and champion of the Incas. One day the brothers convinced him to go into a cave to get food - in Chile - and they sealed him in. They claim Ayar Cachi still shouts in anger, causing the sky and earth to shake. Thus, he is also the god of earthquakes."

"Okay. What has this to do with Jo?"

I answered, "Jo claimed Ayar Cachi was real and that her family had been his unwilling jailors at the command of the other three brothers. Jo said he died in that cave about..."

"About one hundred and fifty years ago?" Sam chimed in.

"Yeah."

"Gods don't die unless physically destroyed by an enemy. No God would die in a cave. He just...disappeared. Jo knew that."

"So, Sam, I got to ask, and yes, I already regret it, but how do *you* know this?"

"I know everything about every God in the Americas. It's kind of my specialty."

"No, Sam. I don't give a shit about your advanced degree in South American Mythology. I'm asking why you think you know that a "God" can't be killed by being trapped in a cave?"

"Oh I know, but you're not ready for that kind of talk yet. You're still fighting the hook."

"Prove it, Sam. Show us you're not a lunatic. Make this real for us."

"I'm about to, Dru, but if you two aren't quite ready to believe yet, there might be a problem. People are amazingly good at fooling themselves and ignoring what they don't want to believe."

"I married a man three hundred years old. I'm pretty good at believing, Mr. Sam." She retorted.

He locked eyes with her for a few seconds. "We'll see. We'll see. Grab the guy in the truck bed and drag his ass into the warehouse. I've got some Mojo to perform."

"Mojo? Really?"

"All real shamans can do some mojo, Dru, it's not reserved for the African Moco'o. And I am one hell of a Sgaaga."

Sarah and I exchanged a glance, and her head nodded a fraction of an inch to the side. I sighed and went to get the asshole in the truck bed.

"Alright," I said once I got the prisoner safely inside and shut the door, "what the hell is a Sgaaga?"

"Me."

"Not helpful."

"A Shaman. Use your context clues. I told you I was a religious man for my people."

"What people?" Sarah chimed in.

"All of them. All of the REAL people of this land anyway. Fuck you white people." he tossed out casually, as if the heat from the thought had long since burned down to embers. "But what you are asking is where am

I from. I currently live in Alaska and the government says I'm part of the Haida people. Pretty funny considering the truth."

"What truth is that?" I asked.

"None of your business. Now let me work on this unconscious guy here so that he doesn't kill himself when we question him about Broadhead, the way the last guy did. Okay? Good."

"Ravens!" I yelled, smacking my forehead.

Sarah and Sam jumped like teens in a haunted house, staring at me like I was the crazy killer jumping out of the wall at them.

"There was a Raven or Crow - some big damn black bird - flying over the house right before we ran into the first group of Broadhead goons. And there was one when I killed those guys right outside in the parking lot yesterday."

Sam seemed to shift on his haunches like a predator of some kind as he squatted over the unconscious guy, and he smiled. "Why Dru, whatever could that mean, do you think? Crows and Druids?"

I stared at him. "There are no Gods running around Central Texas."

"So you hope."

"Ravens? Crows?" Sarah asked.

"Yeah", I replied, thinking furiously. "Broadhead are Druids, right?"

Sam relaxed and settled down as he said, "I think you're starting to get an idea, Dru."

"Ravens, well, Crows actually, are always on the battlefields of Druidic Myth. Sometimes it wasn't a real crow, but actually..."

"Morrigan, Dru. Morrigan, Chooser of the Slain."

"There is no Celtic God running around Central Texas."

"I agree. Definitely not." Sam replied with a laugh.

He stood up and walked over to me, fishing a small plastic bag out of his pocket. He handed it over and said, "But here's an idea: is it so hard to believe that a Druidic organization trains and uses Crows as a symbolic mascot?"

I looked down into my hands to see that the bag was full of my beautiful little painkillers. I looked up sharply at him, uncertainty and suspicion on my face.

Quietly so that Sarah didn't see or hear, he said, "I need you level for what's coming next Dru, you know that I'm right. Take two pills and let's get to work."

Sarah jumped in from her place about twelve feet away, "Wait. Ravens, Crows, and real Gods? Come on boys. Parallel evolution is a thing, and we know it happens, but actual real Gods?"

"Believe it, Missy." Sam said distractedly.

"Missy?" She closed the distance and got right in his face.

Clutching my baggy of opioids, I stepped back and laughed. I couldn't help it. "You done messed up A-A-ron." Both turned and looked at me. "No? Nobody watched that TV show? Substitute teacher skit? It's not nearly as old as Annie Oakley!"

Sarah turned back to Sam, "My name is Sarah, and you'll remember that."

"You bet I will." he said seriously. As she backed off, he commented, "Frank said you were fierce. I see he wasn't exaggerating."

"Frank never even mentioned you before." She said archly.

Before he could reply, the goon started to moan and wake up. While Sarah and Sam were watching him, I opened the bag and got level by taking three pills.

Sam leaned over the goon and grabbed his head with both hands forcing the slowly gaining consciousness prisoner to look into his eyes. He seemed to be searching for something, and as the prisoner focused on Sam's face and got a good look into his eyes, Sam seemed to find what he was looking for because he smiled and mumbled "Gotcha!" quietly to himself.

Still speaking quietly, he said, "Alright little salmon, swim upstream to me. There you go, that's the real you. Come on back and let that mean little tickle slide off your back. That's it. Come up to me. There you go. There you goooo...bingo!"

The guy on the floor shuddered and spasmed once as his whole body went rigid, then he seemed to almost relax and melt into the floor as he sighed and went unconscious again.

Sam uncaringly dropped his head to the floor with a thunk as he stood up and looked over to me. "He'll wake up in about two minutes. I suggest we tie him up good and get ready for a hard Q&A session."

"What did you do to him?" Sarah asked.

"I unfucked his brain. Dru and I discovered that these guys have a compulsion placed on them to go berserk if questioned or even within hearing of people discussing Gods and Broadhead. Isn't that right, Dru?" he turned to me.

"Well, that one guy certainly went crazy while we were talking about it, but one person is not what I'd call a valid sample size."

"Sure. We can keep pretending if you want. But this guy is going to wake up real soon. Maybe we tie him up now and argue later?"

"Fair enough." I said, and went into the side office where we had discarded the ropes from last time. I brought them out and Sam tied up the guy as he started to come around.

As he opened his eyes, Sarah, me, and Sam were standing at his feet staring at him. He immediately recognized Sarah and me, but when he looked at Sam, he got this confused look on his face.

"Hi." I said. "Guess what? You're screwed. You tried, you lost, and now you're done."

He looked at me with a grim set to his face and glanced around the warehouse. This guy was a pro, for sure, but that only meant he knew. He knew he was completely at our mercy and whatever was going to happen, was going to happen.

"Yup. That's right." I continued. "You're here. There's no help coming, no one to hear you yell or scream, and we're going to ask you questions. You will answer."

He chuckled. It was a resigned sound, "I may surprise you."

Sam jumped in, "No. No, you won't. That little Geas you're thinking of is gone. I took it away. No release of madness for you."

Now he stared close at Sam. "Who the hell are you, and how...?"

"How do I know about the Geas? We ran into it yesterday."

"But...how...?"

"How did I remove it? My little secret."

"But...you can't remove it. Can you? It's not possible."

"Of course it is." Sam replied "But here, let's get this over with because you're boring me. Broadhead is a bunch of Druids dead set on bringing back Gods to Earth because they are idiots who don't learn from their own history. They are so stupid, in fact, that they are willing to bring ANY Gods back. Not Celtic. Any."

Then we all stared at each other for a few seconds.

The man was sitting on the floor, eyes wide open and panting. He was clearly terrified and on the edges of real panic. It's pretty common when you realize the other guys are right and you are truly fucked.

Sarah was the first to break the tableau by moving up to the guy and asking him, "Where is my Frank?"

"Frank who?"

"My husband, you monster!" Displaying a surprising level of technique and expertise, Sarah kicked the man across the face with a shinbone round-house, knocking him onto his side. As he struggled to sit up, Sarah went back in for another, but I quickly put an arm out in front of her.

"Sarah. There's a process to this if we're going to get the information we need. This is why you asked for my help. I'll take it from here. Why don't you go outside for a while? What I'm about to do is not nice."

"I can handle it, Dru. I want to know where my Frank is."

"And if this guy knows, so will we. Eventually. But Sarah...what's about to happen is nasty. This is not the nice guys trying to get information from the bad guys. I'm about to torture this man. He will not survive it. It will take hours, and it will be horrible. You do not want to be here."

She was about to argue, but I interrupted her, "You don't. Trust me. If you're a good person at all, the next three hours will make you physically ill and give you nightmares for life."

It finally got through to her, and she looked me in the eyes, "No, Dru. I get the need for harsh actions, but right now we *are* the good guys. We don't need to go that far, surely?"

"This man will die here."

"Dru, I'm okay with that, honestly, but *how* he dies *does* matter. At least to me."

"Didn't you just kick this guy in the face?"

"Yes! I was angry. I'm scared! But I shouldn't have done it, and what you're talking about is much worse. Much more...evil. Yes?"

"I'm talking more efficient and more reliable. But yes, Sarah, this is not good guy stuff."

"But I thought torture was actually unreliable?"

"Nah, that's Television. Torture works great if you do it right. The key is to keep them in such pain that they can't keep the lies straight and they have to tell the truth to get it to stop."

Sam chose that moment to say, "There's a toolbox in the office. It has vice grips, a hammer, some screwdrivers, and more. Let's get started."

Not taking my eyes from Sarah, I asked, "Is there a torch or heat of any kind here?"

"She shook her head in small little turns and whispered to me, "No Dru. Let's ask our questions and move on. I know it sounds crazy, but I honestly think torture crosses a line."

"It's not the movies, Sarah. This is how it works in real life. This guy is going to die screaming answers to our questions. Otherwise, we can't trust the answers."

"No."

"Yes."

Sam walked over to us and looked at Sarah as he said, "Let me take you outside and talk to you while Dru gets everything started. He's right, you don't have to be here. You *can't* be here right now."

In a daze, Sarah allowed herself to be led outside as Sam whispered into her ear while walking. At the door, they stopped and Sarah turned around to stare at me for a few seconds. Sam nudged her a little and she walked out into the parking lot, the door closing with a loud bang behind her.

"You think she believed you?" the prisoner asked from the floor.

"She should. It was the truth."

"You know damn well I'll tell you what you want. Promise me a quick and painless death, is all I ask."

"And you know damn well I can't trust your answers, so I'll have to put you in enough pain you can't keep the lies straight and the truth shall set you free."

"Actually, we have a third option." Sam called across the floor as he came back inside.

"We do?" I asked.

"Of course. I'll do to him what I did to you yesterday."

"Me? What did you do to me?"

"Oh Dru, you haven't figured it out yet? Why did you tell me all that stuff about your last mission in the squad? *How* did you? How did you suddenly remember all that stuff, and then tell me about it? Me? A total stranger to you, and you just...told me everything?"

Somehow a gun was in my hand and pointing at Sam's head. "Yeah. You know, how did that happen, and why am I only now realizing how screwed up that is? Maybe you'd better answer real quick."

"You had a Geas on you. Actually, you have a bunch of them. It's my guess that you're missing lots of memories, my fierce Irish dog. It made it so you could not think about or remember events of that day. I removed it. And it turns out you desperately wanted to remember that stuff, I simply convinced you to say it out loud as it all came back."

"Who are you, Sam?"

"I think you and this guy on the floor have a good idea who I am, and I think you both know that me and mine are real."

"Are you...a God?" The prisoner asked.

Sam kept his eye on me while he answered, "There are no Gods running around Central Texas, right Dru?"

Lowering my gun, but maintaining the stare, I replied, "No, we'd know if there were Gods on Earth. I have it on good authority."

Sam laughed out loud and said, "But there sure are a lot more God-touched running around than we thought."

"You guys are God-touched?"

We both looked down at the poor schmuck on the ground and said, "Yes." in unison.

"Fuck me."

"Pretty much." Sam replied. "But here's what we can do. I can guarantee every word out of your mouth is the truth so long as you willingly agree to what I do. I can lay a compulsion on you to speak honestly and completely, but it won't work unless you agree to it. And yes, I'll know if you agree to it for real or not."

"And if you do it," I added in, catching on to the idea, "I'll ask you questions with no hammer, and when we're done, I'll end your life quickly and painlessly. It's the best deal you'll get. Decide right now or I go get the toolbox. Personally, I hope you decline. I'm feeling a little mean right now."

He decided on the obvious, and we set about getting ready for the interrogation. I went outside to explain to Sarah, but discovered that Sam had told her he was going to offer a plan to question him without torture already. She was waiting for me to come out and get her.

"I knew you wouldn't do it." she said incorrectly. I stayed quiet. I figured I'd let her keep her comfortable delusions about me for a little while longer.

We came back inside to see Sam eye to eye with the prisoner, talking in a low voice with what sounded like chanting. As we walked up to him, he finished whatever it was he was doing and stepped back. "Stay quiet when you talk, ask him questions calmly, and he'll answer everything you ask."

Without hesitation, Sarah stepped up to the prisoner. "Where is Frank?"

"I don't know."

"Sarah", I said, "Let me handle this. It's better if one person questions him. I'll ask the questions and if I miss anything, let me know what you want answered, okay?"

Reluctantly, she nodded assent and stepped back. I pulled up a nearby chair and sat down next to the apparently enchanted captive.

"Do you know who Frank Egils is?"

"Yes."

"Is he alive?"

"I don't know."

"Where are prisoners kept?"

"Lots of places. We can keep them anywhere we want."

"Where would you keep someone like Frank?"

"I don't know."

"Is there a place where you keep the important prisoners?"

"We don't usually keep prisoners long term."

Shit, this wasn't going anywhere good. I paused for a second and Sam came over to me. "Ask him where they question and torture people. If Frank is still alive it's because they need something from him. They'll be asking."

"Great idea." I answered. Turning back to the prisoner I asked, "Where do you keep people you are interrogating?"

"We have a bunch of interrogation facilities."

"Where are the three closest?" I asked in desperation.

"There's one near Dallas, one in Houston, and one in San Antonio."

We all looked at each other. "Where is the one in Dallas?

"The Sanctuary."

"Where is that?"

"Cedar Hill."

I turned to Sarah, "Look that up."

"Already on it..." she replied. "...Found it. Need an address."

"What's the address?" I asked him.

"I don't know. I've never been there."

"Not important." Sam interjected. "I'll find out by the time we get there, if that's where we're going."

"Of course that's where we're going!" Sarah spat out.

"We have more to ask and find out. We can't decide where we're going until we know all we need to know. That's all I'm saying. I'm not trying to start a fight."

Not saying anything to either of my companions, I resumed questioning. "Why do you know who Frank is?"

"I was in the building the day he was taken. Lieutenant Egils and I had crossed paths in Afghanistan while I was deployed about three years ago. He was detained by Broadhead after he came to our Dallas office and asked to see Ms. Byrne."

"Byrne who?"

"Ms. Shannon Byrne."

"What happened?"

"I don't know."

"How do you know he was detained?"

"I saw him walking between Jason and Sean."

"You know Jase and Sean?" I asked, surprised.

"They were friends of mine."

"Who are Jason and Sean?" Sarah asked.

"The first two people I killed yesterday." I answered. Sam smothered a laugh by snorting and covering his mouth.

The guy looked up at me. "You're the one who killed them? You're the Trickster?"

Now it was my turn to be surprised. "The what now?"

"Jason said Frank was working for the Trickster."

I slowly turned my head to stare at Sam. He was smiling, but his eyes were hard as flint.

"I've been called that before. That and worse." he said with a shrug. "It's kind of a code name between me and my associates, of which Frank was one."

Sam was full of shit. I asked my next question, "Who is the Trickster?"

"A real pain in the ass for Broadhead. He's some sort of hacker and environmentalist. He's always trying to sabotage our programs and we have terminate on sight orders if we find him or anyone working for him in the field."

"Why would an environmentalist be after a private military contractor?"

"We contract out to other companies as well. Specifically oil, mining, and mineral exploration."

"They rape the earth." Sam interrupted. "They destroy entire ecosystems. And they do it to prepare the way for specific Gods."

"What?"

"Ask him where the last sabotaged program was located and what they were doing. Go ahead."

"What was the sight of the last Trickster event?"

"Chile mining operation."

"Chile?"

"Yes."

"They were re-opening a huge cave that had been closed in centuries before by an earthquake, Dru. Figure it out yet?"

"Are you honestly trying to tell me they were looking for Ayar Cachi?"

"No. They were opening the cave so that if they could get him back to earth, he'd be free. He'd be a horrifically bad God to have free. So I stopped it. Got the whole mountainside to collapse down on top of itself. He's buried deeper than ever."

"How many died?" I asked Sam.

"Official report lists two hundred and ninety-three people." The prisoner replied.

"That's horrible." Sarah said.

"Better than freeing a God that enjoyed cruelty so vast that both the humans and the God's own brothers conspired to trap him in a cave. A cave, coincidentally, that legend says has windows to the place of the Gods' birth. You're welcome."

"Why did you send Frank into that office alone?" Sarah demanded.

"That was Frank's choice. I wanted him to have backup."

"Then why didn't you back him up?" she continued

"Oh, no. Not *me*. I'm not the kind of guy one wants for backup. I wanted *you*, Dru."

"What? Me?" I was totally caught off guard.

"Yes, you. But Frank wasn't having it. Told me you were unreliable and had too many secrets. He went it alone and he paid the price."

"Well, this is fucked up. When were you planning on telling me this, Sam?"

"Never! It's no longer relevant. It doesn't matter!"

"It doesn't matter that a Native American Shaman slash computer hacker called the "Trickster" was not only aware of who I was, but actually wanted to involve me in this crazy scheme as back up, but didn't, and now my friend is gone and I'm in the crazy scheme anyway? *That's not relevant?!?!?*" I was screaming at this point and about to lose my shit.

Thankfully, it was Sarah who spoke next. "Dru, please. I know this is crazy, but let's finish this and get up to Dallas. I need to find my Frank."

Breathing heavily I continued to stare at Sam while I answered Sarah. "You're right. Let's get some answers." Spinning around, I turned back to our unlucky prisoner who had been watching us all this time and began asking more questions, but now I wanted some answers for me.

"Were you the leader of the strike team sent to kill us?"

"Yes."

"You know why you were sent to kill us?"

"Yes."

"Why?"

"You were considered a direct threat to our operations and Mrs. Egils was a loose thread deemed an unacceptable risk."

"Why?"

"Why what?"

"Why was Sarah considered a risk?"

"She was discovered to be actively looking for her husband by travelling to you and getting you involved. It was decided she could not be counted on to stop on her own. Once you killed my friends and escaped the offices, we were briefed on who you were and we've spent the last twenty-four hours tracking, staking out and planning a clean-up operation of you both."

"What do you know about Broadhead and their activities?"

"I know a lot. I've been in Broadhead fifteen years."

"Fifteen years? Why are you still in the field?"

"I'm not. I requested to lead this team. Jason was my friend."

"Jason? He was an asshole. Sean was way cooler. Until I killed him."

"Fuck you."

Sam interjected, "Don't antagonize, it can break the compulsion if you piss him off too much."

"You've lost talking privileges, Sam. Shut up until I'm ready to talk to you. I'm not joking."

"Dru..."

"Sarah, if Sam talks again, I'm going to shoot him in the leg. You have a problem with that?"

"Not at all." she replied.

Amazingly, Sam said nothing.

"What is the main goal of Broadhead?"

"Broadhead is a huge company with various divisions and differing goals for each of them."

"Does Broadhead believe they can bring Gods to Earth?"

"Yes."

"They do?"

"Yes."

"Actual, real Gods?"

He looked at me and smiled. "Yes."

"How?"

"Make war until the War Gods return. Break down areas of the world that myth say were locations of the Gods into third-world conditions so that the state of existence matches more closely the way it used to be when the Gods were here. Prepare the way to make it easier for them to return. Consecrated actions in the name of the Gods themselves disguised as actions, projects, or events."

"Why would you want that?"

"I don't really care. I like my job and appreciate the incredible income. That stuff is beyond my pay grade."

"Then how do you know any of this?"

"Because they are close to making it happen, and since we work with a lot of Extras in the field, many of us in positions of authority and high up in the decision-making process need to know what's actually going on to prevent miscommunication or screw-ups."

"What about the Extras?"

"What do you mean?"

"Why does it matter that you're working with Extras?"

"Because they know! Many Extras live a long time and they or their parents were actually alive when Gods still walked on the earth! They want their Gods back, because some of the Gods gave them power and protected them. They're tired of being slave labor for humans."

"Have you brought any Gods back?"

"Not yet, but soon."

"How do you know you can bring Gods back? What if they are gone forever?"

"They can be brought back."

"How do you know?"

"Because it happened once by accident."

Sam's head whipped around to stare at the man. "What?"

"It happened once by accident."

Fascinated despite myself, I continued, "When?"

"August 9th, 1945."

Feeling sick and knowing where this was going, I asked anyway, "Where?"

"Nagasaki, Japan."

"What God?"

"Kagutsuchi."

Sam whispered, "The God of Fire and Destruction."

The captive smiled even wider. "Yes."

I carefully tried not to think about that while I finished questioning our prisoner. About the fact that the bomb over Nagasaki was a forty percent stronger explosion than the one over Hiroshima. About the idea that maybe it wasn't actually a stronger bomb as reported in the history books, but rather an effect of calling back and destroying a God in an instant of time.

Chapter Eight

Suspicious Timing

I kept my promise and he didn't suffer.

After we were done disposing of the body in a ditch and back filling it with dirt, it was decided by all of us that going to the Safehouse called "Sanctuary" in Cedar Hill was the right choice. Turns out it's a wealthy gated community in the southern suburbs between Dallas and Ft. Worth.

We had to go, both to look for Frank and to get more information. As is often the way with questioning a captive, we left with lots of answers, but most of them brought up more questions. We were all struggling (well, not Sam) with the idea that this was a real situation. An organization dedicated to bringing back Gods and claims that it had already been done once accidentally? Madness.

But I have to be honest, I was starting to believe them. And it scared the shit out of me. Because I've had a history with a lot of Extras, and the guy was right - Gods are considered fact by them, not "faith". I had never wanted to admit that before.

We walked out to the truck and Sam started going through the bags we had thrown in the back. "Ok." Sam said, "What do we have as far as equipment? We have to break into a safehouse. I assume that's not easy, right?"

"It's basically impossible." I replied.

"Well, how are we going to do it?" Sarah asked.

"We'll try to use their overly complicated safeguards against them, and we'll trust that Sam isn't full of shit about his tech prowess. The recently deceased asshole told us that the safehouses are all essentially the same. Each house was a few improvements over a normal house in the middle of a wealthy neighborhood.

Bullet proof glass is obvious, so it's in hidden spots like on the sides and back windows where neighbors don't look, it's got a sheltered driveway in order to get people in without observation by said neighbors, and basically relies on soundproof inner rooms, reinforced doors, armed guards inside, and a silent alarm that goes directly to their own switchboard in the event that anonymity doesn't work. Truth is, safe houses are only safe until the enemy - that's us - finds out where they exist."

"Why is it impossible to get in?"

"Because there are three of us, not the twelve I'd like to have. It takes a large team to pull off a smash and grab, and reinforcements are about six minutes away once the attack starts. We would be lucky to even find the rooms where prisoners are stashed in five minutes, let alone Extract them. Assuming we're not pinned down in a firefight with a crew of armed soldiers."

Sam interjected, "But we *do* have me and you, Dru. I'm *not* full of shit. There will be no alarm, so there will be no reinforcements arriving. You have a nice rifle here in the truck, so we can at least scope out the place to create a plan of attack - pun intended. And I do trust you to kill a lot of people very quickly once we get inside."

"Which leads us to the other problem. Once a gun goes off, the neighbors will be calling the police, and in a rich neighborhood like this, you can bet your ass they will be there quickly. And that leads to cops shooting anyone with a gun not in a police uniform."

"Yes...well...I can't shut down cell phones," Sam grinned, "but I can shut down the towers!"

"You can do what?!" Sarah exclaimed.

Laughing he claimed, "I really, really can!"

"I really, really don't want to know how, but you better be right." I said. "Regardless, we should try to find a way to get in and out quietly, and that's hard to do."

"Let's go look at our problem." He said, and jumped into the back of the truck and pulled out his phone. "I'll get to work on the way. Those towers aren't going shut off by themselves."

Sarah looked at me and I shrugged helplessly. "It's what we need to do. I need a good look at the house." She shook her head and walked around to the passenger side of the truck and opened the door to get in.

"This is crazy. I need my husband back. All the rest doesn't matter to me."

"Believe me, that's what I want for you as well. All that other stuff? It's his issue, not mine." I indicate, pointing at Sam.

"It'll be your issue too. Real soon." He said without looking up from his phone.

I got in the truck and headed out towards Cedar Hill. After a few minutes I asked Sarah, "Can he actually shut down a cell tower?"

"It's a lot more than that, Dru. He has to shut down several towers in order to create a dead zone in an urban area. Before today I'd swear it's absolutely impossible to do that, short of an EMP or a massive, coordinated, physical attack on the towers themselves. There are a lot of safeguards to prevent exactly this scenario."

"Before today."

"I don't know what on earth is going on anymore."

I rapped on the rear window in the truck cab to get Sam's attention.

"WHAT?" he yelled.

"Can you shut off the power to the safehouse?" I yelled back.

"I'D HAVE TO SHUT DOWN THE WHOLE GRID."

Hmm... not optimal. "NEVER MIND." I yelled to Sam, turning back to Sarah.

"Sarah, if Frank is there, he might not be in good shape. You know this right?"

"Yes."

"If he's in seriously bad shape, it might even kill him to move him. Have you thought about what we do then?"

Staring through the windshield, she said, "If my Frank is there - If he's alive - we take him with us. No matter what. We do not leave him. I can't leave him, do you understand?"

"Understood. But that means get yourself ready. We will not have time to panic, freak out, or waste time doing anything but grabbing him and getting out. Agreed?"

"Agreed. Unless..."

Uh oh. "Unless what?"

"What if there's more than one person there?"

"Huh? There'll be lots of people there."

"I mean prisoners."

"Oh. Shit."

"Yeah. Shit."

"Alright, here's the deal: Frank first, and if it's hot, too bad for anyone else. Frank is the priority. But if there are more prisoners there, and we have time, we release them. We take them if feasible, but we at least give them a chance to flee. Fair?"

"I hate the idea of leaving people in the hands of these monsters."

"Me too, but Frank is the mission. Okay?"

"Yes."

When we reached the historic district of Cedar Hill, and we were about a mile away from the gated community, I pulled into a small retail shopping center and turned off the truck. Sarah and I climbed out of the cab and circled around to the back of the truck, where I dropped the tailgate. Sam sat up in the truck bed and moved over to the lowered tailgate, letting his legs swing off the edge. I started the conversation. "Okay, so let's take a look at a map and make a plan. Do you know what house it is, Sam?"

"Yup, and I think you're going to like it." He pulled up a map and showed us. "It's at the end of a cul-de-sac." and showed us the house at 330 Point View - a house with a cambered driveway conveniently hidden from view by all but their immediate neighbor to the south, and that view was obstructed by a tall fence made for exactly that purpose. More importantly, the back yard opened up to – you guessed it – a greenspace.

"Am I seeing this right?" I asked. "Is that a bunch of empty space between a small electrical substation and the back of the safehouse? Could it be that easy?"

"Well, I'm assuming we're all smart enough to know that the wide open space is a killing field, right?" Sam quipped.

"Only if we try to go in that way." I said. "I'm thinking it's the exit strategy. We kill surveillance at the substation and park 'ole Bessie there, the circle around for a frontal assault when you kill the cell towers. If there's nobody at the house left alive, and no one knows we're there, it's a straight shot to the truck. Hell, the truck is a four-wheel drive. Sarah can drive it over the ground to us if needed. Obviously, we need to recon the site first, but that's the base of a plan."

"We'll recon right from the substation." Sam said.

"How will we do that?" Sarah asked

Sam lifted up a ratty old backpack neither Sarah nor I had ever seen before and said, "I'll take out my drone and we'll send it over there." Looking at our blank faces, Sam continued, "What did you think we were going to do? Hike up the imaginary hill, hide under yon imaginary tree line, and spy on the house through the scope of your rifle? That was a joke! It's the 21st century, catch up. We'll use my drone."

So, that's exactly what we did. We drove out to the substation which was completely deserted, Sam jumped out of the truck bed and walked up to the gate keypad, fiddled with it for a few seconds, and the gate rolled open for us. I drove the truck into the gravel parking area and turned it off. Sam jogged up to the truck and began fishing through the backpack and pulling out his drone and controller.

The drone was a small, well used model with the four propellers and a camera fastened underneath the body. It was completely black and Sam whispered to it like it was alive as he prepped it for flight, "Hello my darling Cutiepie, I'm going to get you ready for a flight now. I want you to go out and have fun. Find us shiny new things to play with, Okay? Daddy loves you."

He glanced over at Sarah and myself and I guess we were both staring at him, because he said, "What?"

Sarah silently turned around and walked away. I shook my head and refused to answer. With a sniff, he turned back to the drone, set it on Bessie's tailgate and picked up his controller.

"You're going to have to catch up with the rest of the world soon, Dru."

"Sam, we used drones all the time. I'm all caught up."

"Not to mention your drone is positively ancient." Sarah chimed in.

"Not ancient. Well loved. That's all."

"Okay, boomer."

We both turned towards her with surprise on our faces.

"What? You two are so archaic, it's the obvious response to your old drones, ancient movie quotes and general weirdness. Boomers."

I laughed. Sam went back to his controller and fired up the drone mumbling, "What does she know?"

The drone took off and Sam expertly piloted it towards the house. We crowded around the controller to watch until Sam got frustrated with our closeness and snapped, "Back away and let me fly! I'll stream it live on my throwaway Facebook page. Like and follow and all of that shit - watch it on your own phone. And yes, I have a Facebook group for exactly this kind of shit. I've been doing this stuff a while."

So, we both went to Facebook, found his group called, "Foods I like to peck at" and joined. There was a question we had to answer to join.

"Am I hungry?" I read, surprised.

"Type yes." Sam answered

I typed yes and I was allowed to join the group. I saw there were one hundred and thirty-seven members in the group and as I scrolled down, I saw nothing but silly little posts about food and a bunch of selfies of Sam eating food. For fucks sake.

Soon, Sam had a live stream started with a note to "everyone" that he needed no help at this time, so no commenting, please.

We watched a livestream of a drone as it took off and flew over the open green space towards the safehouse. As it circled at a high altitude, I was able to see the house was exactly as described.

It was a multistory "McMansion" with a driveway that angled in from the approaching drivers left side of the house with a semi covered carport in the small courtyard like parking space. The garage was an extension to the drivers right that completely hid the parking area from view on that side. To the drivers left, the driveway was parallel to a high brick privacy wall that covered the view to that neighboring house.

The road to the house was basically a boomerang left curve from the locked gates at the front of the neighborhood, all the way to the cul de sac where this house was located. It was well thought out, and a great way to bring multiple people into the house without the neighbors noticing. All it needed to complete the scene was an upscale SUV with tinted windows. Kind of like the SUV I stole from Broadhead a day ago.

Kind of like the one we are watching drive down the street towards the house right now.

Son of a bitch. "Do you see what I see?"

"You mean that Black SUV?" Sam replied.

"No way. Should we get that drone behind them and watch them?" Sarah joined in. "Maybe we can learn something if they are actually going to the house."

"This is crazy timing." I said. "Like, suspicious timing."

"Suspicious?" Sarah asked.

"Yeah, think about it. The drone has been up in the air five measly minutes. We got here fifteen minutes ago. A Broadhead SUV is driving up to the Safehouse? Right now?"

Sam jumped in, "Nah. This stuff happens all the time, Dru."

"No, it doesn't."

"Sure, it does. Trust me."

"Sam, every time you open your mouth I trust you less. What the hell is going on here?"

"Dru, timing is everything. I've got great timing. Impossibly great timing. It's part of my knack. You shoot shit, I arrive at the perfect time. Perfect time to hit a guy on the head with a frying pan, perfect time to catch a ride during a shootout, perfect time to see Broadhead screw up. In this case, I think we lucked out big time. Think about it. If you were Broadhead right now, what would you be doing?"

I thought about it for a second. Slowly, I said, "I'd be freaking out over two people who seem to be looking for Frank, better at fighting than professional kill squads, and who obviously escaped with a prisoner."

Sarah walked between us and said, "I'd be worried that this prisoner might talk, right? I mean, he actually knew stuff we needed. Even if he berserked as planned, they'd have to assume that we might get some knowledge out of him."

"More importantly," I said, getting into the moment, "standard doctrine says after failed ops, you reassess and redeploy to make old intel useless."

"Or even to make old intel a trap." finished Sam. "I'll bet you that car is crammed full of Extra security."

"I'll do you one better," said Sarah, getting excited, "If Frank is alive, I'll bet you they're about to move him!"

Sam and I looked at each other and Sam started to laugh and did a little shuffle that looked suspiciously like an indigenous dance, "I have the perfect timing to upset things! It's what I do!"

"Can you fly that thing while we're driving?"

"Driving, yes. Chasing a car like in a Car chase movie? No. And it maxes out at about forty-five miles per hour. And I can't get too far away from it- say about six miles. But I can bring it in for a landing on a moving truck if we are going slow enough."

"How slow?"

"Say, fifteen miles per hour?"

"Okay, let's get prepped. We'll get back into the truck, watch the camera, and see what happens. There are three distinctly different outcomes we'll face, depending on what we see. We will either be calling the whole thing off because it's now a death trap, we'll be assaulting the house as planned, or we'll be following the SUV because they loaded our... target," for some reason I couldn't bring myself to say Frank's name, "into the SUV for transportation to a new location."

"We will not be calling the whole thing off!" Sarah yelled.

"I don't mean giving up, I mean not dying a horrible death today because we were stupid enough to attack a house with thirty armed men ready for us. If that SUV drops off five or six armed men, we're going to go somewhere safe and make a new plan. Why? Because we have no idea if that's the only SUV coming today, the tenth SUV to already come and drop off soldiers, or what."

Not backing down, Sarah ground out, "We are going to rescue my husband."

I matched her stare and said, "Yes, we are. If he's there, we're going to get him. I promise you that. But it doesn't do him any good if we die stupidly. First, we watch and get intel. Then we decide on a final plan."

We got the truck ready, drove outside of the gate, and sat on the side of the driveway watching the live feed. By the time we did all that, the Black SUV had pulled into the driveway and parked. The driver opened that door, got out, and reached to the back door, opening it. A grim smile spread on my face as I realized there was nobody in the back.

Sarah, unaccustomed to retrievals and actions of this sort, was confused. "Where are the soldiers? I thought you said there were soldiers in that SUV."

"They don't need them," I replied, "because there won't be anything to guard. They either decided a trap was a waste of time, or they think they already have enough people there. This is a retrieval."

"You mean...?" Her breath caught in her chest.

"Yup. You were right. They're here to take somebody away."

As I finished saying that, the front door opened and a security guard came out onto the front porch. Then in what I can only describe as a total twist, a woman was led out of the front door with a hood on her head.

"Okay, that's unexpected," Sam muttered in surprise.

"Wait. That's not Frank. That's a woman or a small man. What's going on? Where's my Frank?" Sarah was edging up towards hysteria with each question.

"Wait." I said. "Just wait, and watch."

After the woman was led into the back seat, the driver closed the door and went to the back of the SUV, opening the hatch. The drone moved to get a better view through the hatch opening, and we could see that the prisoner was in the seat behind the driver, but the other half of the back seat was folded down. The front door opened again and two security guards carried out a covered stretcher with a body on it. It was impossible to tell what was on the stretcher other than "a body".

"Oh my God. Is that Frank? What is that? Is it a body? Is he alive?"

Sam answered her, "Sarah, try to stay in control. Nobody would bother to move a body right now. Whoever that is, they are alive."

I made up my mind right then, "We're taking that SUV and we're grabbing both prisoners."

Both Sam and Sarah agreed immediately.

"Keep the drone in the air, and we'll start heading towards Lakefield Parkway. If they are following standard doctrine, they will turn towards us to avoid congestion and traffic, we can set up at the corner where those cross-walks are and try to get them to stop. Sarah can drive the truck and pull a U-turn and come back to get us after we take out the driver and security. If I'm wrong and they head the other way towards Rt. 67. We'll follow if we can and try to find a spot to interdict them on the road."

Sam said, "There are two Broadhead operatives in the front seat, but nobody else. They've got to be planning on meeting up with another vehicle, right? Two people isn't enough security."

"Most likely," I replied. "It's possible they are running fast and chose speed and anonymity over firepower, but I doubt it. They will probably meet two more SUV's about a short distance away from the Safehouse. Personally, I'd have the escort right there at the gates, but since I don't see any, I have to assume they're trying to save this safehouse and don't want any attention of any sort. They're running scared and overly cautious. I think they're making bad decisions right now.

"The escorts will probably be waiting in a nearby parking lot and will pull out to bracket them as they pass. This is why we need to hit them right fucking now. If this works, there's got to be a check-in they'll miss and the other SUV's will be out looking for blood."

We started driving about the time the SUV reached the end of the neighborhood road and stopped to open the gate. Luckily, I discovered I was right as the SUV turned our way. Sam and I jumped out of the truck onto the crosswalk island and pushed the button to cross.

"They might recognize me, Sam. If they do, they won't stop. Their job is to get away, so we'll probably be safe from harm, but we'll miss this chance."

"Don't worry. Stand behind this crosswalk pole and think thin thoughts. I'll distract them plenty."

Sam walked out into the intersection as the walk sign lit up and the SUV had to stop to let him by. Perfect timing. Damn, that's a good knack to have. Kind of the opposite of my entire life, actually.

Right before he got to the passenger side of the SUV he spun around and slammed both hands on the hood yelling "What the hell is wrong with you white people! You come in here and think you can just run over me and mine? Reparations!"

While the driver was staring at the madman in front of his car, the passenger was far more professional and exited the car quickly and smoothly, drawing his gun and telling Sam to step back. By then, I had my pistol braced on the crosswalk pole and fired two shots into his chest, turned the pistol three inches to the right and put two rounds through the window into the driver who never even got a chance to look my way. My knack is pretty damn useful too.

Being dead, the driver no longer pressed down the brake pedal, and the SUV began to slowly move forward at idle. Sam had already jumped in the passenger side and slammed his foot over the console and onto the brake and then he put the SUV in park.

I rushed over as Sam unlocked the doors, I yanked it open, and he released the seatbelt, so I could pull out the dead driver and dump him on the street. Sarah had completed her U-turn and pulled up as Sam and I picked up the passenger body and threw it into the back of the truck. We ran around to the driver, picked him up, and tossed him on top of the passenger. Sarah took off and drove back to the substation.

Sam and I jumped back into the bloody SUV. It had been maybe thirty seconds. Neither captive had uttered a word. No cars were around.

"Reparations?" I asked.

"Godsdamned right."

I drove back to the substation and Sarah opened the back hatch and jumped into the SUV, feverishly pulling the cover off of the body strapped to the board. Sam jumped out and ran around to the back seat on the driver's side, opened the door, and yanked the hood off of the female passenger.

"Martina!" he cried, "I don't know what the hell, you're doing here, but I found you. You're safe now." Shocked, I looked up into the rearview to see a young lady furiously spit out a gag in her mouth and glare daggers at Sam.

My head seemed to split open for a tiny fraction of a second and before I could even react to the intense pain, a face of a woman flashed through my mind. The face was similar to this Martina sitting in the car, but definitely not really her. It was a white face with blue paint across the cheeks.

The image faded immediately and the pain went away almost as fast.

I heard Sarah gasp and I froze: I couldn't move. I sat in the front seat staring straight out the window breathing shallow, nervous breaths. Please. Be alive. Please. Please. Be Frank. Please. Be alive.

"Frank! It's my Frank! He's breathing! Frank! Can you hear me, baby? Dru, help me!"

I jumped out of the truck and ran to the back of the car. Frank groaned and seemed completely oblivious to the outside world, and I couldn't blame him, because as Sarah pulled the sheets off, we all saw clearly that he was missing his right leg from the knee down and his left foot was gone, both stumps neatly bandaged and looking professionally amputated. Those sons of bitches had been amputating parts of his body as punishment during his torture sessions.

But he was alive, and we had him back.

Chapter Nine

Meet Martina

"Sam, we're going to need a place to lie low for a day or so. Somewhere safe and not an abandoned warehouse we've used twice already. Then you're going to explain exactly what is going on here between you and this woman." We were driving south on the I-35 in a stolen SUV having left behind a truck full of dead bodies and a bunch of gasoline poured all over them. I had shoved a rag into the tank to light it off, but Sam had pulled a boy scout move building some weird contraption that was essentially a delayed fuse inside a closed truck cab filled with gasoline-soaked dead people using nothing more than a cigarette and a piece of leather he cut off his boot laces.

Showoff.

We were almost five minutes down the road before we saw the black smoke cloud we assumed was 'ole Bessie going up in flames. It sucked to lose her, but we had five people now and the SUV could hold us. 'Ole Bessie could not.

Frank was still delirious and half dead in the back with Sarah hovering over him and whispering to him so quietly I couldn't make out what she was saying.

"I know a place, keep driving." he said from the passenger seat.

The mysterious and so far unexplained Martina sat behind me silently, making my skin crawl. It wasn't that I didn't trust her specifically, but I couldn't shake that look she gave Sam when he pulled her gag out. He knew her, she knew him, and she didn't like him at all. On top of that, she was sitting behind me unrestrained, a complete unknown quantity. And she definitely wasn't human. Sarah was ignoring her completely, like she didn't want to admit she was there.

And Godsdamn it, she reminded me of someone I once knew! I could feel it, even if I couldn't remember who it was. In my mind I saw white face, blue paint.

In the here and now, this woman had dark hair with a green tint to it and a complexion straight out the South American Rainforest - a gorgeous dark brown - with brown eyes a good bit larger than typical and a rather fit body. She was bruised and a little battered from captivity, but unlike Frank, she had not been disfigured or tortured. The biggest physical difference between her and us was an obvious case of Syndactyly - the webbing between her fingers was pronounced and extended much farther than commonly seen in human hands.

I looked up into the rearview mirror to catch her eye and asked, "Martina, do you want us to drop you off somewhere? You do not have to stay with us. You are not a prisoner anymore."

Staring back at me with a sneer, she replied, "No habla Inglés."

Just great. I don't speak Spanish.

"Knock it off, Martina!" Sam said. To me he said, "She's fluent in Spanish, English, Italian, and Mandarin. She's just pissed off she got grabbed by Broadhead for some reason, and is blaming me."

"It was your fault, stupid Pombéro! I knew I shouldn't have slept with you again!"

Cue the very uncomfortable silence in the car.

"Soooo...you two know each other, then?" I asked.

Oddly, she looked over at Sarah, who never turned her gaze from Frank.

"She is one of that group of people I work with that I told you about." he answered. "She's not part of my group anymore, but she helps out from time to time. I keep an eye on her, but a few days ago she wandered off and disappeared."

"He's an asshole and son of a bitch!" To Sam she said, "Every time I see you, you try to make me one of your little eco-warriors, so that you can have me around every time you get horny." she snarled.

"And you're a Gods-damned Iara! Fucking is what you do!" Sam snarled back.

"What the hell is going on?" I yelled. "And what's an Iara, damn it?"

"An oversexed Mermaid!"

"Bite me!"

"Uhh...I don't mean to sound ignorant," I said, "but I've seen mermaids. She doesn't look like a mermaid. You know, no tail...or anything...fishy?"

"Get her in the water, you won't regret it."

"If I ever get you in the water again, *Señor de la noche*, you'll never come back up!"

Laughing lasciviously, Sam replied, "I bet you'd try, my lovely little psychopath!"

"Can y'all stop bitching for five minutes and get us to the safehouse?" Sarah yelled. "My Frank needs medical attention!"

Martina looked at Sarah with confusion on her face and questions in her eyes, but said nothing.

"*Is* it a safe house?" I asked Sam.

"Not in the professional sense. It's a private home with great internet connectivity, and nobody bad knows about it. It's also got a boat."

"And you own it? You? A Shaman from Alaska owns a house in Texas?"

Martina jumped back in, "No, the little ass doesn't own it. I do. It's at Lake L.B.J. And as typical, he left out the important part, we have lots of medical supplies there."

To Sam, she said, "They think you're a Shaman from Alaska?"

He looked at her with a frown that was clearly a warning. "Martina, I *am* a shaman from Alaska."

"You're an asshole, Pombéro."

"Why does she keep calling you that?" I asked.

"Pombéro is a Guarani imp. A mischief maker and oversexed legend from the rainforests of Brazil and Argentina. She's trying to insult me. To be fair, pretty much all the Guarani extras are oversexed. Isn't that right, Iara?" he smirked.

Martina leapt from the backseat across the prone body of Frank and punched Sam hard across the jaw, screaming incoherently. She also slammed into my shoulder causing me to swerve the car and almost go off the road.

"Jesus Christ!" I yelled as I wrestled the car back into a straight line.

Sarah instantly reacted. "Enough, Goddamn it!" She twisted around in the backseat, getting on the back of Martina and rather expertly wrestling her off Sam and back into her seat.

"Watch out and be careful! If you hurt my husband I will kill you," she growled into her ear. "I appreciate you're dealing with this jerk, and thank you for the use of your house, but I swear I'll tear you apart if you cause my husband to die!" she turned to Sam, "And Sam, cut it out you stupid child! Stop taunting Martina and grow up! I don't give a damn about your past together, but it's endangering Frank. Cut it out, now!"

Martina had the good grace to look ashamed and apologized, "Disculpá."

Sam, on the other hand, looked angry, and started sulking in the front seat, staring out the front windshield and rubbing his jaw.

So go ahead and imagine the most horrible family road trip vacation in history and understand that our trip to Lake L.B.J. was worse. I turned on the radio and tried to drive. Sarah spent the entire time agonizing over her insensate husband, and the incipient violence in the air between Martina and Sam never abated the entire way to the house. For the remainder of the trip, the only voice heard in the car was the voice of the navigation app (In two miles stay right to take exit for Rt.2471... In a quarter mile stay right to take exit for Rt.2471).

It drove me crazy, but I couldn't stop sneaking peeks of Martina in the back seat. My fractured memories kept showing me a blue painted face matching Martina's attitude and expressions, and I knew it was a lost person from my past. Somebody important.

Lake L.B.J. was out northwest of Austin, but southwest of us. We spent three hours driving through the empty lands of Texas Hill country. We stopped early in the trip at Hico for some gas, food, and supplies as we caught Rt. 281 which took us the rest of the way before we wrapped around some local streets to a nice little row of houses all tucked tightly together on the lake.

As we pulled into the driveway and parked, I basically crashed out the door in my haste to get out of that car and ran around to the back to open the door for Frank and Sarah.

Sarah calmly said, "Martina, thank you for the use of your house. Please open that door and direct us to the medical supplies. We need to check out Frank in detail right now."

To her credit, Martina seemed much calmer and quickly went to the door and typed in a code at the door lock that opened the door and let her in. She left the door open and moved through the house towards a bedroom that had been expertly turned into a first aid station and guest room.

Sarah and I lifted the stretcher with Frank on it and carried it inside.

Sam sat in the front seat of the car still sulking, but honestly, I didn't give a shit. We left him there.

We got the stretcher in the room and I looked around at the well appointed space. It wasn't a surgical hospital or anything, but they had a hospital bed, and some serious first aid equipment. There was a defib mounted on the wall, and some professional looking equipment that reminded me of a field medical tent. This room was meant for emergency medical treatment of serious wounds, but maybe not set up for significant procedures. I figured they could set broken bones, remove bullets from extremities, and perform emergency services to stabilize a person for a trip to the hospital. All in all, I was quite impressed.

I moved out of the way as Martina and Sarah started working over Frank. As I watched them, a few suspicions jumped back up into my mind. Sarah and Martina moved with the smooth confidence of experience as they professionally looked over Frank, giving him a better evaluation than many I'd seen in the field. But it wasn't that they were both good at it, it was that they were so good at it *together*.

There were too many oddities about Sarah and her skills that didn't make sense. Why was she so knowledgeable about medicine and first aide? Why could she shoot so well? And how come she worked with Martina so smoothly? It became painfully obvious they knew each other as they worked on Frank. Shaking my head and disappointed in her, I went to the living room to think it through and wait to hear if my once friend Frank was going to survive. I wasn't sure what would happen if he died.

After they finished working on Frank and got him comfortably ensconced in the bed, the ladies came out of the room and crossed over to the living room where I was sitting. Sarah dropped into the recliner while Martina plopped onto the couch next to me.

"You two worked hard. Is Frank going to be ok?" I asked.

"Yes," Martina replied. "He will never walk again without the help of prosthetics, but he is stable and sleeping."

"Sarah, are you ok?"

She looked down at the floor. "My husband is alive and back with me. I'm furious, and I still want to kill every single one of those bastards," she sighed. "but I'm also on the way to being okay."

She looked up and over at me with genuine gratitude pouring out of her eyes and posture. "Thank you. You helped me get Frank back alive. I owe you forever."

"No problem," I said while standing up and heading to the kitchen. "I'm going to grab a drink. Anybody want something?"

"No, thanks." Martina said.

"I'm good, thank you." replied Sarah.

I kept my voice flat and neutral. The exact opposite of my emotions and my gut. "Cool. Hey Sarah, where are the cups?" I called from the kitchen. I stood there coiled and wound tight.

"...Shit. When did you figure it out?"

"Yeah. Shit" I said, turning around and stalking back into the room to face her. Martina was sitting on the edge of the couch looking like she was about to launch herself at me in attack.

"Don't do it, Martina." I warned. "You won't like the results."

"Let it go, Martina. He deserves to know the truth, and I believe we can trust him."

"You believe?" I asked, incredulously. "You believe? How could you think any different?"

Her voice grew hard. "Because this is about runaway Extras, and you kill them for a living."

Aww shit. The last pieces fell into place then. Married to an Extra forced into service. Angry about it. Lots of money. "You run a Godsdamned underground railroad, don't you?" I started pacing angrily around the room.

"Yes, we do."

"Damn it, Sarah. You're not doing anything that hasn't been tried before. It never lasts. You'll get caught and killed." I paused, "Not by me, you're safe there, but by somebody. Eventually. They always catch the runaways eventually."

"No, you don't." Martina said. "Lots of times in the past, sure. Most of the time, maybe. But since Sarah joined and got us organized with strong finances, we've saved dozens in the last three years. Almost a hundred so far without a single one lost or captured. And we all know how to fight."

"So I've seen. Gods, I am an idiot." I pointed at her, "You three run around saving Extras and sticking it to Broadhead?"

"Hell no!" exclaimed Martina. "Pombéro doesn't work with us! He's a stupid little ass that almost ruined everything!"

"Wait. Where is the damn fool? Where's Mr. Sam?" Sarah asked.

We all stood looking at each other like idiots and then as if from an unheard signal, we all took off and headed to the driveway.

The car was gone.

Motherfucker. I could feel it. I was slipping away into the rage, the fear, the disassociation that comes upon me sometimes when it all goes to shit. Not in combat. Never in combat. In combat I'm relaxed and at ease. Fighting for my life is my natural state of being.

No, this is when I'm betrayed, abandoned, or abused by people I tried to trust. When there's no one around that's an ally. No family I can lean on for support. At times like this I either get away and get alone for a while, or people get hurt. I took a deep breath and started counting. I went with the calming breath of four beats in, four beats held, and four beats to release. I closed my eyes as Martina finally let out frustrations of her own.

"La concha de tu madre!" she yelled at the sky. "That asshole stole our car!"

Sarah answered, "Well, he stole our *stolen* car sweetie, but...yeah, he did."

I opened my eyes on the third breath. After a few seconds staring out at the road, we all turned back and walked silently into the house as only three people completely exhausted with the drama of the day and totally out of fucks to give can do. We made it back into the living room and dropped into our seats, Sarah in the recliner and Martina and I on the couch.

Four in, four held, four out. Repeat.

"So." I said.

"So." from Sarah.

"So." Martina.

Four in, four held, four out.

Trying to stay calm, I asked, "Anything stronger than water in this house, Martina?"

"Oh, hell yes. I'll grab it." I felt my shoulders and chest start to relax, and I thought I might be lucky enough to survive today without killing anyone else. But I kept breathing four in, four held, four out. Just to be safe.

And that's how we found ourselves each quietly drinking a glass of an outstanding Malbec from Argentina and wondering what went wrong in our lives leading us to this moment. We were still drinking that wine and studiously *not* talking to each other when we heard a groan and a muffled series of movements in the room I had mentally dubbed the "medical suite".

Sarah jumped up immediately and charged into said suite, with Martina and I right behind her.

Frank was awake and trying to sit up. He froze, shock writ plainly across his face as he saw Sarah, Martina, and I crowd through the doorway into his room like actors in a Sitcom.

For a frozen moment no one spoke. Then Frank, staring at me and Sarah, croaked out, "What the hell are you two doing here?" Sarah rushed to the bed and threw her arms around Frank and crushed him a hug as a small sob escaped her throat and for a second, Frank forgot all about his question as he closed his eyes and gripped his wife with his arms crying out softly, "It's really you. I thought I had lost you forever. Oh Sarah, I thought I was dead. I thought I had left you alone. I'm so sorry."

"I know, I know," she said. "I thought you were gone too. But I found you. I got you back. Don't you ever leave me again."

"I won't." he said at once.

She pulled back, gripped his shoulders and said, "I mean it. *Never again.* You don't leave me. Not for war, not for a job, not for this slavery. You never leave me, you hear me? Never."

He stared into her eyes and we could all hear the promise and the iron in his words as he grated out through parched lips, "Yes. I hear you. Never again. I promise."

And as simple as that, my friend was a runner. He had promised his wife to be a man hunted to the ends of the Earth by every government on the planet. And he had been crippled by those bastards at Broadhead. I briefly, insanely wondered if I'd be the one sent to kill him. Then I remembered I had been discharged permanently, and for the first time, felt that was good thing.

He looked back to Martina and I with a serious expression on his face and said, "What the hell are you doing here, Dru?"

All that rage from earlier came crashing back. What am I doing here? After all this, I still wasn't trusted? Unwanted?

Feared.

A sick feeling spread in the pit of my stomach and I could feel the entire universe shutting down again. Sounds became muted and I felt like I was underwater, looking towards a blurry, imperfect image in front of me. With a sick smile I said, "Well, Lieutenant, I *feel* like I was saving your life."

"I went and got him, honey. I remembered what you said before you disappeared about reaching out to Dru if there was a problem."

"I what?"

"Baby, you said to me, 'If you need anything while I'm gone, call Dru'."

"Oh...yeah. Uh, Sorry. I'm a little addled still." He looked a little uncomfortable and asked, "Is it only you three? And I'm sorry, I don't know you." he added, looking at Martina.

"No." I jumped in before the others could speak. "Not just us three. Your *buddy* Sam was around, before he stole our only vehicle. You and Martina here apparently know and work with the same people." I said, pointing at Martina. "You sure you don't know her?"

Frank leaned back on the bed and sighed. "Crap. No, Dru, I don't know...Martina, is it? And you have no idea how sorry I am to hear that name."

I was shaking now. "Hey Frank? Maybe you'd better start telling us a story."

Sounding nervous, Sarah said, "Dru...uh...He needs rest, Dru. We can figure all this out later."

Both Martina and Frank seemed way too on board with that suggestion so I put my foot down.

"No way. There are way too many half secrets, lies, and bullshit floating around right now and I want it settled. This is dangerous. Right now not one of you actually trusts me enough to tell me the truth, *so I can damn well not afford to trust you!*" By the time I finished, I was screaming at him.

Still screaming I said, "I packed up, left my home, traveled to Texas, put my life at risk repeatedly, and killed several people to get you into that bed. You sons of bitches owe me! Spill it! What the hell is going on?"

It was at this point I realized that Martina and Sarah were putting me inside of a triangle with Frank at the tip and me in the middle - an effective way to keep someone in a crossfire without accidentally killing your allies with friendly fire, so long as you shoot first. Time slowed way down like it does during a firefight. Even though my joints and muscles felt like they were on fire, my whole body went loose and relaxed. It was almost go time.

"Go ahead. Do it. Try to kill me now that I've done what you wanted. Show me I was wrong to trust you." I turned to Sarah. "Show me I was wrong to help you save your husband. Show me, Sarah, what 'I owe you forever' actually means to you."

Frank spoke. "This is why I didn't want you anywhere near this, Dru. You - and I'm sorry to be so blunt - you are so *profoundly broken*, Dru. Nobody is about to kill you. We're all afraid you're going to kill us!"

"Then why did you tell Sarah to bring me in?" I screamed.

I looked around again, my body rigid with suppressed rage. My fists were clenched so hard they hurt. My legs were quivering with the urge to run, or lash out, or start kicking things until they broke. They still had me in a triangle, but Martina looked nervous and was shifting her eyes between me and Sarah constantly. Sarah...well Sarah was looking at me with tears in her eyes.

"I'm so sorry, Dru. I did lie to you. But it wasn't about Frank. It was about my work with Martina and the others. I didn't know they would be involved. I didn't even know Martina was gone, let alone had once been involved with Sam or Broadhead! Please forgive me. You did save my Frank, and I do owe you forever, and I swear, *I swear by our shared childhoods,* that I'm not going to try to hurt you."

I was breathing fast and heavy and part of me wanted to kill everyone in the room because it would be easier that way.

Safer.

Sarah - how had she gotten so close to me? - reached out slowly and touched my cheek. "Nobody here will hurt you, and if anyone tries, I'll kill them myself. You're my family forever now. Forever."

I stood shaking like a rabbit waiting for the fox to pounce. In my entire life, I don't remember anyone ever calling me family and meaning that as a good thing except once, and they're dead now. So dead I don't even remember their faces.

From the bed a million miles away I heard Frank, "Stand down, brother. We've got your six, and you're safe here. Why don't you rack out."

Martina spoke softly, "Che, you rescued me from captivity a mere four hours ago. I owe you, and if Sarah calls you brother, then I'm your friend too." The blue painted face flashed across my vision again. I couldn't process.

Somehow they had both gotten to the bed and were standing protectively on either side of Frank. I hadn't even seen them move. I couldn't process the moment. The emotions were conflicting, and my mind was reeling. I was shutting down. Standing there without the ability to move, I simply said the truth, "I don't have any family."

I had to leave. My body started up again on its own accord, with no conscious decision on my part. Like an automaton, I turned around and spoke over my shoulder as I shuffled out of the room, "Yeah...Yeah, I'm gonna rack out, LT. Yeah."

As I left, Martina quietly said, "Did you see his eyes? They changed colors! PTSD doesn't do that!"

I could hear Frank whisper to the ladies, "That had nothing to do with PTSD, that was something else entirely. We all almost died. Dru is a very dangerous person to be near when he's like this. And honey, I never told you to call him. What's going on?"

But I couldn't bring myself to feel anything at that revelation. Anything at all. Down in the Zero again. All alone except for a blue painted face without a name sitting in front of my mind's eye, this time she was crying.

Chapter Ten

Dog

I woke up from my nightmare to weak sunlight streaming through a window facing the lake. Despite avoiding violence, I felt physically horrible, like I had finished twelve rounds with a professional fighter. Every part of my body hurt. My muscles screamed at me. My joints didn't want to work. And almost all of it was because I almost killed my only real friends in this world a few hours ago. Friends, but not family. Never that. Family is an empty promise that leads to pain. But still; I almost killed them all last night. I shuddered with the thought of that near miss.

This has happened several times before. But in that moment of peak escalation, there's literally nothing I can do. This isn't some emotional cop out. I am a monster when I reach peak escalation. A monster from your worst nightmares. I spend most of my life trying to make sure I don't reach that point, because once I get there, there's no rational thought, no way back but through it. Believe me, I've tried everything. The only thing that works is prevention.

Like the junkie that I am, I tried searching my pockets again for a painkiller. The little packet Sam had given me had four painkillers left in it. I took two dry.

Judging by the slant of the sun, it was almost dusk. I waited until I felt the pills start their magic and I got up and walked out of the bedroom into the living room and heard voices in the medical suite.

I walked into the room and conversation halted as three sets of eyes turned to me. There was a silence in the room so painful it was almost poetic.

Sitting in the center of the bed, Frank was resting with his leg and injuries exposed above the covers. On his right, Sarah was sitting on the edge of the bed with one hand protectively on his shoulder. Martina was standing off to the left and had been playing with some piece of medical equipment when I came in. Now they were all standing like some gross parody of a renaissance painting.

Eventually, Frank opened his mouth and said, "Hi, Dru. How are you feeling?"

"No idea. Feeling nothing, I guess."

"So, what now?"

"Now we tell each other stories, and we don't fucking leave anything out or tell any lies. And you go first, Frank. How the hell are you here and not in Afghanistan?"

Frank settled himself a little deeper into his bed and sighed, "Sam, though I didn't know that at first."

He fidgeted around a bit more, looked pained as if he didn't know where to begin, but took a deep breath and sighed it all out. "Dru, what do you remember of that day?"

"Until two days ago, I remembered waking up in a mental hospital and being told I was getting a medical discharge - and a bunch of lawyers had me sign papers that said stuff like a "lack of mental responsibility"- because of acute PTSD. Now I know it was all lies because they were hiding the fact that Jo was sacrificing children and I did the world a favor. Sam unlocked those memories for me."

"Yeah, well, Dru, you have to realize something. None of us remembered that. As far as we all remember, you killed Jo and Juan in an empty village for no reason and threatened me as well. We - I - always knew you were a very unhealthy person, but you always wrapped yourself in the structure of the military chain of command and were as reliable as a..." he struggled for any comparison other than the obvious.

"A war dog?" I sighed.

He had the grace to look uncomfortable, but he nodded his assent anyway. "Yes, you were as reliable as a war dog. I pointed, you killed, we all survived another day. Jo called you a dum-dum bullet, but the dog analogy fits better."

I sighed, "It always has...but I remember her calling me Dum-Dum Bullet from time to time."

"Yeah, you were a straight line of death. I've never seen somebody switch on and off so fast. Problem is that you do it all the time. It's your default. You have no middle ground, you're a flipping switch about everything. Point and shoot, no complications, nothing fancy, followed orders immediately and completely. I often loved having you on my team, Dru, but I was also terrified. I always knew you were one bad switch away from something horrible, so this scenario...fit my expectations.

"I had no reason to question it, no matter how bizarre the situation seemed from the outside, because, as you found out, something was keeping us from even thinking about the event.

"Unfortunately for everyone, I was without a team and I had time on my hands while they figured out how to redeploy me. I called home, talked to Sarah a few times, and pestered the doctors at the base about you. And on the third day, I got to see you. They let me into the hospital room where you were strapped down to a table, and you were...raving...I don't know what language you were speaking, but it wasn't English. I assume Gaelic?"

"Yeah, something like that." An image of blue paint on her face.

"Anyway, you saw me and went rigid. Froze like a statue, staring at me for what must have been for ten seconds. Then you deflated there on the table and asked me - in English - what was happening to you. You had no recollection of anything and didn't even know where you were. The doctors told me you had actually broken a restraint the day before and almost killed a nurse. Do you remember that day?"

"No."

"I told you Jo was dead, but the doctors had warned me not to tell you that you were her killer, so I didn't. You simply replied that it didn't surprise you. You honestly don't remember this? You essentially tried to kill anyone who came near you for about a week. Anyone but me."

"No. I remember threatening your life with a gun in the field and waking up to see a doctor, a lawyer, and two SPs standing at the foot of my bed with my discharge paperwork and a threat of incarceration if I didn't take the deal in front of me. But Frank, I totally remember killing Jo. I remembered that as soon as I woke up, and I remembered putting my gun to your head and accusing you of something. But I couldn't remember what."

"Yeah, neither could I, and that's where they messed up. They took too much from me. I have a fantastic memory and I've done this gig four times for America - I knew something wasn't right and it wasn't "trauma-suppressed memories" like they tried to sell me. I started to ask around and was told point-blank to stop asking. Immediately.

I was assigned to lead a new team and sent back into the field for six back breaking months and we were in harm's way the entire time. In hindsight, it's pretty obvious that they were hoping I'd die in the field. Two of us did. You remember Tony and Keith? They were on every mission with me. The last one...I saw Tony come apart in a bomb blast and Keith got shot. We were being evacuated and below the chopper, Keith was lying on his back, drinking something, waiting to die."

"Shit. Keith was a good man. He could shoot almost as good as me."

"Yeah, and Tony was pretty cool."

"This sucks."

"Yeah, I was pretty pissed. I went back assuming I'd be reassigned again. Instead, I was railroaded. I arrived and was escorted from the bird straight to the brig.

"I was shocked. I've served three times over the last century or two, and in the forty seven years these bastards have sent me into harm's way, they've never actually cared that we die. Not in the Civil War, not against the Native Americans, not in Korea or Vietnam, and not this time. They redeploy and send us back out. And it wasn't like I didn't do everything I could to keep us alive, but they used the deaths of my team to trump up some sort of plan.

"Of course, now I know they were determined to get rid of me. Getting killed in the field didn't work, so now they were going to do something bureaucratic. What it was, I'll never know. I received a phone call while in jail from Sam. Not that I knew who he was."

"Hello, Frank! I have saved your life!" a voice said to me over the line.

"Who the hell is this?" I asked.

"Listen, Lieutenant Frank Egils. You were about a week from disappearing forever. Trust me, I saw the orders. You are deep in the shit. You apparently saw a Broadhead operation that you weren't supposed to, and your lunatic friend Drustan interrupted it. He's gone, but you are here and in the crosshairs of people who do not like loose ends. You, sir, are a loose end." he said.

"What are you talking about, and who is this?" I repeated.

"I'm talking about you, Dru, and Jo. Jo worked with Broadhead and when Dru killed her, she was doing something for them. Now listen, in about thirty minutes you are going to be escorted from the brig to a helicopter that will take you to an airplane that will fly you to America. Smile, say nothing, and I will see you when you land.

"Sam had done some computer hacking magic and instead of some dramatic scene, I was loaded into a plane and flown to Andrews and discharged. Sam was there dressed as a Major General, took possession of me personally, calmly walked me through an actual Godsdamned *award* ceremony, and let me call Sarah with my discharge story that technically is false, but the truth is way crazier.

"Sam had me assigned to "recruitment" after being awarded the actual fucking Medal of Honor, Dru. Can you believe that shit? And since we don't actually recruit for the Squad, nor have an office for it, I'm technically free to do what I want while still drawing pay. His idea of a joke or something. I can't figure him out.

"I don't have the medal, of course. That medal means something, and I'm not going to keep or wear one as a scam to get out of a military unit that's full of actual press-ganged soldiers. And Sarah knows the truth too, but she told me that she gave you the edited version."

"Yeah, and she was smart to do so. It was obvious horseshit, but I wouldn't have believed the Medal of Godsdamned Honor either."

"Long story short, I started talking to, and working with, Sam to figure out what the hell happened that day. Sam, obviously, was more about Broadhead as the "Enemy", but I wanted to find out what the hell happened that day in the village."

"So, why the hell would you go to the Broadhead offices?"

"Well, before I get to that, you need to understand that I believe Sam about their goals and activities, Dru. They are trying to bring back the Gods. I've seen enough to believe it. It seems first that Christianity, and later the industrial revolution, kicked their metaphysical asses and our rapid technological evolution pretty much changed this world in profound ways that we don't fully understand."

"Yeah, Sam has been trying to explain it to me a little bit."

"Well, listen, Sam has his own agenda, and I think half of what he says is distorted or lies, but things I discovered on my own support the idea that

Gods exist. In fact, I've got a strong suspicion that there might still be Gods here.

"What?"

"It's like this, Dru; Sam and I were able to hack into a lot of Broadheads information, and Sam tried hard to hide some things we found from me. But I'm not stupid, and reading between the lines, it's obvious that there are three "Head Priests" of Broadhead and that they believe there's a God on the planet. They believe that magic - what little there is - would be impossible if all the gods were gone."

Sarah interrupted, "What magic, baby? There's no magic. Not real magic, right?"

Martina started laughing. "Mija, Pombéro uses magic all the time."

"What?"

"Compulsions." I said. "That's real magic?"

"Yes." said Frank. "There is real magic, but it's nothing like what you are thinking. No fireballs, no lightning from a staff, no dude in New York with a magic stone, no schools of wizardry for orphaned kids. It's nothing more or less than an ability to manipulate reality on a tiny scale."

"That's...still terrifying." I said.

"Not so much," said Martina. "For some, the terror is science. We used to live in a world that was undefined. That makes magic easier. Science sets rules, people believe the rules, people follow the rules, the rules become real. Much harder to change reality now." Then she smirked again, "And magic used to be much bigger and more powerful. Fireballs, lightning from a staff, and even magic stones."

"Um...that's not how science works." Sarah said.

"So say the scientists." Martina replied. "Another rule they made."

"But Martina, the entire point of science is to understand the natural world and how it works. Science doesn't create the rules, it discovers them!"

Martina leveled a stare at Sarah and said, "Wrong, your grade school science is about Socrates and his boxes inside boxes. Big boxes holding ever smaller boxes. Big box is plant, smaller box is leaf, smaller than that is cell, get even smaller and you have the nucleus. Now we're tiny, but inside the nucleus is even more and smaller stuff like nucleolus, but eventually you get to super tiny shit - the molecules. After that you get what most people think it the smallest bits; atoms. But when you break an atom down, you're a level away from the end of the physical rules you know. At a certain point, the tiny boxes don't follow the rules you try so hard to force them to. Your science even admits what I say."

"What do you mean?" Sarah asked.

Martina shrugged her shoulders and said, "Quantum physics, Schrodinger's Cat. The behavior of light. Gravity. Everything related to gods and magic happens at a level smaller than an atom, but the more rules you put in place, the fewer potential expressions of reality there are."

I laughed bitterly, "We all sound like a bunch of freshman college students talking philosophy. None of us actually know enough to even know what we're saying. Schrodinger's Cat? Quantum Physics? Magic? For fucks sake."

Martina smiled, "Well, truthfully, Schrodinger's experiment is almost always incorrectly understood by laymen, but since I do have a Phd. in Quantum Science and Engineering from Princeton, I can assure you I know far more about this than the rest of you. If I spoke more correctly, none of you would have a clue what I was talking about. Might as well say it in Spanish, ¿Comprendé?"

"Well, shit." I said, impressed. "I don't even have a high school GED, so I'll have to take your word for it."

Surprised, Sarah turned to me and asked, "What? I thought you had to have one to be in the military."

"Mine is fake. In fact, my whole identity is like Frank's and comes from the same source; Uncle Sam. I never went to a real school. Homeschooled until I ran off."

Frank shook his head ruefully, "Dru, I learned a long time ago that education doesn't necessarily mean smart, but when you hear your wife with a Masters degree tell you you're being stupid, you probably are. Alright. Martina, if you are the resident expert on this stuff, I'll defer to you. I will say that I've seen many things in my three hundred years of life, and science simply cannot explain all of them."

Martina smiled and said, "Well, I'm only thirty-one, but Quantum science is a young science anyway, and I studied it specifically so that I could try to figure out what's going on with magic and the Gods. I was literally recruited by Sam when I was seventeen. I was about to be pulled into the Argentine version of your Nightmare Squad, and was terrified. I had learned Spanish and English as a child and was teaching myself Italian with some crazy plan of running away to Europe."

"Sam showed up, seduced me of course, the bastard, and took me to Portland. I got a new identity, and I decided to enroll in a local community college as part of that new identity. I wanted to learn languages, and Sam thought a multi-lingual member of his "underground guerilla team" was a great idea, so I started studying Mandarin."

"Imagine when, to everyone's surprise, I turned out to be good at math and decided to study Physics. Quickly, I learned enough to know that Quantum science and engineering presented my best chance at truly understanding the world we were both preserving and the world we were fighting to prevent. I aced my classes locally and applied to Princeton. Sam hacked the college and got me a full ride. The rest was a few years of living on my own and hard study. I got my degree and came back to work with my *lover* Sam, but I learned *Sin vergüenza de mierda* had been banging everything that could consent, and hiding it from me. I don't do secrets and lies, so I left him and his little radical groupies.

"I got involved in the underground railroad for us non-humans and almost lost my life many times. Occasionally, the asshole would find me and we'd hook up for a bit and work together, but about two years ago I found Sarah and we started rebuilding and improving the way we rescued people from their slavery. Then Frank disappeared, Sarah started looking for him and I was left alone and in charge of the whole operation."

"Three days ago I was going to meet a few people that we had been trying to sneak out of Mexico, and Broadhead snatched me right off the street and threw me in a van. They were looking for Sarah."

"Oh Martina," Sarah said, "I'm so sorry, sweetie. I didn't think anything like this would happen. I needed to find my Frank."

I connected a few dots and started laughing. I couldn't help it.

Frank looked grim. "What are you laughing at, Dru?"

"Well, Frank, you getting kidnapped saved your wife's life."

"How do you figure?"

"Sarah was up in Maryland telling me you were missing when Broadhead snatched up Martina, right?"

"Yeah."

"So think about it. Broadhead knew your precious underground was moving Extras in from Mexico. That means they either magically figured out your wife's entire operation in the six days after they snatched you, or they knew all along and were letting her do her thing until such time as they could no longer exploit it. I wonder how many of your "refugees" were actually working for Broadhead or the government."

I started laughing again as Martina and Sarah exchanged horrified looks.

"Yeah. If you hadn't come to me, Sarah, you'd be dead, Frank would be dead, Martina would be dead, and I'd be...uh," I stumbled past my near suicide, "...two more audio books into my series, comfortably sitting on my couch. Poor Sam would probably be pulling his hair out and running in circles."

I turned to Martina, still laughing. "You owe Sam an apology. He had nothing to do with you getting snatched."

There was silence for a minute from the others while I got myself under control. I was putting off the hard part. It was time to find out the most important thing of all. This was going to hurt, I was sure.

"So," I said, coming to it at last, "There are two big questions I still need the answer to."

"What's that?" Frank said.

I swallowed hard, and found I couldn't speak. I tried to ask and nothing came out. I had to stop and try again. I couldn't do it. I couldn't ask. I looked down ashamed and terrified. This wasn't going to work.

"Dru. What do you need to ask? It's okay. Ask it." Frank said.

"LT," I stopped.

"Yes Dru?"

"Frank." I tried once more.

"Yes?"

"Were you ever really my friend?" I finally ground out. "Or were you nice to me because you were afraid of me?"

Frank looked me in the eye, held my gaze, and said, "Dru, you scare the shit out of me, but you are by far the best friend I ever had in the Squad. If I wasn't a good friend to you, I'm sorry."

"You didn't just use me to get the job done?"

"Of course I used you to get the job done, like I used Jo, and myself. But I never became friends with Jo. You are my friend. That's not a lie."

"You got along fine with everybody though. You had lots of friends."

He nodded his head, "I had some, Dru. And I had people I got along with professionally. But you and me? We saved each other's lives so many times. We've been through the meat grinder together more than I can count. And you're a human. You know how many Humans become friends with Extras in the Squad? Even extras like me that look 'normal'?

"None. Ever. But you did. You fought with us. You risked your life for ours. That's rare Dru. But more than that, You broke bread with us. You hung out with us. That never happens. I consider myself lucky to be your friend. Even if you do scare me."

Ok. Alright. I felt a pressure leave my chest I hadn't known was there. Through now blurry eyes, I said, "Okay. Second question. Sarah, why did you come get me? If Frank didn't actually tell you too, why?"

"You heard Frank last night?"

"Yes, I did."

"Well, you missed the rest, and it's not easy to explain, but I did get told by Frank to get you. I didn't lie at all. At least, I thought I did. Best we can figure is that I was the one lied to. We talked a while last night and we think it was Mr. Sam."

"Sam?"

Martina chimed in, "He's good with technology, Dru. Extremely good. If he had film or images of Frank, he could easily do a credible deepfake over a "bad" connection on a video call. He's done exactly that many times for other jobs."

"You think Sam really wanted me involved and when Frank went missing decided to make it happen?"

"Yes." Frank said. "I think Sam is a whole lot more than he seems, and he's up to his eyeballs in this."

"Well," I replied, "he's God-touched like me and an actual Shaman. Priests are always meddling in this shit."

Martina laughed. "Oh no. That Pembéro isn't a God-touched priest."

"No?"

"No." She looked over at my friend. "You are right about Gods on earth, Frank. Sam is that God. The last one. A God that never tells the truth when a lie would do just as well."

Chapter Eleven

Monsters

It was late at night, and I was walking down the street in front of the house with Martina. After dropping the bombshell, Frank had seemed to think for a second and then shrug, accepting Martina's assertion that Sam was an actual God. Sarah and I both wanted to call bullshit, but I had to get out of the house and move. I had been through a bit too much and often when I get this way, I needed to be moving.

Since Frank was still bed bound and recovering, Sara perched herself next to him and they had begun comparing notes and Frank was telling her the truth of what he had been doing with Sam and Broadhead. I found I didn't actually care anymore.

I couldn't sit there any longer, and asked Martina if she would walk with me while they caught up so we could all get a good night's sleep and finish the debrief in the morning over breakfast and coffee. She had agreed immediately and we walked out the front door and randomly turned left and started walking.

I ignored the mental flash of a painted blue face trying to speak to me. It was happening enough that I was getting used to it. "Tell me about Sam, please?" I asked

"Why? You don't want to know about me?" She asked with a sly glint in her eyes.

Surprised and flustered, I said, "What?"

She laughed and patted my shoulder. "I'm teasing, che." She hesitated a second. "And maybe flirting a little."

"Hell of a time to flirt." I said before thinking.

She frowned. "Meh. Pembéro wasn't completely lying when he said we Iara have strong physical drives, but I was actually being friendly. Truth is, we Iara feel very strong emotions all the time. It's one of the ways we're built different than humans."

"I'm sorry, I tend to talk and act without thinking sometimes. I didn't mean to imply anything."

"No problem."

"So...You flirt when under stress? I tend to make wildly inappropriate jokes. And kill people."

She looked up and seemed to realize what I had done and smiled ruefully at herself. "Got me."

"Just giving you a good example." I said while I smiled back at her.

We walked in a comfortable silence for a few minutes quietly looking at the lit houses and occasionally getting a glimpse of the lake from behind fences and driveways.

"Che...I have to ask. Please don't get upset with me, okay?"

"I can't promise anything," I replied, "but I'll try."

"Sarah calls you family, and that makes you my family too. I take that seriously, but..."

"But I worked for the government hunting down Extras."

"For money. You weren't forced to do it, like Frank was. Like we all are."

I paused for a second. I realized I needed to answer this question in a way she could accept or we were going to have a real problem in our group. And I totally understood what she was asking, and where she was coming from. In her eyes, I was a killer of her friends and family while also being a member of her family. Not a lot of people can live with that cognitive dissonance. Of course, I knew it was a normal part of life for some of us. I decided to lead with that.

"I've killed family before. It's not something you ever get over. I've also been a soldier my entire life. I was seven years old the first time I had to kill someone in self-defense. All I've ever been is a soldier." Of course I was lying. I'd also been a victim before becoming a warrior.

"I didn't ask to be in the Nightmare Squad, I was transferred there when I made the mistake of shooting a Taliban soldier from the back of a fast moving truck one too many times in front of my superiors. I got put in for a medal. Got transferred instead. Once they figured out it was a knack and that I didn't freak out when I saw a monster, that was it. I was in for the duration. But I have to be honest. I wasn't forced against my will, Martina. I didn't have a choice, but I didn't actually care. Frank was right about me; I was pretty much a war dog. They pointed, released the leash, and I killed whatever was in front of me."

She was silent for a moment digesting this, and, to her credit, she let me off the hook and asked me, "Why don't monsters freak you out?"

"Grew up with them." Another flash of a blue face, screaming this time. "I'm sorry."

"Everybody always is," I ground out. "Nobody ever does anyfuckingthing about it. In the Squad I get to do something about it. I get to kill real monsters."

She slapped me on the shoulder. Hard. "Che. Listen to yourself. You sound exactly like me. And Sarah. And Sam. About the abuse of all of us non humans. We have less rights and less protection than babies! And nobody ever does anyfuckingthing about it," she repeated my words to me.

I pulled up short and froze. Right there on the sidewalk. I looked at Martina - really looked at her - for the first time. She was scared of me, but she was willing to risk it. She was a true believer, and she was doing something about her people's plight. Every day. And she knew that eventually she'd get caught and die. I could see it in her eyes.

Impulsively, I did something I never do: I reached out and gathered her into a hug, shocking us both, and saying, "I hear you. I'm sorry, too. But I'll help you do something about it if I can. Starting with Broadhead. I'll be your friend if you'll let me."

She hugged me back immediately and spoke into my ear, "You better, because so many are done putting up with this abuse. Some of us are fighting to be free, but many others are trying to bring our Gods back to *make* us free, and if that happens, the world is toast. I don't know how else to say it, this abuse of the innocent is about to destroy the world. Genetics and species have nothing to do with it. It's the monsters created through abuse that will destroy our world. It's that simple."

I whispered back, "I don't want to be a war dog. It was a job I didn't know I could quit. If you can trust me a little, I'll try to be something else."

"Family?"

No. I can't be that, even though it's the thing I desperately want to be. Family. "No, I'll try to be a person, not some animal biting everybody who comes close."

She pulled back and stared into my eyes with a thoughtful expression on her face. "You are a person Dru. But there's nothing wrong with being *like* a dog, provided you're loyal. A good dog never bites family. Their loyalty is absolute. They attack anything that threatens their family. Can you do that? Because that might be exactly what we all need."

I smiled grimly, still in the longest hug of my life. I remembered the one time, long ago, when I had a family of choice worth defending. Before they all died. I decided to ignore the implication of family and answer honestly at the same time. "I've done it once before. And I was pretty good at it."

The Blue face smiled in my head and I realized that she had been part of my first family. I stood stunned, realizing I had known that all along. I even knew her name, but I couldn't bear to think it, even to myself. And like Martina, she had seen my flaws and invited me into her life anyway.

We let each other go, and she sniffed a little and looked at me with that smile firmly back in place and said, "And what's this 'friend' thing? Next, you'll be asking to be 'friends with benefits', I bet."

"Well, I'm sure as hell not going to be asking for your hand in marriage. I barely know you!"

She laughed, "Wildly inappropriate jokes."

"Flirting." I replied.

We walked a few more minutes in silence, trying to get used to each other and this crazy attempt at belonging. I asked, "Can you tell me more about magic?"

"Sure. There's not much left of it today, but it seems to be a side effect of what's easiest explained as multiverse resonance."

"Oh...that's the easy explanation...yeah." We turned around and began heading back up the street towards the house.

"Ok, so bear with me. I'm going to use terms that are pretty pop culture right now, and, to be honest, I'll be using them somewhat incorrectly because it's hard to explain, but these concepts are close enough to make sense for the layman, okay?"

"Like Schrödinger's Cat?" I asked "Existing and not existing at the same time?"

"Exactly." She sighed. "Or should I say exactly wrong. It's all about potential expressions of reality and how observation is connected to those expressions. So, let's start with the fact that everybody thinks they know what a multiverse is, but they're wrong. They almost know what it is, but the math and science isn't sure yet. There's lots of debate and argument. We really don't know. However, what we do know and what makes sense in certain mathematical models is that things we'll call universes but are actually expressions of reality resonate at specific frequencies, and when these frequencies touch or overlap, they can theoretically coexist if they are what I'll call "harmonically balanced". However, that 'balance' actually prevents waveform collapse, or in simpler terms, reality doesn't settle into one expression.

"In pop culture, you'll often have some hero describe the multiverse as splitting off into a new universe with every action or event. In fact, it's the opposite. That universe exists, has always existed, and will always exist in a specific timeframe, and it's the one where that reality manifests itself.

Reality expresses itself, and all expressions are equally viable, until something acts upon it to make one 'more real' than all the others. That something is when we observe. Then the waveform collapses into a single reality. Then that reality is what we experience. Our experience of that reality is what defines our universe, not the other way around. We don't create universes through actions, we create reality in our universe. You and I exist in this universe and we will always exist in this universe, there is no hopping around or alternate timelines, or any of that movie stuff. There is only this universe for us, constantly and uniformly expressed as reality unfolds in what we perceive as time. And again, everything I have told you is wrong, but it's the easiest way to explain it without a whiteboard and eight years of advanced mathematics."

"So. Magic. Remember, we're talking universes overlapping at sub-atomic levels where physics doesn't do what you think it does. This is not supposed to happen. There is something inherently 'wrong' with the Gods. They do something that disrupts our model of reality-based multiverses. At this level, it's my belief that the ability to consciously manipulate potential expressions of reality becomes possible because technically, there are two opposed expressions of reality coexisting already. In effect, physics shrugs, throws up its metaphorical hands, and says, 'Whatever, dude. You decide what's real, I can't figure it out."

"I admit I have almost no idea what you're saying, Martina. What has this got to do with Gods?"

"Well, Gods existing on our planet are the actual nexus points for this overlap. They are not from our universe. That I know for sure. What I don't know is why they can exist in our reality at all. It's the unanswered question. They are the physical location of the resonance, so around them, 'magic' is possible for those that have figured out how to do it."

"And how do we do it?"

"No idea. But Gods themselves had insanely strong magical abilities, and many of their priests were the strongest human mages on the planet."

"But you don't know how?"

"No. But Raven said..."

"Wait, who?"

"Sam. Raven. He is the Trickster God of the Haida people, or maybe of every people in the Americas, though he won't admit any of it to me. But it's obvious. He has pretty strong magic compared to anyone else, and his offspring are all Pembéros."

"Okay - you're moving way too fast. Tell me again..."

She sighed and put a hand on my chest, arresting my forward motion. "Like *Sam* said, Pembéros are what we call a type of mischievous imp in Argentina and Brazil. What he left out was that they are all his bastard sons. They trick, they tease, they screw. Just like their Papá.

"Gods. Are. Real. Accept it, Dru."

I sighed and forced myself to say it out loud, "I do." My body hurt. I needed a painkiller bad.

"Good. Now, if we stick to this idea of 'resonance' we can make certain guesses and develop a few theories. I personally think that way back we used to believe that the only 'real' things we knew existed were Gods. Kind of the opposite of science, you know?"

"Oh yes, I get you. That makes total sense."

"So, if we all believed in our gods, and Gods did magic, the more you believed, the more likely you were to match that resonance and be able to perform magic of your own. You sort of fit into the reality of magic."

"That sounds a little crazy. Like, wish upon a star or close your eyes and say there's no place..."

"Yeah, Dru, I get it. But what I'm trying to say in simple terms is that reality was fluid and could be shaped by will - if the intention was in tune with what you already assumed existed there. And what existed there..."

"... was a God that already created two realities at once." I finished, trying to make this all fit in my head..

"Correct. In essence, there was no set reality *except the God itself*, only belief, expectation, and crucially, *observation* that created what we perceived as real as time unfolded."

"Mass delusions that became real?" I asked.

"Sort of. Remember we're making up imagery to explain mathematics here, and - no offense - you're not educated enough to understand the math."

"No offense taken. This stuff makes my head hurt."

"Well, take it to the next step. A strong will, and matching resonance, and the understanding that you can create a mass delusion, or, even stronger, shape reality all by yourself even if others are not part of what you called that mass delusion."

"Maybe even simpler language?"

"Glamour versus creation. Magic can fool you with illusions, or, if the mage is good enough, actually make real things happen. You know, a God could disguise themselves to mess with mortals, or it could throw a legit lightning bolt. Right in the middle is a powerful function of magic - the Geas. That was what they did to you and Frank."

"Yeah! Explain that to me. I've always hated the idea that somebody could erase my memories."

"Well, based on what I've learned from Raven, you can't. It's not erasing, it's making a tiny change to your perceptions of reality – and remember perception, observation, *is reality-* and laying a strong illusion over it. A Geas in its most basic form is nothing more than an oath or promise of some kind. A declaration about you and your existence that something cannot ever happen or must always happen. And then a magical reinforcement to tie that to reality.

"In this case we're discussing, it is an illusion that something never happened or can't happen or definitely did happen, and that tiny change to your perception so that the illusion becomes more 'real' than what actually happened. You never forgot, you instead believed it didn't or did happen, and who thinks about things that never happened or questions perfect memories? Then add a subtle hypnotic suggestion on top to change the subject whenever it comes up..."

"Then dead villagers and slaughtered children don't show up in your memory of the day."

"Or you lay a nastier suggestion that you will never listen to people talk about Gods and Broadhead together – it's impossible. Therefore, when somebody breaks that Geas by talking about it – you go crazy, they must be monsters, and you have to kill them to fix reality."

"Well shit."

We were almost back to the house when we saw two black SUVs come screaming down the street. There was no attempt at stealth, and it was obvious what was happening. We had been found out somehow.

Standing out in the open or rushing down the sidewalk to the house seemed like a bad idea, so we ducked down behind the neighbor's fence beside us and watched as the cars screeched to a halt, and a man jumped out from the passenger side of each SUV holding something in their hands. I couldn't tell what it was until they both pulled the pins and threw the incendiary grenades at the house. Both had good aim, and the grenades went through the window.

The men jumped back into their SUVs and took off down the street like a pair of scalded cats. As they passed our hiding spot, the grenades went off inside the house and the entire night was lit up with a fiery explosion.

Martina and I stood up and sprinted to the house. As we arrived at the front door, Broadhead's plan became clear as we saw a firetruck come barreling down the street arriving impossibly fast for it to be anything other than a part of said plan to murder us in public and get away with it. No way those were actual firefighters.

The explosion had been confined to the front room of the house and the front door was still attached to the door frame, but it was bent askew and easily yielded to my kick. The fire and heat were extreme and pulled us up short as we tried to get in. It was too hot and we were stymied.

Martina screamed into the house, "Sarah! Sarah, can you hear me?"

Over the roar of the fire we could hear Sarah's voice, "I'm getting Frank and we're going out the back! Help!"

Abandoning the front, we rushed around to the back as the fire engine came around the corner about four blocks away and careened towards the house. We arrived at the back door and Sarah was there, having opened it for us. Frank was in a generic wheelchair and Sarah had a huge field medics bag on the floor next to her.

"What happened?" She asked.

"Broadhead." I replied. "We've been found out. There's a fire truck pulling up outside, but it's full of men coming to kill us."

The house was going up in flames as the fire licked around the door jamb of the kitchen and the heat was extraordinary. We had to go. Now.

"Where are the weapons?" I asked.

"Lost." Frank replied. "We have to go now. The fire engine has arrived. We have no time."

Shit. That meant I had seventeen rounds total. "Time to run." I said, running behind Frank and grabbing the handles of the wheelchair and starting to push. "Where are we running to?"

"Boat house." Both Sarah and Martina said in unison.

We ran out the back and down the long dark path to the boat house as quickly and as quietly as we could. No need to let the mercenaries know where we are. Unfortunately, Broadhead had got their heads out of their asses and planned this one a little better than they had at Sarah's house that first time.

As we arrived at the end of the hundred and fifty foot long footpath and snuck into the boat house, a black flat-bottomed boat with a big damn spotlight motored up towards us and we needed to duck behind Martina's ski boat tied to the dock and take cover. Frank's indignant squawk as I tipped him and his chair over onto the pavement would have been hilarious under any other circumstances, but we had to stay quiet and still as the spotlight lit up the boat house, and only the fact that there was this small ski boat between us and them saved our lives.

Martina quietly wriggled past me and up to the end of the dock behind the ski boat. She looked at me and smiled the nastiest smile I had seen in a long time. I mouthed "What are you doing?" without actually speaking the words, and she smiled wider and stripped her shoes off and began undressing. Momentarily stunned I had a crazy thought that Martina was actually flirting with me until she tossed her clothes onto her ski boat beside us and slid silently - nakedly - into the water and disappeared.

Pretty stupid, Dru. She's a fucking mermaid. I suddenly felt sorry for the guys in the boat.

Sarah waved to get my attention and mouthed, "Do you have the gun, Dru?" while pantomiming shooting with her index finger. I nodded my assent and pulled the gun from my waistband to show her. She held her hand up and pointed to her ear and mouthed "Listen" and put her hand out in a stop gesture while saying, "Wait." Next she tapped her watch and mouthed, "Be ready." and put her hand back to her ear, listening.

We sat like that for about ten seconds, listening to the house burn and faint voices of mercenaries communicating their growing frustration as they found no bodies in the house for them to kill.

I took a chance and slid my head out past the side of the ski boat to get a look at the Broadhead guys, so I was treated to an amazing sight as Martina launched herself straight out of the water behind the boat and wrapped her whole body around one of the killers and simply fell back into the water with him. There was a high pitched scream, a huge splash, and the spotlight began waving wildly about. I popped up over the hull of the ski boat and saw two guys in the boat looking into the water frantically searching for their squad-mate. As I watched, the guy in the stern of the boat lifted his rifle to fire into the lake, so I decided to fire into him at the same time.

As he pulled the trigger on his gun, I pulled the trigger on mine and shot him twice center mass, knocking him off the boat and into the water.

Unfortunately, the act caused their boat to rock wildly and the bazillion watt searchlight fell full onto my face and into my eyes, blinding me with its spectacularly bright white light. It was actually excruciating and I was totally, temporarily, blind.

I felt someone grab me and Sarah spoke into my face, "Are you alright?

"I can't see! Take the gun!" I flipped the gun around and handed the pistol out into the space I thought she might be. A hand took it.

Inexplicably, the last guy on the boat hadn't started firing at us. Sarah didn't start firing at him. I was confused. "What's going on?" I yelled.

I felt a pair of incredibly strong hands grab me and Frank whispered from inches away, "Be quiet! Men are coming down the path! Martina is finishing off the third guy."

Then Martina yelled out to us, "It's clear! Get to the boat! Hurry!

I couldn't help it, "Hurry? How the hell are we supposed to hurry? A blind guy, a guy with no feet, and a woman four inches shy of six feet to carry us both? For fucks sake, we're going to die here."

Frank was still holding on to me and he said, "Roll onto your stomach soldier!" I instantly followed my orders and rolled onto my stomach as my Lieutenant pulled himself onto my back and put his arms around my neck and shoulders. "Get up, Dru and move it! I'm your eyes, you're my feet. Move!"

I pushed up to my feet and struggled to stand up with a human on top of me, but I got it done and Sarah grabbed my hand and pulled me along. "Let's go!" She said.

All attempts at stealth were abandoned and the three of us moved along the pier, Sarah leading, Frank whispering "Move a little to the left" and me walking like a child in the pitch black, blinking furiously, trying to regain my sight.

I bumped into the boat at the end of the pier and turned my body to let Frank off my back. As I did so, Sarah said, "Shit!" And I was shoved violently into the boat, falling on top of Frank, eliciting the second hilarious squawk of the last two minutes right before I heard Sarah fire off three rounds at what I could only assume were the evil fake firemen who had found us.

The boat I was lying in surged forward and sped off into the lake as my vision began to return to me. I looked forward and saw a fuzzy outline of a naked mermaid standing at the helm of the ski boat, legs braced apart, back straight, and hair flying out behind her. Behind us, her house burned to the ground. She was magnificent, and I found myself wishing that she could have been my sister after all.

Over her shoulder she called out to us, "There's a public dock down about five miles. Hopefully we can get there before they figure out that's where we're heading. But we have a big problem."

"What's that?" Frank called out from under me as he extricated himself.

"That first guy I pulled overboard? He was an Hombre el Gato. An ugly guy that looked like a cat standing on its hind legs. They're using Extras in public."

<h1 style="text-align:center">Chapter Twelve</h1>

<h1 style="text-align:center">Why Are You Naked?</h1>

We all tried to digest this piece of news as Martina expertly hauled ass down the lake towards the public dock. Using Extras in the field during military engagements has been going on for hundreds of years, but by and large, anything so obviously different as to be described as a cat on its hind legs was typically...encouraged...to stay the hell out of sight or in disguise if it was going to mix in public.

The willingness to employ them in public - even at night - marked a substantial change in policy for Broadhead. The gloves were off. It seemed that privacy and deniability were now less important than actually taking us off the board. This was a big deal. These rules weren't made by Broadhead, they were made by the fucking world governments that all agreed that humans didn't do too well with the truth and that it was easier to manage things if we didn't have concrete proof that Hombre Gato was real.

For us, it meant that we had enemies that were faster, stronger, and better able to see at night...basically a stacked deck against us now. Great.

We raced down the dark lake using the lights of the houses on the shore and the clear sky as our only aids to navigation. Martina drove with the confidence of someone with long experience on the lake and had us skimming over the lake surface at an exhilarating speed. I swear I caught a small smile on her lips as she turned to Sarah and pointed towards a natural little "bay" in the lake about a mile ahead on the left.

"That's the public ramp!" she yelled over the roar of the huge outboard engine.

"Will anybody be there at this time of night?" I yelled.

"She looked back at me and yelled, "No, why?"

"No reason," I replied with a smile, "It's just that...you know...you're naked."

She threw her head back and laughed loud and long, looking over at me with a smirk and shook her hips a little, and said, "You're welcome!"

Smiling with a fake, yet convincing disapproval, Sarah pointed at Frank and said, "Eyes on me, Mister!"

Frank chuckled dryly and replied, "I'll never have eyes for anything else, darling, don't you worry."

Sarah rolled her eyes, and slapped his shoulder, "Sure baby. Sure."

We were all starting to feel the euphoria of surviving a dangerous encounter and Martina slowed the boat down as we approached the marker buoy about one hundred meters from the public boat ramp. Naturally, that's when we were attacked.

A massive surge of water and a hard slam on Starboard spun the boat around in the water and sent us all sprawling to the deck and smashing into each other, the seats, and everything else that was in the boat. I was on the port side, so I fell across the boat and slammed into a seat that caught me right in the ribs and knocked the wind out of me.

Frank had already been positioned on the floor of the boat so he simply got bounced around a little bit, but Sarah had been standing in front of him forward of the seats and fell back over him and banged her head on the outboard mounts cutting her head and sending blood splashing out all over the place. She wasn't moving, and I was pretty sure she had gotten knocked out.

Martina went right over the side into the lake. I don't know if she was knocked, dove on purpose, or if it was a combination of the two, but she entered the water neatly and disappeared under the surface on the starboard side of the boat.

I sat up groaning and trying to suck in some air and levered myself into the seat I had fallen on.

Frank reached over and grabbed his bleeding wife, "Sarah! Baby, are you ok?" He pulled her unconscious body onto his lap and began inspecting the wound.

"Is she okay?" I asked.

"Scalp wound bleeding pretty bad, but not life-threatening. I need bandages or something."

As he finished speaking, the boat was hit again from underneath and we surged upwards before dropping back into the water with a loud slap and bang as the hull slammed back onto the surface of the lake. The boat had taken some major damage to the hull and I had been lifted right off the seat and slammed back down grabbing at anything to keep me from falling onto Frank and Sarah.

"What the fuck is that?" Frank yelled.

At that moment, Martina shot completely out of the water from the port side and gracefully landed in the boat saying "Shitshitshitshit. There's a Godsdamned horned serpent in the lake!"

"A what?"

"That!" she said pointing to a glowing light rising out of the water about twelve feet to starboard. That glowing light resolved itself into an actual serpent with horns like a ram growing out of its head and a bright jewel revealed as the source of the glow, placed right in between the horns. That head was about three times the size of a humans, and it's body seemed to be about two feet thick at the base of its skull. And it didn't look happy to see us.

Stretching up out of the water about five feet, we could clearly see it was covered with shiny, almost translucent scales that looked more crystalline than anything. Its eyes were hooded and had that snake-like emptiness in them that conveyed a feeling of a big animal looking for prey rather than a thinking, sentient creature looking for us specifically. Not that it meant we'd be any less dead soon.

Bizarrely, Martina said, "Oh, thank the Gods." right before it struck the boat again. Like a ram, it lowered its head and slammed its horns into the boat. This time from out of the water and crashing downward into the front of the boat.

That was it for all of us. The boat pitched forward onto its bow and threw each of us out into the water. Martina turned her flight into a dive, but Frank flew out with an iron grip on his unconscious wife and I, unburdened with anything other than myself, flew twice as far and landed in the water with a slap and an undignified belly flop.

As I came up sputtering and spitting out lake water, I saw the serpent find Frank and Sarah in the water and begin swimming towards them. I began to panic. I'm a decent swimmer, but there's no way I'm faster than a *sea serpent.* I kicked my shoes off and pulled my shirt over my head, before admitting to myself that there was no way I was going to get to Frank and Sarah before the monster got there. But I couldn't let them die. I couldn't let the only people who gave a shit about me get eaten by a stupid water snake, so I only had one option.

I swallowed hard, I began splashing and screaming, "Hey! Sea Serpent! Hey Big Ugly! Look at me you son of a bitch! Look! I'm thrashing around and all alone! Helpless victim right here! I'm swimming right at you, you stupid snake! Look!"

The creature heard me and turned towards the disturbance I was making, but my heart broke as the thing ignored my waving shirt and thrashing around, and continued on towards Frank and Sarah. To add insult to injury, the damn thing smashed me with its tail and damn near broke me in half. I went underwater a few feet while exhaling every bit of air in my lungs and thrashed back to the surface in time to take a huge involuntary gulp of half lake water and half air. Choking and retching, I looked towards my doomed friends with despair.

I screamed, "Frank!" and we made eye contact. I could see the resigned look on his face. He knew what was coming for him, and he knew there wasn't a damn thing he could do while also trying to hold his unconscious wife above water.

Martina picked that moment to make her appearance. Rising up out of the water like a mythological hero of old, she had a huge stone from the bottom of the lake in her hand, and she reared up, smashing the stone down hard onto the jewel right between the horns of the nasty beast.

Three things happened in a most anticlimactic way: the rock fucking broke over the serpent's head, a resoundingly dull yet comical 'THUMP' like a hammer on a log echoed out from the impact, and the glowing crystal dulled as the sea serpent literally crossed it eyes and dropped, flopping onto the surface of the lake.

We all stared at the unconscious serpent until Martina screamed, "What the hell is wrong with you all? Start swimming to shore! It'll wake up any second!"

"Martina," I yelled back "grab Sarah and tow her to shore! I'll get Frank."

"No, stupid, you get Sarah. I'm the stronger swimmer, I'll get Frank!"

Oh yeah. Mermaid. Right. Stupid, Dru. I swam my ass off to Frank and Sarah. Martina was already there and had Sarah in the cross-chest lifeguard carry, waiting to hand her off to me while Frank trod water with his arms. I grabbed Sarah and Martina grabbed Frank and we started swimming to the pier about eighty meters away.

About halfway there, we heard a thrashing in the water and saw the serpent slowly start to move and swirl around in the water. Shit. We were not close enough to shore. Despite hauling the much heavier Frank, Martina was far ahead of me, but she saw it too. Without comment, she released Frank to float on his own and swam faster, effortlessly, than any Olympic swimmer you've ever seen, and raced out past me yelling, "Get them to shore. I'll draw it off."

"Don't die!" I yelled back and redoubled my own pathetic efforts.

"Not today, brother! This is *my* home," she replied and swam straight at the monster snake in Lake L.B.J.

The horned serpent came fully to its senses in time for Martina to swim right up to its face and - I really, honestly, sincerely swear I'm not making this up - slap it right across the mouth.

It reared back in what had to be the horned serpent version of dignified outrage that this tiny Iara would dare do something so outrageous and lifted a full twenty feet of its incredible body out of the water before smashing its head straight down at Martina, who dove underwater an instant before that massive head hit the water and chased after her.

I turned towards shore and swam as fast as I could towing an unconscious body. Frank had never stopped swimming for dry land and was able to beat me by about thirty seconds to the shore where I caught up to him as I pulled his wife onto the paved parking lot where the boat trailers parked during the day while the public used their boats out on the lake.

Frank had been dragging himself up the ramp and I could see his wound on his left stump had re-opened a bit as there was blood on his soaked bandages that had somehow stayed on his calf through all of this.

"Martina will get away from that thing, right?" I asked.

Frank replied, "Dru, she's fast, but I can't imagine she's faster than a water serpent that's fifty feet long."

"Can she beat that thing in a fight, do you think?'

"Without a limpet mine? I doubt it."

We sat in silence for a minute and saw nothing disturb the surface of the lake. I felt a deep sadness and loss for a woman I had barely met. That blue painted face appeared in my head, looking at me with sympathy.

Frank pulled himself together first and said, "We need to get out of the open like this. There's a good chance somebody will come this way looking for us. Plus I need medical gear. Sarah will need some butterfly stitches and a bandage on this scalp cut at a bare minimum."

I sat, looking out at the water. My LT said, "Soldier? I need you on point right now."

Resigned to the loss, I turned to him and bent down to grab Sarah saying, "Let me move her into that area over there by the bushes behind you."

He looked over to the left side of the parking lot where there were some low-lying shrubs and a few scrub oak trees growing right up to the pavement. He nodded his assent as I picked her up gently and moved her over there. When I turned around, Frank was scooting himself over the ground by the simple expedient of lifting his ass off the ground with his arms and pushing backward, dragging his left leg and right thigh on the ground as he went.

I ran over and stood above him with my hands on my hips and forced myself to smile, saying, "You look like you could use a lift, sailor. Headed my way?"

He looked up at me and nodded his recognition that I was trying to keep my mind off our missing Iara, "Get me over to my wife."

"Anything for a friend." I grabbed him under his arms and lifted him onto and over my shoulder and staggered upright. I carried him over to the bushes and trees and was setting him down when we heard a small series of splashes by the boat ramp. I spun with hope rising in my chest, and Martina came walking up out of the water via the concrete steps, looking bedraggled and exhausted, carrying a large bundle or bag I couldn't make out in the dark.

As she got closer, she shuffled into the light made by the single lamp in the parking lot and held up the large med kit bag we had snuck out of the house with us, saying "Is there anything in this bag other than medical supplies? I need a Godsdamned drink."

I felt a release of physical tension I hadn't admitted was there as I ran over asking, "How the hell did you get that!" She shrugged like it was no big deal.

I brought it over to Frank and he dove in without anything other than a terse "Thank you." to Martina and I.

Martina was a little manic, a common reaction to the high adrenaline night she was going through. She explained, "I couldn't outrace that son of a bitch, so I had to stay close to it and we played quite a game of tag. Damn, that thing is fast! I got him all twisted up and dove deep where we stirred up the mud and took visibility down to zero."

Pacing back and forth she continued, "The offspring of Uktena are visual hunters and, in case you don't know, they don't normally live this far south. I don't think this was an accident that we ran into it," she said with a wide smile on her face that was totally out of place with the moment.

I laughed grimly. "No, I don't suppose it was."

Still practically vibrating with suppressed energy, she went on. "Then I shot back up into the boat and rested for a few seconds waiting to see what it would do. I think I hurt it enough when I smashed that rock on its head, that it forgot what it was supposed to be doing and swam off after I got away!"

"So, I guess the big question," I said, "is what the hell is an Uk...Uk..."

"Uktena?"

"Yeah. That."

"Oh, mijo." She walked up to me and put both hands on my shoulders looking me in the eye. "Uktena would have been the death of us. She is a magical and sacred horned serpent that lives in a lake in Georgia. Damn near invincible, smarter than most humans, and the Ulun'suti - the gem on its forehead - is hypnotic. Had we all been staring at the real thing, we would have sat still in that boat until Uktena swam up, killed us with its poison breath, and eaten us."

"So what we faced..."

"Was one of Uktena's offspring. Much dumber, not nearly so powerful. But big. Basically a beast rather than a sentient enemy. Most importantly, its Ulun'suti is nothing but a housing for it's life magic. No hypnotism...thank the Gods."

"Martina," I asked, "for years it was my job to hunt down and kill things like Uktena. How come I never heard of her?"

From back in the bushes, Frank called out softly, "Because Uktena made a treaty with the US Government to stop killing white people in 1836. Uktena is smart, Dru. She speaks the Cherokee and French languages, she plans, and she could see what was happening as America expanded. Also, she's nasty, and she hated the Cherokee people, who often used her and her offspring as a target in quests for their young, would-be heroes. Under the terms of the treaty, She stopped hunting humans, well, white humans at least, and agreed to work with the US government if we asked it of her. In return, we removed the Cherokee people for her. Of course, we were always going to do that anyway."

I sat there quiet for a moment, thinking. "Yeah. The Trail of Tears started in 1837, didn't it?"

Frank looked at me. "Yes, it did. I was there."

Martina interrupted us to ask, "Does somebody want to tell me how Broadhead was able to get a horned serpent, transport it all the way to Lake LBJ, let it loose to go after us, and...oh yeah, train it to attack us?"

We all stared at each other, which was becoming a habit we needed to break.

"No?" She said, looking at us both. Exasperated, she threw her hands in the air and sat down next to Frank and a now bandaged Sarah, saying, "Alright."

Frank spoke up as he began attending to his bleeding ankle, "Honestly, we have bigger problems right now."

His voice was steady as he worked, but I could tell he was struggling to remain calm while tending to the spot on his left leg that had, until a few days ago, had his left foot attached to it. I could see him working through the process of cataloging all the ways he was cooked now that he had lost his left foot and most of his right leg.

"We'll get through this, Frank," I said

His head snapped up and he glared at me, "Will we, Dru? I'm a fucking invalid, Sarah is unconscious with a concussion at the very least, Martina is naked, and you are standing in soaking wet jeans and socks! Thank the Gods at least Sarah had *this* tucked away tight enough that it didn't fall out of her waistband," he said while brandishing my pistol.

With a sense of relief I couldn't attempt to explain, I reached over and took the gun out of his hand and simply held it by my side. Armed and protected. I pulled the mag and counted eleven rounds, plus one in the chamber. A dozen bullets and a wet pair of socks against an international armed security force that had actual monsters fighting on their side. Yay us.

Martina said, "I could use some clothes, honestly."

"Well," I replied, "we can take a chance. I do still have my wallet. We can get to a store, buy some clothes, and maybe steal a car or something."

"It's almost two in the morning. Nothing is open, and we're miles away from anything anyway. Martina, I assume there are some houses along the shoreline this way." Frank indicated by pointing up the road out of the parking lot we were sitting in.

"Yes, there's a few houses along this stretch before we'd get back into a neighborhood proper."

Yeah," Frank continued "It would take hours to walk to a store. It'd be much faster to head back up the shoreline towards those houses, but I don't like the idea of breaking into somebody's house and stealing their shit at gunpoint."

"Well, there's a chance..." Martina started before trailing off.

"A chance what?" Frank asked.

"Well, there's a house not far from here, maybe a mile, mile and a half, that's a vacation rental. The owners live in it during the winter and head out to Colorado in the summers. It's possible it could be empty right now. They don't usually get back until late October."

"But how will that help us?" I asked "We need clothes, money, and a car. Would a vacation rental have that?"

"They almost certainly have clothes locked away somewhere separate from the rooms they rent. This is a high-end rental. The owners probably have their personal belongings locked up downstairs or in the attic or something. I doubt there's a car or money, but it's a place to hole up, get some clothes, grab some sleep, and call an Uber or a taxi in the morning. Sarah is hurt pretty bad and Frank is right, we are all a hot mess right now."

We were interrupted by the welcome sound of Sarah moaning and trying to move around next to Frank. He reached out and put his hand on her shoulder gently while he leaned over to her and quietly said, "It's okay baby, we're right here. Relax and don't move. You took a nasty shot to the head."

"Wha-what happened?" She slurred thickly as she started to come to.

"You got cut and we had to bandage you up. You were unconscious for a bit."

Her eyes fluttered open and she stared around at us standing there in the parking lot with a vacant look until she seemed to realize what she was seeing and she frowned, "What on earth happened?"

I couldn't resist, I counted on my fingers as I said, "House fire, cat men with guns, Horned Serpent, midnight swim. You know - the usual."

She got this confused look on her face and glanced over to Frank and I immediately felt ashamed for putting my foot in it again. "Sorry, Sarah. It's been a night."

"So it would seem," she replied, reaching up to her head and wincing when she made contact with her bandage. She looked at us all again, her eyes locking on Martina last.

"Martina? Sweetie?"

"Yes, Mija?"

"Why are you naked?"

We all waited around as Sarah came back to some semblance of conscious and capable and took that time to fill her in on all she missed while she was out of it. She didn't remember any of it, and even had trouble remembering leaving the house. A bad sign that spelled a serious concussion.

Eventually, she was able to stand up with mine and Martina's arms under hers. A few minutes after that, she was able to walk on her own and we could see her strength returning by the minute.

As we prepared to take the long walk to the vacation house, we were suddenly presented with a pair of headlights slowly winding down the road towards the parking lot.

In a calm voice, Martina said, "Nobody comes down here at this hour. That is going to be Broadhead."

Frank was still sitting at the base of the oak tree and called out, "Honey, get over here and take cover with me in these bushes and tree."

He looked around at the parking lot. It was a simple affair. Essentially, it was a road that went straight to the right of the concrete boat ramp, took a long, gentle U-Turn to the left so that trucks could align their trailers with the ramp which sat right in the middle of that "U", back up to put the boats in the water, pull around completing the "U" and then pulling into large parking spots designed specifically for trucks with trailers that sat in the middle of the pavement.

However, there was one odd little aspect to this boat ramp parking lot; there was a deep ditch that acted as a rain culvert and drain that was in the middle of the parking spaces and was unpaved.

Frank looked at me and said, "See how deep that culvert is and get in it if it offers coverage, Dru."

I ran over to it and saw that it had lots of scrub brush in it and was about five feet deep. I jumped in and lay down completely out of sight, gun in hand.

Martina ran to a large scrub brush right next to the pier by the ramp and hid behind it.

The car came down barely crawling along at a walking pace. It was another black SUV. As it came alongside me I popped up to shoot the driver but slipped in my fucking wet socks as I stood and I went down like a sack of potatoes. This driver was good. With cat-like reflexes, he slammed his foot on the gas and shot forward like a rocket.

Getting to my knees, I swung the pistol forward and fired two shots through the driver's window, but the angle was bad. I winged him twice and was trying to climb out to get a better angle on him when Martina jumped out from behind the bush in all her naked glory, throwing a fist-sized rock she had picked up off the ground and hitting the windshield square in the middle causing a spider web of shattered safety glass to spiral out from the impact point.

And the driver - the fucking stupid driver - kept his foot down and drove straight past Martina, down to the boat ramp, and tried too late to turn away from the lake. He didn't make it, and he shot off the edge of the boat ramp, down the concrete steps Martina had walked up not five minutes ago, and into the fucking lake.

I yelled, "No!" as the SUV settled into the lake. The door pushed sluggishly open and the driver - another Hombre El Gato (which explained the great reflexes and made my thought about "cat-like" pretty funny) staggered out holding his wounded shoulder. I furiously put one more round into his head and ran down to the SUV, but it was too late, it was filling with water and going under.

Nobody else got out of the vehicle, so I assumed he was alone. That was good because we now had nine rounds left in the gun, and we still had to walk to the house. Martina laughed and said, "You should have seen his face as he drove by me! He looked like he had never seen a naked Iara before!"

I was not happy. "Godsdamnit! Can one fucking thing go right tonight?" I yelled to the sky, stomping on the ground and turning around in a circle.

Martina kept the smile on her face, but asked, "What's wrong?"

From the tree line, I heard Frank call out to me, "It's alright Dru. Come over here and let's get organized. We've got to get going right now."

"Easy for you to say," I grumbled "You won't be carrying me on your back for a mile and a half. With no shoes."

Martina, still smiling threw in, "Uphill both ways in the snow, Dru?"

That drew a smile from Sarah, and she muttered, "Back in my day..."

I looked to Frank for help and he grudgingly smiled and held out his arms. I hoisted Frank onto my back and said, "You all laugh it up, but it sure would have been nice to have a car again."

"No point in wishing on what might have been, soldier. Let's get moving," he said over my shoulder. He was right, but shit, there was a car in the Godsdamned lake.

We four started up the road looking like refugees in any war you choose to name. It took damn near an hour to go barely one mile, because I had to put Frank down when he got too heavy for me. A few times I stepped on a sharp rock and almost fell over with Frank on my back, each time letting a little curse out and trying to fall in a "controlled crash" to the ground.

Jokes or not, this sucked.

Chapter Thirteen

B&E

Eventually, we rounded a bend on the road to find a curved driveway on our left curling around to a nice two-story house situated right on the lake. The house was indeed empty, and there was no alarm system on the door or windows. So, for once, one fucking thing went right.

We went in the back door, and in short order had searched the house top to bottom, finding clothes in an upstairs room locked and labeled "off limits". Obviously, none of it fit perfectly, but it fit close enough that it looked like Martina had once been three inches taller, while the shirt and sweater we found for me looked like it belonged to guy about ten pounds heavier than me. Downstairs was a washer and dryer. Jackpot.

Unfortunately, there were no shoes that fit us, but there were several pairs of sandals and flip-flops that fit well enough, so armed with the knowledge that we'd be able to be seen in public tomorrow, we all were ready to crash out in real beds and sleep until the sun was well up the next morning.

I said, "I'll sit up from four to seven am, then wake up Frank, and get him settled into a chair, and we'll take watch."

Sarah disagreed with me, and shaking her head, replied, "No. I have a mild concussion. I need to stay awake anyway, and you and Frank need to be clear headed. Give me the gun and get some sleep."

There wasn't any reason to argue with her as she was right, so I crashed down into a bed and was asleep almost before my head hit the pillow. Even my nightmares were muted, distant things.

The next morning, we looked for a phone to no avail and the house was empty of food. Thankfully, there was a coffee maker. It was one of those abominations that took small plastic cups of coffee grounds and turned them into weak, coffee-like hot water, but they had a box full of plastic cups of espresso roast, and I used three of them on the smallest serving size they offered to make a decent cup of black nirvana.

I stood there in front of the coffee machine and slowly sipped the one true nectar of the Gods; black coffee.

Martina came wandering into the kitchen and eyed my coffee with avarice. I grunted (the closest thing to speech I was likely to use before this coffee was down my throat), grabbed a cup out of the cabinet for her, and moved down the counter to give her access to the abomination machine.

She walked by grabbing the cup out of my hands and grunted a thanks. It didn't sound like a thanks, but us late risers speak a language all of our own. I watched as she grabbed two plastic, environment killers full of coffee grounds, and used them to make one cup of coffee. Great minds and all that, I smiled at her in recognition of kindred souls and tipped my cup to her in salute.

We moved into the living room and sat in silence drinking our wake-up juice for a few minutes and Sarah came walking out of the downstairs bedroom in her now washed and dried clothes and somehow looking wide awake and ready for the world. I narrowed my eyes in suspicion.

She noticed my look and asked, "What's wrong?"

"I don't trust people who stay up all night and are wide awake. It's not natural." I mumbled around my mug.

She smiled sadly, looking at the two of us on the couch, and said, "Frank actually woke up a few hours ago and took over for me. He was in too much pain to sleep. I know it was a bad idea, but I got about three hours of sleep. Plus, I'm a morning person, How on earth are you not? Weren't you in the military for like, five years?"

"Lot more than five," I corrected her. "Seven years in the Squad before the...discharge. And only coffee made it possible."

"That could not have been fun," she replied.

She grabbed a mug of her own and made a cup of hot brown water using only a single pod of grounds and the "large" setting on the coffee maker. Strike two this morning for Sarah as far as I was concerned. I could tell by Martina's frown she agreed with me.

Sarah took the mug of not coffee with her back into the bedroom and I could hear her talking to Frank, but not make out the words. Then I heard Frank's voice loud and clear, "Jesus Christ, is this supposed to be coffee?" Martina and I both smiled at each other while we heard Sarah's laugh followed by more words we couldn't make out.

I had finished and was thinking about another when Sarah called out to us from the bedroom, "Dru, can you come in here and help me with Frank?"

Martina and I both got up and walked into the bedroom where Frank and Sarah had spent the night. It was a guest room with a queen size bed and probably intended for a single occupant, but the master bedroom was upstairs and we had decided last night that it would be easier to leave Frank on the ground floor.

Frank was trying to get dressed in a new T-shirt, compliments of the owners of the house, and we had found a pair of sweatpants last night that fit him well enough to slide on over his injuries and easily fold over and tuck up the leg to his right thigh and the elastic kept the left leg above his ankle. He had done an admirable job but sat looking forlorn and lost on the edge of the bed.

Looking at the four of us, I felt a deep sense of despair. Frank was right when he said last night that we we in trouble. As a group, we were already beaten. Frank was an absolute liability and needed real medical attention and a new wheelchair. After he healed, I had no doubt he'd be able to fit a prosthetic and move about with crutches, but right now he was...defeated.

Sarah seemed much better today, but she still had a small concussion and a big bandage on her forehead. Martina seemed fine, but she was moving around the house with a stiffness that belied that appearance. My shoulder still hurt from where that splinter of wood pierced it a few days ago in the firefight at Sarah's house (God, that seemed so long ago!) but I was probably in the best shape of any of them.

I decided to fall back on my military training and engage in the long-standing tradition of military decision making since the dawn of the modern military. I decided to pass the buck up the line. "So. What's the plan, Lieutenant Egils?"

Not fooled for a second, Frank looked up at me and smiled, "What's next is you get to work, soldier. We need intel. Go walk to Martina's house down the street and stay out of sight. Find out how many people are watching, what condition the house is in, and gather any facts you can. Do not get spotted, are you clear on that? No fighting, recon only."

Martina spoke up from the doorjamb she was leaning against, "I should go with him. If we have the opportunity, we might be able to slip in and grab some stuff we left behind."

He shook his head, "Do not try to get into that house. You're going to have nosey neighbors, possibly real firefighters and police, and an operative or two looking specifically for you both. Observe only and get back here. We'll decide what to do after that."

"Yes, sir," I replied.

"But first," he continued, "pick my ass up and set me on the couch. I'm sick of beds." His face had contorted into a grimace of both physical and emotional pain. Soldiers don't admit weakness very well. That request for a lift took a big bite out of his pride.

After silently getting Frank situated on the couch in the living room like he had asked, Martina and I went back upstairs and went through the room with clothes, each of us grabbing a pair of sandals that fit well enough to not hinder our walking. We also found a large sun hat that fit Martina perfectly and a worn-out baseball cap that had a patch of a hooked bass fighting the line on it.

"This is good," I said, "because you absolutely know we're going to run into those Broadhead bastards on stakeout."

Martina smirked and answered, "A hat? That's the great disguise? What a master spy you are."

"You can do better?" I retorted.

"Yeah. Don't be seen." As we left the house, Martina said, "Follow me, brother."

After we got outside, I said to her, "You've called me brother twice now."

I could feel her tense up beside me and after a breath or two she replied, "Yeah?"

"Why?"

"Because Sarah is my sister, and she called you family."

"Sarah is your sister," I repeated.

"In every way that matters, you'd better believe it. She is my sister, and blood has nothing to do with it. You don't get to choose the people who bring you into the world, but you can choose your family. Frank and Sarah are my family. And so are you."

I walked about half a mile in silence before I said, "I don't think you all know me well enough to take that risk. I'm not your family. I almost wish I was, but I'm not. I'd like to be your friend, Martina, but I don't think any of us are really able to be family. I want to trust you. You remind me of...you remind me of a old friend, but that makes me even more nervous.

I'm not well, mentally. I don't want to confuse you with her. I'm not really your family."

"Yet." I said in my mind. I wanted so badly to say "Yet" out loud, but I couldn't get the word past my lips.

I was ready for Martina to be angry at me for rejecting her incredibly precious offer of belonging, but instead, she once again read me perfectly and let me off the hook. "Good."

Surprised and a little saddened, I echoed her, "Good?"

"Good. You're way too hot to be my brother."

"Ha! Well, I'm damn sure not going to be your Daddy!"

She threw back her head and laughed deeply. "Wildly inappropriate jokes."

"Flirting," I replied.

Martina's master spy-craft of "don't be seen" was comprised of taking a long way around by going down a side street that connected to a road parallel to the street her house was on, and strolling down the street together for about a mile.

The roads and neighborhood were not overdeveloped and there was a lot of scrub brush and Cedar trees growing in wide open plots of land. It wasn't a town, so I was concerned that we would stand out as a couple walking alone, but I needn't have worried. Everybody had been up all night watching a house burn down. They weren't very observant. Because it wasn't built up, we could see past the occasional tree or house and catch a lot of what was going on.

We were walking down the street when Martina pulled up and turned to me. "If we cut through this open lot, we'll come out on my street about three houses away from mine, but do we need to? I can see it from here and...I mean look at my house!" She cried. "All my stuff is gone."

Suddenly she sucked in a small breath, "My necklace from Mama. My brother's watch..."

"I'm sorry."

We could see clearly that there were three police cars on the scene, but that the firefighters had gone home some time ago. Her house was ruined. The roof had collapsed inward, and the front walls were nothing more than a skeleton of burned framing barely standing up. The firefighters (the real ones) had torn great holes in the walls and done their best to get it under control, but this was arson, plain and simple, and we watched arson investigators from the fire department still walking around and poking through the wreckage.

I put my arm around Martina in a sort of side hug as we stared at the carnage and said, "I'm so sorry for this. I know that doesn't make it better, but still, I'm sorry."

She sniffed a little bit and wiped the incipient tears away from her face before she got into a real cry, and asked, "What do we do now?"

"We look around carefully. Try to spot the Enemy. Assess the house from a few different angles in possible, and look to see if this situation has been turned over to the "normal" authorities."

"Alright. What first? Find the Assholes on stakeout?"

"Definitely," I replied. "We need to know where they are so we can avoid them."

What happened next was a frustrating forty-five minutes of wandering around looking for people hanging out in the wrong place, sitting in cars, or otherwise being suspicious. We found nothing. No SUV's. No odd observers on corners. No people looking at people instead of the burned-down house. Not a damn thing.

Nothing except the entire damn neighborhood out gossiping and staring at her house. It's was like a damn town fair out here. People wandering around, meeting up with friends, and telling each other the same things over and over again.

Eventually, I had to admit it, "I'm either not good enough to find these guys, or they're not here. I'm leaning towards not here."

"Why?"

"Honestly? If they were here, they probably would have seen us skulking about by now, especially if they are better at this than we are, which they'd have to be to avoid us so far. And if they had seen us, we'd be either running for our lives or dead."

"You think they left? Why?"

"If I had to guess, I'd say because your neighbors are nosey as hell. The entire neighborhood is out gawking and there's a huge police presence here. I'd bet they decided to get scarce rather than risk a neighbor or a police officer asking what they were doing in the neighborhood."

"Yeah, I did notice that. I'm glad I don't know any of these people. The whole point of my house was to lay low, so I never tried to meet the neighbors or make friends."

"I guess Extras are pretty good at that."

"Yeah, and we don't like that word, Dru."

"What? Extras?"

"Yeah. I'm an Iara. You're a human. Frank is a Jötunn."

"Wait. Bullshit. Frank is a Norse demi-god? I mean, we never ask each other what we are in the squad, but everyone tells eventually. Frank called himself a Homo Superior."

"Idiot." she laughed. "While I love that phrase, All of us, *Extras*," she spat the word, "are classed as Homo Diversus by the powers that be. But Jötunns are tall human beings of long life and great strength. Don't let bad history fool you, they're not giants, they're not blue, and they're not Gods. They're just better than you at everything." she finished with a cute smirk. "Do you know why they were considered the enemies of the Norse Gods? Because they were *humans* who could kickass and take names. The Gods couldn't stand the idea of it! So the Norse Gods decided they must be semi-divine. And I guess being over six feet tall in an era when everyone else was five feet and a few inches made them seem like giants."

"Truth is, they're an evolutionary step up for humans. Genetically speaking, I mean. Frank could try to have a child with Sarah if he wanted to, but there's a fifty percent chance the child will be stillborn, and about a thirty percent chance it'd be born with massive birth defects. Unfortunately, their genetic makeup also leads to lots of trouble procreating. It's absolutely tragic. If they get super lucky, it'll be a Jötunn and have to murder innocents for two decades every hundred years." she ended bitterly.

"So Frank is nothing but a superhuman?"

"Yes, not that the world admits it, but the science seems clear. A Jötunn is a human mutant, not a separate species like me. Homo Sapien...but superior..." she laughed again; this time edged with bitterness.

I was silent for a few steps along the road as we walked together. "Alright. I'm sorry. I'll try to remember to drop the term. I've used it a long time, though, so please forgive me if I slip up."

"Sure thing, Papi Chulo."

"I looked over at her from the side of my eye. "Do I want to translate that on the internet?"

She giggled a bit and said, "Probably not, we don't say it in Argentina, but it's pretty popular here in the south. And you're not my brother, soo..."

"Yeah, I think I'll pretend I didn't hear you, Ms. Homo Diversus."

We decided to walk up and down the street Martina's house used to stand off of and try to get good looks at it like all the other people wandering around gawking at it. We looked the same as everybody else, and the police didn't so much as glance at us.

Without warning, Martina grabbed my arm hard and said, "Oh shit!"

Tensing up and reflexively reaching for the gun I had tucked in my waistband holster, I quickly asked, "What? What is it?" while looking around for the threat.

"The boat house!" She said.

Confused, I replied, "What about it?"

"Dru. My clothes are there, remember? I took them off and tossed them into my ski-boat to keep them out of the way and hidden!"

Slowly straightening up and feeling a mite foolish, I said, "Umm...yeah?"

Exasperated, she threw her hands up in the air and grabbed my head, looking into my eyes, "Dru. Clothes. Wallet. Phone!"

Comprehension dawned and I understood. A phone and more money. Huge game changer. Getting excited myself, I said, "Can you get to it and sneak it out past these guys?"

"Depends entirely on if they are watching the boat house, but why would they? There's nothing there for them to see, and it's far enough away from the house that there shouldn't be any fire damage or anything. I'm sure they inspected it and looked it over, but why would they still be there?"

"Okay," I said, "I think you are probably right, but how do we get there without these police spotting us? We can't stroll on by and down the path to the boat house.

She rolled her eyes, "Oh, I think I've got this covered. Come with me." and Martina grabbed my hand and walked me down the street about one hundred yards to a lot that had a new house under construction on it. "Now keep an eye out for me, Dru. I'm going to go around this house and down to the lake, I'll swim up to my ski boat and grab the clothes.

"It's pretty risky to stay above the water, don't you think? But you'll have to if you don't want to ruin the phone."

Martina looked at me with that smirk I was coming to realize was her primary facial expression, and said, "So pretty. Not too smart though." And then patted me on the head like I was a favorite puppy.

I looked at her, still lost, and said, "Beg your pardon?"

"Dru, think. I. Am. An. Iara. I live underwater more than above. My phone is in a watertight case, you adorable idiot."

"Ahh. Right. Then your wallet..."

"Waterproof too. Yes."

"Makes sense."

She was laughing now, "Yes it does. I didn't strip down last night to save my phone. I stripped down to swim faster."

We went around the construction to the water's edge and Martina ducked behind a stack of lumber and plywood to strip out of her clothes. Straightening up, she turned to me and said, "Look around and tell me if there's anyone in sight."

I looked out and didn't see anyone. "Go!"

She sprinted to the shore about twenty feet away from the lumber pile and dove a shallow dive into the lake and I saw her form disappear as she went down deeper, swimming insanely fast towards her boat house.

I made myself comfortable and sat so that I was pretty much out of sight from the road, but could still see the lake, and waited.

I didn't wait long as about five minutes later, Martina's head popped up about three feet from the shore and stage whispered, "Is it clear?"

I chuckled a bit and said, "All clear. Get your ass up here and get dressed."

As she was getting dressed, she looked over at me and cleared her throat. I looked back and raised my eyebrow at her by way of response.

"Dru, can I ask you a personal question?'

"Sure."

"Are you gay?"

Well, I was definitely not expecting that and I guess it must have showed because she quickly went on, "I don't mean anything, I'm only curious because...well...you've seen me naked a whole lot in the last twenty-four hours, and...nothing...nada."

I smiled at her to let her know I was fine with the question. "No, I'm not gay, but in my past I have had experiences with both men and women."

"Oh! You're Bi like me?"

Lightly, I said, "Nope. I'm what you hip kids call Asexual."

I grew grim and said, "Pretty much all sexual activity I've experienced in my life is not something I want to talk about." I paused for a second, deliberately not remembering the nightmare that was my youth. "I tried. I did. But my relationship with sex was extremely unhealthy. Hell, I had a wife, once," A flash of a blue painted face with a smirk exactly like Martina's crossed my thoughts. "I am capable of performing the act. But I'm not interested in having a sexual partner. At all. In truth, I never was."

"Oh Dru. You and I. We've *got* to talk about this more one day. If you're willing, that is?" she finished that last statement as a question and looked at me to gauge my response.

I swallowed and composed my face to keep my expressions neutral. "I'm not real interested in discussing my past Martina. It's a long way back, and it doesn't do any good to rehash it all." Then I smiled, "But if you're curious about why I'm not trying to have sex with a smoking hot Iara...sure. We can talk later."

She winked at me. "You think I'm hot?"

"Smokin'."

She smiled a huge grin as she pulled her shoes on and playfully said, "I think I love you, Dru."

"You'll get over it."

"Ha!"

It's hard to explain, but after that brief conversation with Martina, I was feeling good. A kind of positive feeling, like things were going to get better for the four of us. Getting that phone and her wallet was a big reason for that feeling too, but if I'm being honest, it was mainly this growing feeling that maybe I had three friends now, and that maybe they were real.

We walked back down to the rental we had broken into the night before and went around back to come inside. Sarah and Frank were in the living room sitting quietly and holding hands. It looked like Sarah had been crying a bit, and maybe Frank too. However, they seemed to have worked through whatever it was and were sitting together in a picture of love that was undeniable.

I know it's cliché, but I was hit with a whirlwind of emotions that punched me in the gut and spread out through my chest as I saw them sitting there doing something so simple yet so profound as holding hands.

I think Martina felt it too, because she paused as she entered the room and crossed her arms over herself in a sort of hug.

Spontaneously, I put my hand on Martina's shoulder and walked with her over to the recliner that was at a right angle to the couch and gestured for her to take it. She reached her hand up and put it over mine in a gesture of thanks and settled herself into the chair. I remained standing but walked over to the floor to ceiling entertainment center that housed the big screen TV and leaned against the side of it.

"Everything go alright, you two?" Sarah asked.

"Smooth as silk, hermana."

"So," Frank said, "go ahead and give me your report, guys."

"It's a good news/bad news situation, Lieutenant," I answered. "The house is a total loss. The police and arson investigation unit were on site, so we couldn't get too close, but there's no point in going back to it. Our guns, supplies, and everything else in the house are lost."

I continued, "The good news is that there was no Broadhead presence we could see. They seemed to have left due to the large crowds of gawkers and the large police presence there. We could walk openly in other places and Martina remembered that her wallet and phone were in the boat house. She was able to go into the boathouse via the lake and get them both." I smiled. "We have a phone and more cash."

Both Frank and Sarah seemed to sit up straighter as an emotional weight was lifted. "Any extra resources are a good thing right now. That's a huge help. But we need to get moving forward. There are some hard decisions to make."

"Not that hard." I interrupted. "Some things are plain as day to see, Frank. You are out. You're done and you need to be in a Godsdamned hospital. Now."

Sarah looked over at him with a look of sad triumph. "See? I told you so, Baby. You can't do this to yourself."

"I'm not letting these motherfuckers get away with this. They cut off my fucking leg!"

Before anyone could answer, I quickly walked over to Frank and knelt down in front of him on one knee so we were eye to eye. "If it was me, and we were in the field, we'd already be headed back to base. The mission as you see it is over. Tell me I'm wrong."

Frank clenched his fists and ground his teeth so hard I could hear them. But he knew I was right and it was killing him. "LT. The mission *as you see it* is over, but we are going to create a new mission, and these sonsabitches are going to die."

He looked at me and said, "You're going to singlehandedly beat Broadhead, soldier?"

"No, I'm not going to beat them singlehandedly, LT., but I am going to kill every single one of them that I can. And I'm not going to do it alone. All four of us are going to be involved, I promise you that. But you're going to do it from a place of safety. You're a REMF now, sir. Get used to it."

He smiled a twisted smile, equal parts sarcasm and self-pity. "Rear Echelon Mother Fucker...I never thought I'd see the day."

In a terribly bad Southern accent, I said, "You've got no legs, Lieutenant."

He looked up sharply, "Did you just mis-quote..."

I cut him off, "No idea what you're talking about. Sir."

He shook his head and sighed ruefully. "Ok, Dru. You and Sarah get your way. We'll figure out how to get me to a hospital that doesn't involve me dead a few hours later when Broadhead shows up to kill me. Any ideas?"

"Oh yes," I said.

"How?"

I turned and looked over to the recliner. "Martina?"

"Yes, Dru?"

"Can I borrow your phone?"

"Why?"

"It'll be faster than Prayer, and I need to talk to a God."

Chapter Fourteen

No Fun at All

The phone rang until it was sent to the Voicemail, which said, "Go fuck yourself. And yes, I mean you. You know who you are." And beeped.

"I don't think so, Sam. You'll call me back and you'll do it now. You owe us, and you want what we're selling, I promise you that. You hear me? You're going to get exactly what you want unless you're too immature to call back. So call back, you baby," and I hung up the phone, handing it to Martina.

Martina smiled and said, "You do know you just made him even angrier, right?"

I grinned at her and said, "Yup."

"And he's a God,"

I grinned wider. "Yup."

Sarah asked, "What do we do while we wait?"

"We won't wait long, but let's clean up a bit and get ready to leave. We should wash up cups, wipe down surfaces we touched, and generally make it hard for anyone to figure out who broke into the house."

We had barely started cleaning the kitchen when Martina's phone rang. She answered and put it on speaker phone before speaking, "Holá, pembéro! We can all hear you!"

"Fuck you, fuck Dru, and fuck this whole thing! You all have ruined so many plans, you stupid fucking...fucks! And you're no fun at all! Don't you get how bad this is? The fucking world is going to end!"

"Sam," I replied, "You are an ass. I don't care about your plans, and I don't find any of this 'fun'. But I agree with one thing."

"What?" He yelled like a petulant child.

"The world is going to end. For Broadhead. We're going to end it, and you're going to help."

"To hell with that, Dru. You don't like me? Fine! Do it all yourself, I've started other plans and have other options."

"I'm sure you have, it's in your nature, Raven."

Silence...

"Godsdamnit Martina!"

"Screw you, pembéro, you stole our car, and you didn't even need it!"

"Why didn't he need it?" I asked.

Over the phone speaker, he warned, "Martina..."

"Because he can fly as a Raven if he wants to."

All sorts of things crystalized in my brain and began to fall into place. There was what can only be called a very, very uncomfortable lull in the conversation as we all stared at Martina. She shrugged and rolled her eyes at us for being so desperately dense.

"I'm not a God! *I'm in tune* with my God. I'm God-touched like Dru."

"In tune with your God?" I asked. "A God that isn't here on earth? How, Trickster? Want to explain it to me?" I was remembering how I had brought up the raven flying over Sarah's house, and how smoothly Sam had led the conversation towards Morrigan, Druids, and crows before handing me a bag of opioids. One hell of a smooth distraction from the truth. "Want to tell me it was a fucking trained crow flying around every time you've shown up in front of me?"

More silence. Then a long sigh. "Shit. No fun at all."

Frank spoke up, "Raven, Sam, Trickster...what the hell do we call you?"

We heard a general mumbling on the other end, "Hell with it, call me Sam. My name is private, and I think I'll keep it to myself for now, but it's way funny to be called Sam."

"Do I want to know why?" I asked.

"Sam means 'God has heard'. That's funny."

"If you say so."

"Maybe one day you'll get it, *Drustan Seta*. But I doubt it."

Frank interrupted, "Sam, we need your infrastructure."

"Infrastructure? Is that a euphemism for something? Has Martina been telling bedtime stories?" We could hear the snide innuendo in his voice through the phone and I didn't like it.

I spoke into the phone, "Sam, we need medical attention for Frank in a safe place that Broadhead can't get to. We need that safe place for us to regroup and plan, we need the godsdamned car back, and we need your tech expertise. Also, shut up about your penis. Nobody gives a fuck, and you are not our friend."

"Oh," he replied as nonchalantly as he could, despite the obvious anger in his tone. "Is that all?"

"No. We need guns."

"Of course you do, little doggy. And what exactly, do I get out of this?"

"You get Broadhead eradicated."

He started laughing hysterically and it took several moments for him to calm down enough to talk over the phone. "Eradicate a worldwide organization. With the four of you. Dru, you still have no idea what is going on."

Angrier now, I spat out, "Okay asshole. You know what I mean. I'll take out the leadership. The company might be worldwide, but their main office is about three hours away in Dallas."

We heard a sigh over the phone, and Sam said, "Look. You all made a mess. It's not completely your fault, because you don't know shit. But things are worse than you can comprehend. Here's my counteroffer: you come into the fold with me and mine temporarily. I explain what's going on, and we make a plan together to save the stupid planet. I'm in charge, though. You work for me, and you don't 'kill ém all' unless I say so."

"Sam..." Frank began.

"Take it or leave it, Frank. You're floundering around with no knowledge of what's coming next. Without me, you'll fail. Shit, without me, you're as good as dead."

We all looked at each other, and I nodded my assent to Frank. Sarah also nodded, and after a brief hesitation, Martina sighed and nodded too.

"Alright, Sam, we'll play along for now, but if I don't like your explanations we'll leave and take our chances. And I think you'll be surprised with how much we do know."

"Why Frank," he replied with a cackle, "don't you trust me?"

"Not even a little."

"Well let me put you at ease. I'm giving you what you want and I'm buying what Dru is 'selling'. Despite your bumbling and smashing everything I've spent years building; you're finally offering what I've been asking for since we met. My ability to plan, your ability to command, and Drustan's ability to kill shit. We might salvage this if you start listening to me."

Sarah jumped in, "Still not at ease, but we've already agreed. Get us to a safe house, Mr. Sam, and get my husband medical attention."

"The private ambulance is already on the way. I sent it as soon as I got your message."

"How the hell did you do that?" I asked.

Smugly he drawled, "You call me and use me for my expertise, yet you doubt my expertise. I tracked your phone's location. It's not like the movies, Dru. If the phone is powered up, I can track it. Plus, I know Frank is injured, remember? I was there when we rescued him. Got your address, and sent an ambulance. The driver is mine and completely trustworthy. Martina knows him."

"You're sending Elijah?" Martina had a smile on her face as she asked.

"Yes, you oversexed mermaid. I'm sending strong, silent, Elijah to you. Like a fairytale. You're welcome."

Martina looked up at us with a big, goofy smile plastered over her face. Huh. Guess we get to meet the crush.

Frank spoke into the phone, "What's the ETA?"

Sam answered, "About twenty-five minutes."

"That soon? Damn, you're good."

"I really do have great timing. Elijah asked to go down as soon as we saw the news on the web about a house fire on Lake LBJ. All I needed was for you to reach out so I could find the address you were hiding at. I called and told him where you were before calling you."

Frank started to wrap it up. "Alright, we'll get organized and cleaned up here while we wait for this Elijah of yours. I feel pretty confident he'll be the only ambulance around, but to be on the safe side, what's he look like?"

"He looks like a human being. A real one, not you soulless white people. Martina knows him well." he chuckled. "He..."

I reached over and ended the call while he was in mid-sentence. "I'm really starting to hate that guy. Martina, what's the story on Elijah?"

"Elijah is one of Raven's three Shaman. He's pretty good to be around and quiet. Smart. We have a history and he's a good man. I trust him as a friend, but he's definitely Raven's man first, so understand he's not on your side. If Raven told him to shoot you, he might ask why, but he'd do it."

"Did he ask to come here for you?"

"Oh yes. He's a warrior, and I'm sometimes his woman."

"Sometimes?"

"It's complicated now that he's basically Raven's enforcer, but once upon a time, I wanted to marry him, and I think he wanted to marry me."

"Not so complicated." I said.

"Dru, I'm an Iara. We have those strong emotions I told you about, and a strong sex drive, and I'm not going to apologize for it. It's not the 1800's. I like sex, and I like sharing intimacy with people I care about. I'm not built to be monogamous. Or celibate. Elijah was fine with that. I don't sleep with people who aren't. I have three relationships that include sex at the moment, and they all know each other well. Elijah and I could have been more, but Raven...well, he chose Raven, and I'm not part of the inner circle. I don't want to be, so I'm an outsider now. I haven't seen Elijah for a few months."

"Hell, Martina, I'm not one to judge. You know my stance on sex. I'm trying to make sure I'm not going to find myself driving down the road with some insecure asshole trying to out macho the new guy sitting next to his girl."

"Not to worry, Elijah is a professional above all. I think you'll like him, actually." She winked over her shoulder as she walked away from me, "And who says you get to sit next to me?"

I smiled and got to work erasing evidence of our existence from the house. Eventually, a shuttle bus-style medical transport pulled into the driveway and stopped by the front door. Martina sprinted outside and jumped off the ground into the arms of an average-sized man with a dark complexion who looked very happy to see her.

"I guess that's Elijah," I said.

Sarah was standing next to me and smiled. "It sure looks like it. She sure seems...happy," she said while glancing at me from the side.

Martina and Elijah went from a happy reunion to making out like a pair of college freshmen in the space of about five seconds. I started laughing and Sarah joined me.

"I heard her talking to you earlier. Strong sex drive indeed."

I started walking towards them, "We should probably stop them before the clothes come off." Sarah followed me and chuckled a little.

As I approached, they broke off from the make-out session and turned to me as Martina disentangled herself from him and he lowered her back to the earth and onto her feet. She grabbed Elijah's hand and turned to Sarah and me.

"Elijah," she said, "This is mi Hermana, Sarah. Her husband is inside and needs help getting out here. This," she said pointing at me, "is my...my very good friend Dru."

"Good friend?" he asked as he put his hand out to greet me.

I sighed as I took his hand in a firm grip. Then he surprised me. No crushing grip, no dominance games, instead he gave me a genuine handshake. I felt the little bit of nervousness that I had been building up dissipate.

"I'm not family material, no matter what these guys want. It's an unfinished conversation. So, yeah. I'm the family's best friend. That's what I can do. That's all she meant."

"I'm confused, but if Martina vouches for you, you're good." He turned to Sarah, saying "I've heard excellent things about you from Martina. Let's get your husband up the wheelchair lift."

The passenger door opened and another guy got out. He was damn near a carbon copy of Elijah, but maybe two inches shorter and ten pounds heavier. He was wearing faded Demin from head to toe with black cowboy boots and a huge, silver belt buckle that definitely started life as an Hors d'oeuvres platter. Martina smiled and ran around to the passenger side yelling, "Mijo! You babysitting your brother again?"

"Of course, my lovely lady! I'm watching him and stealing you. Is today the day you give up on this ugly boy and come back to live with his strong, big brother? Iáxuhke might have some opinions, but at least it will be interesting!"

Judging by the wry twist of Elijah's lips, this guy was indeed his brother, and this joke was an old one.

Martina laughed and said, "We'll have to wait and see. Are you and that wife of yours still fighting over who does the best card tricks?"

Damon sputtered in mock outrage, "Card Tricks? You wound us both, you vicious waterlily. We are Wizards of the highest order. I'll turn you into a newt!"

Martina turned to Sarah and me and pulled the new stranger over to us, "This is Damon, Elijah's brother, and another of Raven's crew. His wife, Iáxuhke, is the third Shaman of Raven's people. And the strongest," she added playfully.

"Too true." He said. He put his arm around Martina and pulled her in tight to whisper in her ear. She laughed and pulled away from him, slapping his shoulder and saying, "Shame on you!"

"It was her idea! You get all three Shaman experiences at once!" He laughed. Then he caught sight of me and his smile slid off his face and all the humor left his expression. I didn't like that, so I turned away and looked over at his brother, Elijah.

Elijah went aboard the big shuttle bus and opened the wheelchair access door at the back. He reached out, grabbed a box attached to a thick cable, and pressed a button. A wheelchair lift slowly unfolded and lowered itself to the ground. Elijah finished by lowering a folded-up wheelchair and jumping out the back onto the lift. As he opened up the chair, I looked him over a little closer.

He was medium. Medium build, medium length hair, medium height. A lot like me. The big differences between us were our eyes, hair, and skin color. Whereas I'm the poster boy for SPF 50 and mixed Celt heritage, Elijah was pure northwest Native American. Bronze skin, Black hair, brown eyes. And he was a damn good-looking dude. I could see why Martina got all worked up about him.

The thing that threw me was that he looked and moved like a special forces soldier. There's a way that men and women trained for the highest levels of combat move. Unlike the movies, special forces soldiers are rarely bodybuilders and giants. They are lithe, average-sized, killing machines. And they move like Apex predators.

Elijah moved like an Apex predator while pushing a wheelchair. Far from concerning me, it made me feel a little bit safer and relaxed. I'm most at home in violent environments and around violent people. I understand them, and we usually live by the same rules, so mistakes and social gaffes are rare. Which is good, because as should be obvious by now, I suck at proper social behavior.

Sarah had run to the front door and was directing Elijah and the chair into the living room, where Frank was still sitting on the couch, and Martina had forgotten that any of us were still alive. She was fussing near Elijah and orbiting around him like a star pulled into a black hole.

It was a little amusing to see the person I knew only as fierce and independent get like this around a guy, but she obviously cared about Elijah a lot. That alone made him okay in my book. It was a little unsettling how fast I had already come to trust Martina's instincts and views considering we'd known each other less than forty-eight hours. But she was so much like...nah, I can't go there yet. Blue face paint and a fierce attitude is as much as I can handle right now. No names.

Damon sidled up to me as Sarah, Martina, and Elijah disappeared into the house and ruined everything. As soon as they were out of sight, he said, "I guess you're the dog?"

I looked over sharply and found him standing tense and ready for a fight, his face stern and his eyes glaring. "Are we going to have a problem?" I answered.

"Not if you start showing some fucking respect and stay in your fucking lane, little doggy."

"That's twice. Say it again and I'll put your dick in the dirt." I replied, stepping back a half pace to make room and provide options. Unlike his brother, Damon didn't signal any apex predator skills, which meant I was going to smash his face in and hurt him pretty fast if he pushed this. "What's the problem, and why do you think you are allowed to talk to me at all?"

"I'm a Shaman for a God, and you're a disrespectful piece of shit." he spat back. "Raven shared your phone conversation with me. Who the hell do you think you are? You think I'm going to let you speak that way, treat my God that way?"

Inside I wilted a bit. Religious zealots are always bad news, but the real problem is that he was right. I'd been verbally sparring with a God and that's a horrible idea. Add into this the entire history of the Indigenous peoples of America and what Europeans did to them, and you've got some seriously righteous anger directed in the wrong direction. Still, I'm not a turn-the-other-cheek guy, and I think I've been clear about my social skills deficit.

"You're picking a fight with the wrong guy. I don't have a problem with you, your culture, or your religion. I have a problem with Sam. It's personal, not general. I don't have a problem with you, Damon, unless you make one." He wasn't listening, though, and I could tell he was working himself up to some pointless gesture.

Again, I said, "What's between Sam and I is personal. He may be your God, but to me, he's a devious, lying asshole, and he started this shit."

"Bitch!" Then Damon hit me. Or at least he tried. He swung his right fist in a huge overhand strike that would have knocked me out cold if it had hit, but as I said, he was no fighter. I saw the punch coming from a mile away and it wasn't hard to cover up and slip it by ducking down and moving forward, which put me in a perfect place to hit him with a left hook as I stood back up.

Which I did.

Which knocked his dick in the dirt. Along with the rest of his body.

A bitch is a dog, and that made three. I may be a piece of shit most of the time, but I keep my promises. Of course, this is when everybody rolled out of the front door and into the driveway. I looked up to see four people staring at me standing over Damon as he was lying in the driveway rolling over to his stomach and trying to stand up with a glazed look in his eyes like some asshole had smashed him with a left hook.

Elijah stepped around the wheelchair and started moving towards me with smooth, gliding steps that appeared deceptively slow while eating up distance.

I put my hands up while standing over Damon. "He started it."

Elijah stopped. Frank tilted his head to the side and stared at me. Both Martina and Sarah sighed in that magical way women can sigh which conveys the incredible depths of disappointment they feel in your bad behavior.

Elijah said, "He started it? With you? Why?"

"I called God bad names and God told on me to his Shaman?"

He sighed and said, "Of course you did. And of course, he did. Back off, or we are going to go."

"Even though you know it was Sam who caused this?"

"Damon is my brother. You will back off. Now."

I looked at Martina and Sarah standing there looking at me with that look. I backed off.

Frank said, "This was a simple misunderstanding, Elijah. It's not serious yet."

"Looks pretty serious to me."

"Nah. If it was serious, your brother would already be dead. Dru does two speeds - misunderstanding, and dead. Load me in the back. Dru and

Sarah will stay there with me, you and your brother up front, Martina can sit anywhere she fits and wants to sit, I guess."

Elijah turned to Frank and gave him a flat stare. "You are not in charge. Raven is in charge, which means right now, I listen to myself, not you. If you want to pretend to be in charge, that's fine with me, so long as your people listen and play nice. Punching my brother is not nice. I came to get Martina and bring you all back to Raven. Get in the ambulance." With that, he went to the front of the truck, picked up Damon, and began dusting him off with brotherly affection and genuine concern.

Sarah and I loaded up Frank onto the back of the wheelchair lift and eventually figured out how to use it. Not a peep or offer of help from Elijah or Damon. Martina seemed upset and uncertain about what to do, but eventually, she got angry at all of us and marched over to Sarah and me to help get Frank onto the shuttle bus.

We eventually figured out how to secure Frank and operate the lift. The bus was laid out like a huge ambulance. It had a space for the wheelchair and a bed with straps, as well as all the gear you'd expect to find in an ambulance: triage equipment, oxygen, a defib, and more. But the layout also had a bench seat against the right side of the van in front of the wheelchair straps that could hold two people, I assume a medic and a patient.

Forward of that were two bench seats typically found in shuttle buses everywhere that could hold two people on the left side of the bus with a single seat beside them on the right side of the bus. I suddenly realized that this entire bus was designed to evac a team after a violent action.

Inside, the converted shuttle bus was amazing. It was a custom job and the interior was both filled with the cutting-edge medical equipment and beautiful artistic touches like real wood trim carved in a Northwest Native motif and varnished over to a high shine. It was gorgeous.

As I stared at the interior, Martina came up to me and grabbed my hand, saying, "Damon did all this woodwork. He's a very gifted artist."

My mouth fell open. The woodwork was stunningly perfect. I have a massive respect for artists who can shape such incredible images out of natural materials like wood, and rock.

In the back of the bus, there was a place to lock in the wheelchair to travel with somebody sitting in it, but after we got in, Elijah came back and pointed to the narrow bed on the left side of the bus, saying, "Do you need the bed?"

"No. No. I...Jesus Christ this bus is incredible." Frank blurted out. Looking around, it was easy to see why we were all so stunned. Everywhere they could fit it, wood trim was fixed to the bus, but every inch was exquisitely carved into designs and animal forms as you would see in the finest examples of Native Northwest art. Imagine gorgeous, mini totem poles and you get the idea.

Elijah smiled and Damon called from the front passenger seat, "Thank you." He didn't turn around or engage with us, but he did seem calmer now than when I hit him. I guess Elijah had talked to him.

Elijah bent down close to Frank and glanced at me saying quietly, "Misunderstanding or dead, huh?"

Frank looked at him square in the eyes and said, "Not really, I made that up to prevent a fight. The Dru I had in my outfit had one speed - dead. I've never seen Dru leave somebody alive before. He's grown a lot since he got out of the squad."

"Not making me feel better."

"So maybe don't poke the bear. Dru is family, whether he accepts it or not."

"I'm right here, fellas." I interrupted. "Look, Elijah, I understand your concern, but you know damn well that this is Sam fucking with me. I get that we might not ever be friends, and I understand that I didn't exactly make a great first impression, but I'm totally capable of behaving like a decent human being.

"Are you a decent human being?"

"Not at all. But I can behave like one." I looked around at the bus again. I knew that Damon and I were never going to get along, but I figured I could try to extend an olive branch or something before we all got out our dicks and started measuring.

"Damon, this woodwork is stunning. I'm impressed."

Staring out the front windshield he answered, "Well that sure makes me feel all warm and fuzzy and oh-so-validated now. White guy likes my little carvings."

Stupidly, and knowing it wouldn't make anything better, I tried one more time, "Yeah Damon, I get it. You don't like me. That's fair. But I'm not kidding, this entire bus is awesome."

"Somebody tell that mutt to stop barking."

I took a step towards the front to feel Elijah's hand on my chest at the same time he yelled, "Damon, shut it!"

Damon shut it, and I looked down at Elijah's hand and then back up at him. I arched my eyebrow while he held the hand there for one long second to make sure I knew he wasn't afraid of me before dropping it. "I think you and Damon should stop talking to each other."

Before I could answer, he turned away and walked up to the driver's seat. As soon as he was seated, he started the bus and put it into drive. We had to scramble into the open seats and Martina yelled, "Elijah! Be nice!"

Elijah didn't answer except to say, "Come up and sit near me if you want, Jáadaa."

Martina frowned but went up to the closest bench seat and sat down behind Elijah. From there, she was able to reach out and put her hand on his shoulder while he drove the bus out of the driveway and onto the road and talked quietly into his ear.

From my single seat in the middle of the bus, I looked back to see Sarah sitting on the bench seat in front of Frank leaning over and talking softly to him. It looked like they were talking about personal things, so I stayed where I was. I turned back to the front of the bus and looked out the side window as the scenery passed me by.

I suddenly had a thought. I got up carefully went back to the triage station and started rummaging through the supplies. It didn't take long before I found what I was looking for; A bottle of strong, medical-grade painkillers. I immediately opened it and took three pills, put the top back on, and shoved the bottle into my pocket. Then I made my way back to my seat, pretending not to notice that everyone else was pretending to not have seen me.

So instead of finding myself driving down the road with some insecure asshole trying to out macho the new guy sitting next to his girl, I got to drive down the road alone, thinking about the man upfront who hated me for religious and historical reasons, and how the other people on the bus suddenly knew I was an addict.

Much better.

<h1 style="text-align:center">Chapter Fifteen</h1>

<h1 style="text-align:center">Meet Dru</h1>

We drove in relative silence for an hour or so until we got to the outskirts of Austin. Elijah drove the shuttle bus onto Rt. 71 and took us around the south side of the city and out towards the airport. Before we got there, he turned down Rt. 183 and drove past McKinney Falls State Park and onto a small street that eventually led to a dirt road that wound around to what can only be described as a compound.

There were four rancher-style buildings all sitting at various distances from a circular driveway loop that we entered as we approached. All the buildings looked like they started life as houses rather than offices or anything like that, but it was clear they had all been altered and repurposed for different things. The one we stopped in front of had a wheelchair ramp and a set of two large doors set into the main entryway. It was situated between a small house that had all the windows covered and a large black steel door in the front, and the biggest house that looked like...well...a house.

At the end of the loop was a long, straight house that was the "guest quarters", but looked to my eyes like a platoon barracks.

We parked and I went back to fumble with Frank's chair and the damned wheelchair lift, but Elijah came back and calmly said, "I've got this. You guys go ahead inside."

I looked at him. "Thank you."

He just shrugged an started unstrapping Frank.

I turned around to head forward and was extremely pleased to see that Damon had already gotten out and left us. As Sarah, Martina, and I left the bus and headed towards the house with the wheelchair ramp, Sam came walking out of the double doors that opened automatically for him.

"Welcome to my humble southern abode."

"I still don't understand why you're here in Texas instead of Alaska." I heard myself say.

He glared at me and said nothing until we got up the ramp next to him. "Because there's some seriously fucked up shit happening here, so here is where I'm needed. Plus - tacos. Remember?"

"Can we stop this now?" Sarah said. "Where are we taking Frank?"

"Right this way, Sarah. This house is both the medical facilities and the tech facilities."

"Medical and Tech?" I asked.

"Yes. Power requirements among other things made it simpler to put them in the same building and upgrade the infrastructure of one house instead of multiple houses. The front is medical, the back is my offices and communications center."

We watched as Elijah wheeled Frank into the building. Sarah and I followed as he took him to the honest to Gods full-sized operating theater. It looked exactly like any operating room in any hospital in America. I was impressed.

The doctor met us there and helped get Frank situated and began questioning him about his injuries. The Doctor. Who worked for Sam. In a compound hospital. I realized that this situation had become much bigger than I thought. Maybe I was in over my head. Great.

Sarah stayed by his side, and as Elijah moved out past me he said, "Follow." and kept walking. I looked over at the front door to Sam, where Martina was giving him a piece of her mind and he was standing there glaring at her with a sullen look that made me think more of a small child than a God. I shook my head and followed Elijah to wherever he was taking me so we could get this over with. We walked out and he took me down a hallway to a side door that opened facing the large house.

He pointed past it to the large barracks-style house and said, "The far house is where you'll all be staying. There's a large open bunkhouse in the front, but if you walk through it to the back, there are a series of six private studio apartments. Pick one." He turned away and let the door close in my face.

I walked over past the large house and up to the front door of the barracks and opened it up. True to his word, there were about five double bunks along each wall with a footlocker at either end. I walked down the middle of the room until I came to the back wall. On my left was a door with a sign showing it to be bathrooms, and on my right, there was an unmarked door I assumed went to the studio apartments. I tried the door and found it unlocked, so I went in. There was a hallway with three doors on each wall. Each door had a number on it, 1, 3, and 5 on my left, 2, 4, and 6 on my right. At the end of the hallways was a door leading to the outside.

I went down the hallway to room six and tried the door. A key was in the lock. I turned the key and the door opened on a room that was essentially a bed, a chair and desk, a tiny closet, and a small bathroom. It was heaven.

I took the key, closed the door, locked it behind me, and then laid out on the bed. My hands were shaking and my body hurt everywhere. I took out two pills from the bottle in my pocket and put them both in my mouth. I was asleep in seconds.

For the first time I could remember, my nightmares included a woman with a painted blue face screaming at me to run. In the middle of the dream, she turned into Martina screaming at me to go away.

I woke up to knocking at the door. I rubbed my eyes and looked at my watch. Three hours had passed, so I guessed it was time for a late dinner.

"Who is it?" I called out.

"Your fondest wish," Martina called from the other side.

I smiled, letting the nightmare go, and said, "A rare steak and a baked potato with a good Italian Red?"

A mock outraged, "Italian? You mean Argentine, you uncultured savage!" was her reply.

I got out of the bed and padded over to the door, opening it to see that wry smirk I was growing to appreciate. "I stand corrected. Argentine wine."

"Of course."

"Of course." I echoed.

She looked me over and said, "Get your shoes on and wake up. It's time for a working dinner. We need to plan out the next steps. Frank is done with the doctor for now, and Sam has dinner almost ready.

Still half asleep. I asked, "Sam is making dinner?" I slipped my shoes on and pulled my shirt over my head.

"Don't be obtuse. He has people for that. There's a full-time staff here, Dru. This is one of four compounds Sam owns and utilizes in the Americas to do whatever it is he does."

"Fight Broadhead?" We started down the hallway and out into the barracks.

"Among much more," She turned to me and put her hand on my chest, stopping me as we got halfway down the room. "Dru, he's a God. Remember that. More, he's Raven. Raven is, among many things, the Trickster God. Trickster. Do you understand? Dangerous, secretive, and prone to impulsive action. And a lot of his grand plans have unintended consequences. Assuming they don't just go tits up."

"I thought the trickster was a Coyote."

Her eyes got wide and a quick look of genuine terror crossed her face. "Dios mio, don't *ever* say that, Dru. I mean it. He is not the Coyote and he will kill you if you call him that. Raven considers himself far more than Coyote, and to compare them is to court death. I'm serious, Dru. Please, never even say the word aloud around him."

"What, is it some kind of professional jealousy?"

"Dru, Raven was one of the first American Gods, possibly *the* first. Try to wrap your head around the idea that human beings sailed into the North American continent led by a God long before the white archeologists admit people were here. Then thousands of years later, that same God led a new bunch of humans across a land bridge through Alaska. A God we're about to eat dinner with.

"In every Pantheon, some Gods came earlier than others. The only gods mentioned before Raven are personifications of creation.

"He was considered an equal or even leader of all the Gods of the Americas that followed. He *is* the human creation myth for the Americas! He brought humans here and put men and women together. He was the God who interacted with humanity. He taught humans how to fish, build houses, and find fresh water. He genuinely cares about his humans, Dru. As far as he's concerned, Coyote played cruel practical jokes on one small group of his children in the Southwest, while he shepherded all of humanity for half the world."

She put her hand on my chest to stop me as she said, "Mythology tends to simplify things. Raven is called the Trickster of the Haida people now, but his name – the one he wouldn't tell you? – is Nang Kilslas, which means *The-One-Whose-Voice-is-Obeyed*."

It dawned on me why he liked the name Sam. Bitter irony.

She continued, "Can you comprehend that, mijo? All these hippy white people walking around America incorrectly calling Coyote the Trickster God of the First Nations People – as if they were all one nation? There were more nations of people on these continents at one time than all of Europe. Do you get that?

"And Raven wasn't like Europe's Odin, or Zeus, or Osiris, some leader of a single peoples pantheon. He was the God who brought the ancestors of every living Indigenous person in the Americas across from Eurasia. He is known in all except a handful of Indigenous pantheons.

"Yeah, it's professional rivalry, but it's a lot more. Being the Trickster doesn't mean that's all he is. He's much more complex than that. But he'll absolutely kill you if you call him Coyote, Dru. Please don't."

"Consider me warned and I will not use the "C" word around him." She relaxed a little and dropped her hand to her side as she turned back towards the front door and started walking again.

After a few steps, I asked, "Speaking of 'C' words, do you know anything about the Celtic Gods?" She looked over and nodded a negative. "According to the mythology, our Gods had all sorts of jobs that often overlapped each other too. Our scariest," I said while swallowing hard, "was Morrigan. She often appeared as a crow, and when she flew over the battlefield, she was the chooser of the slain. Related to that, but different, she was an agent of chaos. Not the chaos of the battlefield, but chaos in general. But here's the thing, she was also intimately related to childbirth and childhood. In legends, she loved to help women give birth, give boons to the babies, and," I smiled bitterly, "often looked out for the kids."

Martina looked at me. "So, you do understand what I'm saying. Sam is complex. Assuming he's nothing but a practical joker would be a fatal mistake." We passed the medical facility and kept walking.

"Yeah. Morrigan was often referred to as the Triple Goddess, and the trick was figuring out why she was around – what aspect she was when you faced her. At least that's what the legends say. And honestly, most of the Gods had all sorts of overlap."

As we approached the house that looked the most like an actual house, Martina asked me, "What would happen if those Gods came back, Dru? Based on the tales, what do you think would happen if they were real?"

I didn't have to think. "It'd be a nightmare," I replied. "A fucking nightmare."

"We have to stop Broadhead."

"We will."

We walked into the house and Martina led me to a large dining room with a table that could comfortably fit ten to twelve people. At the head of the table was Sam. On his left, Frank was closest to Sam, with Sarah seated beside him. There was an empty place after her, and Elijah was in the last chair on that side. On the other side, seated across from Elijah, was Damon. He glowered at me but said nothing.

Sam was sitting there looking happy to see us. I was pretty sure he wasn't, but I can play the game too.

"Hi, Sam!" I called out. "Where should I sit?"

He gestured to his right at the three open seats on that side. I headed over that way and Martina, after glancing at Elijah and the open seat next to him, squared her shoulders and walked with me to the other side of the table. I pulled up the chair at Sam's right hand, and Martina sat down beside me.

Looking across the table at Frank and Sarah, I smiled and winked at them both, saying, "Hi guys, how was your visit to the hospital?"

"Fine," replied Frank. I was not fooled. His eyes were haunted by the loss of his limbs, and there was going to be a long road ahead to recovery. I was afraid of what a three-hundred-year-old warrior might do if he couldn't come to grips with the new reality.

Sarah said, "They took care of his wounds and started the process for prosthetics already. After the...wounds...heal, they will create a socket for his thigh and Mr. Sam says they have some good above-the-knee prosthetics my Frank will be able to try. The other leg will get a similar treatment for the foot." She looked over to Sam and said somewhat coolly, "Thank you again for stepping up and making good on your responsibilities for my husband's injuries."

Sam's mask slipped a tiny bit, but he continued to smile and said, "It's no problem. Frank got hurt working with me, and I take care of my friends.

"Good," I replied.

Servers came in from a door off to the side of the room bearing small bowls of mussels that smelled like the brine of the Sea with a hint of spices and butter. Others came in with bottles of white wine and proceeded to pour us all a glass. I took a sip. It was an amazing Riesling and it paired with what were the most delicious mussels I've ever had.

Conversation ceased as we dug into the appetizer and devoured the mussels. As we finished, Sam looked up at Frank and said, "Frank, you and Sarah are free to stay here as long as you need, and I assume that will be a few months at least. I want to make sure you get the proper prosthetics and physical therapy. Also, you are safe here."

"I appreciate that," he answered, "but how can we be sure that Broadhead won't find us yet again?

He sighed, "Because this is my land, and I said so. In this space, I am the very law of reality, Frank."

"You're reality?" I interrupted.

Sam's head whipped to me and his eyes bored into mine. It's impossible to explain, but the room seemed to waver like a glitch in an old VHS tape, and his voice became a **Voice** - capital V, bold letters - and I was rooted to my chair and abruptly terrified beyond the capacity for words. "**Yes, _Drustan Seta_, I. Am. Fucking. Reality**.

And every one of us believed it. Hell, we didn't believe it, we _knew_ it. Fuck me, "One-who's-voice-is-obeyed" is too right. I suddenly understood that Sam could destroy us all utterly and there wasn't a Godsdamned thing I could do to stop him. A shiver went down my spine. I was returned to that impotent feeling of powerlessness from my childhood. My throat constricted and my heartbeat started to soar. The painkillers stopped working and my entire body began to ache with that bone-deep pain I live with every day.

While I was rooted to my seat and unable to move my eyes off of Sam's, Frank gasped out through clenched teeth, "Then why the hell do you need us?"

Sam slowly broke eye contact with me and turned lazily to Frank and Sarah, saying, "Because Broadhead isn't here. They are elsewhere. My power is almost comically limited in the modern world. Away from my people and my locus, I'm much reduced. When I'm out there I am not much stronger than Damon or Elijah. Or you, Dru."

Time seemed to start up again. "Locus?" Sarah asked.

"I'm not going to try to explain an eternity of Gods and seventy-eight thousand years of American history over dinner. Know that there are a few places in the Americas where I...belong. Places that have kept me alive, alone, and the only survivor of all the Gods on this plane of reality. I have some believers, some priests, and a small, but zealous religious following, all of which gives me enough 'oomph' to work some of my *mojo*." He smiled at me out the side of his mouth as he glanced over and winked.

Damon spoke up from the bottom of the table, "My wife Iáxuhke, Elijah, and I are Shaman – Shamans – and all the people you see with us are *our* people. Raven has God-touched the three of us," he said, gesturing to himself and Elijah, "though Iáxuhke had much power even before. We use this power to help the world survive the destruction wrought by the European man and the industries of the wealthy," He glanced at Sam guiltily and went on, "and despite our God's loneliness, we follow his guidance and keep the other Gods locked away from us all."

I couldn't help myself. I tried to change the subject. "Eco-terrorists?"

Before Damon could respond, Elijah said, "Yes." and there was a short, pregnant pause at the table.

Right on cue, the servers came in bearing plates of Salmon fillets, baked baby potatoes, and asparagus. As the plates were set, I said, "I notice we're not being served some special Haida menu."

Sam smiled as Damon replied, "We are not all Haida. We are Indigenous and we follow our God. My wife is actually Apsáalooke and was a strong two-spirit healer before I was lucky enough to meet her. But, there's nothing more Haida than salmon. Without Raven, there wouldn't be any."

"And I love asparagus." finished Sam.

"Well, I love potatoes, so I guess this is the perfect meal," I said. Martina snorted and hid her laugh behind her hand.

"Well, I'm sure you do, Dru. Stereotype much, my Irish war dog?"

I pointed my fork at him, growling, "I'm not your Dog, Sam. I'm theirs." I said, pointing the fork one at a time to Frank, Sarah, and finally Martina. "And you'll be wise to remember that."

"I didn't mean you were mine..." He began

"...No, you meant to insult him." finished Sarah.

Sam immediately held up his hands saying, "Sorry, sorry. No. I apologize. I'm not trying to insult him, I'm trying to see how he reacts." He looked over at me with narrowed eyes. "You, Drustan Seta, are a giant secret wrapped up in trauma-informed behavior. You're a mess, but you're also far more than you're telling. I honestly think I might know more about you than you do."

I slowly put down my fork and wished for my gun, but the knife at my right hand might have to do. "You want to expand on that?" I said quietly.

He looked over at Frank, "No, I'll keep my thoughts to myself right now, but how about you, Frank? Want to tell him about all those talks we had when I tried to get you to listen to reason and bring Dru in on this mission?"

Every one of us turned to look at Frank and none of us except Frank knew what he was talking about. Sarah put her hand on Frank's arm and asked "What does he mean?"

Frank glared at Sam for a solid three breaths before replying, "Sam and I both think there's more to Dru than simply God-touched. Look," he said glancing around the table at everyone but me, "Dru's talent is amazing, but plenty of god-touched descendants still exist in the world, and working in the Nightmare Squad means I've met a bunch of them. That's not what is strange, though your talents seem extremely consistent - far stronger than most."

He shrugged and set his cutlery down as he explained, "Most knacks are watered down over the generations as the descendants get farther and farther away from the original family member who was God-touched. Their knacks are small things that barely tip the balance in favor of the touched in some way, but Dru...Dru has an absurdly strong and useful knack. It's almost unfair to the enemy to have him in the field with a gun. I mean, he never misses!"

Sarah said, "That's not true. I've seen him miss."

"No, you haven't." Frank said with confidence, "You've seen him not kill. If he aims, he hits the target, but that doesn't mean they die. In a combat situation, most bullets never even hit their intended target. All of Dru's shots hit. They might hit an arm, or a non-lethal area, or body armor, but they hit."

"But in the house, he shot an entire magazine from your AR and only one bullet hit."

My body did that prefight relaxation, but I knew whatever I did, as long as Sam was here, I was as good as dead if I fought. I was trapped. I started breathing heavier, and the pains in my body started to get worse in my joints, but I think only Martina noticed. She seemed to move closer to me in her chair.

"I wasn't aiming, Sarah, I was using the gun for suppressing fire," I admitted.

Frank looked over at me, saying, "Dru, what's weird is you. Your consistency is damn near mythical, yet...You do realize that Sam can get anything he wants via the computer, right? He looked you up, after the incident, of course. You received an all-new identity the day you became a member of the Nightmare Squad, like Extras do, yet you're not an Extra. Why?"

I looked around the table. Both Sarah and Martina were looking at me with trust and confusion on their faces. I took strength from that and said, "I needed a new life. Nothing that happened before was worth remembering or holding onto." I could see the comprehension and agreement from Sarah, my sister of the Secret.

"Alright," said Sam, "But why did they agree? Also, I can look anywhere, Dru, and I did. Your previous existence is gone. Completely. They don't do that for humans. Hell, they don't do that for Extras. There's always a past, and a complete scrub is impossible in this day and age. Impossible. So, where were you before the nightmare squad?

"The US Army," I replied truthfully.

"How?" Sam retorted. "Frank told me what unit you claimed to come from. You only appeared in their rosters one day before you were transferred, the rest of their rosters are all intact, the files and paperwork of the other soldiers are easily obtained, and if it had been scrubbed, I'd know. You didn't exist until twenty-four hours before you were sent to the Squad."

"Yeah, that was a lie."

"What did you do?" Frank asked.

I looked around one more time. I was judging the distance to Sam's neck. Maybe I could cut his throat before he could say anything that caused my head to explode and then take out Elijah before anyone else could stop me. Ha. Wishful thinking. Violence wouldn't save me here. But I started shivering, pain locking up some of my muscles now, ready to flee or fight or...

Martina put her hand on mine and said, "Dru, you don't have to say a thing. I don't care who you were. What you are now is all I care about."

"But what am I?" I whispered. "Do you know? Does anyone?" I said, looking around the table.

"You're my family," she answered. I turned to explain to her for the last time that she couldn't be my family, but she put her finger to my lips to stop me and stared into my eyes. The look on her face was such pure acceptance it rocked me back onto my ass in that chair, and for the first time, I believed her. She sincerely meant I was worthy of being in her family. It hurt so bad I had to turn away. I looked over the table to Frank and Sarah.

Sarah's eyes were glistening with unshed tears, and she nodded her head the tiniest bit in the affirmative and I realized she was casting her vote once and for all for family. Again. She was not interested in judging my past, she just wanted to help me. All at once, something inside me broke, snapped under the pressure of decades of abuse and repression, and I made up my mind. I was going to tell a part of my story for the first time since my childhood.

I turned to Sam as tears formed in my own eyes and said, "I didn't transfer. I died. If you go back about two weeks before my transfer, you'll see a death from an IED. That was me."

Down at the end of the table, Elijah snorted, "Nice trick."

Sam and Frank sat with serious looks on their faces, waiting for more explanation.

Damon unironically muttered, "Jesus Christ" in disbelief and I couldn't resist.

Laughing through a hitch in my voice, I replied, "Not Quite."

Frank was not amused. It looked like this conversation was as hard on him as it was on me, and I realized I didn't want Frank to feel that way. I don't know why now, of all times, I believed I had some people willing to choose me to be part of their family, and most importantly, why I actually believed I might be able to keep it despite the truth, but I did. I knew and believed with every fiber of my being that blood had nothing to do with family, but to choose, to say "You, Dru. You are worthy of being my brother." That's the most powerful event in a human life. To find your family in every way that matters is profound. It can save souls. Not mine.

I knew it was far too late for me, but that didn't mean I couldn't help the man who would be my brother.

Frank dropped his head like he was too tired to hold it up any longer and stared at his plate as he asked, "Dru, what the hell are you, and where did you come from?"

After a short pause while I wiped tears from my eyes and gathered the strength to do the hardest thing I've ever attempted, I said, "I'll tell you. I'll tell you *some* of the truth. About my adult life." I looked over at Sarah. "My childhood may be relevant to my personality, but it's not necessary to answer what you're actually asking. Fair?" Sarah, of course, was already nodding.

Frank said, "Absolutely, Dru."

I continued, "But after I tell you about my life, about what I am, we make a plan to take out Broadhead, and we execute that plan. Deal? Please, after I tell you this you might not want to be my family. You really might not. But please don't say so. Work with me to take down Broadhead. All the rest can wait until after that. "

Sam, eyes glinting, immediately said, "Deal." but I wasn't looking at him, or Elijah, or Damon. They were irrelevant. This was potential family business. I was looking at Frank.

Frank stared back. "Deal, brother."

I looked over at Sarah. "Deal, brother."

Finally, I turned to Martina. "Deal, hermano."

"Elijah and Damon can go. They don't need to know, and I'm not telling them." I looked at Sam, "Understand? This stays between the five of us."

"I love secrets, Dru. Deal."

Damon complained, "But we haven't had dessert yet."

Sam called out, "Bring in dessert! Make two of them to go!"

Dessert came in shortly thereafter and Elijah took his dessert and his brother out of the room.

As we five sat down to eat a chocolate torte, Frank said, "Tell us every-thing, brother, we're listening."

So I did.

"I, personally, am God-touched. Two of them, in fact. And before you ask; yes, it was a long time ago."

<h1 style="text-align:center">Chapter Sixteen</h1>

<h1 style="text-align:center">Just the Relevant Facts</h1>

R aven leaned forward over the table and asked, "How long ago are we talking?"

I needed to stay in control of this conversation as there was absolutely no way I was going to tell them everything about my past, so I said, "No. No questions. I will talk. You'll need to listen. If you interrupt me, I'm afraid I won't be able to start again. Please."

To his credit, Raven remained silent, and the others mutely shook their heads in affirmative. I took a deep breath and started over, "I am the second oldest being in this room."

I looked over at Frank and said, "Yeah, I'm older than you. Before all the Gods disappeared, It seems that my mother attracted the attention of the God Lugh and he gave her a gift for her son. Me."

Raven's eyes gleamed and he started to ask, "You mean you really are..." before Martina leaned over the table and slapped her hand over his mouth.

She glared at him and said, "Shhh! No questions!"

I went on, rushing past the painful origins of me, "I'm God touched by Lugh. He gave me my ability to never miss, and a few physical gifts for warfare. I'm faster and stronger than most human beings. My step father was a monster. I learned to fight early."

I wrung my hands together, looking away from everyone, afraid to make eye contact. "Obviously, I became a warrior, but Gods are a shitty bunch of assholes," I looked over at Sam to see him frowning and looking distinctly offended, "and as my reputation as a warrior spread, a certain Goddess took interest in me."

I shuddered and glanced guiltily over at Martina, "The Morrigan. Goddess of War and Death. Chaos and Sovereignty. Chooser of the Slain. She saw me, loved what I was doing on the battlefield, and decided to give me a gift. A 'Get-out-of-hell-free' card."

I paused for a second to get my head straight, "I had lost everything. I was alone, all my friends and family dead. I was about to die and there was a sound of wings, a pulsing of a dark purple light, and the Morrigan paid me a visit. She declared that my soul could never be chosen on the field of battle. At first, I thought that meant I couldn't die, but after she flew away, I met my end. I died, my guts around my feet."

Frank looked confused, "but..."

"Three days later at sunrise, I sat up gasping for air, body healed, mind still broken. Morrigan sat there at the foot of my deathbed laughing." I slammed my hands down on the table, "Laughing!

"She explained it to me. I will die. Everything dies. However, I have to die in combat. When that happens, she will refuse my soul, and since I'm also God touched by the Sun God Lugh, I will wake up at sunrise on the third day at the age of my first death, twenty-seven fucking years old.

"So," I swallowed hard and ground out my sins through clenched teeth, "I have fought and killed non-stop for the entirety of my existence. I don't do twenty years on, and sixty years off. I go from army to army, unit to unit, country to country, fighting, killing, and dying. Over and over. I can't even remember most of my life; it's one set of barracks after another. The uniforms, the weapons, the scenery, it all changes, but the core remains the same. I kill people until they kill me, then I do it again."

I sat there quietly, lost in my own fractured memories of death.

Sarah was sitting there shocked into immobility. She murmured, "What about friends, family?

"I don't have any. They've been dead a long time."

She raised her hand to her mouth in anguish and leaned against Franks shoulder as she started to cry. I think she got it even before Frank or Martina. She understands the long-term trauma of being on your own in hell. She lived it too.

Frank held his hands up, "Wait. You've been a soldier *non-stop* for centuries?"

"Yes."

"How?"

Martina asked, "For who?"

"Anyone who'd have me. I don't really remember."

Sam looked at me closely as he asked, "You don't remember who you fought for?"

"I don't want to remember."

Martina started to reach out to grab my hand, but stopped short as if she couldn't cross those last few inches of space, "How many times have you died?"

"I'm not sure. Dozens? Hundreds? That last time was about seven years ago. IED shredded my legs with shrapnel. It took about twenty minutes to die that time. I woke up on a hospital bed in Afghanistan and was informed I'd be going to some special branch."

Frank looked sick, "Hundreds?"

"I started killing long before gunpowder. Getting killed hurts a lot with a sword through your guts or an arrow in your eye, but it comes quick and easy once bullets start flying."

"Bullshit. It's me you're talking to, Dru. Killing and dying hurts." He unconsciously rubbed his right stump as he said it.

I shrugged, remembering flamethrowers, "Some hurt worse than others."

Martina started crying too, "Screw the dying. I'm so sorry, Dru. I'm so sorry you've had to do that. I'm so sorry you've had to fight alone for so long."

There was a hitch in my breathing as I tried to process what she said, "It's all I've ever done, Martina. I'm a butcher. I've literally done only two things in my entire life. I've died, and I've killed. That's what I am. Right LT?"

He was nodding his head slowly in negation, but I knew he was only denying the truth to himself, not absolving me.

"I'm a monster. A murderer. A professional killer."

I turned to Martina, who was sobbing now, "Thousands, Martina. I've killed thousands."

Frank spoke loud enough to interrupt me, "Hey, there's no way for a person to do that for that long and stay sane, Dru. No way."

"I didn't," I shrugged.

Sarah gasped out, "Didn't?"

"Stay sane. I didn't stay sane. I think that's why I can't remember stuff. I had to forget in order to function."

Sam muttered, "Maybe."

"I think I remember most of my first twenty-seven years of life. Then whole decades start to disappear. Nothing but fragments of battles, deaths, fights. Killing over and over."

Frank swallowed hard and asked, "What about..."

I looked at him as he stared at his own legs and knew what he was asking, but I didn't want to answer, "What?"

"Well...what happened when you got wounded. Really bad? Lot's of us don't die, we just..." he shrugged helplessly and swung his arms to indicate the missing leg and foot. "There has to be a time or two you lived through...this!" He slapped his thigh in anger.

"I only remember once. I lost my right arm somewhere hot and dry. India? Africa? Not sure. They tried to send me home. I snuck out and started fighting the enemies until they killed me. Three days later, I was alive and whole."

Frank ground his teeth together as he said, "Good trick."

"Frank," I said. "Frank, look at me."

He stared at me with red rimmed eyes full of self-loathing and despair.

"It's not 1700. I know what you're thinking, but you're wrong. This doesn't make you useless. It doesn't make you less. I know what you are thinking, and I was around back then too. I remember when the disabled were sent away and hidden from sight. I remember when physical challenges were tied to your character and worth. But those days are gone. Humanity is better than that now."

"So you say. I'm not so sure about society. Plus your legs would fucking grow back!"

"And yours won't, but I know which one of us I'd want planning this fight, and it ain't me or this lunatic Sam. I need my Lieutenant!"

Martina finally grabbed my hand, "Do you hear yourself, Dru? A monster wouldn't even think to comfort his friend, his brother, at a time like this. There is good in you, a man worth loving and saving."

"How can you say that? So many have died at my hands. What kind of redemption is possible for a creature like this? What kind of people would invite that into their family? How could they? But this is what I am. What I have always been."

Sam muttered, "War Dog indeed...Dru, you might not be as evil as you think you are, but you also might be far more dangerous than you believe."

I blinked as I tried to figure out what the hell he just said, "What?"

In lieu of an answer, he leaned forward and asked, "What's you first memory?"

"No."

"No?"

"No. I will not answer that."

He seemed to understand me and rephrased the question, "Think back in time from today and go back to the last memory you have before you reach a blank spot. What is that last memory of?"

"Oh. That's easy. I left the Military at the end of the Korean war to live in Myanmar for about sixteen years. I fought in the civil wars there."

"Do you remember the Korean war?"

"No. I remember going AWOL in 1953 after waking up in a MASH unit morgue and scaring the shit out of the doctors. I stole a jeep and made it to the shore, where I stole a boat and island hopped to the Philippines before heading to Thailand and eventually Myanmar. I was there until the Vietnam war got hot, so I started fighting for the French, then back to the Americans."

"Do you remember any of the combat in Korea?"

"No. Well...bits and pieces."

Sam sat back and crossed his arms, thinking. "Did you fight for America?"

I was stumped, "You know what? I have no idea."

Frank was shell-shocked, but trying to keep up, "Sam, what are you thinking?"

"You were in Korea and Vietnam too, weren't you, Frank? With the unit?"

"Yes."

Sam smiled and stood up.

Chapter Seventeen

A Good Plan

A week had passed since that night. After Sam stood up, he had crowed, "I knew it! This changes everything!" and abruptly left the table and room. He, being what he was, had no problem adjusting to my history.

"Where are you going?" I had asked.

"I'm going to find your past. Now that I know two times you died as a soldier, I should be able to answer a few questions that have been bothering me about you. That was a good story, but I'm the Raven, I've been telling tales since the sun first rose over the planet. I hear what you don't say as clearly as what you do, Dru."

"I don't doubt it. "I said. I sat with my head down, numb and shut down by the agonies of my past brought back to the surface, still raw after all these years.

Frank had sat dazed with glassy eyes while Martina had bawled her eyes out, hugging me tightly and refusing to let go, saying, "Oh hermano..." over and over again. Sarah, who had covered her mouth with her hand about five minutes into the reveal reached out to Frank and hugged him, crying into his shoulder.

The next day, Frank had come to me and tried to talk. I had quietly said, "No. After Broadhead." and he had deflated a little bit, nodded his head, and gone away. It was the only way I could process and handle the new reality of four people knowing my sins, my history. I hadn't felt this raw or exposed since...well...the first time I'd died all those years ago alone and facing an entire army.

We spent six days developing a plan and putting it into action. It was brilliant, mainly because I didn't have anything to do with it. Sam and Frank spent some time discussing logistics and assets, then built a diabolical plan to take down not only the Dallas headquarters, but, if everything went right, potentially identify, locate, and take out the three head Druids who ran the whole show. They went by the titles of CEO, CFO, and COO, but they were Druids, and Druids ran councils of three. The thing is, companies that want to look real and honest and all that stuff have to list those people who hold those positions. Broadhead was no different, so Sam was able to find out who these people were.

Our CFO, the Chief Financial Officer, was one Ms. Shannon Byrne. I smiled when I saw that, and so did Frank.

"She was the one who had me taken and tortured," Frank said. "She works out of the Dallas office, she'll almost definitely be there."

She was a stern-looking woman with dirty blond hair and a cleft chin. Her photo showed her unsmiling and serious.

Our COO, The Chief Operations Officer, was one Mr. Dillon Carrick. He was unknown to all of us, but his smiling headshot on the Broadhead website showed a well-proportioned face that was clean-shaven with green eyes and a knowing smile.

Last but not least was our CEO, the Chief Executive Officer, who was identified as Louis Hughes but disappointingly, had no photograph attached to his bio.

We spent three days with Elijah explaining and practicing the plan with his small group of ex-special forces soldiers and private attack squad made up entirely of Raven's followers.

Today was the last day of training and tomorrow was the action. I sat watching the final meeting until it ended then went over to Elijah.

"You and your guys are up to this?"

"Yup."

Elijah was not much of a talker, but he rarely replied to me with anything more than a syllable or two. It was starting to bother me. "How come there are so many former military in your group? Aren't you all from a tiny Nation of people?"

"Indigenous."

"Yeah? What's that got to do with it?"

He didn't even bother to sneer at me as he walked off, but good old Damon was right there sneering for the both of them. "We're all indigenous, but we're not all from the same nations. Culturally we're as different as any other people. But when it comes to Raven, he's the God of all the Americas.

"I still don't understand."

"The Native peoples of Canada and America have always been warriors, even for the countries that stole their lands. We make up a disproportionate amount of active servicemen and women."

"Ah. Gotcha."

"Do you? Do you understand anything at all about us?"

"Damon, you won't believe me if I say yes, so why do you ask?"

He turned his back on me and walked away.

That night, I prepared for my part in the plan and packed up. Sam's equipment was fantastic, and I was able to outfit myself in pure MilSpec gear that was as familiar to me as breathing.

One interesting thing happened the last night we were there before the action. Sam called us all into the medical suite where the doctor was finishing up crafting a mold of Frank's stumps for the creation of a cutting-edge set of carbon fiber prosthetics.

Frank looked so depressed I was actually scared for him. The reckoning was coming. I realized suddenly that I intended to be there for him when it arrived.

Sam had declared, "We don't have the facilities to make the fittings here, but we'll send off the molds tomorrow morning and the prosthetics will be built and shipped to whatever address you want."

Sarah had answered for Frank, "We don't know where that will be yet, but thank you for this. It actually means a lot."

Sam had the grace to look uncomfortable and said, "I know we're not really working together, but sincerely respect what you are doing, Sarah." Then he turned to Frank, saying, "And I am sorry that this happened to you, Frank."

Frank looked at where his missing leg should be and said nothing.

The next morning, we all woke up early, had breakfast, and headed out to our respective locations. Frank and Sarah went into the communications center of the house and sat down to run communications and oversee the operation.

The plan was pretty simple. The primary goal was to remove the ability of Broadhead to utilize their Dallas offices and severely impact their operating efficiency worldwide through that disruption. The secondary goal was to take out one, two, or even all three of the Druid Triumvirate if the opportunity presented itself. This was trickier because we didn't actually know if any of them were in Dallas, but it seemed almost certain that at least one would want to be physically present during this clusterfuck we had caused already.

We were going to do a variation of the classic bait and switch. Sam, a few of his guys, and I were going to go way out into Texas Hill country and call out Broadhead for a little parlay.

How? Technology, baby.

At 9:30 am, every monitor, television, and piece of technology connected to the internet in the Broadhead building began showing a recording of Sam as he played the "Evil Eco-Terrorist" known as the Trickster. I got to watch on my own phone as he broadcast it on his FB page at the same time. Sam, of course, was sitting right next to me in an SUV as we drove out into Hill Country towards a sacred space called Enchanted Rock. That is where we hoped to meet at least one of the Triumvirate to "talk."

The video was inspired. Sam was ranting and raving on the camera. "Enemies of the Earth!" He screamed over every TV, computer monitor, and cell phone in the building, "Prepare for your last day! Mother Earth has said, "Enough!" Enough of your raping the planet for profit. Enough of your bombs, bullets, and destruction! Today you reap what you sew! Today I blow up your building!"

Through the cameras we hacked and streamed, I could see some people who had started watching this with bemusement slowly start wondering if it was real. Some people had already started heading towards the exits. Then Sam locked the automatic computer-monitored locks on the doors.

"Nobody gets to leave their fate! You all will die as soon as I have pronounced the sentence! This building is locked and we have placed explosives in the foundation. This building will go down in five minutes. You all will die!"

At that precise moment, the soldiers that had snuck in an hour before and led by Elijah set off a few remote explosions on the lower floors of the building and in the carport. Nothing that would actually take down the building, because that wasn't the real plan, but more than enough for people to accept that this was real and that they were about to die. It also closed off the exits of the garage, to impede anyone trying to leave.

Pandemonium ensued as hundreds of employees rushed to the elevators, stairs, and the lobby. We watched as the tide of people turned into a tidal wave of panic rushing towards the locked doors. As the security guards saw the crowds, three of them put up their hands and began yelling for calm and orderly behavior. The fourth guard turned to the glass doors and windows and drew his gun. His first shot went into the door and did fuck all because the doors were bulletproof. His slug sat there embedded in the door about a quarter of an inch.

He turned to the window beside the door and it shattered with the first shot, falling into pieces smaller than a pencil eraser. Safety glass.

I started laughing and Sam reached into his pocket and pulled out a dollar. I took it as he asked, "How did you know?"

"Broadhead had a lot of security, but none of it was coherent. Metal detectors to look at my guns, but then they handed them back to me. Stupid. I saw on my visit that the place had bulletproof doors. So what? I was positive that they built to code, which only required safety glass for windows. So what if they upgraded the doors? What were the odds they ever bothered to upgrade the first-floor windows? The whole damn building is glass. It would have cost them millions. So, basic safety glass."

The recording of Sam was still going on with him ranting and raving and calling down the doom of the ages. "By now the primary charges have gone off and prepared the building for implosion. Say your prayers to whatever God you believe in. You will meet them soon!" People were flooding out of the now three broken floor-to-ceiling windows.

"You're sure that the real message was sent to the right offices?" I asked.

"I sent it over the private, 'executive' intranet they have in their building. It's reserved for the most senior people. They got it."

The "It" he was referring to was the short, recorded message that outed Sam as the Trickster and told the Broadhead Triumvirate that we knew who and what they were and that we wanted a meeting on a neutral ground to discuss alternatives to destroying each other.

"Hello Druids," the video began, "I am the man you call the Trickster. I am going to destroy your building, but I'm sure all of your people will have time to get out. I'll tear it down completely unless you come meet me. I want the Triumvirate. Yes, I know what and who you are, and I have to tell you, a few real Gods around wouldn't upset me." He shrugged at the camera and winked.

I'm only concerned with the destruction of the earth, and I only recently learned what you're actually doing, and I have to be honest, it might be that we're actually on the same side. I dream of an Earth returned to its pristine shape, the earth from when humans were shepherds and stewards of nature. You might be able to bring that about, yes?"

"Then why fight? Meet me at the top of Enchanted Rock. If my people see the Triumvirate head out towards Fredericksburg, the building will remain standing. What have you got to lose? We may become allies, maybe even friends. It's good business, after all. I'm already there waiting with two people you've been eager to meet these last few days." He panned the camera out to show Frank and me seated and relaxed in two chairs beside him.

"That's three of you and three of us. No need for soldiers or staff, that way we can have a serious discussion and see what accommodations we might be able to reach. See you there?" and the video ended with Sam smiling, arms spread apart in an eloquent, questioning shrug.

Back at the Broadhead offices, we watched as a large group of well-dressed executives rapidly bustled out of the elevators and rushed towards the windows. Several of the group were security, and at the center was a woman who was a VIP. It was clear to see that it was our murderous CFO, Shannon Byrne.

At the same moment I recognized her, we heard Frank's voice come over our headsets, "Target one, CFO identified. Watch her and task drone..." here he paused and ground out "...drone *Babycakes* to surveillance. Let's see if she's running, or going to meet Sam."

Sam giggled and said, "I love my *Babycakes*. You keep her safe, Frank."

"You really had to name them all?" He replied.

"Of course."

The flow of terrified employees had trickled off to nothing and Frank said, "Elijah, it's a go. You have five minutes before the bomb squad arrives. Get to work."

Elijah and his crew had already been in the building thanks to Sam's ability to override the electronic locks of the loading bay side doors and other locations of secure egress. They had spent that hour dressed in business suits or janitorial garb riding the elevators and planting incendiaries out of sight.

Now they stripped, pulled out guns and a final few firebombs from the custodian carts, and sprinted to the elevators. Elijah and three others went to the upper floors to throw incendiaries into the offices of the executives, while another group went to the server rooms. Sam, meanwhile, removed the video and installed the virus that started wiping all the hard drives and servers of everything they contained.

Franks said, "Three minutes" over the headsets.

Elijah replied, "Munitions set. Leaving now."

As Elijah met up with his second crew, they dumped all their guns into the custodian cart and pushed it into the elevator.

Frank switched our view to the garage cameras as a four-person security detail in a classic security diamond formation led COO Dillon Carrick into a Black SUV. Two more were already in the vehicle and immediately drove towards the exit after Carrick and one of the diamond jumped in the back seat. The three others jumped into the next SUV and immediately followed.

Frank said, "Target two, Dillon Carrick positive ID leaving with one escort. Task drone *Cutiepie* to follow. Elijah, one minute until first responders arrive.".

"We can hear them from the street. Exiting from the building." Then Elijah and all his crew ran out as if they were the last terrified employees finally getting out of a bomb threat, sprinting away in different directions as the fire department and police arrived simultaneously.

One cop looked at the running soldiers dressed in suits suspiciously until about thirty incendiary bombs all went off within five seconds of each other throughout the building. After that, he and every other first responder were running like hell away from what they thought was a terrorist attack on a building in downtown Dallas.

By the time they realized the building wasn't going to collapse, the entire thing was an inferno battling against automatic fire suppression systems.

Phase one was a complete success. If any equipment survived the fire, the hard drives would be wiped anyway. There was nothing left for Broadhead there.

We were still driving down the road out towards Enchanted Rock and had nothing to do but listen to Frank run the operation from the communication center on Sam's compound and watch the cameras on our phones.

There were four of us in the truck. Up front Damon was driving while Sam sat in the front passenger seat. It was a brand new Dodge truck with a huge rear cab for myself and the other guy, a friendly, quiet soldier who had introduced himself as "Jesse's my easy name. You can't pronounce my real one."

I smiled and said, "Hi, Jesse. You're with us today?"

"Yup-yup." he answered. "I'm kind of Elijah's number two guy." He proceeded to tell me his life story from the time he was born to the Nez Perce people, to the five-year hitch in the army, to finding an actual God running a group he could get behind.

We got along great and were sharing my phone to watch the antics. Right now, we were watching a split screen of two drone cameras following three cars heading out to Enchanted Rock. This had made Sam happy because our biggest fear was that they'd turn around after we torched the building, but we had a plan for that as well, though it looked like we wouldn't need it.

"Shame we don't have those drones armed," I said.

Sam explained, "They're little drones for surveillance. They're at the limits of their capacity now. We're going to lose the feed soon when they fall behind and their batteries die."

"I know," I replied, "I was just thinking out loud."

Jesse looked over at me and asked, "Are you going to be able to do your part of this insane plan?"

"No problem," I answered. "You guys hit your marks and get those two standing at the edge of the summit, I'll do the rest."

"Not until I tell you, Dru. We absolutely have to get this right, and I need to question them first." Sam said.

"I understand," I growled out. "Don't tell me my job, Sam."

Over the headsets, Frank spoke up, "How long until you are all in place? They will be there in about three hours if they don't stop on the way."

"We're about an hour out from Enchanted Rock, but we have to drop off Dru first. Then say about thirty minutes to hike to the top. We'll be in place in plenty of time."

"Alright. Make sure you send up drone *Sugarplum* before they get there so I have eyes. Dru, you have everything?"

"All good, LT." I replied. "Just like old times."

"Be safe, brother."

I swallowed. It was going to be a long time before that felt right or normal to hear. "You bet."

"Sam, Damon, and Jesse, when this pops off, it's gonna get loud and you'll need to move your asses. Even assuming they don't try something nasty the second they see you, they're going to try to kill you all as soon as Dru starts. Make sure you get down and hustle. There's no real cover there, so if Sam isn't as smart as he claims, your asses are going to be hanging out on a bare rock surface."

"I'm smarter than I claim, trust me."

Damon added, "I'll take my chances with my God over you two hired guns any day."

Jesse frowned and looked like he was about to say something but settled back into his seat and looked over at me apologetically. I nodded to him to let him know it was all good. Frank didn't even bother replying.

About ten minutes later, they dropped me off to do my thing and the three of them went off to Enchanted Rock to set up an ambush that the damn Druids would hopefully literally never see coming.

As I got into place and settled down, Frank came on the headset again. We've lost the drones, but based on their progress, they should be about ninety minutes out. Is everyone in place?"

I looked at my wrist with the old Speedmaster watch, it's scuffed and battered body sitting on a relatively new black NATO strap. It was ticking along slowly. "Affirmative," I replied after marking the time.

"You bet." replied Sam. "I'll send up my baby when we see the cars arrive down below, and we'll get into final positions. In the meantime, picnic!" Then I watched through my spotting scope as Sam lifted an honest to Gods wicker picnic basket and set it on the top of a large stone and proceeded to pull out Fried chicken, potato salad, and cans of coke for the three of them on top of Enchanted Rock. I snarled a mild obscenity under my breath pulled a granola bar out of my pocket and ate it. I swear I could see Sam looking right at me through the spotting scope and grinning as he lifted a chicken leg in salute.

Fucking asshole.

Chapter Eighteen

A Plan Comes Together

About an hour later, the first SUV pulled into the parking lot of Enchanted Rock, and Sam set his little drone, *Sugarplum* up into the air and handed control over to Frank back in Austin. I had my phone propped up in front of me to my left so I could watch.

As the drone flew into the air, I could see the three men standing on the amazing massive pink granite dome of rock sitting there in the middle of Hill Country and rising to over 1800 feet of elevation. Besides Sam, Damon, and Jesse, there were about fifteen people wandering around the massive surface of the dome and exploring the edges and split layers of rock sitting along the edges of the incredible geological feature.

A little over a billion years ago, a pink granite batholith was created by cooling magma. It sat there undisturbed until weathering and erosion exposed what is called an exfoliating dome of the stuff. When humans showed up, it quickly became an important geographic marker and the Indigenous peoples used it as a focal point of their religious rites for centuries. Sam called it a locus of power.

It was a huge mound of pink sitting in the middle of flat, desert scrub and cedar trees. The biggest thing around, sitting there majestically dominating the scenery for miles.

All along the edge of Enchanted Rock were fissures and granite flakes that had peeled off the main formation like layers of an onion over the last millennia or two. Deep fissures, dangerous cracks, and chimneys created some great technical rock climbing at the site, but what we were more interested in was avoiding falling off the steep sides and edges into what would be a fatal drop onto the boulders below.

Sam and crew had picked a huge, semi-detached flake with a large flat surface to stand on. The flake had a rather large gap of about twelve feet at its widest separating it from the rest of the summit, but it tapered down to nothing as it angled in towards where it remained attached to the dome. Behind where they were standing the flake slopped steeply about four feet down to another small ledge about twenty-four inches wide before ending at a sheer drop of about seventy-five feet to the boulder field at the base.

The drone moved off towards the parking lot at the base of the trail to the top.

The first car was alone. We watched three security exit, and one of them opened the back door to let Shannon Byrne step out and into their protective circle. She looked up the mountain and said something while pointing to the trail, the guard looked at his watch and said something back. She looked agitated and pointed at her feet while yelling at him, and realizing what she was angry about, I started laughing.

"What's so funny?" Sam asked.

"She's wearing heels. Her feet will be killing her by the time she gets to the top."

Frank laughed over the headset and said, "She'll start up soon then, so she doesn't embarrass herself by holding up Carrick. It'll probably take her about an hour instead of the forty minutes it took you guys."

She was about halfway up with her three men when Dillon Carrick arrived with his entourage thirty minutes later. Two vehicles pulled in and eight people got out, including the aforementioned Carrick. He immediately pulled out his cell phone and made a call. *Sugarplum* showed us Ms. Byrne looked down at her suit jacket pocket and pulled out her phone.

After a quick conversation, Carrick sent four men running up the trail while three stayed with him and began the hike.

"Okay everyone," Frank said "we have twelve hostiles. Ten soldiers and two principles. As we discussed, they are not here to talk, they are going to try to take you three by force, but I don't see any rifles, so we have the opportunity we planned for. It's a public place and they are unlikely to display weapons unless they need them. Don't spook them, just do what we planned."

"We've done stuff like this before," muttered Damon.

"No we haven't," replied Jesse. He put his hand on Damon's shoulder in a friendly gesture of comradery, "Get your game face on brother, this relies on you more than anyone."

"Everyone relax and try to have some fun. If this works out right, this is gonna be hilarious," said Sam. "They'll never know what hit them."

Damon sat down and started praying, while Sam and Jesse settled down to wait for the Druids and their men to arrive.

I moved the phone a tiny bit further away from me and made a few final adjustments to my surroundings and my position. I said over the headset, "I know this is the best place for me, but I wish I was there on that rock."

"We discussed this, Dru," replied Frank. "You and I can't be there, because they are expecting us to be there."

"Understood, but I still wish I could get my actual hands on those two shithead Druids."

"Dru. Are you making this personal?" Frank sounded shocked. "Remember your orders, soldier."

He wasn't wrong. I had never made anything personal in the entire time he'd known me until that day in the village. I was abruptly uncomfortable in my own skin. Who the hell was I? What the hell was I becoming?

"Dru? You understand me?"

I shook my head. Focus Dru! Get your shit together! After a few seconds, I said, "Yes, LT I'm back."

"You good?"

"Yes, LT."

"Alright. Stick to the plan, do your job, keep your promise, kill those bastards."

"Understood," I growled.

Watching on the drone camera, Damon stopped praying and stood up. He extended his hands towards the big crevasse separating the flake they were standing on from the main dome of the summit. Nothing seemed to happen on camera, but Jesse started laughing and clapping his hands, and Sam turned to Damon and put his hands over Damon's. On the headset, I heard Sam say, "Your skills are progressing quickly, Damon. Maintain your focus and remember that this is your one essential job. Don't let this slip away until we spring the trap." Damon lowered his head and closed his eyes momentarily in a posture of gratitude.

"I won't, Raven. I have it locked down. The power here is…astonishing. I feel so strong."

"Don't let it fool you. There's a price you'll be paying later because that power isn't yours, it belongs to the mountain and the hundreds of years of sacrifice and prayer of those who came before you, and you are only borrowing some. If you don't pay attention to your body, you could cook yourself from the inside out. Try to send the power directly from the locus to the illusion and not through you."

"Understood."

Jesse looked over at Damon with awe and said, "You are one scary Shaman, Damon. I'm glad you're on my side."

On camera, I saw Damon smile and move to the back edge of the flake, where it dropped to that lower ledge.

We sat and watched as four security guards ran up the trail to catch up to Ms. Byrne and her trio of guards already with her. Mr. Carrick and his three tromped steadily on, slowly eating up the gap between the two parties.

Eventually, the four caught up to the front party and became eight fish out of water hiking up a state park mountain in business attire. They drew a few looks, but nobody on the trail said anything to them. I guess the grim looks and angry semi-permanent snarl on Ms. Byrnes's face as she tripped her way up the path in heels discouraged communication.

As the large party arrived at the summit, Mr. Carrick and his three remaining guards were about five minutes behind. Ms. Byrne talked to the group she had and they spread out around the summit looking for us. Sam started waving his hands over his head when the first guard came into sight, and after doing a quick double-take, he turned around and ran back to report.

In a short time, the guards fanned out and approached Sam, Jesse, and Damon. As they neared the Flake, they seemed to ignore the large gap and spread out into an arc of bodies designed to prevent escape.

"That's far enough!" yelled Sam as they got within feet of the gap.

Standing behind her men, Ms. Byrne said, "It appears you weren't entirely truthful with us, Mr. Trickster."

"How so?"

"I've been told our building is completely destroyed."

"I never said I wouldn't destroy it. I said I wouldn't tear it down. It still stands." Sam said with a huge smile on his face.

"What about Mr. Seta and Mr. Egils? You said they'd be here."

"I also told you to come alone as the three High Priests, yet I count eight of you in front of me, and four more are coming, Ms. Byrne."

If she was bothered by the fact that he knew her name, she didn't show it. "Please, Mr. Trickster, you knew we'd bring our security. And you are of course armed?"

"One pistol for my associate Jesse, here. We come in peace." He laughed "But where are the two others of your Triumvirate? I don't see them anywhere."

"One will be along in a few minutes."

"You mean, Mr. Carrick of course, but where, I wonder, is Mr. Louis Hughes?"

She ground her teeth together for a moment before she said, "Mr. Hughes is in our East Coast Office. He couldn't possibly make it here in time for the meeting."

"Well, I guess we'll have to wait for Mr. Carrick, and we'll see where this fun little conference leads, won't we?" replied Sam

"Where are Mr. Egils and Mr. Seta?"

"Well, much like Mr. Hughes, Mr. Egils is too far away to get here in time. He's recovering from your torture quite nicely, by the way. Shame on you."

Completely unmoved, Shannon asked, "And Mr. Seta?"

"Drustan doesn't play nice. I decided it was better for all of us to put him somewhere safe. If he was here, he'd be trying to kill you."

She laughed as three more security men arrived and Mr. Carrick stepped up beside her. "You should have brought him. You might have had a chance to make it out of here. As it stands now, you and your two subordinates will be coming with us, and after we'll go get Mr. Egils and Mr. Seta."

"How do you think you're going to pull that off?" Sam asked.

Into my mic, I said, "Sightline clear, target acquired."

Frank replied with a terse, "Roger." while Sam only smiled wider.

Carrick spoke for the first time, "Come now, Trickster, you have to know how this is going to work. We are going to take you. We don't want to make it violent here in public, but you either walk with us down this mountain or these ten men surround you three with their stun guns and we carry you down. "Victims" of heat stroke or dehydration or whatever story gets people to shut up and look the other way."

"Do you think that would work? There have to be two or three dozen people wandering around this rock right now. We'll fight, and we'll be loud."

"And we have one pistol," Jesse added with a smile.

"Pull your gun and we pull our ten. We have more than stun guns, I assure you. So, yes, it'll work. We have a few skills we use in these situations. It's been done many times before. Believe me, you three are coming with us."

"Ah yes. Your magic." Sam replied. "Which God is it? Who is so close to returning that they have given you the means to shape reality?"

There was a dead silence while Carrick and Byrnes looked at each other out of the corners of their eyes quickly and then turned back to face Sam. It was brief, but even over a drone camera, I could see they were rattled.

"Magic?" Carrick asked.

"Enough. No lies. Let's not waste each other's time. I know far more than I let on in my little video. You're extremely close to bringing a God back, that much is obvious. Is it a South American God? Celtic? Certainly not Norse?" Sam asked, "My money is on South America, but I'm really only guessing that because of all your work in Peru and Chile. I guess Celtic would be the obvious choice though."

Byrnes smiled a nasty smile, "You're not as smart as you think, Mr. Trickster." She looked over at Carrick and they stepped back behind the line of security surrounding Sam, Damon, and Jesse.

The goons started forward, but Sam held up his hands again and said, "Wait! Isn't there something we can do to negotiate some sort of coexistence? I'm serious when I say I'm not against a God or two here on Earth."

They paused, and Carrick said, "Sure. Give us the two troublemakers right now and come with us to Baltimore. As our guest."

Sam smiled, "Guest? What are my assurances? I have no love for Dru, you can have him as far as I'm concerned. He's been nothing but a pain in my ass. Mr. Egils, on the other hand. Well, I've kind of grown to respect him a little bit. Are you sure you need him?"

I snarled to myself, I knew he was bluffing for the sake of getting knowledge, but screw him. I didn't have much love for him either.

"Non-negotiable. We get them both," said Carrick.

"As far as assurances," Byrnes said, "What would work for you? What could we say that you'll trust?"

"Well, first I guess you'll need to tell me why Baltimore?"

"Because some asshole terrorist destroyed our Dallas building today." cut in Carrick.

Heh. That was actually pretty good.

"Plus, that's where Mr. Hughes is." finished Ms. Byrne.

Off to the side, Damon grunted and swayed on his feet. In all the fun, I hadn't noticed him. He was sweating and looked like he was barely able to stand. I didn't understand what was going on, but it was clear Sam did. His face turned grim and he looked back to Byrnes and Carrick. "We need to move this along; my associate isn't feeling well."

"What's wrong with him?" Carrick asked suspiciously.

"Fever, I think. He's worked too hard planning a surprise party," Sam answered. "He needs rest."

"Well then, Trickster, decide. Are you coming peacefully, or are my men coming to take you?"

Sam sighed dramatically and struck a pose like a boxer out of the 1800s, fists raised and arms moving in small circles. "I guess you'll have to *come and take it.*"

Carrick and Byrnes blinked with incomprehension and Sam shook his head sadly, "Nobody appreciates the classics anymore. You're standing in Texas, damn it."

They stood there for a few more seconds so Sam added, "No. It means no. Come get me, you sons-a-bitches." Jesse moved up and stood in front of both Sam and Damon with his hands up like he was going to fight ten trained soldiers from Broadhead, all of whom were pulling out their tasers.

Behind the soldiers, Byrnes and Carrick reached out joined hands as they started a quiet chanting. Sam said out loud, "Now would be a good time. They're about to throw some magic at us."

Over the headset, Frank said the single-word command, "Go."

I pulled the trigger and watched through the scope as Jesse smoothly reached into his waistband pulled out the pistol and started shooting at the soldiers on his left, closest to where the flake was attached to the main rock. Sam turned and jumped off the flake onto the narrow shelf behind him.

Then my bullet finally got there and took Mr. Carrick in the head, which then disintegrated all over Ms. Byrnes.

Almost as one, the Broadhead soldiers disguised as security guards in suits dropped their stun guns, reached for their pistols, and charged Jesse, who had grabbed Damon and turned to jump down onto the shelf with Sam. Two soldiers managed to pull the triggers of their guns and they ran forward, one striking Jesse with a glancing blow, turning him away from Damon.

And then those poor sonsabitches enthusiastically and professionally ran off the cliff into the gap between the flake and the main summit. Like they never even saw it there. Because they hadn't. Damon had created an illusion that it was solid rock.

Five of them were near the outer edge and they never even made a sound as they almost comically sprinted off into space and fell seventy-five feet onto the rocks below.

At the other end of the flake where the gap was much smaller, three ran off the edge and smashed into the flake on the other side. Two of them slipped down the gap and fell to their deaths. One held on to the flake and began pulling his way up.

Jesse had put the two on his far left down with double taps, and straightening up, he walked over to them, putting one more into the skull of each. I could see blood on his left arm. He walked over to the man hanging on to the flake for dear life, said "Sorry about this." and shot him in the head.

I think it barely needs to be mentioned that tourists all over the summit started screaming and running down the trail. Many reached for their cell phones, but Sam had taken care of that right before the Druids had arrived at the top of the rock. There was no cell reception for about twenty miles around the Rock. Fredericksburg was down entirely.

Damon swayed one more time, collapsed onto the flake, and would have fallen off if Sam hadn't been standing on the lower ledge behind him laughing hysterically. He reached up and grabbed onto his body after he fell down on the rock.

Ms. Byrnes had been standing there in shock, staring at the carnage of what had once been her cohort, and her eyes widened even further as she seemed to see the large gap between the flake and the summit for the first time and she turned to stare in horror at Sam.

Sam looked at her with a malice I had never seen on his face before and he said a single word as if passing a death sentence upon her, "Magic."

She screamed and turned to flee. She made it about five steps before she twisted her ankle and crashed down onto the granite surface of Enchanted Rock.

Sam stalked over to the edge of the flake and leaped to the summit. He walked to Shannon Byrnes and stood over her, saying, "Not what you were expecting, you Druid bitch?"

Terrified, she asked, "Who are you? What are you?"

Using his **Voice**, Sam said, "**I am Raven, and you are my enemy.**"

Everyone flinched as massive feedback blared through our headsets and they all went dead.

Because the headsets died, Frank was cut off from communicating with us, and I could not hear what Sam and Ms. Byrnes were saying, but the drone had stayed up in the air despite a moment of static from the camera and a steep, but momentary dive from the drone itself. So we were at least able to watch what transpired next.

Sam turned to Jesse and said something to him. He shook his head yes, walked over to Damon, and began helping him to rise and walk off the flake and back onto the summit. Damon looked completely exhausted, but he waved to Jesse in affirmation of whatever Jesse had asked him.

Sam turned back to Shannon and knelt. He reached out to her and she flinched away from him, still visibly terrified. He roughly grabbed her chin, turned her face to look up at him, and began speaking. Her terror soon melted away and she visibly relaxed.

Then, the most incredible thing happened. She smiled. And she started talking. Sam listened.

As I said, all the tourists on the rock had run off screaming as soon as Jessie fired his gun, so I figured we were short on time, but Sam sat there next to her as if he had all the time in the world.

He asked a few questions and she answered them. On the third answer, he stood up and rocked back as if he had been slapped. Jesse looked shocked and turned to stare at Ms. Byrnes and Sam started yelling at her. Shannon looked confused and upset that she was being yelled at, and tried to explain to Sam whatever it was they were talking about. Her expression was earnest and she seemed desperate to make Sam understand what she was saying.

Sam stood up and screamed to the heavens. Jesse, Damon, and Shannon slapped their hands over their ears, and I, from almost a mile away on Dutch Mountain, heard it clear as a bell. It was a scream of rage and loss. I felt it on a visceral level that almost turned my bowels to water, and I was forcibly reminded that Sam was a God, whose voice was a Power. Suddenly, I was very happy to be so far away from him.

Sam turned away from Shannon as if she no longer existed and gave a single terse order to Jesse that was something along the lines of "Let's go" because they both helped Damon and started walking down the path to the base of the mountain.

After walking about a hundred feet, Sam turned back to Shannon and said something that must have broken the spell because she looked at him and her face took on that terror again as she huddled up, turning her back to Sam. He, Jesse, and Damon turned back to the path and walked away.

The three of them left her curled up there on the top of the granite mound. After they got out of sight, she struggled up into a sitting position put her head into her hands, and sobbed for a few seconds, getting herself under control. Eventually, she struggled to her knees and gingerly stood up to put some weight on her injured ankle. She looked around at the now empty space of Enchanted Rocks summit and limped a few steps towards the trail down. She wobbled in obvious pain and she seemed to realize something that made her stop and turn to look out in the general direction I had sent my sniper fire at them.

The bullet took her in the center of her chest and flung her off her feet and onto her back. Through my scope, I watched her take three shuddering breaths before her chest stopped rising and falling. I took out two painkillers and dry-swallowed them while I watched her die. Then I quickly broke down my rifle and spotting scope and hauled ass down Davis Mountain to await pickup from Sam.

That made two-thirds of my promise to Sarah finished. I had to kill one more asshole and he was in Baltimore, a few hours away from my house. Phase two of the mission was complete. Time to plan phase three.

Chapter Nineteen

A Plan Gets Revised

When Sam arrived in the truck driving with Damon slouched asleep in the passenger seat, I expected to be regaled with his version of events and had steeled myself for a noisy trip home, but instead what I found surprised me.

Both Sam and Jesse were grim as death, and neither wanted to talk at all. Sam silently pulled over to the side of the road where I was standing and unlocked the doors. His head never even turned my way. I climbed in and sat next to Jesse and looked over at him. He wouldn't even make eye contact and I began to get a little worried.

"What's going on guys? This was a success. Yeah, we missed one of the three, but we know where he is and I'm going to go kill him."

Jesse clearly looked torn, like he desperately wanted to tell me something, but instead, he glanced up to the front of the truck where I could see Sam glaring at him through the rearview mirror. His eyes shot over to me, and instead of answering, he settled down crossed his arms apologetically and slouched deep into his seat, and leaned against the door, as if he was trying to get as far away from this situation as possible.

"Jesse," I said, "You're a good man. Don't worry about it. I understand being told to shut up and say nothing by my superiors. No worries. And good shooting back there."

He still wouldn't look at me, but now it was more due to shame, I think. He did seem to relax a little though and I believe it helped ease the tension a little bit.

I turned to Sam, "But you, you bastard. You have no excuse to hide anything from me. What the fuck is going on?"

He said nothing for so long I was about to jump back in on him, when he said, "I'm going to explain it once. Wait until we're all back and safe at the compound."

"Why can't you give me the condensed version right now?"

"Because some things shouldn't be said aloud at all, Godsdamnit! I know what I'm doing, and you'll just have to wait! This is dangerous shit, Dru!"

So, I waited.

We got back to the compound and Jesse went into the medical center to get his arm looked at. It was merely a flesh wound, but it would probably take four or five stitches. Elijah was there to wake up his brother and escort him back to the house they stayed in. Damon seemed a lot better after waking up, but his eyes were sunken in and his skin had a pallor to it that did not look healthy.

Elijah walked close to him and asked, "You okay, brother?"

Damon looked over at him with warmth in his eyes, and said, "Yeah, little big man. I'm good."

"I called your wife and told her you have the record. That illusion must have been epic."

Damon chuckled. "Now you've done it, she'll be inventing a spell or something as we speak. You know how competitive she is."

"Yeah, but you're the only one who can keep up with her, I suck at magic."

Damon spoke as they turned the corner and disappeared down the hallway, "You're too literal for chaos magic, bro. You're a soldier. We're compliments, always have been, and always will be, forever."

Martina, Frank, and Sarah were standing outside waiting as well and all three came up to me right away to say hi and see how I was. That unnerved me quite a bit. I was used to Frank and the squad all hanging out, talking, and decompressing after an action, but it was a whole new thing to have a family looking out and asking after me. I wasn't sure what to do, or what my responsibilities were. It had been so long since the last time I had people like this, I wasn't sure how they did it.

Sarah asked, "How are you, Dru? Everything go well?"

"Easy," I replied. "Good vantage point. Had to shoot upwards a tiny bit. That makes it harder, but the sightline was clear. Two shots, two kills."

Frank was smiling. "Dru, she's not asking for a report, she's asking how you are feeling."

"Oh. Good. Fine." I said looking at her. "Um...how are you?"

Martina laughed. "Dru, you're funny. Relax and come drink a beer with us."

Sam spoke up, "Don't take too long. We need to talk. Five minutes. Grab a beer and bring it to the war room."

Frank spoke up again, "Dru, push me into the war room." He looked over at Sarah and said, "You and Martina grab a six-pack for Dru and me, whatever you want for yourselves, and bring it to the room, okay?"

Sarah looked at him levelly, and he blanched. "I did it again?" he asked.

"Yes, dummy, you did it again. But it's fine. I'm happy to help out."

"Did what?" I asked stupidly.

"I told the girls to go 'make us a sandwich'."

I laughed. "Oops. You in trouble now. Sarah, I can grab the beers if you want."

"And leave me to push that big oaf up this ramp and to the war room? No way, that's work for donkeys and boys named Dru. Get to work and push that husband of mine. I'm going to grab a bottle of wine for Martina and me, and a six-pack of beer for you guys."

I must have looked confused because Martina jumped in with a big grin, "A lady likes to be asked, how hard is that to understand?"

All smiles disappeared after we got to the war room to find Jesse and Sam looking distressed and Elijah looking curious. The ladies arrived in good spirits, but it tapered off immediately as they looked around and picked up on the vibe of the room. We all sat down and silently passed beers to Elijah, Damon, Sam, Frank, and myself, while Sarah popped the cork on the wine and served both Martina and herself a glass of something red.

"We've got a big problem." Sam began. "Ms. Byrne, Carrick, and this other asshole Louis Hughes had access to real magic. They could use it in multiple areas. I thought..." he paused and then started again, "...I prayed that we had a religious group about to bring back a God."

"I was wrong." Sam looked absolutely sick. "Turns out that I am not completely alone after all." He turned to look at me with pure hatred and with venom in his voice said, "It appears one of your fucking Gods," he said pointing at me, "has been able to manifest here and it put together a group of dedicated mortals to enact its will on this plane of existence."

He clenched his fists, "Ms. Byrne said it manifests during their rituals and talks to them. Total bullshit. That's not how it works. There's a second God on Earth."

Except for Sam, Damon, and Jesse, we all sat stunned, even Elijah. Sam dropped his head into his hands and rubbed his eyes.

I sat cold, a deep dread spreading through my guts. Frank asked the question we were all thinking, "Who?"

"Don't know, but definitely Celtic."

"How the hell don't you know?" I blurted out. "Didn't she tell you?" I asked, referring to the late Shannon Byrne.

"She didn't know! The God is secretive and apparently appears only as a ball of light. Seems only the head Druid knows which God it really is."

"With Louis being the head Druid, of course," I said.

Elijah spoke up and asked, "Raven, how bad is this?"

"It's very bad, my friend, but how bad depends entirely on who it actually is. Celtic Gods are complicated. There are actually three main 'families' of gods, isn't that right, Dru?"

I paused with a bottle of beer halfway to my lips. Looking around, I saw everyone was staring at me. I sighed and lowered the bottle to the table.

"Yeah. In general, there are three families of Gods, but parents don't matter because parents rarely raised their kids. Surrogates, Aunts and Uncles, and others raised the children. That leads to lots of conflicting loyalties. Our Gods are called the Tuatha De", I said, using the Ulster pronunciation that sounds a bit like "Two-a-day".

"The Gods these days are all lumped into the Tuatha De Danann, but that's because we don't know where the first six Gods came from, so we assume they are related, but they break down into three families. The families are: Tuatha De Danann, Tuatha De Ernmann, and Tuatha De Domhain."

"Why does it matter which God we face?" Frank asked

"Because some of them are hard-core nasty, some are smart as hell, and some are psychotically violent. Like many groups of Gods you might be familiar with, Celtic Gods tend to be associated with certain things. The Tuatha De Domhain - the children of Domhu and Cernunnos - are pretty much classically Evil. Called the Fomor in legends. They are creatures of nightmares, mainly. Perhaps the first Gods of the British Isles, they got their asses kicked out by the Tuatha De Danann, who are supposed to be Goodness and Light, but let me tell you, they operated under a different version of 'goodness' than we recognize. Smart, ruthless, egotistical, and proud.

"The third family are the children of Ermas and Viridios and are called the Tuatha De Ernmann. Their family tree is essentially 'pure' as they didn't mix with the others, but they are every bit the equals of any other Gods.

"Take, for instance, one of the first Gods of the Tuatha De Ernmann. We call her Morrigan and she's a holy terror."

I looked over at Martina to see that she remembered our earlier talk and was nodding along. "Personally, I think she'd be the worst-case scenario, but this doesn't sound like the kind of thing she'd do. At least according to the legends and myths."

"Who would?" Sam asked,

"Well, another trickster, I guess," I answered and looked at him. "Isn't that exactly what you did here; build a group of religious fanatics to do your will on earth?"

Martina spoke, asking "Who is the trickster?"

"It's not that easy," I replied. "Remember when I told you there's lots of overlap in Celtic Mythology?"

"Yes.

"Well, there's no real 'trickster' God of the Celts, but two or three Gods would often do tricky things. Clever Gods that liked mischief from time to time."

Sam suddenly looked even worse, if that was possible. "Aw shit," he said.

"What is it?" Elijah asked.

"Nothing." He replied quickly. He looked over at me and asked the question I'd been dreading, "Can you go against a God and win? Because he...or she... might be around when we go for *Louis Hughes*."

"Not a chance," I answered. "You all know what happened the last time I even said 'No' to a God. She killed me."

Elijah and Damon looked up with surprise, but said nothing.

Frank said, "Then we're done here? Are we calling this off, because I think leaving enemies alive and at our backs is a horrifically bad idea."

"No," I replied. "We are not done. Louis dies by my hand. I made a promise to Sarah and I'm going to keep it."

Sarah looked at me and said, "Dru, I'd rather you be alive than Louis dead. You don't need to do this, it's O.K."

I looked over at Frank and said, "You know we have to do this. We need to stop these guys and put that God back beyond the...the...veil or whatever the fuck we are calling it."

Frank nodded and said to Sarah, "He's right, honey. We leave this unfinished; we're as good as dead anyway." Turning to Sam he said, "Let's put that big brain of yours to work, and let's figure out how to use our God to trump their God."

Elijah cleared his throat and we all looked over at him. "I think we can move forward. I mean, Damon and I can both sense magic and even throw some of it. I'm not in Damon's weight class, but we're both sensitive, right Raven?" Sam nodded.

"Okay, we can plan a raid. Not at the building in Baltimore, that would probably be suicide now, but this Hughes guy lives somewhere, right? We bring about twelve guys, find the house, plan a raid, and we do it so long as Damon and I don't feel any strong magic around the house."

Sam shook his head, "There is zero chance his home isn't protected, Elijah. He'll have wards, alarms, traps, and probably a healthy dose of armed personnel as well."

Elijah sat back thoughtfully.

Frank said, "I don't see how it matters, we're talking about moving fast, but it doesn't have to happen tomorrow. We can find the house, go look at it, and then see what plan might work."

"Uhh, Frank?" I asked.

"Yeah?

"What's the 'we' thing you're talking about? You aren't going anywhere."

"Yeah. I get that, Dru. Thanks for shoving it in my face."

I felt ashamed, but Frank went on, "I'm far more than a soldier, Dru, but even without legs, I'm still the best soldier in this room."

I snapped to attention, saying, "Godsdamned right LT. I'm sorry."

"I'll be here and I'll run it like I did for the Enchanted Rock action. I'm sure Sam has all the satellite communications equipment we'd need.

We all looked over at Sam as he said, "Of course I do, but magic makes it more complicated."

"I get that..." Frank began, but Sam interrupted him.

"... No you don't Frank. Real magic is the altering of *reality.* Damon did a Glamor today. An illusion. He altered what the eye saw, not what was actually there. Those poor suckers saw solid granite all the way to us because Damon made it appear that way. Strong magic can change the laws of physics. If this God is present, you won't be facing glamour and spells, *you'll be facing a God. The very reality of the universe will be against you.*

"Today I got so angry I lost control," Sam said with a look of chagrin. "I spoke with my power, and later I screamed. That was dangerous. I was angry and scared and I didn't want what I heard to be true. My scream was a scream of chaos and for a few seconds, I altered reality. I altered reality around me and everything was destroyed, including our technology. Hell, Jesse's gun probably doesn't even work anymore."

He looked at me and said, "Imagine, Dru, how long your headsets would last facing Morrigan, a Goddess of entropy and chaos? How about that steel gun?"

Hell, not one second. I knew that for sure.

"Wait, how the hell can you break a gun?" asked Frank.

"Iron," I said grimly.

"Huh?" said Frank.

Raven shook his head, "Not quite, Dru."

Surprised, I said, "What?"

"That cold iron myth of the Fae is just that - a myth."

"The What?" Frank asked.

I answered, "There is a myth that the Fae can't stand the touch of cold iron and that if they come in contact with it they are harmed and the iron is destroyed."

"Propaganda," Sam said. "The reality is that it's about alloys. Any alloys."

"I'm so confused right now," Sarah said.

"The myth about iron is a misinformation campaign. It's both exactly true and completely misunderstood. It isn't iron, it's the fact that iron isn't an alloy, like bronze was, or steel is."

Fascinated despite myself, I asked, "Why does that matter?"

"Alloys are a product of technology and industry of man. They are fabricated by man, and thus they can be unmade by gods quite easily. Changing an element present in nature is hard by comparison."

"I'm still confused," Sarah repeated.

"A God could literally unmake a bronze sword being used against him or her. Turn it back into copper and tin. In practical terms, the sword would fall apart in the hand of the wielder. We could not do that against iron. Iron is. It exists in nature. So an iron sword could hit us and cause harm. We American Gods worked hard to prevent iron from being discovered and used. In fact, about three thousand years ago, I had to convince a whole culture in the Midwest of what is now called the United States of America that stone and bone worked better than pure metals." He smiled at the memory, "That was a good trick."

Sarah looked aghast. "Why?"

"They got way too adept at working with pure copper. A God could get hurt fighting that. Carbon steel? Iron? Near impossible for us to deal with and dangerous as hell. Gods love alloys and hate pure elements"

"So, back to guns?" Frank asked.

"Guns are steel alloys. I told Jesse to throw away his pistol when we got back today even though steel is not made like Bronze. The melding of iron and carbon works at a molecular level, but the fact is, it's still negatively affected a tiny bit by magical energies.

"If you add metals like zinc or nickel to make it stainless, we can tear it apart. Also, there are some significant alloys in a steel barrel because they have trace elements of manganese, beryl, etc. Add it all up and you can't trust the gun to work right.

"However, the big risk with guns is that most bullet shells are brass, and there are lots of parts these days that are plastics and polymers. Any energies focused and employed by Gods will make them less than reliable. Fragile grips and compromised bullet casings."

"Magic destroys technology?" Sarah asked.

"No, not as such. As you can see, I love technology. But I have to avoid large workings around sensitive circuits and I keep my electronics in Faraday cages to be safe because I'm an agent of change and chaos. It's what I am. My actual intent and action lead to chaos. Pretty much always. Other Gods? Not so much."

"A God of order and rules," he continued, "would probably have almost no effect on electronics at all. It's not the magic, it's the intent. But I can promise you this," he finished, "If the God was around during the Bronze Age, it hates iron, and sure as hell knows how to break down alloys. That spells the end for any electronics in the way."

"Alright, we can't count on technology or eyes in the sky to direct us. Guns will probably work, but might not if the God shows up and intentionally goes after them. That's not ideal, but we've cleared houses and taken out targets before, Frank. And we won't go if the God is there because none of us want to suicide. We can do this with a good team." I indicated Elijah.

"Hello? Excuse me, Dru?" Martina spoke up. "You better point those pretty little hands over here too. I'm coming along."

Surprised, I asked, "Why?"

"Because, you silly man, it's my ass on the line too, and I've got years of fighting experience. I'm on the team."

I wanted to argue but realized I had no reason to say no except that I cared about her, so I said that. "I don't want you hurt, Martina. It's selfish, I know, but it's the truth."

She smiled at me gently, then her features hardened and she said, "Tough shit, hermano. I'm coming." Elijah covered his face in an attempt to hide the laugh. I guess that settled that.

It looked like Sarah was about to say something when Frank lovingly said, "No, honey. No. You're with me. Trained fighters only. You don't have the skill set for this, no matter what you think."

She glared over at him and opened her mouth, but Martina chimed in, "He's right, mija. I've trained with Sam's people and I've fought real actions. You'd be a liability. Please, stay and help Frank."

"Alright, listen up." Sam said "Here's the deal, Elijah, you and Damon pick a team to go with Dru. Make one of those picks Martina. We'll help as best we can here to develop an assault plan, but plan on going in alone. After you all arrive and recon for Magic, we'll finalize and decide if we can go."

"I'm bringing Jesse too." Elijah replied.

"You're not coming?" I asked, turning to Sam.

Sam looked at me levelly, "You do not want me there. That is not my place of power, and all I'd do is alert them that a strong magic presence is in the neighborhood. Plus, I've got somewhere to be. I'll be leaving tonight, but I'll be on the headsets and in the loop for the action. But hey, I'm a God and all. I'll be ready to try to create a miracle if you need one. Call it plan 'Z' if you want."

Flustered and suspicious, I asked, "Where do you need to be at a time like this?"

He didn't answer me. Instead, he winked at Damon and smiled.

"Timeframe?" Elijah asked.

"Put the team together now. You'll fly charter to Baltimore tomorrow morning and set up..." Sam looked to me for confirmation, "...in Dru's house?"

"It's small, but we'll all fit," I said.

"One more thing," Sam said with an expression that made me reflexively reach for the pain pills in my pocket. "plan for things to get ugly. Carry some iron weapons that don't go bang. It could get prehistory inside that house."

That made me smile involuntarily. Hopefully, nobody noticed.

Later that evening, I was two extra pain pills into a pleasant buzz when I walked over to their armory with Elijah to gear up, and I was not surprised to see that there was a wall of large cutlery made of wrought iron. I smiled again.

"Old school, just the way I like it."

Elijah looked at me funny but held his questions in. That was lucky, because feeling as good as I was, I might have accidentally answered him.

Right away I saw a bundle of three iron throwing knives. I picked them up and felt their balance. They were surprisingly good and I nodded to myself, putting them into my pocket.

Elijah laughed and said, "I thought better of you. You have to know that throwing knives are only good for movies and idiots who want to arm their enemies by tossing them a blade."

I smiled back at him and said, "For you maybe. I'm built different." And gave him a wink to show that I was having fun. He shook his head and smiled at my folly.

I was patient while looking over the bigger weapons, trying to find the best fit for my needs. I spent that time reminding myself all about the benefits and limitations of wrought iron. Much stronger than bronze, wrought iron was susceptible to rusting quickly and badly, and it was damn near impossible to repair after hard use.

Weapons could be made thinner, lighter, and longer in wrought iron than bronze, but after a point, they were at risk of bending, breaking, and dulling quickly. It wasn't until man accidentally invented steel that it ended the argument for all time about what metal was better for war.

A thought struck me and I asked Elijah, "If Gods hate Iron, and prefer alloys, why isn't this table full of Bronze weapons?"

"Because Raven wants us ready to kill a God. He trusts his people completely." He hesitated for a second, "But Dru?"

"Yeah?"

"You are not his people."

"What are you saying?"

"I'm asking you not to bring any iron weapon near my God. I trust you to fight with honor and I know you're a stone killer. I recognize that in you, and I'm glad. Arm yourself with whatever you want, but please respect my wishes in this matter, and don't go armed with iron around Raven."

"That might be the most you've ever spoken to me at one time. You have my word. No iron near Raven."

"Thank you."

"Can I ask you a question? About Damon?"

He looked at me carefully, "Maybe. Ask. I might answer."

"Is there a scenario where we learn to get along?"

He actually took a minute to think about it. "I love my brother. We practically raised each other when our mother died. But the world has not been kind to him, and it's been worse to his wife. He does not harbor anything but hate for the European colonizers."

Then he shrugged, "You aren't a colonizer, but you share the skin. Give it time." He smiled, "A lot of time."

"Fair enough. Thank you."

"My turn. You and Martina?"

"No. Not that way. She reminds me of the only person I've ever loved. Same wit and attitude, but I'm not built the way she is. Actually the opposite."

"Gay?"

"Why the fuck does everybody ask that?"

He laughed, "It's cool if so. I have no issues with anyone being who they are. Martina and I were once...something special, but she's polyamorist, right?"

"Yeah."

"So, she had another boyfriend and a girlfriend."

"I'm aware."

"You know what a two-spirit is?"

"You mean besides Damon's wife? No."

"A two-spirit is a person who takes on the traditional roles of both sexes. They are almost always strong Shaman's due to their unique outlook and access to the spirits. Iáxuhke is not only a two-spirit, she is also transgender. Damon loves her so deeply it's like looking at the best version of him whenever she's around. I'm so happy for him, but it's also hard. Prejudice exists everywhere, man."

"I get you."

"Do you? An indigenous guy married to a transgender two-spirit from another First Nation group inside of a white man's world? You get that? You get the white man's obsession with oppressing transgendered people? You understand the self-destructive tribalism of first nations people ostracizing those who marry outside of their nation?"

"No. No, I don't. But I get a foreign government forcing their language and Gods on you, letting your people starve to death when a potato blight hits, rounding up those that might be trouble and shipping them off to a penal island in the South Pacific, and stealing half their country. Not the same, but similar. I think we could at least not be enemies, even if we can't be friends."

He stared at me for a few seconds before smiling and changing the conversation, "So, not gay?"

I laughed, "Not anything. Not interested."

He grunted and turned back to the rack of weapons.

I went back to looking over short blades, inspecting a cool looking gladiolus, a score of leaf blades, and some long daggers, when I came across a sight so beautiful it almost brought tears to my eyes. Sitting on the table, half hidden under an errant leather scabbard sat a wrought iron kukri with a blade about fifteen inches long.

My breath caught in my throat and I grabbed the blade, lifting it up to eye level. It's hard to call anything made out of wrought iron exquisite, but that was the only word for it. Exquisite.

The entire blade and tang were iron, of course, but the tang was a full one, and the handle was black bone riveted onto it in the traditional style. The scabbard was the traditional two pieces of wood wrapped in black Ox hide. Everything was black except the finely honed edge, and it screamed *"Built To Kill."* It was perfect.

Like all kukri blades, it was forward curving with the edge on the inner belly, with this particular version shaped fairly narrow for the weight considerations and perfectly balanced in my hand.

I looked over at Elijah and said, "This is mine now. Forever."

He grunted a smile at me and said, "Ah! You're a liar. Clearly you need some alone time with her."

"Maybe," I replied, laughing. "She's gorgeous."

"You know how to use that thing? Nobody here has ever used it before." He paused, "You can't throw it, you know. It's not a boomerang."

I laughed out loud.

"Oh yes," I breathed, "Oh yes, I know how to use it. Learned how some years ago. Trained with a Gurkha for a while."

Elijah raised an impressed eyebrow and said, "So, yeah, I guess you do. I met a few Gurkhas myself in Afghanistan. Toughest SOB's I've ever seen, and I was a Marine."

"Bullshit. If you were a Marine, you were Force Recon."

"Sort of."

"Holy shit, you were Special Operations Command?"

He grinned.

"No way. You were a Raider, weren't you?"

"Guilty."

The Marine Raider Regiment were the toughest Godsdamned Marines on the planet. No wonder Elijah moved like an apex predator – he was one. "Have you ever seen Ghurka fight with their Kukris?" I asked. "It doesn't happen much anymore in modern warfare, but every once in a while..."

"Yeah," he replied, "I saw it. Joint operation with the British. We were overrun by the Taliban once at an outpost. Used up every round, every grenade, everything that went bang. It got old school. By the end, I was swinging my gun like a club and he was carving up the enemy like it was Thanksgiving dinner and he was an overly enthusiastic Pilgrim."

I looked at him and said, "I wouldn't think you'd like a Pilgrim."

He chuckled, "Different Nation, same problems. But there's nothing that can describe seeing a Gurkha fight."

"I know, I've seen it too."

"Where?"

"Burma."

He looked at me funny. "You mean Myanmar, right?"

"That's what they call it now, yeah."

Give the man credit, he held back his questions again.

Chapter Twenty

A Plan Falls Apart

The next morning, we were up early and headed to the airport. We all carried two huge bags full of gear, and I lamented the loss of all my luggage and belongings that got left behind when this whole shitstorm kicked off. I was especially sad about the loss of my clothes as I had spent most of this trip to Texas wearing whatever fit the best from the closets of others. I was excited to get back to my house and my own damn wardrobe.

I wasn't sure how we were going to be able to move all of this ordinance through an airport, but we left all the bags in the two shuttles as we got dropped off at the entrance to the terminal for private flights out of Austin Bergstrom International Airport.

Sam had smiled when I brought it up last night and said, "We have ways to move the equipment. Most of it isn't illegal at all, and I have several legitimate identities that have the right and privilege of traveling with gear such as this. Relax, nobody will go to jail or get stopped."

I didn't trust him at all, but if I wanted to go to Maryland and kill this guy I had to accept his word, and as he said, we boarded and left on time with no problems.

I was anxious and my hyperactivity was making it near impossible to sit still, but across the aisle and two rows ahead of me, Damon and Elijah were sitting and talking like it was any other day.

Elijah asked, "How is Iáxuhke doing with you gone so long this time?"

Damon's face broke out in a genuine smile and he answered, "She is positively joyful at my absence. She said I'd been driving her crazy messing up her spellcasting with my incompetence."

Elijah laughed, "She's still kicking you ass in the magic department?"

"Not as much anymore now that Raven is taking a personal interest in our growth, but yeah, she's still the best there is. We're different. I'm more of a shaper, she's casting legit workings man. It's incredible."

"How's everything else?"

Damon hesitated and glanced at his brother, "She wants a baby."

Elijah whistled quietly, "Wow brother. Are you ready for that?"

"I'm ready. I've been ready for a while. I've been waiting on her because...well you know."

"Yeah. You think you'll find a place that will let you both adopt?"

"It's hard, man. She doesn't care what kind of child she adopts, you know? But..."

"But you do?"

"Nah. Well, yeah. I want to adopt one of ours, you know? The whole thing we're doing here is to help our people, right?"

"Right, but nobody can help the way they're born, Damon, and every kid deserves a loving family."

"You think I don't know that? I married a woman that half the world refused to call a woman because of how she was born. I'll love and care for any child we decide on adopting, but I do admit I'm partial to our own people."

"So, am I brother, but we are more than genetics, aren't we? We're real people, and any kid lucky enough to have you as a father will grow up right. Your child will be our people. You know that."

Damon was quiet for a moment before putting an arm around Elijah's shoulders. "Love you, brother."

"Love you too. And Iáxuhke would be the greatest mother the world has ever seen. I think we both know that."

Damon snorted with suppressed laughter and said, "I do feel bad for the kid in one way, though."

"How's that?"

"Have you met the guy who'll be his uncle? Ughh..."

I stopped listening after that, feeling ashamed as if I had eavesdropped on something sacred and not meant for me.

When we landed at Baltimore Washington International, several emails were waiting for us. Sam had found the house. We took two rental vans Sam had reserved for us to my home and we started to get organized.

When we got to my house, a wave of bone-deep sadness hit me after I walked in the front door and tried to turn on the light and remembered I had called and turned everything off not six hours before Sarah had shown up at my door. I had been that close to attempting my suicide.

I explained it away to everyone as a precaution in case I had been killed trying to find Frank, and I called the Electric company and the Gas company and scheduled a resumption of service with a fat fee to expedite the electricity so we could have it in the next three hours. Martina was staring at me thoughtfully, and I was worried that she knew, or at least had guessed, what I had been about to do that day. So, I ignored her and went about organizing the group.

We moved all the furniture in my living room against the walls and assigned floor space to each person. I gave the training room to Martina and a Cheyenne woman who everybody called Hahkota, and my Master Bedroom would be both the sleeping space for Elijah and myself as well as the communications room that I still called an Air Operations Center in my head.

I invited Damon to stay in the room too, but he looked at me and said, "No. I'll stay with my people."

Elijah called out, "Damon..."

"No bro. Just no."

After getting ten adults settled into the space, the lights suddenly came on, so Damon, Elijah, Martina, and I went into the bedroom and gathered around my laptop. I dialed up the compound back in Texas and put it on speakerphone so we could all hear Sam, Sarah, and Frank.

Frank started without any preamble, "It appears Louis Hughes has a compound of his own. It's a large house with a pond and about fifteen wooded acres behind it. It's surrounded by a stone wall about twelve feet high and the driveway is gated and has a guard house."

Sam spoke, "He normally has guards stationed in the guard house twenty-four hours a day, and a small patrol of two guards with a K-9 working the perimeter."

"That's not so bad," Damon said.

"This is not a normal time," answered Elijah. "How many does he have now? Is he holed up there?"

"There isn't a satellite over his location right now, so I can't tell," replied Frank. "I'll need you to get a recon team together and head over there to scope it out."

We planned out a recon for tonight.

After talking it through, we decided that because the target was in Monkton, Maryland almost four hours away from my house on the Eastern Shore, we should bring the whole team with us in case we saw an opportunity to perform the elimination immediately.

This type of operation didn't need an overly complicated plan to achieve our objective since the goal was the death of the target. The trick was to get away with it and not wind up in a shootout with local authorities. Speed, shock, and awe were the goals.

We weren't going to get much more intel than we already had. Sam had grabbed the blueprints on file for the house and we went over them briefly and came to a consensus of the most likely places we'd find the target, but blueprints can be essentially useless in cases like this. After all, the target was stupidly wealthy and involved in massive conspiracies against the whole world. He had the money to build things without official permits. Things like panic rooms, reinforced doors, and bulletproof windows wouldn't be on the plans, so we had to have a smash-and-grab that took them by complete surprise.

Assuming they didn't have a God there hanging out waiting for us.

We'd bring everyone, and if we could see a way to perform the elimination tonight, we'd do it. If Damon and Elijah felt the mojo of a God, we'd haul ass out of there and back to my house to figure out if there was a feasible option in the short term to take Mr. Hughes.

We were driving Rt. 50 on Kent Island and about to cross the Bay Bridge when Frank called and we had a group chat.

I was driving in Van One with Martina and Jesse, while Elijah and Damon were in Van Two. I had two more soldiers in my van with us and they were studiously looking over the limited intel we had and talking about their areas of responsibility. Professional, and it made me feel good about our chances. I assumed the same thing was happening in Van Two.

My two soldiers were as different as night and day, but they seemed to be good friends with that easy and relaxed camaraderie that comes from long deployments together. One of the guys was called Russell, and he had introduced himself to me as, "Russell, as in Means." I hadn't understood what he meant, and after staring at me for a second or two, he grimaced a little bit and shook his head as he walked away.

Russell was a tall guy well over six feet, with a strong build, and would have been handsome if not for a nasty slice that started above his left eyebrow and went to his left ear. It was an ugly scar that marred a strong face. His buddy, on the other hand, was named Yaz, had relatively pale skin despite the unmistakable features of a man from the southwest of the U.S.A., and stood a lanky five foot five inches tall and smiled all the time.

Martina leaned over and spoke into my ear, "Russell is Lakota and Yas is Diné." after they had walked away.

"Hey guys," I called into the back of the van, "listen up, we've got some more info coming."

Sam and Frank appeared on the tablet Martina had, and she turned around to hold it where everyone but I could see them. Being the driver, I figured watching the road was more important.

Sam started with, "This guy has serious pull, gentlemen. There is essentially a "no-fly zone" over his property for satellites, so I'd have to hack a Chinese or Soviet satellite to get a look. That simply can't be done in time, so you'll have to do it the old-fashioned way."

Frank took over the talk and began with "Monkton, Maryland is pretty much horse country, so the compound is on about twenty-five acres of a working horse ranch in addition to the fifteen wooded acres behind the house. You can see from the intel that the driveway is gated with the guard house and it has a low stone wall along the entire length of the property where it faces the road. Behind the stone wall is a more modern fence high and strong enough to discourage horses from leaping over. It's also electrified.

Sam interrupted, "We're going to bring down power in the neighborhood, but you'll still go straight through the front gate. However, we need to do it stealthily. Any alarm gives them way too much time to get organized, run to a panic room, or whatever."

Over the speaker in the tablet, we could hear Elijah ask a question, "Will there be cameras? Because we have to assume generators will come on, right? Damon can't fool the cameras, just eyes."

"We're working on that right now," Frank replied.

"Well, that fills me with confidence," I said aloud from the front seat. "Your little illusions don't work on cameras? I guess that explains why I never saw your illusion on Enchanted Rock; I was watching through the drone camera."

"Sugarplum." Sam corrected absently.

"What. The. Fuck. Ever." I replied

What followed was about an hour of discussion and evasions from Sam about how, exactly, we were going to be able to get down an eight-hundred-meter driveway lined with trees and cameras without alerting the entire compound that we were there.

But that's not important since nothing we planned went right anyway.

As dusk fell, we were driving down the aptly named Monkton Road about two miles away from the compound, planning on doing a drive-by and scouting the surrounding area for a close recon, when we came around a corner to see three local police cars across the road with their lights on.

A big, pot-bellied man with a bigger cowboy hat and a sheriff's uniform was standing with his hands up, indicating we should probably slow down and stop for a second or two. Beyond him, and using the cars as cover, were five more guys in the same costumes pointing AR-15's at us.

"Heads up!" I called out. "Hostiles on the road ahead. I'm stopping here and will get out and walk up to him. You all get ready to deploy about as rapidly as you've ever done. This looks a whole lot like an ambush."

I pulled up about fifty meters short of the cars, slamming onto the right shoulder of the road, edging up to the trees there, and was out the door before the van stopped rocking on its suspension. I was dressed out for the op, had my gun in my holster, and looked exactly like what I was; a mercenary ready for combat.

The Sheriff smiled and said, "Hey there son. No need for concern. You are with the Trickster, I presume?"

Stopping about fifteen yards away, I answered, "That depends entirely on who's asking."

He frowned, "Son. I'm asking. This is my town, and Mr. Hughes is a good friend to this community. We've been expecting you, and Mr. Hughes has a message for you."

"If that message involves those rifles behind you, you won't like my reply."

That got a smile from him, and he turned his head back towards his men as if only now noticing them. "These fellas? Naw. You don't need to worry about that. Mr. Hughes wants you to know he's expecting you, and that you're welcome to come on up his driveway and onto the property.

"Oh really? Are we now?"

"Yes sir. Mr. Hughes and I have come to an understanding that's worked out quite well over the last seven years. He doesn't make a mess I need to clean up, and I stay away from his business."

His smile faded and a grim look replaced it. "You look like a mess waiting to happen. So, get your vans off my road and onto Mr. Hughes' property before I decide that my boys and their rifles need some target practice."

"I would, but some asshole parked three cop cars in my way."

He glowered at me and ground out, "We're leaving, son. Now, how about you get back into the van and follow us to his driveway? If you turn off onto his property, we'll keep right on driving, but if you don't, I guess we'll use you for that target practice after all."

I was about to go back to the van when a thought struck me.

"I have a better idea, why don't you drive us up there? We'll drive in between your cars all the way to the house, then you can turn around and drive away."

"That wasn't the agreement Mr. Hughes and I made."

"Please. Get on the radio and give him a call. Tell him I hate claymores and ambushes and hope he likes you guys enough not to kill you along with us as we go up a driveway custom-made for both."

A shadow of uncertainty flickered across his face and he went back to the car without comment and grabbed the radio. He began talking into it, and while I couldn't hear what was said, apparently, it was amicable enough, because, after only a few moments, he put it back and walked over to me smiling.

"Mr. Hughes says you keep poor company if you think he means to kill you. He wants to offer you a job."

"And you believe that?" I asked incredulously.

"I don't care, son. Get in the van. Let's go."

"I'm not your son, old man."

He ignored me and walked back to his vehicle, so I turned and walked back to mine.

"Okay folks," I said, "we've been invited in. Anybody else think this is an astonishingly bad idea?"

Frank and Sam both said at the same time "Yes."

But Sam continued, "However, I think it makes sense if there's strong magic available to this Hughes guy. And if there is, then our plan to attack is out the window anyway."

"We abort," Frank said.

"I wouldn't," Elijah said over the headset from the van behind me.

"Why not?" asked Frank.

"Because our plan is tits up, and we're not going to get another shot, like, ever. The game has changed and we need to learn how."

Damon joined in, "Raven, shouldn't I have access to the magical flow here too?

Sam took his time replying, " ...Yes...Practically speaking magic is magic. If it's available, you don't need anything but your training and your will. It'll 'taste' a bit different to you, though."

Damon seemed to understand that as he said nothing, but Martina wasn't having it.

"Damon, you'll be at a significant disadvantage. This Hughes guy will have familiarity and be aligned with his God's desires. Assuming my theoretical model of magic is correct in any way, he'll have much easier access to the magic, while it will fight you. You have to assume he'll be an order of magnitude stronger than you."

"I still think my brother is right. We need information, and we have been invited in."

I was getting anxious. "Again, am I the only one here who thinks he's going to kill us all with claymores?"

"No, my friend," Jesse chimed in, "I'm right there with you."

"Um...not to belabor the obvious, but do we even have a choice?" asked Russell. "I mean, we either go, or we start killing Sheriffs. Is that a thing we're willing to do?"

There was silence for the final few seconds as the police cruisers got sorted out and lined up on the road to lead us to the compound.

Frank said, "I want a consensus. Go or No go. Elijah?"

"Go."

"Dru?

"No Go, boss."

"Damon?"

"Go."

"Martina?"

She looked my way guiltily and said, "This is too important to pass up. We need to learn more. Go."

Long story short, Frank asked everyone, and I was the lone dissenter. Even Jessie caved and voted to go on.

And so the way we successfully got past the eight-hundred-meter driveway lined with trees and cameras (and most likely Claymores) was by following a police escort. And apparently everybody knew we were coming. And they didn't care.

We immediately went live with each other via headsets and body cams as soon as we started following the police escort. Sam honestly did have great stuff. We discussed what was going on the whole drive with the notable absences of both Elijah and Damon. They were sitting in their van doing whatever it was they do when trying to feel the presence of a God.

We turned up the driveway and Damon said, "Holy shit."

"Yeah." breathed Elijah.

"What?" I asked.

"There's tons of magic everywhere. This is as strong as Enchanted Rock. Stronger."

"Not possible," Sam replied, "Enchanted Rock is ancient magic; a sacred space for over fifteen hundred years. There's nothing like that in Monkton, Maryland. I'd know."

Elijah spoke up, "Raven, it's massive. Whatever is here now is like...I can't even explain it. It feels so strong, but...linear. Straight?"

Sam replied, "You are used to my chaos magic, it's more...unconstrained. It flows..."

"Circular," Damon said.

"Yes. You're describing what its opposition feels like. Our Enemy has a God of creation and order on his side."

"Watch your gear closely, people. We might lose our tech and our alloyed arms quickly." I said.

Martina turned off her cell phone and shoved it into the glove compartment, looking at me and saying, "Just in case."

"Ok. Ok, this is a good sign." said Sam, "He's probably feeling quite secure in his power but he doesn't know exactly what happened on Enchanted Rock, so Damon and Elijah; you two should be prepared to give him a nasty little shock. Embrace the magic and don't fight it, try to come to an accommodation with it, and remember it will respond better to straight-line visualizations, not arcs."

Frank interrupted and gave directions to all of us non-magical people. "Proceed as planned and don't show your hand early. Act as if you know nothing about the magic or the entropy concerns, but don't forget that your guns might become as dangerous to you as to them."

As we got to the top of the driveway, I said, "Now." over the headset and we turned a hard right as the van behind me turned a hard left and we both accelerated for about two seconds as we drove off the driveway and onto the neatly manicured lawn, tearing up the grass and leaving deep tracks where the tires tore through. We hit the brakes, slammed the doors open, and exited the vehicles rapidly, raising our rifles and searching out cover via the vans themselves and rapidly approaching the sheriff's vehicles with our guns raised and calling out for them to show us their hands through the windows.

The front door to the house opened and a voice called out, "Please let Sheriff Crouse and his men go. There's no trap here. I'm going to come outside, please do not shoot me."

Then a butler straight out of central casting walked forward with his hands up and looked at us with an epic level of disdain. He walked over to the police cars, ignoring all of us with such effortless snobbery I couldn't hope to match if I had a thousand years of practice as he leaned over to talk to the sheriff and said, "Mr. Hughes thanks you for your service, Sherriff Crouse. Have a good evening."

Elijah quickly approached the butler, gun still up. "Pardon me Jeeves, but you're not currently in charge here. The Sheriff leaves when I'm sure your boss just wants to talk."

The offended sniff from the butler was so comical I started laughing and several of the guys grinned along with me.

"My name is Liam, sir, and I assure you that I would not be here if violence was imminent."

Then I swear he muttered under his breath, "Ruffians."

He faced us and said, "Allow me to send these cars of armed men away from you. In return, I suppose you can have me as your 'hostage' should you still want one."

Elijah looked my way and mouthed "Ruffians?" as Frank said, "Let them go." He looked back at Jeeves and nodded his assent.

The sheriff and his men turned around and quickly drove away down the driveway without comment like all little men who had sold their souls do.

Liam looked around at us and said, "Three men are about to come out and lead you to Mr. Hughes. They carry no firearms. Please don't shoot them."

"What about dogs?" I asked.

"I beg your pardon?"

"There are K-9's on the property, where are they?"

"They are kenneled, sir." He sniffed, "In anticipation of your team's arrival."

Three men who were clearly Broadhead soldiers came out in tactical gear and, true to Jeeves' word, they carried no guns. What each carried was a riot baton about three feet long and a huge knife on their hip that most rational people would call a short sword. I bet they weren't steel.

Frank's voice came over the headset. Or at least it tried to, but there was strong interference as he tried to communicate.

"Dr...yo....mera isn't wor...an't see...atic."

Shit. That was fast.

"You can take the headsets off and your cameras have probably stopped working by now, sir." said an insufferably smug Jeeves.

As we had already agreed to pretend we had no idea why we were having these issues, Elijah replied, "We'll keep them on. I'm sure we'll re-establish communications quickly." while we all surreptitiously turned off the headsets to prevent static or feedback. Now they were props.

"As you see fit, I'm sure. These men will take you to Mr. Hughes."

I pinned the man with my gaze and said, "You're not taking us, Jeeves? Forget your offer of hostage? What kind of butler are you? Do you even buttle?"

He stared at me like I was the freshly discovered shit on the bottom of his shoe, sniffed epically yet again, and turned around, leaving without a backward glance.

Elijah let him go, and I couldn't blame him. Liam was a prick.

We were all led up to the front door and ushered inside. The foyer was a huge, gorgeous, ornate killing field. It was round and about fifty feet in diameter. The walls were eggshell white with tasteful impressionist oil paintings of landscapes mounted on the walls. Between each painting stood a man with a bronze crossbow pointing at the ceiling. We entered guns up and pointing right back at the soldiers with the ancient weapons and my stomach sunk as the implications were clear.

A voice came out through an open door on the far side of the abattoir, "Hello Trickster army. Please put down your firearms. You may keep your 'sharps' if you desire, but I'm afraid I do not allow firearms past this room. Not even for my own security guards."

"Why should we disarm ourselves?" Elijah asked.

"Please, sir. If you intended to attack, you already would have. You are here to learn something about me. I'm happy to oblige. On the flip side, I could have killed you several times over by now, but that is not my intention. Please, I ask again, put down the guns and come in for a talk."

I shrugged and started disarming. I dropped my rifle, pulled out my pistol and put it on the floor next to the AR-15. Then I dropped all my magazines of ammo and adjusted my kukri on my waist as well as felt my pocket sheaches for the throwing knives. Everyone else had done the same and we filed into the door. As we passed through, I stopped to put a hand on Martina's shoulder and asked, "Help me out. Is this an appropriate time for 'Ladies first'?"

She grinned a quick smirk and swatted my hand away, walking past me into the room, muttering "Inappropriate jokes". Thu, I was the last person to enter the room. Elijah and the voice of Louis Hughes had already started talking to each other as I came in behind Martina and Russel.

"Hello soldier, my name is Louis Hughes and you are?"

"My name is Elijah, and I am the commanding officer of this team."

As I entered the room and we all continued to spread out a bit, I saw that two men were standing behind a large desk where a seated figure I couldn't yet see but had to be our Louis Hughes resided, and four men along the walls all holding bronze and wood crossbows pointing upwards at the ceiling where an accidental discharge wouldn't kill someone.

Professionals to the core, we all spread out to avoid clumping into big targets and eased our way close to the potential hostiles in case we needed to fight. A Crossbow might be old-fashioned, but a heavy bronze bolt will kill you dead in a flash.

I moved to my left to get close to the nearest guard when the view cleared and I got my first look at Louis Hughes.

He was speaking to Elijah, but looking around at everyone. "Well, Elijah, I'd like to clear up some misunderstandings between your boss and our group and maybe see if we can't..." His eye fell upon my face and he stopped short. My heart froze in my chest as he threw back his head and started laughing hysterically.

My despair must have been plain to see on my face because I heard Martina as if from a thousand miles away ask, "Dru? What's going on?"

"Oh this...this is funny," Hughes said between laughs. "Ah...Hysterical..." He finally got himself under control long enough to ask me between deep breaths of recovery, "Does Raven even know who you are, my son?"

Chapter Twenty-One

Meet Louis

I was already moving. My kukri had cleared the scabbard and the blade flashed toward the startled guard's neck as I screamed at Louis, "You don't get to call me that!"

The guard's head leapt from his shoulders in a fountain of scarlet as my cut went straight through and I followed up into a spin and leaped towards the desk. The world slowed down as it always does in combat for me, so I watched everyone get shocked into action at my unplanned attack.

I saw Hahkota turn and leap for the door behind us to close it before the men in the foyer could charge in, while Martina pulled two, eighteen-inch-long knives from scabbards on her belt and dove behind me into a roll on the floor.

Over on the other side of the room, Russell had drawn an ugly, wicked-looking hatchet of iron and threw it as hard as he could at the crossbow soldier farthest up the wall to my right, while Yaz pulled a monstrous Bowie knife and charged the closer guard on the same wall.

A soldier named Willie, who had traveled up in the truck with Damon and Elijah, had drawn a Gladiolus and launched straight for the desk. He was met with a crossbow bolt fired by a soldier behind Louis Hughes' desk that slammed straight into his chest and passed halfway out his back before getting stuck in his shattered scapula. The force knocked him backward off his feet into Damon, who survived the bolt aimed at him by the other desk guard because he fell on his ass.

Hahkota jerked back as three bolts punched their heads through the oak door and stopped there, her life saved by quality construction.

I took my third long step toward the desk.

Somehow, Martina managed to reach the guard far up the left wall as he released the bolt at Russell across the room. She was able to jostle him the tiniest bit and the bolt whistled past Russell's neck and buried itself into the wall beside him. He never noticed as he closed into hand-to-hand range with his own guard as the man panicked and tried to reload his crossbow instead of facing the six-and-a-half-foot Sioux warrior in full-on attack mode. He was slammed into the wall and all but crushed under the onslaught of Russell's fury. Too late, he dropped the crossbow and tried to fight back, but by then it was already over as Russell punched him in the throat, crushing his larynx and voice box and cross-stomping his knee, destroying it. The man fell to the ground already dead, through his body would take about sixty seconds to figure it out and stop trying to breathe through the crushed airway.

Yaz wasn't as lucky. The guard had the crossbow down and aimed before I had even finished killing his friend, and was going to shoot me, but Yaz became the bigger threat, so he turned his shoulder a fraction and pulled the trigger sending the heavy iron bolt straight through poor Yaz's head, exploding it like a ripe melon.

Elijah had not been idle. He had stooped low and pulled two long knives in a style similar to Martina's and had charged the desk with me, Jesse, and the now dead Willie. As Yaz fell, Elijah altered his trajectory and attacked the guard. The doomed man attempted to use his crossbow defensively and swiped it across his body to block Elijah's thrust, but as he did so, he opened himself up for the second blade, which Elijah punched up under the armpit and into the heart of the guard stopping it at once.

Martina had used her blades to open the neck of her opponent and he was bleeding rather profusely all over her as I reached the desk at the same time as Jesse with my kukri high over my left shoulder for a killing blow and...

BOOM

Whiteout.

Ringing ears.

Vision returned slowly and I saw all of us - our team, the two remaining guards, the five dead bodies - all fetched up against the walls as Louis Hughes stood furious, eyes on me, his face glowering, teeth gnashing, and his hand extended towards the door we had all come in.

I looked over to the door and saw Jesse transfixed like a butterfly pinned to a board. A shining ivory spear was holding him a foot off the ground as it had crunched straight through his chest. A look of utter surprise was on his face as if he couldn't believe his life had ended because of a fucking spear. And the spear was on fire, burning Jesse from the inside out.

And then, like magic, the spear pulled itself out of the door and flew back to the hand that had thrown it, leaving Jessie's body to crumple bonelessly to the floor. A smoking sack of meat for carrion birds. I felt it like a punch to the gut. I had really liked Jessie.

Holding a burning spear without so much as a blister, Louis Hughes screamed, "I invited you into my home, Setanta! This is not how we behave! You know better!"

My face twisted with bitter defeat and my impotent rage. Gods how I hated this asshole. "It's not fifty B.C. anymore, you piece of shit."

Martina, my brilliant sister, made the connections. I could see it in her eyes and they widened and she looked from me to him, an expression of terror and revulsion growing in her body posture. "Are you," she swallowed and tried again, "You are the God?"

He slowly turned to her, thunder still smoldering in his eyes and he nodded once, saying, "I am Lugh." before dismissing her and turning back to me.

"Fifty B.C.?" His mouth twisted down into a wry expression of disgust. "You don't even get the irony in that yet. But you will soon." He seemed to shrink back to merely human and said, "Plus, technically you were born in eighty-seven B.C., my son."

"I've told you repeatedly. You don't get to call me that."

"Wait," Elijah said, "That Byrne woman said the God manifested as a ball of light during rituals."

Lugh looked at him bemused, "A Shaman of the Raven fell for that old trick? The ball of light was from me, fool. I wasn't ready to show myself yet. You all have forced the issue."

His two remaining soldiers were getting themselves off the ground and Lugh pointed his spear at Elijah as he left the room, "Stay on the floor or die. All of you."

We believed him and stayed on our asses. But we did scoot around a little to get closer to one another. I looked around the room and saw poor Yaz, Jessie, and Willie. Right on cue, I heard the question I had been dreading.

Damon looked over at me with fresh depths of distrust and antipathy evident in his face and said, "Setanta? Who the fuck is that? Who the fuck are you?"

I deflated like a balloon. I guess it's time to explain more.

"About a week ago," I began, "I sat at a table in Raven's compound and told Sam and my Family who I was and what I had been. I told them all my family was God-touched once before I was born and once again right before I died.

"Truth is, this asshole who goes by Louis Hughes is the Celtic God Lugh. And he's technically my father.

"See, he raped my mom way back in eighty-seven B.C. Afterwards, he skipped right out, leaving me with Mom and my abusive stepfather. I've only met Lugh a handful of times in two thousand years.

"But him being a God, I was always going to be born with a couple of knacks. You already know that I don't miss...Ever. Neither does he, by the way. We may not always hit the bullseye, but we always hit the target somewhere.

"But I also have agility and speed a good bit higher than the average professional athlete, and every once in a while I can pull out a trick or two in battle. Unfortunately, I attracted the attention of the Morrigan. She tried to seduce me. I said no. She killed me.

"All this is well-known about me. I was somewhat famous for a few centuries after I died that first time."

I swallowed hard and went on, "My mother named me Setanta. I prefer Dru. The people of Ulster called me something different.

"What most people don't know about me is that, as I stood tied to a standing stone on a field of battle, trying to die on my feet, the Morrigan paid me another visit. Legends say she came to gloat and peck out my eye. The truth is hidden from history. What she gave me was a curse disguised as a gift. See, she had learned what my stepfather had done to me as a child. Then she promised that she would not choose me to be among the slain. Ever. Seemed a good deal at the time, but after a while, I realized it meant that if I wanted to live forever as a healthy young man, I had to join an army, kill people, and make sure that I died in combat. I've never died in bed, or at rest, or peacefully. I've spent my two thousand years killing others until they got lucky and killed me.

"She told me it was an apology for not understanding why I turned her down....ha."

Equal part furious and aghast, Martina said, "You didn't tell us that. You only said that before the Gods disappeared, you were a warrior who had his skills given to him as a gift from the God Lugh to your pregnant mother, and the first time you almost died, the Morrigan gave you an immortal 'get out of hell free card', I believe you called it. You made it seem like you were a few hundred years old, like Frank. And it was still the most horrible life I had ever heard of. Fighting, dying, reborn alone for hundreds of years. You mean to tell me that's been happening to you for millennia?"

I turned to Martina. "I didn't tell you all of this in detail because I didn't want to get into it. My youth was brutal and evil. I was killing people by age seven, Martina, remember? But what I told you was the truth. I've spent hundreds of lifetimes fighting as a soldier, and every time I'm mortally wounded in combat, I 'die', wake up, and I'm essentially a healthy twenty-seven years old again."

Frank said, "Why didn't you stop and let yourself die? You're not a maniac. Why stay alive forever?"

"Ha. I tried. Turns out I just age. I don't die. All I do is get older. The first time I realized it, I was almost an objective seventy years old in an era where everyone died by age fifty. I looked pathetic trying to fight my way to death, but finally, I found a thief and got him to knife me in the gut for a handful of coins. I fought back, died, and woke up twenty-seven years old. Tried again a few hundred years ago. Got to one hundred and seven years old before I had my servant put me in my old armor, strap me onto the saddle of my horse, and then charged a bunch of English archers across a muddy field in France. Twenty-seven years old again.

So soft, I could barely hear her, Martina asked, "Why not suicide?"

My brain got fuzzy and had a hard time understanding what she said. "Whenever it got that bad, I'd go join an army."

"That's not what I asked."

Confused, I said through the haze, "But that's what I did."

Martina said, "Dru. You're not making any sense."

"I'm making perfect sense! You're the ones asking weird questions!"

Martina stared at me and quietly asked, "Were you going to kill yourself before Sarah found you?"

I looked down at the floor in shame, pressure building behind my forehead, "There wasn't any war left to fight."

"Can you kill yourself? Won't you come back?"

A sharp, shooting pain went across my head from behind my eyes to the base of my skull. "If I die in combat, yes."

"What about if you die peacefully?"

My head was buzzing loudly and I put my hands over my ears as I said, "I never did. My destiny was to die young and famous as the greatest warrior in Ireland."

There was quiet then. I looked around and everyone was staring at me in confusion. I asked, "What?" but got no answer.

We all sat in more silence for a few moments, until a dry, bitter laugh escaped from Elijah. "And Raven knows this about you. Knows exactly who you are."

The pain and noise subsided a little bit. "I had hoped not, but...Yeah. It seems so."

He chuckled again and turned to his brother, "Raven had you pick a fight with the Hound of Chulainn by calling him a dog..."

I slumped wearily against the wall as my head finally cleared and the pain subsided. "Cú Chulainn is a mythical character."

He stared at me. "Based on you, right?"

"Some of it."

All eyes turned to me again.

"Alright, yes." I hated that fairytale. A happy go lucky boy of unblemished success and victory. A boy loved by all for killing every motherfucker that got in his way. I envied and despised that imaginary, simple version of me. A boy doesn't kill at age seven unless he's got really bad reasons to.

I was saved from explaining more by the entrance of the Evil son of a bitch that called me son. The door opened and Lugh stepped into the room glancing around to see that we were all still on the floor and not up to some sneaky plan. He was holding a leash that was connected to a harness around the body of a gorgeous German Shepard with a very dark coat and was followed by four new security guards all holding short spears with large, sharp, bronze spear tips mounted on oak staves.

While I had been talking, we had shifted around a bit because we were professionals and weren't going to miss the opportunity to retrieve lost weapons or clean them, but our asses will still firmly planted. Russell had his hatchet back and the soldier whose name I couldn't remember - Tony? Travis? - whatever, had moved over next to Hahkota and had helped each other get organized as neither had bloodied their weapons in the incredibly short melee.

Elijah and Damon had not shifted, but rather had sat and listened to me, unmoving the entire time except for Elijah's cleaning of his long knife.

Lugh looked around the room at the dead before turning to Martina. He pointed to the throat-cut guard and said, "You killed this one?"

Her eyes fired up with defiance and she said, "Yes."

He nodded and pointed to the guard who had choked to death due to a crushed throat and looked at Russel. "This one is yours?"

Russell smiled, "Yes."

He pointed at the man slumped over with a small amount of blood on his stomach and looked over at Elijah, "This one was yours and it was well done. Quick."

Elijah nodded an affirmative.

He looked at me and sighed. "And of course, you made the biggest mess of all. The whole head?"

"Maybe you're next," I said.

He frowned as if I'd disappointed him, and I sincerely hoped I had.

He looked to Damon and a ghost of a smile touched his lips as he ignored him and turned to Hahkota, "Where is your kill?"

She swallowed nervously and said, "I pinned the door shut so the guards outside couldn't get in" as she pointed to the oak door with three bolts stuck through it. "The fight ended before I could get mixed in."

Lugh stared at her for a few seconds before nodding again and saying, "Smart."

He turned to Tucker – Tommy? I'm gonna call him Tommy – and repeated, "Where is your kill?"

He glanced at me and over to Elijah as he said, "It happened too fast, I was going to charge the guys behind you after they fired off their bolts, but you..."

"Enough," Lugh said. "You have no kill. Only excuses."

I knew where this was going. "He did not flee the field of battle. This was too short a fight for him to get it stuck in. He is no coward. These men and women are warriors, everyone."

With a calculating stare, he rubbed his chin while thinking, eventually saying, "Fine. You all may come in. Follow me." At the door behind the desk, he turned to Tommy, "Cowards have no place here. I am watching you."

Tommy squared his shoulders and said, "I am no coward."

That seemed to please Lugh and he swept through the door first, turning his back to us with a total lack of fear or concern for his safety.

Elijah swept up next to Tommy and said, "Smart move, Tobias. I think it'd be an extremely bad idea to back down in front of this God."

Tobias! Of course. Knew it all along, only needed a hint. "Tobias, Elijah is right. In Lugh's era, cowards were ostracized and exiled. I have a feeling here you'd be killed out of hand. Arrogance and bravado are celebrated. Don't ever back down. This whole thing was a throwback to the days when we Celts boasted our deeds after battle."

Elijah turned to Damon and said, "Plan Z. Do it. Get started now."

Damon nodded, tapping his head, and said, "Already on it."

The rest of us acted like we had heard nothing.

We entered a hallway and continued walking down until we got to another well-made oak door, which a guard opened and ushered us all through.

In this room was a wall of floor-to-ceiling windows and a huge sliding glass doorway to the outside patio and pool, except that "patio" and "pool" were wholly inadequate words for the Edenic garden outside. It was a verdant scene out of the past. His backyard looked like a portrait straight out of the far distant past of the East Coast of America. Large, old-growth trees, sun-dappled little spots on the ground where the sunlight managed to trickle down through the leaves to reach to the grass and a quiet hush of peace.

The pool was actually a beautiful natural pond, but even that is a pathetic image compared to what we saw. A gentle slope into the water, with artfully grown rushes on shore and reaching out into the shallows, with clear water showing the hints of large fish swimming below the calm, idyllic surface. We all instinctively walked over to the gorgeous water feature, and I could see the longing on Martina's face to jump in and swim. It was almost painful. I briefly, insanely, wondered if it was an enchanted pool of water. It was that stunning.

In fact, if it wasn't for the large standing stone in the middle of a small clearing next to the pond showing obvious signs of ritual sacrifice, it would have been a wonderful paradise. Or at least a nice spot for a picnic. Unfortunately, there *was* a large standing stone with iron manacles hammered into it for both feet and hands, as well as a dark stain that nobody here could pretend was anything other than blood all over the lower half of the stone.

I looked from that stone to Lugh's face to find him staring at me knowingly. My face must have given me away, because he said, "Yes, Setanta. That's for you."'

"The hell it is."

"You'll walk over there and chain yourself up, or you'll be responsible for the deaths of each of your friends here. "He saw my face set in denial and he went on, "You'll do it because I have no intention of killing them all unless you fight me. You're all too late already, and there's no need to kill them because I am quite sure their boss is going to fall in line and tell them to play along. The only other option is an all-out war between the only two Gods on Earth, a thing we want to avoid since it basically means we have to start the whole damned world all over again. Too much work, trust me."

"Why chain me up at all?"

"Because you're staying here when they leave. It's time you and I had a talk. You are coming home to your family."

"The fuck I am." My vocabulary was somewhat limited at the moment.

Martina reached out to me and whispered, "You're already with your family."

Lugh continued, "And I know you'll fight me because it's what you do. Frankly, you're too messed up to trust. You and I both know you won't behave." He gestured at the gorgeous German Shepard at his feet, "Do you see my hound, Tynan? It is well trained and well behaved, raised on the blood of a God, but she still requires a leash, as do you."

He laughed and said, "Go chain yourself to the stone, boy."

"I'm not doing it."

He sighed, showed a hand signal to the dog and it promptly dropped to its haunches and sat still, staring at me. Then he dropped the leash and walked over. "Alright," and moving faster than I could react, he shoved Martina into the pond. When I say "shoved", it doesn't adequately describe the lightning-fast strike he threw with his open hand into Martina's sternum. He knocked the breath out of her as she flew about twelve feet into the pond, her eyes searching me out, wide and scared.

But before she made contact with the water, a horror leaped from the pond and grabbed her, dragging her under. It was an ollphéist – A nightmare water worm from the British Isles. I had killed a few in my day and knew they were hideously strong animals and always, always, hungry. It had wrapped its long, grey-mottled body around Martina twice and splashed back into the pond, dragging her down so fast she hadn't even been able to scream.

I spun towards Lugh in a rage, planning on attacking him right then and there, everyone else be damned, but without even appearing to try, he slapped me with that open hand and sent me reeling to the ground, seeing stars, feeling like I was going to vomit, and completely disoriented.

Yet all I could think was that I had lost my sister. It was crushing me.

"Put on the manacles!" he yelled over his now barking dog.

I was still unable to stand, so Lugh pointed to Damon and Tobias, "You two, drag him over and chain him up."

Elijah, sick with silent grief for what he had witnessed, reached out to Damon to stop him, but Damon shrugged him off and helped Tobias stand up. Tobias looked around, but refused to make eye contact with Elijah or myself. I guess he was a coward after all.

Then those two bastards did it. They chained me to a fucking standing stone. Full circle to the first time I died. I didn't fight back. All I did was mutter "Martina", over and over while I waited for the world to stop spinning and my stomach to settle down.

In my head, a blue painted face appeared and for the first time in centuries, I heard her voice. It was quietly saying, *"Let go and do it, my love."* over and over.

I dropped down, absolutely devastated. Martina was gone, and I was chained to a stone. I was suddenly so tired! The pain came roaring into my body, every old injury, every ache and pain I'd been hiding under painkillers for the last year; I didn't have the will to hold it all back anymore. Dully, I looked out at the scene playing out in front of me.

"So, now what?" Elijah asked, his shared grief plain to see on his face.

Lugh looked over the group. "Now we wait."

"For what?" asked Damon.

"Plan Z, of course." He drawled slyly.

"Well, I guess that's my cue," said Raven as he walked out of the wooded fringes of the yard. "Hello Lugh, sorry to see you again." Raven was no longer speaking English, but I could hear him clearly in English and Gaelic. It was bizarre.

He was also no longer "Sam", he was Nang Kilslas, Raven God of the Native people of the Americas. He was clad in a shirt made from woven cedar bark, with a cape made of the same material featuring a giant Raven laughing at the sun. His leggings were leather and he had on a simple pair of unadorned moccasins, but he positively reeked of magical energies and he shimmered in the air like a city street in August.

Beside him walked a beautiful woman in traditional garb I would associate more with the Indigenous Plains people of North America than the Haida people, but it was clear this had to be Damon's wife, Iáxuhke because she was shimmering with magic as well.

I wasn't even surprised. Well, I was, but I also didn't care. About anything. I mumbled, "Your Plan Z was to show up after all? Shit, you could have done that right away."

"Let go and do it, love," said the woman dead two thousand years but who had loved me.

Raven looked over at the dog standing by Lugh and used his Voice, "**Sleep**." The dog dropped instantly to the ground, asleep.

Bemused, Lugh looked around at Tynan and asked, "How long will she be like that?"

"Forever, unless someone wakes her up. I'm sure you could figure out how soon enough."

Lugh seemed to shimmer like a mirage and a God was now standing there in a red silk tunic and linen wraparound skirt held up with a leather belt. The only other thing on him was an exquisitely wrought torque of gold around his neck. I felt a momentary, stunningly strong pang of homesickness for Iron Age Ireland. It passed through me, leaving me bereft, and I realized there wasn't a single person I cared about present at this moment. Martina was gone, and the rest of these bastards could all die and go to hell as far as I was concerned.

But that is my normal. It was almost comforting. And it gave me options.

"Let go and do it, my love," said the woman from my past, who had understood me and never asked me to be what I wasn't.

"Should I kill yours to make it even? Maybe kill that two-spirit Crow medicine woman beside you? I have to hand it you Raven. I haven't seen power like that in a mortal in over a thousand years. Wherever did you find it?" Lugh asked.

"She found me. No need to kill anyone, you know what's going to happen now."

"Yes, we're going to bring back our Families. All of them."

"No we're not, Lugh. The whole point of this was to get rid of them all except yours and mine. We're not letting the others back."

"No Raven. You still think I don't know? The point was for you to trick me and Loki into getting rid of the European and Asian pantheons for you so that you could kill my family at your leisure with the entire might of the American Gods behind you."

With undisguised disgust, Raven replied, "You honestly think so?"

"I know so," His body went rigid and his face twisted in hate, "but you fucked it up!" he screamed. "They all went away! Every single one, even yours! You and I are alone!"

I stared at Lugh. He was crying with rage and loss and had forgotten our existence entirely. His entire focus and concentration was on Raven. For his part, Raven actually looked ashamed and more than a bit angry himself. I started noticing my pain. Especially the pain in my head and my joints, they felt good to me. It had been centuries since I welcomed this pain, but I did so now.

"Let go and do it, my love," whispered the ghost of a blue painted warrior who had been my family.

"It wasn't my fault! That bastard Loki set us both up! All I ever wanted was for my people to be left alone!"

Lugh sneered. "Loki wasn't even a real God! How could you let him screw this up?"

"That's exactly how! I needed three Gods to make reality bend to the working! Three! You know this! Loki had the world fooled! He was nothing but a God-touched Jotun Mage!"

"It's your fault for being fooled! This was your idea!"

Raven answered with disdain dripping from his voice, "You were fooled too, but pointing fingers is a waste of time! If I had known you were still around, we might have been able to fix this by now!"

"No! We need three Gods to make a safe and controlled change, and there are but two of us. It's time to break it asunder completely and let them all back. Your plan failed. Now we do it my way. I want my family back."

"And we can get them! I want mine back too, and I have three Shaman here! You see what power this one holds," He said, indicating Iáxuhke.

"Together, they will be enough to fix the working, but if we break it, they'll all be able to come back and they will destroy everything. You know this! Your family and mine are similar, Lugh! We have watched our people displaced; our lands overrun in the name of a fake god we created!"

I looked up sharply, motivated at last to make a few final decisions here. A fake God they created? What the hell was Raven on about?

Let go and do it, my love, said the painted woman, who had been the only one who understood me.

"But the others, our enemies, they're all gone now! We can bring back a balance! A return to the way it was before steel, before the One True God con became real!"

"I don't care!" Lugh screamed. "I have set it all up, it's happening with or without you, Raven. Everything is in place. Join me in bringing them back, or die right here."

"Why are you doing it this way?" Raven asked.

"I want my family back!" and held his right fist out to the side willing Gáe Assail – his magical spear – to appear in his hand.

As it did, he drew back to throw, but Raven pointed at him and said, "**Attack**." Elijah, Hahkota, Toby, and Russell launched themselves off the ground and attacked a God with their iron blades, while Damon and Iáxuhke took a stance next to Raven and began chanting.

Instead of throwing the spear, Lugh switched into a two-handed grip and set his feet to fight as his four guards dropped into fighting position on either side of him, pointing their spears straight at Elijah and his team.

But you know what? I had decided to put my pain to use. Raven's command made it easy, because the smart ass included me in his intention. I felt an overwhelming urge to jump into the fray, so fuck it, I did. But I don't think Raven was expecting how, or he never would have asked.

"Let go and do it, my love," said the woman who had been named Emer.

See, there's another power that Cú Chulainn – that I – have. In the stories about me, I inspired terror in my enemies because of a trance-like fury that would come over me before battle. It's known as ríastrad, or 'contortion'. It literally broke and reformed my joints, reshaped my jaw and mouth, and turned me into a berserk beast that killed everything in my path, friend and foe alike. It was an outward expression of all the rage, pain, and fear of the years of abuse, rape, and suffering I had endured. The first time it happened I was seven years old, and I killed all three guests of my stepfather who had been taking turns with my body.

"Let go and do it, my love," said the woman who had been my wife.

I tore three famed warriors apart with my bare hands. At age seven. By turning into the beast they had made of me.

I had hated it and tried everything I could to suppress it, and my painkiller addiction was a conscious effort to prevent it from happening, but as I said, there was nobody left alive I cared for here, nobody I needed to worry about. No friends. No Family. Nothing but that ever-present rage. My old friend.

So, I finally listened to my wife, Emer, the blue painted woman of my memories. *"Let go and do it, my love."*

"Alright, my love, I will," and the beast was let out for the first time in decades.

Maybe you remember me saying that in that in peak escalation, I am a monster? A monster from your worst nightmares? Yeah. That was literal.

Martina was right all those nights ago when she said we create the monsters that will destroy us. I'm living proof. Right now, I couldn't remember why I had ever feared it. It – I – was beautiful. I was justice and vengeance in one. I was the judge, jury, and executioner for these bastards and their crimes.

My joints broke with audible snaps and my knees actually cracked backwards and healed in the backwards shape like an animal, my head felt like it was bursting, and my jaw elongated, breaking and healing over and over as my teeth grew, filling out the new, larger mouth. I started screaming as everything in my body exploded in searing, unfathomable pain and my higher brain functions began to shut down. My torso filled out, ribs breaking and growing and reforming. My fingers elongated into claws, and I flexed my arms and the chains holding me to the rock shattered. I saw Lugh look over at me and his mouth formed the words, "Oh no."

Then, to my own horror, I saw Martina break the surface of the pond and throw the head of the ollphéist onto the bank.

As the beast took over completely, and everything went red, my last despairing thought was, "I'm going to kill my family. Again."

Chapter Twenty-Two

Martina's Battle

I woke all at once and sat up in bed taking a huge, gasping breath of air into my lungs. Gods, it hurt coming back to life!

Then, as I caught my breath and the blood took oxygen to all the parts of my body that needed it, the blessed cessation of pain settled on me and I remembered. I was whole again, injury-free, pain-free, and physically twenty fucking seven years old.

Again.

I had been killed somehow while transformed, and now I was back; physically seven years younger than three days ago.

My eyes didn't work right yet, and it was dark in the room, so I couldn't see anything, but I heard sounds from outside the room.

As I adjusted to being alive again, my vision slowly returned, and I picked out a low, narrow line of brightness ahead of me and off to my right. It resolved itself into light bleeding under a door about ten feet away. I rolled carefully out of bed and tested my strength as I stood up. I felt a little weak, a little off balance, but everything appeared to be working as I settled my weight onto my feet and slowly, quietly, shuffled to the door. I put my ear against it but didn't hear anything. The sounds had stopped.

Then I remembered my last memory of seeing Martina alive. I began to cry as I realized the beast had killed her. It always did. I killed everything around me when I change. No friend, only foe. I stood there and almost gave up. I almost slid to the floor in the darkness. But I needed to be punished, and punishment waited outside the door. It had to.

Beside me, the memory of my long dead wife Emer put her hand on my shoulder and said, "It's alright, Setanta. Go face it." I shouldn't feel her hand of course, because she wasn't there. I knew that, but it sure felt real to me.

I groped around for the doorknob, found it, and slowly twisted it in my hand, pushing the door open to reveal the living room of my house. Seated on the couch was Sarah and Frank.

And seated in my favorite chair was Martina.

I must have looked awful because all three were staring at me in varying degrees of distress.

Martina was the first to speak, "Are you okay, hermano?"

"You're alive?" I cried incredulously as I staggered over to her, dropping to my knees and wrapping her in the most important hug of my life. "You can't be. How?"

She pulled away from me and looked me in the eye, "Sit down. I have some hard things to tell you."

I looked away in shame, "I'm sure you do. Is everyone else...?"

"I'll tell you everything. Sit down."

I sat, head hung low, "Tell me the butchers bill."

She took a deep breath and looked up at the ceiling before slowly letting the breath out.

"Let's go back to when Lugh tried to kill me." She stood up and began pacing, then she seemingly spoke to herself as she recounted the price she paid to call me brother.

"I felt that crushing blow to my chest as the hijo de puta punched me, hurling my body out over the pond. Before I could even try to draw in a breath, some disgusting worm reared out of the pond and wrapped its slimy, nasty, gross body around me and squeezed, taking me under the surface of the water with it."

She shook her head and began pacing, "That was a huge mistake. Water rushed past my gills on the underside of my jaw and I felt a welcome surge of strength as I got my wind back.

"Of course, my arms were still pinned to my sides and I knew this worm was going to turn its open maw of teeth towards me any second and take a bite right out of my face, so I had to think of something fast. But then the worm made its second mistake, it leisurely took me to the bottom of the pond and bounced on the mud and stones as it began adjusting its grip." She grinned wryly, "That might work perfectly fine against fish, but I had two arms, opposable thumbs, and – oh yeah- two iron short swords strapped to my hips."

She stopped pacing and her head cocked to the side as she remembered, "After about thirty seconds of fighting the constriction, I was able to grab my sword with my left hand and work that arm free by pulling my right arm across my body and getting my hand up between me and the disgusting coil of worm flesh adjusting itself. As I pushed, it constricted in response, but I shoved a foot of iron into its guts and pulled sideways with kind of a savage glee."

Here she stopped and admitted to us all, "I love fighting underwater! Even covered in all those stupid clothes, I feel more free and alive underwater than above." She shook her hands at her sides, "And that electric sizzle of combat - Gods it was almost erotic." Frank and I shared a look. We recognized that strange crossover from terror to joy that can happen in combat.

She pulled herself back to the story and continued, "The worm recoiled from me and at last decided that biting my head off would be a good way to stop this pain I was inflicting. So, it spun around and launched itself right at me. You know, it all changed then: I almost felt sorry for the beast. It had no real reasoning skills, it was simply a large predator that couldn't understand it was already dead." The frown on her face turned to anger, "I realized I had to kill this poor thing because that asshole up above wanted to keep it for a pet. It wasn't so fun anymore. Erotic? What was I thinking? This was butchery.

"Resigned now, I darted to my right and it shot past like a deranged underwater version of a bullfight. It turned around and came back at me. This time I shot to my left and neatly slammed the blade I had drawn into its body about a foot behind its head. It didn't have a neck, so it sunk into and through the worm, and I pulled the second blade out and slammed through the worm from the other side and it wheeled around to run away from the mortal wounds I had delivered. I rode the spin and the turbulence caused by the sudden twist and used it to help me pull the blades up and around to meet at the "top" of the worm's head, effectively cutting about three-quarters of the way through the body.

"The worm went into death spasms and I arced the most graceful circle around the twisting corpse I could as it finished its death throes." She shrugged an aside, "Can't really be graceful with a battle harness and shoes on."

She started pacing again and she continued, "I looked at the dead worm. Then, I got mad. I remember snarling as I finished cutting off the head. It took a lot longer than I thought it would, and I decided I was going to force-feed this head to that asshole Lugh."

She stopped and looked at me with some small fear on her face. "I cautiously and slowly swam up toward the plants and rushes extending out into the water to use as cover as I exited the pond. Still mostly submerged, I tossed the head up onto the bank and popped my shoulders out of the water for a quick look, ready to dive back under if I was targeted. I needn't have bothered. Everyone was in the middle of killing each other, with everything happening all at once.

She lifted her hands in the air and looked up at the ceiling, saying, "And where the hell had Raven and Iáxuhke come from?"

She looked over to Sarah and Frank as she continued, "My Elijah was closest to the enemy and he brandished his two swords in the flowing pattern of a Philippine fighting system known as Silat. I recognized it from the countless hours he had spent teaching me those same drills."

Miming the actions as she described them, she went on, "He used his left blade to catch and parry the spear being thrust at him and spun along the shaft as the soldier finished and began to withdraw the thrust, but it was too late. Elijah was close and he backhanded the right side blade into the soldier's exposed throat, ripping it out in a welter of scarlet spray.

"Russell tried to parry the spear aimed at him, but the mercenary adjusted and the deflection was only partially successful as the spear punched into his right shoulder, sending him staggering back with a shout of pain. The merc stepped forward with a strong thrust at his belly and Russell tried to spin to the side to avoid it while pulling a small combat knife with his left hand, but wounded, he was too slow, the spear punched into his stomach, and the soldier gave it a twist as he removed it, spilling Russell's guts to the ground. His eyes opened wide and tried to say something as he stared at his insides unspooling at his feet."

She focused on me and walked closer. "Hahkota saw this and adjusted her trajectory with a scream as she lunged for the soldier who had mortally wounded Russell. He turned his spear on her, but she had a better angle and knocked the spearhead aside with the flat of her actual hand and brought her iron machete down so hard on the oak shaft it splintered and broke. She followed that strike up with a backswing that planted the machete deep into the soldier's face and he fell gurgling to the ground."

Then she kind of fluttered her hands and clasped them together as she remembered, "Russell finally toppled over and stared up at the sky as he died."

She shook her head and got back to the story after a beat, trying to look at me but failing. "Tobias had engaged in a smart dance of combat with a soldier and had gotten inside his guard with a thrust when a...a...beast out of nightmare smashed into both of them wielding a kukri and literally split Tobias in half from the shoulder to the waist with a downward chop. Stunned by the violence of that act, even in the middle of combat, the soldier who had an instant ago been fighting poor Tobias gaped at this monster as it dropped the kukri and grabbed him by the neck and arm." Martina looked like she was about to cry. "It screamed with pure rage as it pulled the poor soldiers fucking arm off of his body and used it like a club on him as he died."

I whispered, "I'm sorry."

She didn't hear me, lost as she was in the memory. "Raven, Iáxuhke, and Damon did something I couldn't understand, and a wave of "wrongness" washed out from them and over us all. I faltered in my steps as a queasy feeling washed over the battlefield. Lugh, for his part, wasn't even paying attention to it, he only had eyes for the beast behind him as it was clubbing a dead man with his own arm. He drew back to throw that flaming spear at the beast," she looked at me guiltily, "and I honestly wished him luck as that thing terrified me, but the magical wave hit him before he could throw and he staggered, dropping to one knee. Snarling, he turned to the three and pointed his left hand at Iáxuhke, and a piercingly bright light washed over them all, causing Raven to throw his hands up in front of his face, but it knocked Damon onto his back and made him scream as he covered his eyes. Poor Iáxuhke was hit dead center and blasted onto her back, either dead or unconscious, already taken out of the battle.

"Lugh turned to the beast and stood back up. I cried out and started running towards him because I realized something horrifying." now she looked full on at my face, "That beast hadn't stolen your weapon. No, I saw the torn clothes, and the mangled uniform as it picked the kukri up off the ground, and I realized that beast *was you*, and I had to save you."

I started crying again. Save me? What in the hell was she thinking? You can't save that creature.

She knelt down beside me and put her hand on my leg, speaking barely above a whisper, "Everyone else had frozen and stopped fighting as they watched the beast kill two men in as many seconds, and I suddenly understood why people who didn't freeze when they saw monsters were so rare and sought after by militaries around the world. Another pang of sadness went through me as I sprinted towards a nightmare that was probably going to kill me, but I had to try Dru. I had to try."

She sniffed back a few tears of her own and said, "Hahkota got there first and swung her machete at you. I can't blame her. She had seen you chop her friend in half."

I nodded understanding.

"You used the Kukri in a reinforced block over your head to deflect the machete and then swung it head high, parallel to the ground. You took Hahkota's head off at the shoulders. I skid to a stop as her body slumped to the ground.

"My Elijah recovered, of course, and he lunged into the last guard of Lugh's with both blades sinking up to the hilt in his chest. The guard seemed to suddenly remember where he was and he stared at Elijah in shock as he died. I was close enough now to hear him sigh out the word "Monster" as he collapsed.

"Lugh drew back his arm again to throw the spear into you, but you had pulled out a throwing knife and was in the process of throwing it at Lugh. Raven took a deep breath and spoke the word, '**MISS**.' And by doing that, I think he may have doomed us all."

She stood back up and looked around at all three of us. "The best I can theorize is this: The spear was magic, clearly, as it radiated light and heat yet didn't burn Lugh's hand. Lugh is a God whose abilities include never missing. Dru never misses either.

"But Raven is a God whose voice creates reality. A Chaotic God by nature. Raven sent opposing chaos magic at you both to create a different reality. One that required you to miss their target. I'm pretty sure that magic fought back."

She looked at us to make sure we were following her logic. "What I do know is that I felt an oppressive, crushing, disjointed warping of the air, the land, and the very gravity of the planet as, on one side there was a spear that desires nothing but death, thrown by a hand that never misses, passing in air a knife thrown by another hand that never misses, all fighting against the other side that only accepted a reality where they both had to miss."

"What happened?" I croaked.

"Your knife creased Lugh's neck, drawing a bead of blood and a flinch of shock from Lugh himself, but nothing more. The spear that was pure death was forced to wound, entering low on your abdomen. You began to burn as you staggered and fell to your knees and toppled face first to the ground, driving the spear up through your side and out your back. The spear burned so hot it cauterized the wound as it passed, and you screamed."

She addressed us all as she continued, hands still at her side laughing helplessly at the absurdity she had witnessed, "The universe, meanwhile, became violent as three realities and two gods were a few too many things to entertain at one time. An explosion of light and sound washed over the battlefield, and a thing impossible to describe appeared in the middle of the air between Raven and Lugh."

She put her hand to her head. "Maybe it was a black door on the ground. Perhaps a miniature sun burning right in front of us at eye level. Maybe it was both of those. Or none. I can't make myself recall.

"But I do know Raven screamed, 'No!' and Lugh smiled and yelled, 'Yes, finally!' and they both focused all of their magic on the impossible box of potential reality, trying to bend it to their will. It immediately morphed into a ball of what I can only describe as "realness" or potential, and it swirled with an impossibly bright darkness of destruction and creation. It pulsed like a heartbeat, and on every beat, the whole world shuddered at our feet."

She looked at me and then sat on the arm of my chair, resting her hand on my shoulder, "That battle of wills left the rest of us alone with you. I was about fifteen feet away as you pushed yourself up to your feet. You were clutching your left side with one hand and Lugh's spear in the other. You seemed oblivious to the fact that the spear was severely burning your right hand."

She shuddered just a tiny bit, but forced herself to continue, "You glanced my way and locked eyes."

"I tried to talk to you, 'Dru, It's me.' I stuttered to a stop as I stared into those eyes and recognized...nothing. You weren't there, only a beast that knew me not at all. I was terrified. I'm sorry Dru."

"Don't be. I understand."

She continued, "Off to my right, I heard Elijah scream at me, 'Martina! Run! Please run! That's not Dru! Cú Chulainn will kill you. He'll kill us all!' The beast snarled at me, lifted the spear, and prepared to throw it right through me. I knew I was dead. But then a different kind of magic happened. Absently, without even looking our way, Lugh decided he needed the power of the spear, so he held his hand out and the spear ripped itself from your burning hand and it flew back to Lugh.

"At the same time, Elijah tackled me to the ground and rolled with me. We both came up to our feet, as we had practiced so often in the good old days when we fought together, trained together, and loved one another. Before Raven made us choose him or each other, and we had made different choices. I knew we still loved each other, of course, but Raven would always come first for him, while I never believed in the cause the way he did. But old habits die hard, and we were working together like the well-trained partnership we once had. And we were running our asses off towards Damon to escape the beast behind us.

"You, on the other hand, seemed far more angry that Lugh had stolen the spear and was roaring challenge at him.

"Lugh was ignoring him, talking to Raven."

Martina seemed to disappear into herself for a long moment, and when she began again, she wasn't talking to us anymore, she was reliving the day. Sarah, Frank, and I stayed quiet for the rest of the tale.

"I'm impressed, Nang Kilslas. I would not have thought you could fight me this long. Even here on my own Locus, you are almost...equal." He sneered, "I think I'll kill both of your Shamans and we'll see how well you do without their help. Hell, they look half dead already," he joked, looking at Iáxuhke prone on the ground. "Maybe I'm doing them a favor."

Raven looked nervous. I guess Lugh had figured it right. Raven was barely matching Lugh with the help of Damon. And Damon looked almost spent as he knelt over his wife desperately calling out to see if she was alive, while still throwing magic at Lugh. How would Raven fare without him? I thought we were all going to find out because Lugh was starting to raise the spear and it was obvious from the looks on both Raven and Damon's faces that they knew what was about to happen.

That's when I realized I was running towards Damon alone. Elijah had curled off and sprinted towards Lugh. I watched as my lover, my precious Elijah, threw himself on top of a burning spear held by a God. Elijah screamed in anguish as the spear lit his clothes on fire and I could see from my vantage point that Elijah was literally burning to death wrapped around Lugh's right arm and the spear, preventing him from throwing it at his brother, but he wouldn't let go.

"What's happening?" Damon screamed.

The big ball of potential reality had flared darker and bigger as Elijah had distracted Lugh momentarily and the view between Raven and Lugh was obscured by a giant, impossibly black vortex. A sort of blackhole, though that's a hopelessly inadequate description of the swirling black tendrils of chaos and creation. On the side of the phenomenon closest to Lugh, he redoubled his efforts, ignoring Elijah hanging from his impossibly strong arm immolating himself, and the darkness began switching to a pale light that grew brighter and took on the colors of a sunset over the ocean before beginning to coalesce into an open circle of flames, empty in the center.

That restored the sightlines between Lugh and Damon, in time for Damon to see Cú Chulainn stride up to Lugh in a towering rage and smash both arms down onto Elijah, crushing his skull and body, along with the spear, to the ground.

Damon screamed, but I couldn't hear him over my own.

Cú Chulainn bent over, picked up the burning spear, and shoved it into Lugh's back.

BOOM.

Static across my eyes.

Ringing ears.

Sensory overload and pain.

I had been knocked on my butt, and as I regained my senses, I could see all five of us left alive were down, even Raven and Lugh. But the ball of potential? It was still there, and it had stopped moving. One side was a ball of black and purple swirling inky depths, and the other side was a bright, fire-circled ball of plasma.

As we all watched, a giant Eagle flew out of the ball of fire and screamed an exultant cry that made all of us, Raven included, slap our hands over our ears.

Raven cried out, "No. Not you. Why you? WHY YOU?" He screamed, and for the first time, I saw Raven transform from man to bird as the Eagle spied him and immediately turned into an attacking dive at Raven.

Raven flew. The Eagle God – I can only assume it was a God – chased him. Quickly, they both were gone into the sky and out of sight.

And then Damon and I were the only two conscious people left on the field of battle, facing a God and a monster. He rushed over to me and grabbed my arm, pulling me to where Iáxuhke lay unconscious on the ground. The monster that had been Dru ignored the eagle entirely and stabbed Lugh over and over with the spear. Without stopping, he looked our way, searching for us. Lugh was feebly trying to fight off the stabs, but Cú Chulainn had the burning spear in both hands and kept stabbing over and over as fast as he could into the body of the God, screaming in rage and vicious victory as his hands burned down to the bone.

Damon, looking like he was about to pass out with exhaustion, held onto me and whispered "Don't move. Don't make a sound. I've put the three of us under a veil. Hopefully, they can't see us."

"Wha.."He clamped his hand over my mouth and pointed with the other. The most incredibly beautiful woman I have ever seen walked calmly out of the black vortex and forward toward Cú Chulainn and Lugh, smiling. She was almost a caricature of beauty, she was so intense.

It was impossible to look at her and not fall back on clichés. Her hair wasn't black, it was the black of the space between stars. Her skin wasn't pale. it was alabaster. Her body wasn't perfect, it was womanly perfection itself. She was what poets threw words at, hopelessly trying to describe "woman."

I hadn't dated a woman in a while, and I'm not into casual affairs. Still, I felt an aching to be seduced by her. Damon slowly dropped his hand away from my mouth and stared stupidly at her. His face seemed to hold more terror than lust. I wondered what he saw because I knew we couldn't be seeing the same thing.

Her clothes were black, and evocative of ancient Ireland, yet somehow modern and practical. Whatever the black outfit was, it showed her body off to an amazing degree while still looking like it was good for everyday use, whatever that meant to Gods.

"It's been a long time since I got to choose a God amongst the slain, Lugh." She wasn't speaking Spanish, English, Italian, or Mandarin, yet I understood every word as if it came in all four languages. It was all very confusing, yet somehow completely understandable.

Cú Chulainn looked over as the muscles and tendons in his hands finished burning away and the spear fell to the ground. Despite the wound through his side and two hands that were essentially charred bone and sinew, he screamed in challenge and rushed the Goddess.

With a grace that was both ethereal and deadly, she danced to the side as he rushed her and shoved a thin bronze blade through his neck as he passed.

"Sorry, my love," she said as he staggered to a stop and turned around ready to attack again before he wobbled and fell to his backside on the ground. Blood was gushing out of the holes in his neck, and he put his burned stump of a hand up to it and looked at the blood in shock as if he could not comprehend how any of this had happened. His eyes rolled up and he dropped to his back, shuddering out one last breath, and went still.

I couldn't help it, I whimpered, "No. Dios mio, not you too, Dru."

Damon tensed beside me as the Goddess snapped her head around and that gorgeous face stared right at us, despite the veil.

"A little advice, mortals. I can hear you well, and you're pulling magic right to you to power that veil. Inefficient and obvious to those who can see the magic. I can tell much has been forgotten over the centuries." She seemed to consider those words for a moment before saying, "That's probably a good thing."

She dismissed us from her thoughts and turned to Lugh. "What should I do with you? I didn't get back here because of you, you know. Whoever you were fighting was calling to the Chaos, not you. I owe you no favors."

In what was perhaps the most incredible thing I had seen all day, the perforated and bleeding-out God managed to talk, "It was both of us, he was calling Chaos and looking for an ally from his American pantheon, I was calling Order and the Tuatha. It worked, of course...heh."

She threw back her head and released a laugh that sent shivers down my spine. It was tinged with more than a hint of madness. "Yes, I see how well it worked, you each got what you wanted. I wonder what American Sun god came back."

"It was an Eagle, and it hated Raven on sight."

"Ahh, Raven. Of course. Who else." She paused, a deep belly laugh of genuine amusement burst from her perfect, red lips. "It was an Eagle? And it hated Raven? Ha! It had to be Huitzilopochtli."

I gasped again. The Goddess looked up and raised an eyebrow at us.

Coughing blood, Lugh said weakly, "Who?"

"For pity's sake, cousin, do you not remember anything at all? Huitzilopochtli is the most powerful *Mexica* God. An Ascended, no less. He was a bitter rival of Raven because they fought for dominance of the peninsula that became known as Mexico. Huitzilopochtli won that war, by the way. Something Raven never forgot nor forgave because it cut him off from the South American Continent, allowing those Incan usurpers to establish their hold over the people there."

Lugh said "Who cares. Are you going to heal me Morrigan?" Then he paused for a moment before nervously adding, "Or are you going to choose me?"

"Well, I suppose you are half responsible for my return. And you have a lot of knowledge about what's going on. I'd like to know that information." she paused, "Also, I admit I've been lonely."

A shudder passed through her body and her smile slipped, "You don't know what it was like being stuck back home. The Fomor and their allies have taken over everything left, and many of our family have gone mad. We need to bring back the ones that are still sane before it's too late. It's so much worse than the first time, Lugh. Worse. We need access."

"Then heal me enough to move. We have to go."

"What about the mortals?"

"Who cares about mortals? There is nothing they can do. This entire fight was a distraction. I have already won."

She snorted in disbelief, looking at his bleeding body and then at the carnage around the field. "Is this what winning looks like to you?"

"Druids are strong again, Morrigan. We have a congregation and an army. By this time next year, every human being on earth will know that they are not alone and that all the creatures of myth and legend are real. And now that you are here, we will work together to bring back our family."

She frowned thoughtfully at him, "Fine, cousin."

"Let us be on our way, please. Heal me."

"Yes," she said, looking down at Cú Chulainn "but first..."

She kneeled next to Elijah and Dru, and I couldn't stop myself. I walked out of the protection of the veil and asked with as much bravery as I could force through my mouth, "What are you doing to my family? ¡Dejarlos solos!"

The Goddess smiled and squatted back on her heels. "I'm doing nothing, and yes, I'll leave them alone, don't worry. I wanted to see who you were. Do you call both of these warriors' family?"

"Yes."

Her smile fell, "In that case, I am sorry for your losses today."

I looked pointedly at my Elijah, dead on the ground. I tried to speak through the hitch in my breath, took a moment, stared into the flawless green eyes of the Goddess, and said, "You mean loss."

The Morrigan held my stare and a sly smile played around her mouth, "Good girl. You are clever." She put her finger to her lips indicating quiet and glanced first down to the beast of Cú Chulainn and then over at Lugh.

I got the point and stood quietly.

"Let's go, cousin," she said as she moved over to Lugh's supine body. She kneeled again, placed her hands on his wounds and the Gods were just...gone. And Damon and I were alone.

Damon, exhausted, struggled to walk over to the dead bodies and knelt beside Elijah, weeping. "Oh, my brother, what am I going to tell Iáxuhke when she wakes up? She's going to be heartbroken, Elijah. Why did you leave us?"

He looked over at Dru's body through his tears and a snarl formed on his face as he grabbed one of Elijah's short swords off the ground and raised it over his head screaming, "You killed my brother you piece of shit!" and began slamming the sword into Dru's chest over and over again. I tackled him to the ground and wrestled the sword away from him, crying and yelling, "Stop! Stop it, Damon. He's dead, leave his body alone!"

"He killed Elijah! He killed your lover! He killed my brother! And he killed Tobias, and Hahkota! Shit, Martina, he killed more of us than that bastard Lugh did! Fuck him! I want to chop his body into pieces and burn him!"

"I know you're angry," I cried, "but it won't bring them back. They're all dead, our Elijah is dead, Damon. Nothing will change that."

"He looked at me and my heart broke as a man I loved and respected grew disgusted with me and said, "You think I don't know what you're doing? I was there when he told us, Martina. Your new piece of shit brother will come back from the dead, won't he? And you would hide that from me?" He started crying again, but this time in rage. "I was your family, Martina! We were your fucking family, not this animal!" he said, pointing at Dru's corpse.

"No!" I screamed back "You acted like my family, but you and Elijah chose the Raven over me. Your family is a God and humans. I was just a token Iara. You gave me an ultimatum you knew I couldn't accept. I am not one of Raven's toys! Your family is his family, indigenous humans only, and I forgave you all for choosing him over me. Hell, I even understood why you did it, but I had to find a new family after you all turned your backs on me, and I found it! I found Sarah and Frank, and yes, I found my brother Dru!"

He sat back and all was quiet for a few breaths. Eventually, he said, "I'm going to chop that monster up and burn the pieces before I leave here, Martina. He's not coming back this time."

I felt an even deeper sadness settle over me as I realized this was it, I was going to make an enemy out of a man I had once had the highest respect for. A man who had had me over for countless meals and good times in his house even after Raven had radicalized them all. "No," I said firmly, "You will not."

"Are you going to try to stop me? Are you going to be my enemy too?"

"Yes," I whispered.

He sighed. "There's a lot of magic here, Martina, this isn't a fistfight, I'll..." Tears blurring my vision, I punched him as hard as I could across his mouth as he was speaking. He crumpled to the ground unconscious. I looked down at his body on the grass and said, "Yes, I know what you would have done to me with all that magic. I'm sorry, my old friend."

I dropped to my knees in the grass and tried to reach out to Elijah's body. I couldn't bring myself to touch him. I felt like I had betrayed him by choosing to protect Dru, but I think Elijah was first and foremost a soldier. I think he wouldn't hold a grudge against the monster that ended his suffering. For God's sake, he was burning alive, and in the end, Dru had saved Damon's life at the expense of Elijah's and that's exactly what Elijah had decided to do as well.

"I still love you," I said to Elijah.

I knew the beast hadn't done it benevolently or out of a sense of empathy. No, he had killed Elijah because he wanted to kill everything in sight, but that didn't matter. When we create monsters, we have no right to expect them not to act monstrous. But Damon would never forgive. I knew that. I had to get Dru out of here before he woke up, or Damon would destroy us both.

Still crying, I grabbed the body of my brother by the damaged straps of his combat rig and pulled him along the grass. In death, he was no longer a monster. Just a slim man of about seventy-two kilograms.

I paused only once along the way; when I got to the form of the sleeping dog Lugh had named Tynan on the ground. It was impossibly sad to see it like that and know it would sleep until it died. Eventually, I was forced to leave, and I pulled Dru into the house. I had reached the giant circular entryway when I saw a door open from the corner of my eye and I dropped Dru's body and spun in a crouch, pulling my blades to face the new threat.

The piece of shit butler stepped through the door with a Godsdamned shotgun and pointed it at me. I dove into a roll to my left and towards the butler as I heard the thunderclap of the gun go off. Immediately I felt the sting of pellets tear into my hip. At the same time, I heard the butler scream a high-pitched cry of pain and surprise as I finished my roll, lunging towards the asshole when my right leg gave out and I collapsed to the floor in a heap, screaming "¡Mierda!".

I would have died right there on that floor, but I looked up at the butler to see him holding his bloody face and leaning up against the wall with an exploded shotgun at his feet.

I guess nobody warned him about the effect of Chaos magic on alloys.

I rose up to my feet and tested my weight to make sure I could support myself. I could, I just hadn't been prepared for the injury when I came out of that roll, so I limped my way up to the now whimpering butler and shoved my sword up from his navel into his heart. "Just fucking die." I snarled as he slid to the floor.

I limped back to my brother and dragged him out to our rental van sitting in the driveway. Then, despite my pain and bleeding, I decided I needed to go back in there and retrieve one or two things we desperately needed.

After, I drove about five miles down the road before stopping to address my wounded hip. I wanted to be far gone when Damon and his wife woke up, but I was bleeding all over the place, and I didn't want to pass out from blood loss on the way to wherever I decided we could hide out.

As I pulled once more onto the road, I checked the phone I had turned off and stashed in the glove compartment before we had started this nightmare mission. It worked, thank the Gods. I made a call to my sister Sarah for help.

Chapter Twenty-Three

The Price of Family

A few hours after Martina finished, I was sitting alone on my bed, where I had retreated after the story of my newest crimes. I couldn't fathom how she could stand to look at me, let alone forgive me for killing Elijah, but she had emphatically denied blaming me, and instead insisted that I had released her lover from the agony of being burned alive and finished his efforts at saving Damon.

She fucking thanked me.

I didn't deserve it, and somehow it hurt even more than the blame would have. Gods I'm a mess.

When I came back out of the room, they were all seated in the same spots, waiting for me to come to grips with what had happened. All four of them, Frank, Sarah, Martina, and Emer. I closed my eyes and took a deep breath. When I opened them, Emer was still there, but her face was superimposed over Martina's. That can't be good.

"Do any of you see Emer, my wife, right there?"

"They all looked to where I was pointing. Frank quietly answered, "No, just Martina."

"I didn't think so." Slowly, she faded from sight. "I think I might be in real trouble." I said, tapping my head.

Martina walked over to me and took my hand, "We'll figure it out together."

"What now?" I asked, leaving the doorway to head for the couch.

Clearing his throat, Frank said, "Now we figure out what's next for all of us."

"Wait. First, tell me how come we're all at my house. Seems pretty dangerous, what with both Broadhead and Damon knowing where I live. In fact," I said as the thought struck me, "how did you avoid him while I was dead?"

"After I called Sarah, she called a friend in Baltimore. One of our underground friends. You'd like her. She and her husband teach self-defense to runaways. They took us in and helped patch me up."

"And Damon didn't find you? Didn't do some...I don't know...magic person finding thing?"

"I don't think it works that way except in your audiobooks, Dru." She said with a small smile. "Anyway, he didn't."

Sarah stood up, moving towards my kitchen and pointing at Frank, "We were still at the compound when Raven got back. He looked like he had been in a fight and come out behind."

Frank interrupted, "He got his ass kicked, Dru."

Sarah continued as if Frank hadn't spoken, "He started issuing orders in a hurry, and the entire Texas compound was evacuated in a matter of about an hour. He left everything behind; locked it up and ran. He offered to take us with him, but we turned him down."

"Where did he go?"

"To Alaska, apparently."

"He has another compound there. Far from Mexico." Martina added. Her smirk was back on her face. I took that as a good sign.

"Mexico?"

"Huitzilopochtli."

"Ah. Right. Another Sun God to shine with Lugh."

"Worse, he's the main God of the Mexica – you call them Aztecs. Sun. War. Conquest. Sacrifice."

"Of course he is," mumbled Frank.

Sarah was making herself a glass of ice water and added, "Anyway, while Damon and Iáxuhke were driving around Maryland looking for you two, he called Raven to ask for help. Instead, Raven told him to get to the airport and fly to Alaska. There was a big argument as Damon didn't want to leave his brother's body behind sitting there, so Raven got angry and made them both drive the van all the way back to Anchorage." She shuddered with the memory, "He used the Voice."

"On his own Shamans?" I asked. "Because that's like..."

"Compulsion. Yeah. No free will. It's pretty ugly."

Martina stood up and walked to me, "He's never done that before to my knowledge. He's scared, I think."

"That's an excuse. He took away the free will of his own Shamans. Not a good look."

"No, it's not, but it might have saved our lives."

"True. So," I looked around at the three, "That explains why we don't have a Shaman mage killing us. How come there isn't a Broadhead team here?"

"Broadhead is in a mess right now," Frank said. "They are reeling from the publicity of a bombed-out building, two murdered executives found on top of Enchanted Rock the same day, and a third executive nowhere to be found."

"Good. Fucking serves them right."

"I don't know," he continued, "There's also some disturbing news gaining traction around the world."

"What?"

"Sightings."

"Of?"

"Monsters, myths, and legends. They're getting caught on film. There are about five minutes of perfectly clear video of our lake monster in Lake LBJ on the news. It battered a pair of jet skis into wreckage and killed one of the riders. A Yeti tore a hiker limb from limb while his girlfriend was filming a bird. She dropped the camera and ran away screaming, but the Yeti picked it up, chased her down, and gave it back to her. Crystal clear footage."

"Holy shit."

Martina grabbed my hand. "Yeah, mijo. In Argentina and Brazil, there are multiple reports and camera footage of El Hombre de Gatos terrorizing the slums of Rio De Janeiro and Buenos Aires. And more. Cherufes raiding villages and stealing children in Chile and Peru."

"Over in Europe, evidence is mounting too," Sarah said as she walked back to the couch to sit with Frank. "I think Broadhead isn't here because Lugh is too busy winning. I think this was his plan all along." She looked hesitantly over to Frank, who seemed grim and was avoiding looking at me.

"What?" I asked, "What is it?"

Martina was the one who answered. Standing right next to me, she quietly said, "Ireland."

I went still. "What about it?"

"Last night, Ireland literally went dark. All the power grids failed. Cell towers, radio, television. All of it. Only satellite communications stayed up. Then the reports started filtering out. Nobody believed it at first, but..."

"But what?"

"A nightmare."

"How?"

"Druids, Fae, riots, creatures of myth and legends, and two Gods throwing around magic. They are scouring Ulster. Wholesale slaughter and people running through the streets of Belfast looking for shelter. Morrigan and Lugh have gone home and are taking back what they think is theirs."

"Jesus Christ!" I stood, stunned at the implications raging through my head. Indisputable proof worldwide of Extras. Real Gods out in the open, a televised war between Extras flocking to the side of the Gods, and deserting our Units like the Nightmare Squad. Chaos. How long before Huitzilopochtli decides to do the same thing in Mexico? How long before more Gods make it back?

We had thought we were stopping Lugh, but he had already won the war.

A phone rang.

We all jumped about a thousand feet straight into the air and stared around wildly for a second until we realized what it was. Sheepishly, Sarah reached into her pocketbook and pulled out her cell, looking at all of us for confirmation. We all nodded some form of assent, and she answered, putting it on speakerphone,

"Yes?" she said.

"Who is with you?" came a smooth, silky, feminine voice of a person I didn't recognize.

"Depends on who this is, I guess." Sarah replied.

"That's Iáxuhke, Damon's wife," Martina said. "Hola, Iáxuhke."

"Hello Martina. I tried calling you first. Got rid of your phone? Smart. If you are there, I can assume the Beast is there too? Is he alive?"

"I'm doing fine," I said.

"Too bad. I had hoped you'd stay dead. It would have made everything easier. Now my husband is going to waste time trying to kill you."

Putting on my best tone of polite disinterest, I said, "Is there a point to this call?"

She sighed, "Yes. We want to know; who's side are you on?"

We all looked at each other and Frank took over the conversation, "What sides are there, in your opinion?"

"Is this Frank I'm talking to?

"You're talking to all of us, I'm the one answering."

"There is our side, that would like to save this planet, and there is the other side, that wants to bring back all the gods and destroy this universe in the process."

"Hmm. How simple it all sounds."

"It is that simple, Frank."

"No. No, it's not Iaux.."he stumbled over her name "shit, sorry, Iáx-uhke?"

A bitter laugh went out over the line and she said, "You're almost adorable. Apologizing. How polite. My name means Fox. Call me that, if you need to."

There was no humor in Frank's voice when he replied, "Whatever Iáx-uhke, but let's cut to the point. The way we see it, there are a bunch of sides. There are the world governments, which want the Status Quo. We are not on their side. There's Lugh and, apparently, Morrigan who want all the Gods back. We are not on their side. There's Huitzilopochtli's side..."

"Oh sure, get his name right the first time." she interrupted.

Annoyed, Frank continued, "We have no idea what his side wants, so for now, we'll stay silent on him. But your side? Your side wants whatever Raven wants, and he hasn't been honest about that. In short, we don't trust him at all. Hell, he doesn't even have the decency to make this call himself."

"Thanks to your beast, I have been forced to take over the duties of my brother-in-law. I'm Raven's head Shaman and leader of his people. He's too busy training new Shaman right now to talk to you. Don't question my God."

"I'm not questioning him, but you're proving my point about sides. His side is whatever whim takes him. That leads us to the side everyone is ignoring. The side of the underground. The side of live and let live. I think we're on that side, honestly."

"Where does that leave us, do you think? You harboring a monster that killed three of mine, including my brother-in-law, and allowed a bunch of gods to return?"

"That isn't true!" Martina yelled. "Those Gods got back because of Raven! And there would be a whole bunch more if not for the sacrifice Elijah made and the fact that Dru defeated Lugh before he could bring back more Gods!"

"I know nothing of the sort!" Her voice had become vicious and sharp. "I know my friends, Hahkota and Tobias are dead at his hands. My husband's brother is dead at his hands! I know! My husband saw your monster do it with his own eyes. And two more Gods have escaped into our world."

Martina got even angrier, "You may be the strongest mage on the planet, chica, but you don't know the mechanics of it. I do. I am the expert, and I'm telling you, Raven messed up like he always does. Study your own tales. He sent so much opposing magic at Lugh that he broke reality! I've had three days to think on it, and I'm positive. The fight between Gods opened the way because Raven wasn't trying to stop Lugh, he was trying to beat Lugh and bring his own Gods back."

"Martina, I don't trust you anymore. You've chosen your side and you chose a monster. I don't believe you."

"Monster? Who stole your free will and made you drive across the country with your brother-in-law's dead body in the van next to you? Who's responsible for this whole mess in the first place? Ask your Raven why the Gods really disappeared, because we learned some interesting things that day, didn't we? You were there, you heard what Lugh said."

Uncertainty creeping into her voice, Iáxuhke shouted, "I don't believe you!"

Frank broke in and said, "So, what are you going to do about it? What do you want, and why did you call?"

Breathing heavily over the open line, Iáxuhke took a few seconds to compose herself. "First, I'm going to honor our dead." I saw Martina bow her head and a tear slid down her face. I wrapped my arm around my sister and gave what little support I could. "Later I am going to ask you if you're going to help us save this world. But not today. Today I am too angry at you all to accept your help."

"What makes you think…"I started.

"You shut up, Beast! I will not talk to you! Raven has said we must leave you alone, though only he knows why, but I *hate* you. Do you understand? I hate you for what you've done to my husband and my family, and there is no forgiveness. Orders or not, my husband will kill you one day, and on that day, I will smile."

I remained silent because she was right. There is no forgiveness for me.

Frank, on the other hand, wasn't having any of it. "You'll watch how you speak to my brother, Shaman. You asked what side we're on? I'll tell you. We're on our side. This is our family," he glanced at me, "our pack; this is our side. And it's clear you'll be needing our help. You don't have to like us, but you better remember that we don't like you either, and you're coming to us for help at the command of your sneaky little God, so you'll Godsdamn well come to the table with respect. You hear me?"

There was silence on the other end of the line for a few seconds before Iáxuhke hung up the phone.

Outside, a dog suddenly started barking in my backyard.

Epilogue

I put the finishing touches on the window treatment in what used to be the training room as Martina came in and stood taking it all in.

"Everything look good?" I asked.

She smiled as her gaze swept the newly remodeled bedroom and said, "It's exactly like I pictured. Thanks for doing this, hermano."

"Thank you for staying with me, Emer. I...need the company. The world is on fire, and only a few of us know what's really going on."

Her smile faltered and I saw a sadness and pain deep in her eyes, "Martina."

"That's what I said."

She looked like she was about to say something, but changed her mind, "I hear you, but I honestly expected it to be a lot worse out there right now than it is."

"Me too. I don't understand why Ireland went quiet and why the sightings have tapered off lately, but I'm glad it's given us some time to get our feet under us."

"I'm a little scared of what it might mean for the future, though."

"Me too."

Martina suddenly looked a little uncertain and timid, but she put her hand on my arm and asked, "Dru. Do you think you might be interested in trying some sort of therapy?"

"How?" I shrugged "Who would even believe me?"

She smiled and said, "Hey Doc, about two thousand years ago I had a really bad childhood?"

I laughed, "Yeah. Imagine that conversation."

Then a gorgeous black German Shepard named Tynan padded into the room, all eighty pounds of war dog, and began sniffing around the freshly painted walls and the new bedspread. I put on a lighter tone and said, "At least we may have found a new place to train Tynan here and work out at the same time, so this room belongs to you now."

Martina was looking at Tynan as she said, "You still have a long way to go before she's going to be comfortable in our family. This was pretty traumatic for her. Big life change. "

I wasn't fooled for a second. "For all of us." I replied. "I still can't believe you went back into Lugh's house for a sleeping dog."

"I didn't. I went back because she didn't deserve to die like that, and I think we could use a war dog, and that's not you. Not anymore."

"But I'm going to have to train her to be more than that."

"Sarah gave us the number to that couple that patched me up, John and Betsy. Said they could help with Tynan and you."

"Big life changes." I sighed.

The bedroom was one of the things happening in the big life change. We had been pleased to discover that Martina still had access to one of the operations bank accounts of Raven's group, so we stole and transferred a small amount to an offshore account in Martina's name. Raven's account had contained almost two hundred and fifty thousand dollars, so we took two hundred and forty-nine thousand. I'm not sure why, but Martina thought it would be hilarious to leave a few hundred in the account. I would have taken it all.

When Raven found out, he sent an email that said only, "Well played, you oversexed mermaid. $$$"

We used the money to reinforce the entryway and windows, add a security system, and have a large pool with a hot tub installed in the backyard. That backyard was all Martina, of course. But in exchange I got to live with family again for the first time in almost two thousand years. Me, my sister, and our dog.

Sarah and Frank were already wealthy, plus Frank was drawing pay - for the next thirteen years no less - due to that ridiculous trick the Raven pulled with his Medal of Honor, so it was easy for Sarah to transfer from Austin to an office in Baltimore and use her position to help run the underground full time with Frank. They're making a few changes to it. Now they're using cutting edge tech to purge the spies from Broadhead and the government and stay organized.

They are trying to help what we're all calling the Homo Diversus population stay safe from the upcoming war and trying to keep them from running from one uncaring group to another, but that's a hard sell to people who have been abused their whole existence. I don't envy them, but Frank and Sarah are my family, so I'll be there when they need me.

We walked outside to the backyard to see the big hole in the ground where Martina's pool would soon be, when a huge black bird flew by overhead. I grabbed my pistol out of my waistband holster and pushed Martina behind me, about to yell "Get in the house!" When the bird gracefully circled in front of us and landed on the lawn, transforming as it did so into the most beautiful woman I had hoped never to see again. Tynan was suddenly there by my side in a fighting position and growling, teeth bared and hackles raised. I put my hand out in the sign for hold, and she held.

The Goddesses presence washed over me and I had the sudden urge to drop to my knees and bury my face in the ground. I clenched my fists and forced myself to stand there and maintain eye contact.

It seemed to amuse her.

"Hello, lover."

Eventually I was able to answer. "Hello Morrigan. And if I recall correctly, the reason I'm in this mess is because I'm not your lover, and never was."

"I apologized for that, Setanta."

"Dru."

"Excuse me?"

"I'm Dru now. Setanta has been dead for a long time."

"I've said that I was sorry, Dru. I didn't know what that bastard of a stepfather had done to you. If I had, I would have chosen him for death much sooner than I did. I understand now why you spurned me. I'm over it. Mostly."

"Why are you here?"

"To warn you."

"Of what?"

She looked down at Tynan for the first time and a ghost of a smile flitted over her face before she looked back up to me, all signs of levity gone. "Lugh. He is insane. As are many of the Gods back home. And yet he wants to bring them all back."

"Why are you telling me this, Morrigan?"

"Because we've had a falling out, Lugh and I. If he brings all the Gods back, it will be the end of everything, even us. He can't see it. I can. Haven't you wondered why there aren't a hundred Gods back already? Between us, we could do it. I refuse to help destroy myself."

"That makes sense, I guess, but I have to ask again, why are you telling us? Emer and I have no part in your little games."

Her eyes narrowed in confusion for some reason, and she looked over at my wife before continuing, "Because Raven and Huitzilopochtli are slowly becoming less antagonistic towards one another for some reason, so Lugh can't use either one in his plans."

"And?"

"Well, that leaves only you."

"What the hell are you talking about?"

"Setanta...Dru...You are the child of a God." As if that explained everything.

"Yeah, I'm God-touched, so what?"

"No, you impossibly dense child, you are both God-touched – by me – and you are the *son of a God*. That makes you a Demi-God; a source of power. Your father needs that power."

I stood there rooted to the ground and shocked to my core. I knew that. I always had. How come I hadn't remembered until now? Is there still a Geas on me?

The thought seemed to occur to her at the same moment. She looked again at Emer and then back to me, "Come here, Dru, let me see your mind."

"Oh, hell no..."I began.

Morrigan said, "Waterborne, I'm trying to save your brother's mind. Trust. Restrain the dog." Then she reached out, covering the twenty feet between us in an instant and grabbed my chin, staring into my eyes.

I felt a huge weight fall from my mind and a waterfall of thoughts, memories, and trauma came crashing back into my brain, driving me to my knees. My vision went yellow and I almost passed out as images painfully kaleidoscoped through my brain like a jackhammer.

"You're killing him!" Martina screamed and would have launched herself at the Morrigan except she released me then and stepped back. Tynan was going crazy, straining at the leash and barking.

"That poor man's mind is a mess. He is quite insane, and it will kill him if we are not careful. There are so many layers of Geas placed upon him, It's like a tangled nest of threads and knots. From where they all came, I do not know, But I think I've been able to start a slow unraveling. And be thankful it will be slow, Waterborne. I believe that if Dru had these Geas lifted all at once, his mind would be lost forever. Let it come back slowly, for his sake."

As I recovered, I looked up from my knees to see something suspiciously like concern on Morrigan's face. "I am the son of a God." I said as I stood up. I looked over at my sister, "You're Martina, not Emer. Have I been calling you Emer?"

I put my hand out and Martina let the leash go as Tynan ran to my hand and rubbed her head in my downturned palm for comfort.

Morrigan nodded, relieved. "Lugh will be coming after you with these new 'Druids' of his." she shuddered. "A most distasteful abomination of a once beautiful source of worship." She looked away from me and nodded to Martina.

"Get ready," she said to Martina, as she shifted into a Crow and took flight.

I felt my sister's hand slide into mine overtop of the dog. "We will be," she whispered.

Acknowledgements

Thank you, my family. You know who you are.

And thank you deeply to all who read this book. This series is a labor of love that has been kicking around in my head for a decade now. It is my sincere hope that you love the story and these wonderful characters as much as I do.

Special thanks to my Beta readers, ARC readers, and my editor, Kathleen Howard.

To everyone who's name appears in this series – you probably earned it, but I'm sorry anyway...lol

About the Author

Daniel Nick is a lover of the Written Word. His preference to write is Dark Fantasy and Science Fiction, but he'll read anything. He's also been a fierce advocate of inclusion and child protection for his entire professional life, and he spent most of it trying to walk the walk, not just talk the talk.

The author has been called many things. The ones safe to repeat in public include special education teacher, sailor, martial artist, biker (the kind with loud engines and leather jackets), world traveler, rock climber, sculptor, writer, actor, ADHD adult, husband, dog lover, and more that would probably bore you. The author also embraces the honor of being the representative of the International Thiang Boxing Association for the Americas. Daniel Nick prefers to be called an artist, and maybe a good person.

In real life, he created the 501-(c)-3 Non-profit, One World Martial Arts Federation, which creates fully inclusive and adapted martial arts and self-defense programs for students of all abilities world-wide. Every dollar of profit that his writing produces goes to this cause. Your book purchase changes lives. Thank you!

Also by Daniel Nick

Café Muse – in the Anthology, Coffee and Dreams Volume 2
Doubly Blessed – in the Anthology, Coffee and Dreams Volume 3
Root of all Evil – in the Anthology, Coffee and Dreams Volume 4
Seven Degrees Off Horror – A Horror Anthology
War Dog – Book One of Hound of the Gods
The Hands That Feed (August 2026) – Book Two of Hound of the Gods
Mad Dog Mean (Spring 2027) – Book Three of Hound of the Gods
They Called Me the Hound (forthcoming) – A Novel in the Hound of the Gods Universe
Trapped for a Dog's Year (forthcoming) – A Novella, Book 3.5 of Hound of the Gods
Kicking a Dead Dog (forthcoming) – Book Four of Hound of the Gods
Strays and other Stories Vol. 1 (forthcoming) – Anthology in the Hound of the Gods Universe
Sleeping Dogs Lie (forthcoming) – Book Five of Hound of the Gods
Brought to Heel (forthcoming) – Book Six of Hound of the Gods
Strays and other Stories Vol. 2 (forthcoming) – Anthology in the Hound of the Gods Universe
And More!

Afterward

I want to take a moment to personally thank all of you that care enough about my book to leave a review somewhere – every author in the world cherishes those stars. But more than that, I am what the industry likes to call (sometimes with a strong side dish of snark and disdain) an Indie Author. *Reviews are literally the most important things you can do for me besides reading the book.* When you give my book a review, you aren't (just) feeding my ego, you're telling the world my book is <<<insert number of stars here>>> good. And for an Indie author, that's priceless. That's community.

Just what is an Indie Author? Well, it's a writer that wants their books to be published and enjoyed by you. Yeah...sounds familiar. Kinda like every other author, huh? The difference is that we don't want to spend a decade waiting to publish the book. The traditional publishing world takes TIME, and I'm already 53 as I write these words. So, an Indie author does everything by him or herself. Everything. If we don't do it personally, we pay a professional to do it for us...personally. For example, I hired a developmental editor and paid a design house to create my book covers. The Indie author (me) pays that cost.

Not a publishing house.

So, we Indies have to create for ourselves all that the publishing house brings to the process – the editing team, salesmen, publicists, and cover designer – just to name a few. We don't have any of that provided for us.

What we do have is a love of the art form and a desire to share it with you so strong that we pay to get this book in your hands. And we do it with a clear understanding that we'll probably never make that money back.

Unless.

Unless the story is good enough that you share your enjoyment with the world. That's what a review means to us. It means we can stay in touch and share our stories. It means we can keep writing.

So, thank you from the bottom of my heart for that review, and I invite you to join my newsletter (www.danielnick.com) because I love to send out free short stories and ramble on about my life, my dog, my travels, and my writing progress. I also love to answer questions and emails. Please drop me an email! Yes, you!

Indie Authors build communities, and I invite you to be a part of it. I will absolutely personally answer every email I receive. authordnick@gmail.com

Now, go ahead, turn the page, and read the first chapter of the next book!

The Hands That Feed – Chapter One

The Hound of the Gods Book Two

I was on fire, and I assure you I was quite pissed off about it.

This entire meet had gone wrong from the get-go. My brother Dru had come up with what was, for him, a pretty solid plan that didn't involve walking in the front door with a gun and killing everyone, but we had some crappy luck.

The situation was this: there were three children to rescue, and the easiest way to do that while keeping them safe involved impersonating the buyers and giving the child traffickers their money. Then we'd kill them when their backs were turned, because fuck child traffickers, and doubly fuck the ones that had decided to get into the kidnapping and selling of these sweet, innocent Canoti wood sprites. They had been kidnapped from the trees that grew in the ancestral lands of the Lakota, Nakota, and Dakota peoples. You probably call them Sioux Indians.

Canotila were children of the peaceful, tiny, tree-like creatures that rarely got bigger than four feet tall even when full grown, but these particular predators had made a reputation by selling only the "real thing"; Child Extra's under the age of thirteen. Extra is the slang term for Homo Diversus (that's every one of us not "human") like the Canoti and other sentient species like me. I'm an Iara from South America, which means I'm a mermaid. I live underwater as much as I live on land.

So, the fact that I'm currently on fire is ironic as well as extremely painful.

My human sister Sarah had found out about these poor children when their parents approached her for help. There were several reasons the child traffickers went after the Canotila. One was that because they were incredibly hard to find and capture, they were very rare. A second reason was that they are tough as...well...trees. Durable. The monsters buying these three kids could sate their degeneracy for a much longer time with Canotila children than with human ones. So Canotila were considered both a prestige purchase and a good investment.

The parents came to Sarah for help because she and her Jötunn husband Frank were the most trusted people on Earth to those Homo Diversus who objected to slavery and were on the run from the world governments. That trust was earned because they had organized a modern version of the Underground Railroad worldwide.

When we were told about the issue, Dru had squeezed his hands in to balls of compressed rage and said, "As long as I get to kill them all. I'm not taking prisoners, and I'm not wasting my time with jail for 'rehabilitation'."

Sarah had replied with iron in her voice, "I know what rehab is worth as well as you. They don't have any information I need, and I already have their entire organization uncovered. Go do what you do, brother, but know that they use Diversus as enforcers. You can expect a Troll or an Ogre."

"Troll would be too damn big, but I hear you."

We put together a simple plan. Step one included ambushing the real buyers. We killed them in their hotel room and rolled into this meeting pretending to be them. There was no evidence that these two groups had done business face to face before, but they must have, because they got one look at us and the ugly, nine foot tall troll picked up a large barrel full of something that turned out to be flammable and threw it at us, Donkey Kong style. The human next to him shot at us with his shotgun as we dove for cover and a spark set everything off.

Dru lost his composure entirely. He jumped on me, all five foot eight of him, and began smothering the flames on my pants, pointlessly screaming, "I got it! You're okay! I got it!" I was bemused, because usually it was me with the emotions running high. Of course, I am an Iara, so big emotions kind of come as part of the package. It's one of the many ways I'm not human.

The Troll and the human shooter were on the ground too, and the warehouse had a hundred little independent fires all over the place. I saw them struggle to smother the flames on their clothes.

I guess everyone except the two other humans at the back of the warehouse carrying three screaming children out the back door were on fire.

I pushed Dru off me, yelling "Hermano, stop smacking my ass and shoot those fuckers!" as I pointed at the crispy troll and the accidental shotgun pyromancer.

Dru sat up, wild eyed and panting, "Okay, okay." He reached behind his back and pulled out his Colt Python .357 revolver, putting a nice big hole in the chest of the burning human before turning the gun on the troll and putting two into the body, knocking him over and onto his back, where he stayed.

Still smoking, but not currently on fire, I started to get up when I noticed Dru was sitting there with the stainless steel gun braced and pointed at the Troll. His dark brown hair smoldering. Literally. Smoke was rising from his hair, and I had a momentary burst of manic laughter escape my throat as I imagined flames in his hair matching the red in his facial stubble.

"Everything OK?" I asked

Sitting still despite the flames licking at his pants and boots, Dru kept his grey eyes pinned to the troll as he said, "We'll see. Trolls are incredibly tou..."

"YEEAAARRRGGGGG!" The troll screamed as it rolled over onto all fours and sprinted impossibly fast straight at Dru. Panicked, I reached into my waistband to grab my own gun, but the Glock 17 wasn't there. I started searching frantically along the ground, trying to find where it had fallen, but I knew it would be over one way or another before I could reach it. "Shit!"

Dru didn't bother trying to get up or evade the charging monstrosity, he simply began pulling the trigger in a measured cadence of about one shot every half second.

Boom!

Boom!

Boom!

The troll slid up to Dru's smoking feet and its head stopped about ten centimeters away from his boot soles.

I saw that It had a crease down one side of its face from where one of the bullets had gouged through the skin but failed to penetrate the skull. There was a chunk out of the very top of its skull where a second bullet had taken a piece out of it, but I didn't see a third wound. Shocked, I asked, "Did you miss him?"

He looked up at me with a sly smile on his face, "I don't miss, remember? Look on the front of his face."

I moved around, and then I saw it. One eye was missing. Dru had shot him through his left eye. That troll's head was so freaking tough the bullet was still in there.

Impressive as it was, we didn't have time to congratulate ourselves. Two bastards and three children were still out there needing our intervention. "Help me find my gun."

"I'm sitting on it, I think."

Exasperated, I turned back to him, still sitting there on the floor, "You're sitting on my gun? The one with seventeen rounds? And you used that stupid six-shooter?

"Nine-millimeter isn't enough for a troll."

"Nine-millimeter in his eye would work fine and you know it. Give it to me and get up, hermano. "

"I hoped two in the chest would be enough. Troll eyes are tiny," he pulled my gun out from under him saying, "and get a Godsdamned holster like I told you to."

I smacked him on the back of his head as he stood up, "Argue later. Kids are still in danger, and we're about to be burned alive."

He handed me my gun, "And we've only got a few hours before we have to be under the Elder tree." He shook his head ruefully as he dumped his empty shells and reloaded, pulling out a speed-loader and putting six new rounds into his pistol. "I never thought I'd be back doing all this nature magic shit. There hasn't been any real magic since the Crusades."

"Dru! Kids. Kidnappers. Burning building. Focus, mijo!" We ran out the back door where I had seen the two child traffickers run out carrying the poor Canotilas.

I'm pretty quick, but I'm built more for swimming faster than a fish as opposed to running faster than a deer. Dru, on the other hand, had a few advantages over normal people, such as the ability to haul ass for short distances. Like, world record in the one hundred meters fast. It's a benefit of being the son of an actual God. Legends said he was so sexy all the girls of Ireland swooned, but to me he looked like your basic fit guy in his late twenties. A medium build, easy to look at, and all-around average trending towards good-looking, though never in danger of being mistaken for a movie star. But he could sprint like a deer!

He got there first and knocked the door open with a textbook front kick next to the doorknob. He went through and darted to his right as I followed behind him and cut hard to my left, clearing the door and separating to make us harder targets to shoot.

We needn't have bothered as the two traffickers were in the process of jumping into the front seats of the van. I assumed they had already loaded the three children, so I yelled to Dru, "Don't shoot unless you have a clear shot, the kids are probably in the back."

"I fucking know, Godsdamnit! Get the car, I'm going to try to cut them off at the exit to the parking lot."

I knew my brother wasn't angry at me; he was pissed at the two bastards that were effectively using children as Canotila shields, so I ran for the car without comment, but he'd hear from me later. Right now, I wanted to save those poor children. My emotions were running full steam, and I gave myself over to the chase.

We were in a large parking lot surrounding two sides of the now very obviously burning warehouse. The entire property was surrounded by a large chain-link fence with slanted fittings holding barbed wire. The only way in or out was through two entrance exit points for cars, and one access point for delivery trucks around the other side.

I jumped into the front seat, started the car, and slammed it into drive as off to my left I saw Dru sprinting towards the exit while the van careened around the corner of the parking lot row and accelerated towards the same place. I couldn't cut through the parking lot because each spot had those damn concrete wheel stops designed to prevent exactly that, so I had to take the long way there. The good news was that the bad guys had to do the same thing, which is why we even had a chance to save the Canotila. Dru is fast, but he's not faster than a vehicle.

I watched the van as I drove around the row and accelerated down the parking lot towards the exit, but I was definitely behind them. I wouldn't get there before they did. I looked for Dru and found him as he ran straight for the exit with a huge grin on his face I could see from all the way back here.

I quickly realized why as he pulled up, sliding on his feet across some gravel, bending down and grabbing a huge chain sitting on the side of the exit to this warehouse. He lifted it and ran across the exit, stretching it tight and fastening it around the opposite side fence post.

"Ha, pendejo! Got you!" I drove my car to the nearer exit and pulled it across the opening closing it off. The Van driver saw what we were doing and slammed the brakes before it got close to Dru's chain barricade. It then turned my way, and I could see through the windshield both humans were yelling at each other and pointing at my car blocking the second exit.

Then they turned my way and floored it, rapidly accelerating. It didn't take a genius to see that they were going for the only opening left – the truck access – but to get there they had to drive straight past me while Dru could run across the parking lot to the exit in a straight line, which he immediately started to do.

I couldn't ram them because I might hurt or even kill the children, but they didn't think that way, so maybe I could use their sociopathic lack of empathy against them. I snarled to myself and aimed right at them, flooring the accelerator. As I hoped, they fell for the bluff and turned off to avoid the collision, zig-zagging their way over to the last exit.

All I had to do now was stay between them and my exit and trust Dru to take care of them. That would be the smart play because my brother Dru had been killing people for over two thousand years, and he is really good at it. I had no fear that those two assholes could beat him in life and death combat, but I was too Godsdamned angry to let this go, so I closed the distance and brought up the rear of this soon-to-be-over car chase.

With no chain to pull across this opening, Dru grabbed a chain-link gate on a track that he slammed shut, standing in front of it with his gun drawn and pointing straight at the van. A clear message: stop or die before you get past me.

The two assholes decided to stomp on the brakes hard, well short of Dru, and I breathed a sigh of relief that they didn't think to try to circle around me and run for the now abandoned exit I had been protecting. I was smiling as I too smashed my brakes and stopped behind them, effectively reducing their options to surrender or attempt to drive through Dru's gunfire.

Or so I thought.

Instead, the driver opened his door and jumped out of the van with his hands up smiling.

The other human dove into the back of the van and grabbed a hostage. I could hear the three kids screaming.

Still smiling, the driver said, "Hey, what is this? You've already got the money; you want these kids too?" He was fidgeting nervously as he continued, "Are you sent from DeMarco? Because I got no beef with you if so. You can buy these kids with the money you stole, and I'll never say a word about what happened. But if you try to take them, Derek will kill all three before you can get into the van. And then this whole thing is nothing but a waste. Give me the cash and the kids are yours. Fair deal, hey?"

Dru and I stayed silent, him because of his rage that threatened to overwhelm him, and me because I had started praying Dru didn't just start shooting.

He frowned and licked his lips. "You're not from Petrus, are you? Shit. Because I'm not kidding about Derek and the kids, man."

Dru was still silent, but as I looked at him, I realized he wasn't looking at the driver, he was looking at me. When I met his eyes, he slid them over to the van and back, willing me to understand whatever it was he trying to say.

I looked over to the white, solid mass of the back doors and back to Dru, not understanding. I mouthed, "What?" and shrugged my lack of understanding at him.

His face took on a frustrated expression that would have been comical in any other situation, and finally, he spoke. "Kill those kids and I'll kill you both, that's a promise. I don't care if I can't see in the van and...Derek, is it? I don't care that your buddy Derek can't see out, he emphasized while looking at me. "But if I even suspect those kids are hurt, I'll start pulling the trigger. You won't survive, I promise."

"So, what do you want, hey?" the man asked.

"I want to see Derek in the van, facing me and showing me three living children. Then we can negotiate a price."

Suddenly, I got it and smiled. I winked at Dru and crept slowly out of sight of the van driver and behind the rear doors of the van. Rear doors that did not have windows.

Relaxing a tiny bit, he replied, "Fine. Derek!" he shouted, "Show the man his merchandise."

I heard a shuffling of bodies and a small child started crying before it was cut off with a sharp slap and muffled, "Shut the fuck up." from inside the van. Oh, I was going to enjoy killing this asshole.

Dru's voice reached me from the front, "Nice. We might salvage this after all. Now that everybody is in front, bring them out so I can see them clearly. Tell Derek to open the door and let them out."

I crept up to the door and carefully tried the back door, pushing the door release slowly and softly, trying to avoid noise. Thank the Gods, the door was unlocked, and I felt it unlatch, but I didn't open it up, because I assumed a light would go on.

"Ha. Sorry friend, that's not going to happen. Inside that van, we have full control. You've seen the kids. They're alive. Nothing else matters."

"Bullshit." Dru replied, "They have to be healthy enough to do what they are meant to do. Send out two. If Derek is scared of being alone in the van, he can keep one in the passenger seat next to him or something."

There was a pause before the driver said grudgingly, "Fine. Derek, send out the little one. You can see one. Derek keeps the other two."

Another long pause as a door opened and what I had to assume was the smallest Canotila was passed out to the driver. "You happy, guy?"

Dru replied, "Well, I'm happy they look uninjured, but no, I'm not happy."

Then, in what had to be for my benefit, Dru said, "Hey Derek, you sit right there in the driver's seat with those two kids beside you in the passenger seat while I give your partner his payment."

I risked a quick glance around the van to see Dru throwing the bag of money at the driver's feet. I gave him a thumbs up. He caught my action and looked at me as he said, "Now send the three kids over to me, and I'll count them as they arrive, one, two, three."

The driver was getting uneasy; I could hear it in his voice. He said, "You sure talk a lot, hey? Why don't you back way up while I get the little shits ready. In fact, you open that gate and your partner...wait, where the fuck is the woman?"

I heard Dru yell "Three three three!" as a loud BOOM sounded from out front.

I yanked the rear door of the van open to see Derek lifting a gun and lunging across the seats to pull the little girl across his upper body. He pointed the gun at her head and held her between him and Dru's weapon. The kids were screaming and it was chaos. I launched myself into the van and lunged the full length towards the front.

Derek looked over his shoulder and must have seen his death coming because he screamed, but he couldn't do anything else because I grabbed his gun with my right hand and lifted it up as I drew my blade with my left and rammed it through the seat and into his lower back.

His gun went off insanely loud in the cab of the truck, but the bullet went harmlessly through the roof of the van,

My blade is about an inch and a half wide at its base and sixteen inches long; a delicate, steel blade designed for killing. It had a sister blade that matched it in size, but was made of pure, black, wrought iron. I let go of the steel blade I had stuck through the seat and reached across my body for that sister blade. I pulled it out and drove it through Derek's neck and his scream of anguish went silent. He dropped the child and spasmed violently in the seat, wrenching the iron blade out of my hand.

Dru reached the passenger door, grabbing the closest child and pulling him out of the van. Quickly he reached back in and together, we pulled the

Canotila shield from the hand of the quickly expiring Derek and got her safely away from the scumbag.

I looked out of the window and saw the dead driver with half of his head missing. Dru's knack of hitting what he aims at could be positively terrifying sometimes, but in times like this, it became easy to accept it as the God-given gift it was intended to be, rather than the curse it usually was.

Dru jumped back out and gathered the three children together and was talking quietly to them, his arms around all three as they hung onto him as if their life depended on it. My brother has a severe case of self-loathing that has shaped his life in very horrible ways, but while he couldn't see it, I sat there with the now dead Derrick, staring at the small part of Dru's soul that had survived two thousand years of abuse, killing, and death. I knew there was still something in him worth protecting, and maybe, just maybe, something we could save. My eyes welled up and I viciously wiped them dry, mumbling, "Not now, dummy. Cry later."

I wiped my hands dry on my pants leg and called out of the cab. "They have to be healthy enough to do what they are meant to do?" quoting his words back to him.

He looked over at me, "Yeah, they need to be healthy enough to play with each other, run around, and get into some mischief like kids do. Not my problem if those two assholes thought something else."

I pulled my blades out, only to discover the steel blade had somehow gotten bent badly during Derek's death throes. Ruined. I got out of the van and threw the steel blade down disgustedly and began cleaning the iron sister.

Dru straightened up and said, "Petrus and DeMarco."

I nodded in understanding. Two names. Two organizations involved in child trafficking. Sarah would be turning her resources towards these two bastards soon.

www.ingramcontent.com/pod-product-compliance
Lightning Source LLC
Chambersburg PA
CBHW051231050726
47594CB00001B/122